THE AUDACITY
TWO MASTED FRIGATE

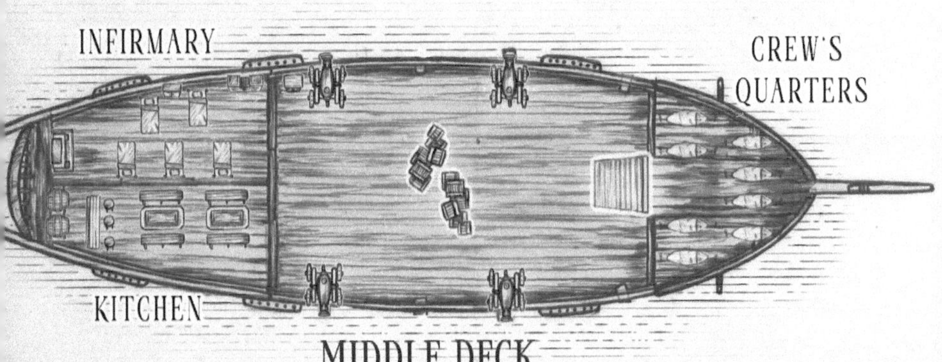

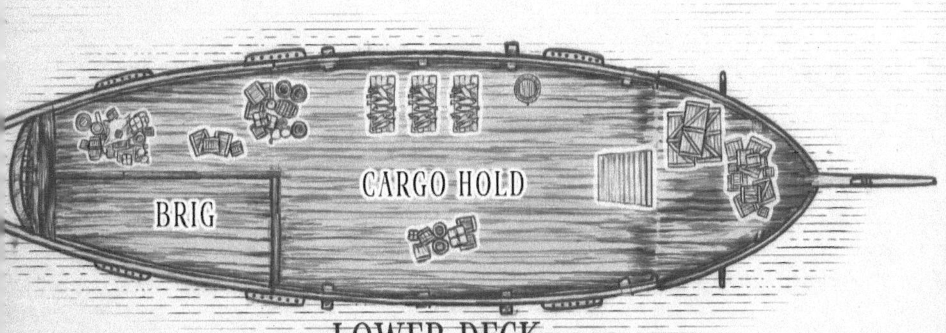

KAILANI

N
W
E
S

LILISA
ABYSSUS
ORABEL
THE BARREN SEA
SEA OF RAIDAN
THE BORDER

JOKUL
AR DOMHAN FIACLA
WORLD'S TEETH
KEAN
AEDAN
IRON MINES
IRON MAW
AUDRYE
DAIRE
WHITE WOODS
THE FRINGE
DORNWELL
TALA
EVERWYN
SCORCHED SEA
VESPERA'S
ISLE
BRIMLAD
RUHETTE
CATIA
BAZYLI
ANTILLIA
DEIVI
ESAI
LIMANI
JYRI
CICERA
DRYAS

Also by K. J. Cloutier

<u>Beyond The Horizon</u>

Beyond The Horizon

Beneath Crimson Sails

Behind Shattered Shores

Beneath Crimson Sails

Beyond The Horizon
Book 2

K. J. Cloutier

First edition August 2024

Front cover image/design by Natalia Junqueria
Map design by Natalia Junqueria
Character art by Alana Meyers-Echegaray

ISBN: 978-1-7778562-6-7 (paperback)
ISBN: 978-1-7778562-9-8 (hardcover)
ISBN: 978-1-7778562-5-0 (ebook)

Published by Meraki Books

www.kjcloutierauthor.com

Part One

A Black Flag

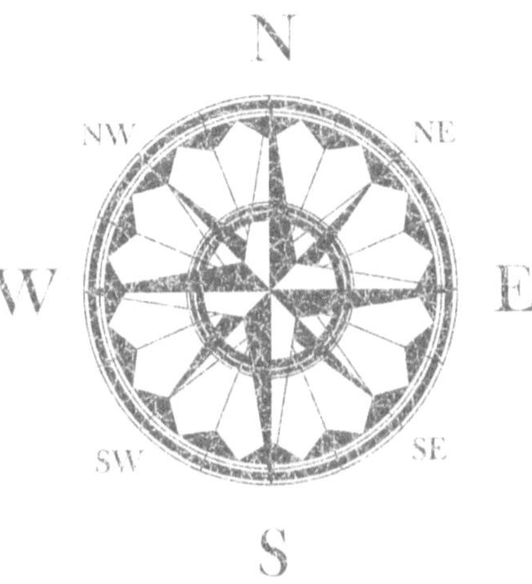

Chapter One

L iam Aalokin was dying.

The sun baked his skin until it peeled, glared off the ocean until it blinded him. The wind cracked his lips until they bled, seared his throat until he could scarcely suck in another breath of hot, salty air.

His stomach cramped with hunger. His fingers blistered. His body ached. And all that was fine.

But the boredom—it was killing him like a slow disease, eating him from the inside out. Soon, his brain would begin to ooze from his ears.

Licking the salt from his chapped lips, he squinted with watery eyes and glared at the distant horizon, forever out of reach. And empty. Always empty.

"Did you mark the tally today?" Caelin's voice was rough, quiet, nearly lost on the wind.

Liam turned on his stupid plank bench, his butt so chafed it was mostly numb. Caelin stood at the helm, leaning on the wooden wheel more to stay upright than to steer their sorry excuse of a ship. He looked back at Liam with glassy eyes.

Liam grunted and hauled himself towards the mainmast. He ran his raw, blistered fingers across the collection of nicks in the wood. Twenty-eight of them, at least. One for each day they'd spent on this gods' forsaken ship. But had he made a mark today? Or was that yesterday? Or the day before?

He stroked the wispy beard that had sprung up on his chin. Last time he marked the mast, the sun had been low over the horizon. But had it been rising, or setting?

"Hm," he answered, staring at the nicks, his head aching.

"Well," Caelin mumbled, his face red and shining in the afternoon sunlight. "What are we at now?"

Liam made a show of counting every single scratch in the mast. "By my calculations, we've been sailing for all of eternity, plus a day."

An eternity of staring at an empty horizon, of walking no more than twenty paces before running out of ship, of eating stale food and drinking stale water, of resisting the urge to fling himself into the ocean to end it all.

Before the boredom killed him first.

He stabbed his knife into the mast and stomped off towards the prow. The deck rocked under his feet, but by now, he hardly felt it. The salty wind caught his thick curls; the sea spray spat on his skin. His tunic and trousers where so thick with salt, they felt like stone.

He stared at the horizon again, at the smudge of grey clouds forming in the distance.

"Please, Eldoris," he whispered, his lips cracking again. "Let there be another storm."

A storm meant water and shade. A storm meant excitement and action.

They'd hit one several weeks ago, nearly capsized the ship as they rode the giant swells and battled the fierce gale. Rain had pelted them like needles, wind had torn at the rigging, at their skin, and waves clawed their way onto the deck, hoping to drag them into the sea's merciless depths. All night, they'd clung to the masts, having tied themselves in place. All night, Liam's heart had raced.

In the morning, the storm had melted away, leaving nothing

but gleaming puddles on the deck, nothing but adrenaline in Liam's veins and a smile on his face.

Since then, the weather had remained hot and boring.

Not long after the storm, Liam had spotted a ship on the horizon. His fingers hovered over the *lim* strapped to his back as he'd watched it glide along the sea. But then the ship vanished. Three times that happened, three times Liam's heart had leapt, and then withered.

Since then, no ships had appeared to give Liam something to look at.

A few times, they'd passed masses of green and brown lands, never getting close enough to see much more than blobs of colour breaking up the endless blue. But Caelin refused to stop. It was too dangerous, and they had to get home. Immediately. So Liam watched the last of the land pass with hungry eyes; that had been at least a week ago.

Since then, nothing. Nothing, nothing, nothing.

He tied knots. He climbed the rigging. He patched the sails. He picked weevils from the hardtack. He threw the weevils at Caelin. He sharpened his knife. He paced the ship, around and around. He stared at the sea. He stared at the sky. He stared at nothing.

He waited for his brain to ooze from his ears.

And he worried.

Constantly, he worried, mostly about whether he'd made the right decision in letting his twin sister stay behind—though it hadn't been his decision. It had been Emery's, and she had been certain. He trusted her. But with nothing else to occupy his time, he had nothing to do but worry.

He closed his eyes and pictured his sister the last time he saw her, standing alone on that rotting dock in Brimlad, growing smaller and smaller as he sailed away without her. Leaving her in the mercy of a man who was a wanted criminal, a man who was known as one of the cruelest Forbiddens of their time. It had been her choice, but he felt like he'd abandoned her.

His stomach clenched with nausea, and for the thousandth

time, he had to remind himself that Captain Sean Denzel had saved their lives, had rescued them from the depths of Tavor's dungeons after weeks of torture. If it wasn't for him, they'd be lost in Abyssus right now. Or dead.

Emery trusted Sean. And Liam trusted her...

"Please, Tadewin and Teralyn," he whispered again, "Let her be safe."

He closed his right hand into a fist and pain seared through the scar on his palm, still raw and blistered. The one Tavor had given him before Sean had rescued them. And on the heels of pain, his nerves flared into fury.

The rage pushed him to his feet, and he stomped towards Caelin, who kneeled near the stern, leaning over a ragged map and a spinning compass, the wind tousling his dark hair, which had grown out some since he'd cut it short a few months back.

"Please—*please*—tell me we're almost there," he said in a growl.

Caelin studied the map and tapped on the compass until the two spinning arrows stopped moving. He gritted his teeth.

Liam glared at the map, at the black swirls of ink that were supposed to tell them how to get home. "Caelin?"

His friend's shoulder's slumped. "I don't know."

Liam snatched the map from Caelin's fingers, not that he could read it any better. They'd entered a section of the map that looked to be nothing but open ocean, and without a single landmark, it was impossible to tell where they were. Sean had tried to teach them how to use a sextant to figure out their longitude and latitude—whatever *that* was—but the demonstration had been quick and, apparently, neither of them had retained much of the lesson. For all they knew, Orabel, their intended destination, their home, was behind them now.

They had severely underestimated how challenging this journey was going to be.But they had to get home, to warn their friends and family that they might be in danger.

Liam's stomach clenched with nerves again. Because when they got home, he was going to have to confront the Arch-

Elemists, the leaders of their people. He was going to have to demand answers. Had they known that Tavor planned to destroy Orabel? Had they known they were sending two children out into the world to get tortured? Had they *lied?*

Or had they been wrong, for the first time ever?

Worse than the boredom, worse than the knowledge that he'd have to confront the Arch-Elemists, was the fact that he'd have to tell his Grandparents he left his sister behind. Gods, he could only imagine their reactions.

He blew out a nervous breath.

And Fia, one of his best friends... A whole new set of nerves wiggled in his stomach at the thought of returning home to her...

"We'll get there," Caelin said, snatching the map back and glaring at it.

As soon as the words left his mouth, the wind died.

The sails fluttered and fell, the air turned heavier, hotter. The ship slowed to a crawl.

"Uh, what the—?"

"The doldrums," Caelin whispered, his eyes sparkling with shocked hope. "We've reached the doldrums."

Liam clutched the railing so hard, his knuckles turned white, and stared at the horizon again, his breaths sticking in his dry throat.

"The Barren Sea," he said into the stillness.

Where the wind never blew, where the land never appeared. Where his elders raised their home from the depths one hundred and forty-nine years ago.

Caelin grinned, his chapped lips splitting. "Well, grab an oar!" He settled into one of the worn, wooden benches and grabbed a paddle with his already blistered hands. "Tadewin's wind won't help us now."

Liam dropped beside Caelin, grabbing his own oar. He stared at the mass of nothingness stretched out on all sides, imagined rowing its entire length.

There it was, the first of his brain oozing from his ears.

Chapter Two

Emery Aalokin didn't flinch as the Scourge of the Sea launched himself at her, his blade gleaming gold in the light of the rising sun as it arched towards her. She held her stance and managed to block the first blow. But the sword in her hands was so heavy, way heavier than the weapon she was used to.

She dodged the second swing, but the third...

The Scourge's sword hovered just over her belly button, and he stood so close, she could count the different shades of green in his eyes. "Dead," Sean whispered.

She glared, unwilling to back down, but also wondering what she had gotten herself into. It had been her idea to try to duel him with an unfamiliar weapon, and now, she couldn't remember why that had seemed like a fun challenge.

Earlier that morning, she'd awoken to find Sean already gone from his cabin, as usual, though dawn had barely broken. As she strode onto the deck after practicing some statera movements, throwing her hair into a haphazard braid and strapping her lim to her back, she'd heard the clank of steel and followed it to the waist of the ship, where Sean was busy training Seadar and Ranit with a blade.

Seadar, at only fifteen and the youngest of the crew, was new to the training. But Ranit, a few years older than Emery's seventeen and Sean's first mate, had been adept with a sword—until he'd lost his arm.

Now, as Emery dodged another slash of Sean's sword, she couldn't help glancing to where Ranit sat watching them. He squeezed his left hand into a fist over and over, as if it cramped from his earlier lesson. She tried not to look at the hook where his right hand used to be.

Still, the sour taste of guilt filled her mouth. She never forget the way the varen – intent on capturing them dead or alive – had barred down on them, how he'd shot Ranit with the blunderbuss and almost completely blown his arm off, how their medic, Aleksy, had to cut off the rest herself to save Ranit's life.

Now Ranit had to learn how to use a blade all over again, because he'd stepped in front of that gun for her.

Unaware of Emery's inner turmoil, Sean stepped back, tossing his blade from one hand to the other, and grinned wickedly.

Without warning, he swung his sword at her ribs, and instinctively, she parried with Tortoise Shell, one of the moves she'd learned from home. But with the awkward angle and weight of the blade, she was too slow to deflect the stab to her heart.

Sean stopped the blow inches from her chest. "Dead again."

She stepped away first this time, grinding her teeth with anger and humiliation. Especially since Farley - a young man Emery's age who spent most of his time in the crow's nest - had wandered on deck to watch the fight. He perched on a crate, sketching on a piece of parchment with a stick of charcoal. This was a common sight, but Emery's humiliation grew. He was probably making a drawing of her epic loss. Camulus joined him, ruffling her brother's icy-blonde hair as she stepped up beside him. Farley swatted her hand away lightly. Cam's own icy-blonde hair was mostly hidden under her tricorn hat, as usual.

Over the last few weeks, Emery had only observed the sparring as well. But the shoulder wound she'd recently suffered had finally healed, and she'd been itching to try her hand at a blade, curious to see how she'd stand up to the notorious Scourge of the Sea. Like a fool, she'd challenged him to a duel.

Now she glared at the cutlass in her hand, so heavy and awkward and useless.

Sean circled her, letting the tip of his sword scrape across the deck. He rolled up his sleeves, revealing one arm covered in tattoos. "You need more speed."

He swung his sword low, aiming for her calves. She hopped over the blow, slashed her cutlass up and out, then swiftly in towards his navel in a sloppy rendition of Lightning Strike. Sean danced out of the way, but his brows shot up with intrigue. Steel flashed to her right, but when she shifted her blade to block, she met open air.

An arm snaked around her belly, dragging her back against a solid chest. A sword hovered over her throat, so close she felt it when she swallowed.

"Too slow again," Sean whispered, his breath tickling her ear.

Shivers that had nothing to do with the blade at her throat rippled up her spine. He lowered his sword a few inches, but neither of them stepped apart.

"Where did you learn to fight like this?" she asked.

She felt him shrug against her back. "Lessons as a kid." His breath ruffled her loose hair this time. "And necessity. You learn quickly when everyone's trying to kill you."

She stepped out of his embrace so she could face him. A half grin twisted his lips. He meant it as a joke, but they both knew it was no such thing.

Glaring again at her cutlass, she swiped sweat from her brow and waited for Sean to attack again. The early morning air was not quite hot, but it held the promise of heat to come.

Sean lunged.

This time, she danced out of the way and hurled the blade off to the side, where it stabbed into the deck and stood quivering. She yanked her lim from its sheathe on her back.

Sean paused, eyed the quivering sword, and then the slender staff of wood in her hands. He shrugged and lunged forward. The lim vibrated as she stepped into Solid Oak, deflecting the assault. She slashed her stick up and over in Waterfall. They spun around each other, their wood and steel clashing, and though Emery did not care much for outsider weapons, she had to admit, there was something beautiful about the way Sean fought with his blade—the way he evaded with the grace of a dancer and struck with the precision of a falcon.

The way his frown deepened as her moves confused him.

She twirled behind him, jabbed him in the left side with one end of her lim, and then the right. She hooked his leg, and he lost his balance, stumbling to one knee. She paused with her weapon a hair's width from Sean's temple.

He froze, eyes wide. Behind him, most of the crew—Ranit, Seadar, Cam, Farley, and now Billy—all stared with open mouths.

She grinned. "Dead. Or at least, very unconscious."

"Interesting." Sean stared up at her, sweat dripping from his forehead, his chest heaving. "Where did *you* learn to fight like this?"

"Home."

She wished she could give him more than that. She wished she could tell him that everyone in Orabel began training with a lim at age twelve, so they could protect themselves from potential attacks from outsiders while they waited for their elemental abilities to surge.

She wished she could tell him anything about her home.

But she couldn't.

Sean climbed to his feet, but halfway there, he grabbed the end of her lim and yanked. She staggered forward, nearly crashing right into him. But she spun, and as he swung his sword, she ducked into Falling Falcon. His blade missed as she twisted out of reach.

"What is this?" he panted.

Instead of answering, she sprinted right at him. Instead of striking, she dropped and rolled. Springing up behind him, she locked her lim around his neck, dragging his spine against her chest. He dropped his weapon so he could use his hands to keep her lim from crushing his throat.

Emery had to stand on her tiptoes to murmur in his ear. "The reason I don't need to use a blade."

This time, she felt him shiver against her.

This time, the crew cheered. Ranit whistled through his fingers.

But on her toes, she was off balance. He whirled, yanking the lim around and her with it. She let go of her weapon, throwing *him* off balance. She hooked her ankle around his, and he fell, but not before he grabbed her arm. They tumbled to the ground together. Sean landed flat on his back, and she on top of him.

They stared at each other for a moment, chest to chest, and then she snatched his fallen sword from the deck and held it to his throat, kneeling on his sternum.

"Definitely dead."

She grinned, panting, pride flowing through her veins. But then she noticed the silence. The crew stared at her, all of them now, with wide eyes and opened mouths. They'd stopped clapping. And she realized perhaps holding a weapon to their captain's throat while they all watched might not be the best idea. They'd accepted her, but she was still new, after all.

Then Seadar cheered. "She did it!"

The crew broke into a round of applause.

Emery smiled, looking down at Sean. He gazed back up at her, his eyes bright. He smiled a wolfish grin she'd never seen before, one that sent fire through her entire body. "I can't think of a better way to die."

Farley must have gone up to the crow's nest at some point, because he suddenly shouted. "Sail ho! Three points off the portside."

The jovial air aboard the *Audacity* immediately grew tense. The ship's crimson sails still sat furled in the rigging, and the anchor hid in the turquoise depths of the sea, having kept them from floating off in the night while they had slept. This meant if it was an enemy ship heading their way, they were sitting ducks.

Emery immediately stood, offering a hand up to Sean before they both headed for the railing. Indeed, a white spot marred the distant horizon. Emery took out her telescope and peered through, but even then, she couldn't make out much. Farley had the best eyesight out of all of them, which was partly why he was almost always on lookout duty.

"Colours?" Sean shouted up to Farley, not bothering to take out his own telescope.

"Andillian, Captain!"

"What is she?"

"A merchant's ship, I think. She's a deep keel."

Rooney stepped up beside them, his large frame literally blotting out the sun for Emery. His grin of delight flashed through his red beard. "This is perfect timing. We've only a week's worth of water. And the food—she's looking sorry."

But Sean did not look happy at all. He fiddled with the time-piece hanging around his neck. Emery knew now that this was his tell. Anxiety gripped him.

"Isn't a cargo ship a good thing?" Emery asked carefully.

"Aye..." Sean hedged.

"Are we raiding her?" she asked.

Sean closed his eyes, took a deep breath, and said, "We're raiding her."

Chapter Three

Captain Sean Denzel knew the cargo ship on the horizon should have felt like a blessing.

He knew they were dangerously low on food and water. It had been a while since their last raid, and though Rooney's small garden, their fishing nets, and Cam's slight skill at siphoning fresh water from the ocean kept them alive when things got truly dire, it wasn't enough.

And there was only so much fish they could stand eating.

The cargo ship should feel like a blessing. But it felt like a curse.

Still, he raised his voice, and gave the order. "All hands on deck! Weigh anchor, ready the topsails, and bring her about!"

His crew immediately dashed to follow his orders, all of them knowing exactly what they were supposed to do. Within minutes, the sails were let loose, and the *Audacity* was skimming across the water. Sean marched to the helm but couldn't quite meet Billy's eye when he relieved the older man from the wheel. His stomach was churning. With shame. Guilt. Dread.

Still, Billy said nothing as he raced off to help Ranit, Cam, and Emery with the topsails. Sean pushed it all down. Down,

down, down, into his deepest crevices, where he couldn't feel anything anymore. He couldn't afford to.

He wrenched on the wheel, swinging the *Audacity* about so the cargo ship was two points off the starboard bow, and the sails were angled across the eye of the wind, giving them more speed.

Long, tense minutes passed as the distances between the two ships diminished league by league, until Sean didn't need a telescope to see the square sails and the deep keel, the broad prow and the fluttering red and orange flag. Farley was right: a merchant's ship from Andillia.

Sean couldn't help it; he looked up into the rigging to where Emery sat on a yardarm, ready to loose the topsails. To where he hoped she'd stay.

He gripped the pegs of the wheel so hard, his fingers ached, but he forced his expression blank. The energy aboard the *Audacity* crackled as the crew readied their weapons for a battle that would hopefully never come to pass. Billy marched up the stairs, a sharp cutlass in hand, the sight of the old man gripping his weapon cutting through Sean as surely as the blade would have.

Again, he pushed the dread down, down, down.

"She's turning about, Captain!" Farley shouted.

Sean cursed, tightening his death grip on the wheel. Sure enough, the cargo ship had changed its course. The vessel skimmed across the azure ocean, away from the *Audacity*.

Sean wished he could give the orders to abort the mission. Instead, he turned to find Seadar standing at the ready. "Let fly the Jolly Roger."

Seadar dashed off, and within moments, a huge black flag rose into the sky. The white skull grinned in the wind, the red slashes like bloody cuts. A warning flag.

Flee and die. Surrender and live.

Please, for the love of Roark, surrender, Sean prayed.

But the merchant's ship never slowed, and Sean swallowed the bile in his throat.

"Let loose the topsails!"

Above, the highest sails unfurled, and the *Audacity* picked up speed. The frigate's shallow keel and narrow hull gifted her with speed unmatched by most ships, and sure enough, the dwindling leagues between the two ships slowly vanished.

But Sean's veins thrummed with energy, and slowly wasn't good enough. He closed his eyes, pushing himself deeper and deeper, until he felt nothing at all. Nothing but the wind tugging at his hair and clawing at his skin, roaring in his ears, his blood. He grabbed hold of that wind, molded himself into its mercilessness and fury. Until he became part of the wind, screaming through the rigging and filling up the sails.

And the *Audacity* raced across the waves towards its prey.

Sean popped an eye open, half of him still up in the rigging with the wind, the other half clinging to the helm. The merchant ship was right there, but she wasn't slowing down. Sean's grip on the wind slipped, just a little, his strength already ebbing. It was times like this when he wished he was more skilled with his abilities.

"Ready the starboard cannons!" He shouted.

He knew without looking that Aleksy, Seadar, and Rooney would be racing belowdecks. The *Audacity* caught up to the merchant's ship and sailed up alongside the vessel's port side.

Sean closed his eyes again, and shouted, "FIRE!"

The ship lurched as booms tore the sky apart, followed by the sound of cracking wood and screaming men. The air reeked of gunpowder. The merchant's ship slowed. They'd managed to take out her mizzenmast.

Sean ripped himself from the wind and slumped against the wheel, momentarily dazed. The *Audacity* slowed and he brought her about to drift alongside the other vessel.

Billy relieved Sean from the wheel, and Sean stepped up to the starboard railing. He felt Cam and Aleksy stand at his back, the two women as fierce and fearsome as any man. "Surrender," he called across the remaining sea separating the two ships. "Or receive no mercy!"

As he spoke, his gaze darted about the enemy ship. Three

men at the prow, four at the stern, twelve at the waist, three in the rigging. Twenty-two men total. But how many down below? If a fight broke out, Sean's crew would be dangerously outnumbered.

The captain of the cargo ship, a bulky man wearing a violet jacket with golden buttons that gleamed in the sunlight, brandished a sword in the air. "We will never surrender to you, Sea-Wolves!"

But Sean noticed the way the captain's crew looked uncertain, like they weren't sure if they truly were willing to die to protect their cargo.

Sean's pulse raced, but he forced his expression empty, dead. "Are you sure about that?"

Right on cue, Smythee stepped into the middle of the *Audacity's* main deck, a flaming torch in hand. With his wispy white hair blowing in the wind, and his leathery skin looking as if it might disintegrate at any moment, the old man didn't look like much. Until he started cackling, and the flames from his torch danced brighter and brighter, encircling him in a ball of fire. This move almost always worked—if the old man stayed lucid long enough.

"Sean." A whisper in his ear tore Sean's attention from Smythee. Emery had climbed down from the rigging. "Sean, we should try my idea."

"No," he said without hesitation.

"But it's a good idea!"

"Absolutely not."

"Captain, with all due respect," Aleksy said, the beads in her dark braids tinkling as she stepped up next to Sean, "it *is* a good idea."

Sean glared at his medic. "It's too risky."

"But if it works, the risk for everyone else will be so much less!" Emery pleaded, her deep blue eyes impossibly bright.

"Let's vote," Cam said, stepping up to his other side, her axes already unsheathed.

"What? No," Sean snapped.

"All in favor?" Cam said, raising her hand. Emery, Aleksy, and Seadar raised their hands as well. "All against?" This time, Sean raised his hand, as did Billy. No one else. Cam smirked, swiped her tricorne hat from her head and plopped it on Emery's. "Don't lose this."

Sean turned his glare to Cam and part of him wondered if Cam had sided with Emery, for once, because she secretly hoped Emery wouldn't come back.

Aleksy tossed Emery her long coat.

"I'm going!" Emery turned for the nearest mast, but before she could, Sean's calmness cracked.

He caught her wrist and tugged her close. "What if it goes south? What if—"

She shook her wrist from his grasp. "I can take care of myself. You know that."

He did know that. But it didn't mean he didn't worry.

But Emery turned and scaled the rigging. With his heart hammering against his ribcage, Sean turned back to the scene below, where Smythee was blasting the cargo ship's sails with flames, burning them to ashes so they had no escape.

"Hooks," Sean ordered. Within seconds, grappling hooks flashed silver in the sky, linking the two ships together.

Sean hopped onto the railing, drawing his sword and letting it dangle loosely at his side. "This is your last chance!" he shouted. "Surrender now, and live!"

The captain of the cargo ship spat into the ocean separating them. "Never!"

His crew roared their agreement, their blades and pistols glinting in the sunlight. So many weapons. Too many. But again, Sean noticed fear in their jerky movements. They didn't really want to fight.

Perfect.

A short sailor pushed their way to the front of the crowd, a tricorne hat covering their face, a bulky coat hiding the shape of their small body. The sailor hopped onto the cargo ship's railing, facing Sean. Her blue eyes were just visible under the shadows of her hat as they locked with his.

His heart flailed harder, but he forced his face empty, empty, empty.

"We aren't afraid of you!" she shouted, and the sailors raised their weapons in approval, oblivious to the fact that she didn't belong. She pointed right at him, and he felt it almost like a physical shove to the chest. "Do your worst, Scourge!"

Though Sean knew it was all an act, the word almost made him flinch. Instead, he schooled his features and shrugged. "If you insist."

Smythee cackled again, and this time he released a torrent of flames straight at Emery. The fire engulfed her, swallowing her whole, until she disappeared into a blur of red, orange and gold. The fire roared, and Emery screamed. Screamed like her flesh melted and her hair burned, like every nerve ending in her body was on fire. Like she was really dying. Like it wasn't a trick.

Sean gripped the pommel of his sword so hard he though his fingers might break, his heart pounding so fast, he thought it might rip itself right out of his chest.

It's not real, it's not real, it's not real.

The screaming cut off abruptly, and the silence that followed was almost deafening in comparison. Emery, still bathed in flames, toppled from the railing into the sea. Both crews stared into the ocean's inky depths, but she did not emerge again.

Sean tore his gaze from the ripples where she vanished, and sighed loudly, as if bored. "Anyone else?"

Not one sailor on the cargo ship spoke. One by one, they dropped their weapons. One by one, they dropped to their knees.

A beautiful sight.

Except for the captain. He glared at his crew. "You're all a bunch of cravens!"

But then he, too, lowered to the deck, his violet jacket flapping in the wind. "We cede."

A beautiful sound.

"Then you're not as stupid as you look," Sean drawled.

The next moment was a blur of activity as Sean's crew pulled the two vessels tight, and a gangplank was set between them. Aleksy and Rooney rounded up the sailors and shoved them together on the main deck. Cam kicked their weapons out of reach and Sean strolled across the gangplank himself, his eyes darting over everyone and everything.

No sailors in the rigging; none at the prow or the stern. Twenty-two men at the waist. Aleksy and Cam were guarding the sailors, with Ranit and Rooney scouting below. Smythee, Seadar, and Farley waited for the go-ahead to start hauling the goods, and Emery—

Nowhere. No sign of her.

"There are a lot of goods, Captain!" Rooney's booming voice snapped him back. He was nearly dancing with excitement, no doubt already planning meals for the next few days. "Some avocados and plantains. Garlic, paprika, chiles—"

Sean cut him off, unable to share his enthusiasm. "Take whatever you think we need. You decide."

"Aye, Captain." Rooney raced belowdecks again.

Sean circled the sailors, watching their every twitch, their every blink, his muscles coiled tight, his hands hovering over his weapons. He counted again, twenty-two sailors kneeling on the deck, Aleksy and Cam guarding, Ranit, Rooney, Farley, Smythee and Seadar unloading, Billy at the helm of the *Audacity*, and Emery—still no Emery.

He couldn't help it. His gaze flickered to the water, searching for any sign of her, and as Sean strolled past the captain, the idiot man lunged for Sean's pistol. Sean sidestepped the man and cracked him over the head with the pommel of his blade.

The captain fell back to his knees, blood pooling on his forehead. Aleksy and Cam started forward, but Sean held up his hand. He turned his face to stone, his voice to ice. "Perhaps you *are* as stupid as you look."

The captain glared and spat on Sean's boot. "You bloody Sea-Wolf. You are *scum*."

Sean scratched the stubble of his chin, sheathing his sword. "You got me there."

Because he couldn't afford to have any more men fighting, he reached for the air, and he stole it straight from the captain's lungs. The man's eyes bulged, and he clawed at his throat, choking on nothing.

Sean clung to the air, forcing it away from the man as he fought to breathe, to live. He steadily turned purple, matching his violet cloak, until finally, he slumped face first onto the deck.

Not dead, just passed out. But that captain's crew did not know that.

Neither Sean nor his crew had much skill with the abilities with which they were condemned for having, but this small act would be enough to reinforce his villainy in the eyes of these Ungifted.

They murmured in horror, crossing their hearts and edging away from Sean as he strolled through their midst, his head held high.

"By the gods, he killed him!"

"Demons, they're all demons!"

"Bloody Forbiddens!"

And one man—no, a boy—looked right up at Sean with eyes so wide with fear Sean nearly stumbled. He emptied his expression and stared back.

"Are you an Ashborne?" the boy asked.

It was like the boy had shot him through the chest.

Ashborne. The name he hated most in the world. Even more than Tavor.

"No," he said, squeezing his fists tight so the boy didn't see them shake. "I am the Scourge of the Sea. And I'm worse."

Because he needed them all to believe it, he shoved the boy with the wind, hurtling him into the nearest mast. Not enough to really hurt him, but enough to make it look like he had.

The rest of the sailors cowered, shutting up.

By then, his crew had finished unloading, and half of them had already made it back to the *Audacity*. Sean strolled across the gangplank, his chin high, not looking back at the man he'd suffocated into unconsciousness, or the boy he'd traumatized for life.

When he glanced up at the rigging again, finally spotting Emery crouched in the crow's nest, he thought he'd collapse with relief. And when he counted his crew one more time, making sure they were all accounted for and safe, he nearly lost the careful calmness he'd forced himself into.

But not yet.

He stepped onto the *Audacity's* deck as the grappling hooks were cut and the gangplank was taken down. He didn't shout any orders because he didn't need to. The crew knew what to do.

He didn't look back at the wreckage they left behind.

Sea wolf. Scum. Demon. Forbidden.

He was all those things.

And he thanked all the gods for that, because it meant nobody else died that day.

Chapter Four

Ranit strummed a careful tune, plucking awkwardly at the strings of his lute. The whale oil lantern burning in the middle of the circle cast his face in a white glow, sharpening his cheekbones and flashing off the metal of his new hand.

Emery couldn't look away as he sang.

"In a pirate's heart, there's a tale to tell,
of life upon the rolling swell.
Of a love as deep as the ocean's song,
in the dance of waves, where we belong."

He stumbled over a chord, his tongue poking through his teeth as he concentrated on his metallic hand. A few weeks ago, Rooney and Aleksy had fashioned a sort of hook that Ranit could attach to the stump of his arm, so he could at least strum with it again. Ranit had spent every spare moment since practicing his lute.

The entire crew sat in circle on the main deck, listening to Ranit play and allowing his music to sweep away the stress of the day—at least, almost the entire crew.

Emery glanced towards the bow yet again, where Sean had

vanished hours ago. After the raid, he'd strode across the *Audacity*, checking on everyone and everything, his face impossibly blank. When Emery had dropped to the deck, still soaking wet from her swim in the ocean, he'd been at her side immediately.

"Are you hurt? Did you get burned?"

"No, I'm fine."

He'd swept his gaze over her body, as if he didn't quite believe it. Without another word, he headed for the bowsprit.

Emery had left him alone, mostly because the rest of the crew had. They'd spent the early evening unpacking their booty and daydreaming over the delicious meals they'd get out of it during the next few days. Rooney had been positively giddy. Soon enough, the sun set, and Ranit placed the lantern in the middle of the deck. He sat down, strummed a few notes on his lute, and the crew joined him. Not long after, Rooney brought them all a bowl of steaming rice with fried plantain, peppers, garlic, and a melody of spices. Everyone else also had fish, but Emery had once mentioned to Sean that she didn't eat meat—no one in Orabel did but she didn't say that part—and Rooney had always made sure to leave meat out of her meals.

Apparently, Rooney had once cooked in the king's kitchen before he was found out as an elemist and captured. Emery took an eager bite and groaned with pleasure. She'd had several of Rooney's unreal meals since being aboard the *Audacity*, experiencing firsthand his incredible cooking skills. She'd even helped him with the little garden in the galley, a project he had started so he'd be able to offer more varied meals. But fruits and vegetables don't grow well on ships, and no one aboard was particularly skilled at manipulating the earth with their abilities; Emery was only able to help due to the years she'd spent tending the garden that kept her people fed back home. The freshness of the ingredients they'd taken from the cargo ship made that night's meal shine particularly bright.

Emery glanced at where Rooney sat enjoying his meal beside Aleksy, trying to imagine the burly, bearded man in a royal kitchen. Aleksy whispered something to him, and his answering laugh was booming.

She had also recently learned—after accidentally catching Rooney and Aleksy entangled with each other behind a pile of crates in the bilge—that the two were married. Emery had been mortified upon finding them in such a position, and Ranit had teased her, saying that everyone aboard the *Audacity* had walked in on them at least once, since it was tough for a married couple to find a place to be together on a ship when everyone slept in the same room. Now she was officially part of the crew, he'd quipped.

She'd refrained from asking what being married actually meant, as the term was unfamiliar to her. She assumed it was similar to when couples became soulbound back home, when they expressed their eternal love and commitment to each other.

> *"A sweetheart's kiss on distant shore,*
> *but the sea calls forevermore.*
> *Life's adventure and a tempest's quest.*
> *Love's compass guides, to east and west."*

Ranit continued to sing. Seadar sang along quietly, casting shy looks at Emery. It had taken him a while to even speak in front of her, so she considered this progress in her pursuit to befriend everyone. Smythee rocked back and forth, singing his own words to the same tune. Billy switched from humming along to tugging on his salt and pepper beard and glancing towards the bowsprit. Farley sang along while also sketching something with charcoal on a piece of parchment, something Cam smiled at as she watched over his shoulder. When she looked up and met Emery's gaze, her smile fell and she glared, her pale blue eyes hard.

Cam was no longer hostile towards Emery like she'd been before they all realized Emery was on their side, but she still glared. A lot.

Emery avoided her gaze and looked to the bowsprit again.

"You should go to him," Ranit whispered during a pause in his song, pushing back the scarlet band of lace that kept his dark hair out of his angular eyes.

"Doesn't he want to be alone?" she asked.

"Sometimes what we want and what we need are not the same things."

Emery fiddled with her rope bracelet, the one Sean had made her as a goodbye gift not long ago. "Why me?"

Ranit smirked, cocking an eyebrow. "You can get away with more than the rest of us." Then he sang the next verse.

"But in the deep, where shadows cast,
a pirate's journey might be the last.
Whispers of tales in the ocean's breaths,
about a dance with death, in the cold sea's depths."

She stood and only took a few steps before Billy stopped her. He held out a bowl of food. "Can you bring this to him? He needs to eat."

Emery had the sense of déjà vu, remembering a time, months ago, when Billy had asked her to do the same thing. She was surprised then. She wasn't as surprised now. She smiled and took the bowl. Ranit's song drifted after her as she wandered to the prow.

"Onward we sail, though the tempest's roar.
With love as our anchor, forevermore.
In the heart of the sea, where stories are spun.
Life, love, and death, until our voyage is done."

A cool breeze whipped Emery's hair as she stepped up to the railing next to the bowsprit, the long beam of wood jutting out into the open sea. Sean sat on the platform at the very end, so still one wouldn't notice him if they weren't looking.

Carefully holding the bowl, Emery leapt onto the bowsprit and climbed to the small platform. She sat beside him, her shoulder skimming against his. He didn't look at her, just stared at the black horizon in the distance.

She allowed her legs to dangle over the water, inhaling the salty scent of the sea and the musty smell of wet wood. Before them, the ocean stretched open and vast, a swath of black in all directions. Above, the moon and the stars twinkled silver.

From the corner of her eye, she glanced at Sean's face, just visible in that silvery light. His expression held no hint of emotion, as if he wasn't even there at all. But Emery knew by now that the emptier his face, the more he was hiding inside.

"May I ask what you're thinking about?" she asked.

After a few breaths, he closed his eyes. "I was thinking about a place I used to dream about, where elemists were safe. An island far away from everything else."

Emery's stomach dropped and it was all she could do to keep her jaw from doing the same.

Sean continued, "I used to dream about finding it, so I could take my crew there and we'd never have to steal or be in danger again."

She struggled to find words. Tavor had mentioned that he'd first learned of Orabel from rumors. It made sense that Sean could have heard these rumors too. But it was still shocking hearing him speak so casually of her home, a place only its residents were supposed to know about.

"Do you...think such a place exists?" she asked carefully.

"Not anymore," Sean said. "I don't think there's anywhere safe for us anymore."

Emery swallowed a lump in her throat. He sounded so exhausted, so defeated. She wanted so badly to tell him that a safe place *did* exist, but fear stopped the words from forming. What if the Arch-Elemists where listening? And what if... What if Orabel wasn't actually safe anymore? What if the illness had destroyed it? What if Tavor was still out there, plotting its destruction?

Emery's stomach twisted with the horrible thoughts.

Sean opened his eyes and looked at her, frowning. "Are you certain you're alright? Smythee didn't accidentally burn you?"

She realized he misunderstood her silence and laid a hand on his arm, schooling her features in the process. "I'm fine, Sean. Smythee was in control. He knew what he was doing."

But even as she said it, her stomach twisted again, this time with the same terror she'd felt as she stood on the railing of the cargo ship, waiting for Smythee to wrap her in flames. She'd gotten the idea from the nightmares she'd been having, wanted to help Sean and his crew so badly she thought she'd be able to handle it. But when those flames swallowed her, she'd almost forgotten it wasn't real. Because the heat on her cheeks was real, the way the flames sucked away her air was real. And her scream had been partly real too.

But it was worth it, because it stopped the fight before it even began. It kept anyone from getting hurt.

Except for the man Sean had choked out with his wind, and the boy he'd shoved into the mast. Although Sean held his ground afterwards, holding his head high and his back straight as he stalked amongst the rest of the crew, there had been a moment when he walked across the gangplank, and he'd looked up to see her watching from the crow's nest. The moment their eyes met, his face had cracked, his horror showing for just a split second. And then it was gone.

She'd heard the things they called him. Sea wolf. Scum. Demon. Forbidden.

"Sean," she said, still holding his arm. "You're not scum. You *know* that, right?"

Sean dropped his gaze to the dark ocean below, his hand rising to play with the timepiece forever present around his neck. His dead sister's timepiece.

Emery continued, "You're protecting your family the only way you—"

"The boy called me *Ashborne*," he cut in, his voice cracking.

Emery blinked. It took a moment for the name to register in

her head. "That hardly seems fair, you didn't start the Elemental War over a century ago."

"He didn't mean that Ashborne."

"Then who?"

"There's been more than one famous Ashborne over the years since the war. His sons, and his sons' sons. Ever since elemists were banished, they took to the seas and created as much havoc as possible. Destroying everything. Killing anything. They were the original Forbiddens."

Emery took a moment to digest this. Back home, she'd always heard stories about Forbiddens, who were essentially elemists who used their abilities for evil things, ensuring no peace between elemists and the Ungifted. She'd always hated them. Until she met Sean and understood not everything was so black and white. Sean did what he must to survive. "Why did they do that?"

Sean shrugged. "They were angry, I guess. Wanted to prove they were still more powerful than the Ungifted, even if they were banished from the realm. Every generation seems to have an Ashborne."

Emery shook her head, sighing. She'd never realized so many of the stories she'd heard about Forbiddens were about the same family.

"I've always hated the name," Sean whispered.

"Because they're the reason we have to keep hiding?" That's why she had hated Forbiddens before.

"That, and..." He ran his fingers through his already windswept hair, the gold dyed silver in the moonlight. "He killed my parents."

All the air whooshed out of Emery's lungs. "I-I'm sorry," she stammered. "That's horrible."

Sean shrugged again, his shoulder brushing hers. "I never knew them, so..."

Emery couldn't suck in another breath. "Me neither."

Sean frowned. "What?"

"I never knew my parents either."

Sean dropped the timepiece and gazed back at her, his empty expression finally cracking with curiosity. "Really?"

She nodded.

"What happened to them?"

"I don't know," she admitted. "They just vanished one day, and never came back."

Of course, she couldn't tell him that this was after her mother had already left their home island, even though it was forbidden to do so, and after she'd shown back up in the dead of night with her outsider lover, Emery's father, to dump her children with their grandparents before leaving again.

Sean let his head fall back against the mast and the corner of his mouth quirked up. "I guess we have something in common."

"I guess so." She still felt a little lightheaded from the revelation. All her life, she'd wanted to meet someone besides her own siblings who never knew their parents. To talk to someone who knew what it was like. And here he was. Questions exploded in her head, the when, why, and how of it all. But she'd come to distract Sean from distressing thoughts, not add to them.

"That must be awful," Sean said, before she could change the subject. "The not knowing. At least I know."

"It is," she whispered. Awful enough that she'd dreamt about them all her life and wondered about them every day. Awful enough that she stayed in a world that wanted to kill her on the off chance that she could find out what happened to them.

She reached into her pocket and squeezed the little wooden box she'd carried around for months. The box that contained a scrap of parchment that might tell her everything, if only she could read it.

But she couldn't read it, and she hadn't been brave enough to ask Sean to read it for her.

"Who raised you?" Sean asked, his voice soft.

Emery looked up at the stars so he couldn't see the way her eyes suddenly burned. "My grandparents."

Gods, she missed them. The way Grandmother always fussed, and Grandfather always had a tiny smile on his face, as if the trees themselves just told him a joke. Had Liam made it back to them by now? Was Caelin reunited with his sister? Was Ayana even still alive?

She shoved the thoughts of home away, clearing her throat. "What about you?"

Sean's mouth quirked again, and he glanced over his shoulder towards the main deck. "Actually, Billy raised us. And his wife, Luana."

"Ohh." She peered over her own shoulder and could just spot Billy. He still sat in the circle, his mane of silver hair shining bright in the lantern light. He looked in their direction, the concern on his face visible even from a distance. "Well, that certainly explains a lot."

Sean raised a brow. "It does?"

"He wanted me to give you this." She held out the bowl she nearly forgot she'd been holding this entire time and Sean took it. "He says to eat."

"Thank you," he said. He eyed the rice and vegetables for a moment, before taking a bite. His head fell back against the mast as he closed his eyes and chewed. "Gods bless, Rooney."

Emery watched him take another bite, her heart breaking a little more for him as she realized he had no family left. His parents, gone. And his sister, the last of his family, taken away so brutally.

Rage and sorrow filled her veins at the thought of what Tavor had done to Sean's sister. And she thought back to a conversation she, Ranit, and Billy had shared only a few days prior.

They'd been standing together on the main deck. Across the way, Seadar and Sean had been in their own conversation, and they both burst out laughing, catching Emery's attention. Sean had laughed so hard, he'd doubled over, something Emery had never seen him do before.

When she glanced up at Ranit and Billy, they were watching him too. Ranit was grinning, but Billy looked as if he might cry.

He'd turned to Emery and placed a hand on her shoulder. "Thank you for bringing him back to us."

Emery had been momentarily perplexed. "I think he brought me here?"

Billy shook his head. "I don't mean physically..."

Billy had squeezed her shoulder and then walked off, leaving Emery a little off kilter as his words sunk in. Now, knowing Billy was Sean's adoptive father, they hit her even harder.

"How bad was it?" she had asked Ranit, keeping her voice low.

Ranit's face had fallen. "I don't know how much of this is for me to tell, but it was...awful. He's never been the same. He's closer to himself, but for months after...it was like a part of him died that night too. Like he was a ghost haunting this ship. He didn't eat. Didn't sleep. And he..." Ranit swallowed, glancing back at his captain. "I think he should be the one to tell you the rest."

Emery had watched Sean as well, her heart aching for him. He still smiled at Seadar. The younger boy looked delighted to be getting such reactions out of his captain.

"Has he ever talked to you about what happened that night?" Ranit had asked.

"Once, a little bit. I know Tavor took him and Lily, tortured them both, and shot her."

"He's never talked about it to any of us. Ever."

Emery had turned to him in shock. "Never?"

Ranit shook his head sadly. "It's like he can't. We know what happened, but he refuses to talk about it. But I think he needs to. He's doing better. But I think it's still killing him a little."

"Have you ever asked him?"

"No."

"Why?" Emery asked.

Ranit frowned. "Well, have you?"

"No..." she had admitted. And she understood. After finding out what happened, she'd never dared bring it up again. She didn't want to be the one to bring his pain to the surface. She still didn't, especially not right now, when she was supposed to be cheering him up.

She waited until he was nearly finished his meal before speaking again. "Billy must have been a wonderful father."

For some reason, Sean's expression slipped into nothingness again. He gazed down at the ocean, his food seemingly forgotten. "Aye, he is."

The sight of that nothingness launched Emery to her feet. The gods all knew how badly she wanted to ask him about his parents, how much she wanted to tell him about her own, but now was not the time. Now was the time to make him smile.

"Alright, let's go." She hung onto the mast with one hand and held out her other in an offering.

His gaze flickered from her hand to her face and back again. "Go where?"

"Ranit has practiced that damn lute for weeks. The least we can do is go listen."

Sean hesitated, and Emery was certain he'd refuse. She'd never seen him at one of their after-raid gatherings before. But now, he grabbed her hand and stood. He didn't let go as they headed for the circle.

Ranit grinned as they approached, never breaking from his song. And when they sat down, a moment of stillness settled upon the circle. The crew stared at Sean. Aleksy and Rooney recovered first, turning back to Ranit and singing along with his gaudy song. Billy and Seadar beamed.

Farley dropped his drawing charcoal. "Captain, you haven't sat with us since—"

Cam slapped her brother upside the head to shut him up.

Emery wondered just how long it had been.

Cam, of course, glared at Emery, her eyes narrowing into slits when she spotted their clasped hands.

Ranit whistled, and plucked a rowdier tune, strumming as fast as he could with his new hand. Smythee scrambled up and started dancing. He wheezed as he clapped his hands and stomped his feet to the rhythm of the tune. Seadar and Farley jumped up to join him, and Billy followed soon after. When Billy smiled and offered her a hand up, Emery took it.

Billy twirled her around and around, her hair fanning out around her, the beads clinking musically.

She spun to Sean and smiled, breathless. "Dance with me?"

He shook his head. "I don't dance."

She whirled around again, incorporating a Whipping Willow into the steps because she didn't actually know what she was doing. "And I can?"

And there it was, a real smile, as bright as the moon shining above. "Not really."

"Your loss." She twisted away from him, glancing over her shoulder as she did, because he kept smiling, and it was impossible to look away.

Chapter Five

Emery opened her eyes and watched the lanternlight dance with the shadows on the beamed ceiling. Her body ached with exhaustion, from sparing and climbing and dancing late, late into the night. She'd fallen into a deep sleep, the exhaustion keeping her nightmares at bay for once. Now, she wasn't sure what woke her.

The sky outside the window was an ominous grey, thick with clouds and fog. The first hints of dawn barely broke through the mist.

She rolled onto her side, ignoring the mild throb in her shoulder wound. On the bedside table, a lantern turned low flickered against the darkness. She went to sleep with the lantern lit every night, because she couldn't handle the darkness anymore.

A few paces away, Sean lay in his nest of pillows and blankets on the floor, his breathing slow and even. Even though Emery had fought against it—even though she had been part of the crew for nearly a month now and her recent shoulder injury was healed—he still insisted she take his bed.

If she was being honest with herself, she hadn't fought very hard the last few weeks. She couldn't bring herself to go sleep in the crew's quarters without him, where he wouldn't be there to wake her from her nightmares. Not yet.

Emery grinned to herself as the memories of the night before flashed in her mind. She'd made it her mission to keep a smile on Sean's face all night. As Ranit played his lute, Emery danced as ridiculously as she could. Spinning and jumping and twisting with Seadar, Farley, and Smythee.

Her mission was a success. He did smile, and he even plucked the lute from Ranit's hands to play his own tune, an upbeat song with a nonsensical rhythm that Emery and Seadar tried to dance to, earning tears of laughter from the rest of the crew. Even Sean chuckled. And Emery felt stupidly proud that she'd been the cause.

But her pride slipped now as she watched him toss and turn in his sleep, tangling his legs in his sheets.

"No," he muttered. "Please, don't."

She was on the floor and by his side in seconds. "Sean, wake up."

He bolted upright, his fingers grasping for the blade he always kept under his pillow. Emery didn't even flinch this time as he shot the dagger up between them, breathing hard.

"It's just a nightmare," she murmured.

If they didn't plague her in the night, they plagued him instead.

He stared at her, his face white as snow and his golden hair mussed from sleep. With shaking fingers, he dropped the blade in his lap. "Oh god, I'm sorry."

"It's alright. You didn't get me."

Sean closed his eyes and fell back against his pillows, throwing an arm over his face. She stretched backwards to snatch the book they'd started the other night off the bedside table. Letting the book fall open in her lap, she sat cross-legged, and began to read.

The first time she awoke from a nightmare full of fire to a room full of darkness, she'd been in a full-blown panic. She couldn't breathe. Couldn't think. Couldn't fall back asleep, no matter how many times Sean repeated that she was safe, no matter that she could *see* she was safe. Her body had been convinced she was back in Tabor's dungeons.

"Can I try something?" Sean had asked, and he'd sprang to the bookshelf, grabbing one at random. "This usually helps me fall asleep." He flipped the book open to a random page, and read a random paragraph, and it had worked.

The rise and fall of his voice, the lilting of his strange accent, the rhythm of the words, it had all lulled her into calmness. And so it went, for so many nights, on and off. And he never seemed bothered. Even when she'd apologized for being afraid of the dark like a child, saying she knew she was being silly, he'd told her it wasn't silly, and that he himself feared small spaces. He hadn't elaborated, and went back to reading, leaving her to wonder if he'd developed that fear the same way she acquired her terror of the dark...

When the nightmares struck him instead, she always attempted to return the favor of comfort with no judgment or questions. But her reading was slow, and she stumbled over every other word. Without looking up, Sean corrected her on a few words, and slowly, his breathing returned to normal. He removed his arm from his face and watched her instead as she butchered the story, until she got so stuck, he sat up to glance at the book himself. "Ah, we haven't gone over that letter yet. Hold on."

Sean reached sideways to grab a bottle of ink, a quill, and some parchment from his desk, and as he did so, his tunic rode up, exposing golden skin and hard muscle. Emery averted her gaze to the window.

During one of her first days as part of Sean's crew, she'd discovered he spent a few hours every evening teaching Seadar, Farley, and Cam how to read and write with the little symbols she'd seen in his books. He'd been delighted to teach her too. But the others were much, much farther along than she was, so they often did their own little classes, mostly after one of them woke from a nightmare and reading alone didn't do the trick.

Sean's hands still shook as he dipped his quill in ink and

scratched a mark onto a piece of parchment. "This makes a 'ja' sound."

He passed her the quill, their fingers brushing briefly, and she copied the letter over and over. "Ja," she mouthed.

And so, she learned her seventeenth letter. Yet, none of the symbols she'd learned so far matched any of the symbols on the parchment in her wooden box. And her frustration was rising.

She glanced at him as he scratched out a second letter, yet another that didn't match. Clearing her throat, she ran a finger over the dried ink of the symbols she'd already written. "I used to dream about my parents a lot."

He looked up sharply, his quill pausing halfway through a letter. Though they'd woken each other up from countless nightmares, they'd never spoken of what they dreamed of. She'd always felt silly about hers, but now...

"Me too," he said. "Still do."

She let out a slow breath, still not quite meeting his eye. "I used to dream up ways they may have died."

Sean dropped his quill and sat up straighter, cocking his head to the side. "Me too. Though, Ashborne was always there."

She licked her dry lips. "And now..."

Now she dreamt about Tavor, and how he'd locked her away in the darkness. How he tortured her, branded her, and had planned to ship her off to a prison where elemists entered and never emerged again. But she couldn't bring herself to say his name. It could lead to questions about why she'd been sailing with him in the first place, questions she couldn't answer without revealing her home. And telling Sean about Orabel would be akin to a death sentence—for both of them.

Telling outsiders about Orabel was simply not allowed.

Besides, she already knew Sean dreamt of him too. She'd heard him yelling in his sleep.

She cleared Tavor's name out of her throat, and before she could stop herself, she sketched another little symbol on her parchment, one of the jagged ones from inside her wooden box. "What is this?"

Sean squinted at the mark, and then picked up the parchment so he could examine it closer. "Where did you see this?"

Emery tapped her quill on the floor, anxiety burning through her veins. She didn't even know why she was so scared to let Sean read the clue. Before, she'd thought she was worried he'd think her childish for obsessing over her parents. But now, she realized, after sixteen years of wondering, that she was afraid to have her questions finally answered. What if she didn't like the answers?

Plus, she felt guilty about going after her parents instead of searching for a cure for the Withering. But she didn't have any leads for a cure. She already knew no one aboard the *Audacity* even knew about the disease. Meanwhile, she did have a lead for her parents. And she'd promised her sister she'd find them, too.

Taking a deep breath, she pulled the box from her pocket and held it out in her palm. The curling symbols etched into its surface flickered in the lantern's light. She grabbed Sean's blade and poked the end of her finger, drawing a bead of crimson blood.

Sean snatched the dagger back and held it out of her reach, as if he thought she might stab herself again. "What are you *doing?*"

She let a drop of her blood land on the box's wooden surface. A series of clicks sounded, and the box split in half like a cube egg.

Sean cast it a sideways glance. "Well, that's quite the trick."

He handed her a cloth from his wardrobe, and she wrapped it around her finger, staunching the bleeding. With a deep breath, she plucked the curled, yellowed piece of parchment from within the box and passed it to Sean with shaking fingers.

He took the paper, brow arching with curiosity, and Emery watched as his gaze skimmed over the jumble of jagged, black symbols inked upon it. When his eyes met hers again, his brows were even higher. "Where did you get this?"

She took a deep breath and finally told him how, while they'd been in Brimlad and Sean had gone to fetch medicine for Ranit and the grimy men had chased Emery away, she'd met an elderly lady who claimed to be her great aunt.

"She gave me the box, told me it was from my parents, and then vanished. The box only opens if I spill my blood on it."

Sean scanned the parchment again. "Interesting. Is this the reason you wanted to learn how to read?

"Partly."

He chuckled, the lovely sound so startling, Emery stared. "And here I am teaching you the wrong language."

"What?"

Sean flattened the crumpled piece of parchment on the floor next to their new ones. "I've been teaching you the Royal Tongue. But this... I believe it's old Aedish."

Hot disappointment poured into her belly. "You can't read it?"

"I can. I just need a moment." Sean pulled a fresh piece of parchment towards him and began to scratch out more words. This time, Emery actually recognized most of the letters.

She held her breath until he was finished. He handed her the parchment, and feeling like she was on the precipice of life changing information, she read the transition out loud:

> *"Clues, maps, and puzzles of the kind*
> *Chase to seek the treasures that they bind*
>
> *For the blood of some, secrets will reveal*
> *For all else, they won't but conceal*
>
> *The next clue is hidden under a stony memory*
> *The year of 1507 takes love s key*
>
> *The isle of a god will bring you said charms*
> *Which may cause the seeker significant harm"*

Emery sat back against a pillow and blinked. "What did I just read?"

"It's sounds like a riddle," Sean said, "and a poorly written one at that."

"A riddle? By Tadewin's Wind, why would they leave me a *riddle?*"

Sean leaned closer, his cheek brushing her shoulder, and read the parchment himself. "Perhaps it leads to your parents?"

"It sounds more like it leads to some sort of treasure."

Sean shrugged. "Perhaps both?"

Hope sparked in her chest. Did that mean her parents were alive? Did that mean they wanted her to find them?

But she had no idea how to crack this riddle. And more importantly, she needed a way to get to wherever they were once she figured it out.

She cleared her throat, her mouth suddenly dry. "Sean... would you be interested in making another deal?"

"Hmm?"

"Will you take me to wherever this leads? In exchange, you can have all the treasure we find. All of it."

Sean gazed at her, cocking his head to the side. "You don't want any of it for yourself?"

She shook her head. Truly, she had no need for treasure. "I just want to find my parents. But the treasure could mean you never have to steal again—that *none* of you have to steal again."

Sean slowly shook his head, and for a moment, disappointment tightened Emery's stomach. But then he smiled, a little smile that made her heart flip. He clasped her hand and shook. "It's a deal."

Emery grinned and stared down at her tiny piece of paper, at the dark jumble of words that could finally give her the answers she'd been seeking all her life.

"Now we just need to decipher the riddle," Sean said, leaning back against his pile of pillows.

She fell back against the pillows with him, and together, they read and reread the riddle, but they didn't get anywhere. At one point, Emery glanced at Sean, and found him watching her with one of his rare, lopsided grins. Her heart skipped a beat.

"What?"

"You're getting ink all over your face."

Confused, she looked down and realized she'd been nibbling on the wrong side of a quill for the gods knew how long. Heat crept into her ink smeared cheeks. "Well, at least we match now."

Sean frowned. "How?"

She reached an inky hand for his face, but he snatched her wrist before she could wipe it on him.

His grin deepened. "Nice try."

Smiling, she tried again with the other hand, but he snatched that one too. With their hands entangled, she leaned forward to rub her inky cheek on his face instead. He tried to dodge, but they both feinted to the same side, and somehow, she caught her lips on his. They both froze, Emery half in his lap.

He moved away first, his eyes wide. "That was an accident. I'm sorry."

She held his gaze, a whole new heat creeping up her neck. They'd kissed before. Twice. But both times, *she'd* kissed *him*. And without the fire of adrenaline gifting her with bravery, she'd been too nervous to do it again. Especially since he'd never showed any sign of wanting to kiss her over the past month. But the way he was looking at her now, his gaze lingering on her mouth...it made her feel bold.

"I'm not," she whispered.

Something shifted in his emerald eyes as he stared back at her. Something that made her heart hammer.

She slowly leaned closer, and then paused, their faces just a breath away again, their hands still entangled. "I'm not sorry at all."

Sean made an almost pained noise. Then he released her hands and cupped the back of her neck, burying his fingers in her hair and pulling her fully onto his lap. They're lips crashed together—

A knock sounded at the door, loud and jarring as thunder.

Emery jumped and Sean jerked back.

"*What?*" he practically growled at the door.

"Captain!" Ranit's fearful voice doused Emery with ice. "On the horizon—there's a ship you should see!"

There was a moment when Emery and Sean stared at each other. And then they leapt up, racing for the door.

Chapter Six

Emery and Sean burst from the cabin, nearly knocking Ranit off his feet. The bard's gaze flickered from Emery's ink-stained face to Sean's, and he arched a dark brow.

"Forbiddens?" Sean asked. "Varens?"

Emery's pulse raced. Which would be worse?

Forbiddens – elemists who used their elemental abilities to wreak havoc across the sea – were dangerous, but they might just sail on by.

Varens – officers of the law who hunt elemists – would not just sail by. They'd chase the *Audacity*, and if they caught up, they'd either kill everyone aboard the ship, or take them to prison.

"We're not sure..." Ranit said, looking apologetic, as if he knew he'd just interrupted...something. "She's three points off the starboard stern."

Sean cast him an exasperated look, and then climbed the stairs to the afterdeck, Ranit following at his heels and Emery just behind, breathless. She touched her lips with trembling fingers. They still burned.

"I didn't see it right away through the fog!" Farley shouted

"

down from the crow's nest. "The ship just floated out of nowhere!"

Indeed, the horizon disappeared in blankets of grey mist, and the unfamiliar ship bobbed along the edge of the fog, too close for comfort.

Sean stepped to the railing and peered at the ship. It was close enough they didn't need a telescope to see it, but far enough away that details were difficult to make out.

"Huh," he murmured, then shouted, "Colours?"

"She ain't flying any!" Farley answered.

"Huh," Sean repeated.

Emery climbed onto the railing and scrutinized the ship's broad hull, square sails, and two masts—no, there should have been three.

"One of the masts is broken," she noted. "And...there's smoke."

Indeed, a streak of grey drifted above the ship, nearly lost in the white fog.

"It looks adrift," Ranit said, standing next to Sean.

"It could be a trap," Sean muttered, his gaze darting along the entire horizon as he slowly spun in place, his jaw clenched. But the sea was empty, save for them and the drifting ship. And Farley did not call a warning.

Rooney joined them, his blood-red beard bright in the sun. "There may be cargo, Captain. Might be worth a look."

"What if someone needs help?" Emery added.

Sean sighed. "We approach slowly and carefully."

The going was indeed slow as the wind was not in their favour. The closer they got to the ship, the worse the acrid taste of smoke and gunpowder tainted the breeze. The haze settled heavy in the air, blanketing both the ship and any view they might have.

Gripping the ratlines, Emery leaned out over the ocean as they finally neared the vessel. She blinked as the smoke drifted into her eyes. When Sean cast a breeze to scatter the smoke and reveal what lay underneath, her stomach recoiled.

One of the masts was indeed broken, snapped in half like a jagged bone. The fallen half had crashed through a portion of the top deck, and wood splinters littered the floor. Frayed ropes snapped in the wind, and the sails that weren't still smoldering dangled in tattered ribbons. Ominous stains dyed huge portions of the decks crimson, along with black streaks that appeared to be scorch marks.

And yet, Emery saw no people. And no bodies.

"Fire and brimstone," Rooney said with a whistle.

"Burn! BURN!" Smythee swung down from the rigging and landed cross-legged on the deck behind Emery, startling her. He cackled and clapped his hands together, his mismatched eyes fixed on the smoldering sails. "BURN!"

Emery swallowed the taste of smoke and tried to ignore him like everyone else. "Did Forbiddens do this?"

"Could just be pirates," Ranit suggested.

"No. It couldn't." Sean glared at the hull, and Emery followed his gaze.

The ship turned lazily in the water, revealing massive spikes of ice stabbing up from the surface of the sea into the ship's starboard side. If Emery hadn't known any better, and if they were further north, she might have thought it only an iceberg.

"Certainly, an effective way to slow a ship down," Ranit mused, grimacing.

Farley appeared in the ratlines above them, his face nearly the same colour as the smoke. Emery didn't know the tall, gangly man well, but so far, she'd noted that he seemed to be afraid of everything, including, evidently, empty ships. He said, "Ain't no one aboard Captain. She's derelict."

"We should check for survivors," Billy said, appearing on Sean's other side. "Someone could be stuck below deck."

"And check for rations," Rooney suggested. He shrugged when Billy cast him a look. "What? May as well; they aren't using them."

Emery hated to admit it, but she agreed.

Sean nodded, his gaze still roving over the mess before them. "Prepare to board."

Grappling hooks flashed silver in the air, connecting the two ships. The *Audacity's* anchor was lowered to keep them from drifting any farther than they already had. Long planks were placed between the two vessels.

And then the commotion stopped. The crew looked to Sean for further instructions, waiting for the go ahead. Sean still eyed the empty, blood-stained decks with mistrust, and fiddled with the timepiece hanging from his neck.

"Billy, man the helm in case this is a trap. Ranit, get ready to cut the lines and kick off the planks if we need to make a quick escape. Rooney and Farley, once we board and confirm it's safe, search below decks for any survivors. If you find no one, grab whatever rations and supplies you can. Cam and Aleksy, search above deck for any provisions or hiding survivors. I'll search the captain's quarters."

A round of "Aye, Captain"s chimed across the *Audacity*. But Sean had already turned to look at Emery, his expression as serious as she'd ever seen it. "You. Stay with me."

She stared up into his emerald eyes, the urge to bristle and insist she could take care of herself dying at the intensity in them. Right then, he evoked the image of a true captain, of the Scourge of the Sea. A man not to be trifled with.

It was hard to believe his fingers had been buried in her hair just minutes ago, his lips on hers...

She swallowed, and when he tracked the movement of her throat, her pulse leapt.

Not breaking eye contact, she pulled her lim from its sheathe and whispered, "Aye, Captain."

His own throat bobbed, and then he cleared it, finally looking away. He unsheathed his blade and metal sang as his crew followed suit. He stepped across the gangplank, never taking his eyes off the disaster before them. Emery gripped her lim as she followed him onto the blood-soaked deck, for once wishing she'd thought to put boots on.

The frayed ropes snapped in the wind, and the sea sloshed against the ship's hull, but otherwise, it was silent and still.

The crew spread out across the floating vessel, weapons ready and waiting. Rooney vanished below decks, a pale Farley following at his heels. Cam and Aleksy moved towards the bow.

"Clear up here, Captain," Cam shouted after a moment. "A lot of blood though."

Emery's stomach clenched as she side-stepped another crimson stain herself. "Where are all the bodies?"

"I don't know," Sean said, leading the way to the captain's quarters, his eyes darting over every surface. "Thrown overboard, most likely."

"Wouldn't we have seen someone...floating?"

"Not if the sharks got them first."

Emery blanched at the thought.

One of the doors to the captain's quarters lay on the floor, ripped clean off its hinges. Black scorch marks streaked the other. Using his sword to poke the remaining door open, Sean peered inside, motioning for Emery to stay put.

He let out a long, low whistle, and Emery peaked over his shoulder.

The room was trashed; pillows littered the floor like bodies, their stuffing spilling out onto a rumpled, bloodstained rug. A bookshelf rested on its side, half shattered. Books lay scattered across the room. In the corner, a desk was smashed in half, and in the other corner, a bed sat stripped of its blankets, the mattress slit open to reveal straw and feathers.

But no people.

"It looks like someone was looking for something," Emery whispered.

Sean paced around the room, occasionally pausing to read a piece of paper on the floor or flipping something over with the toe of his boot. "Hard to say if they found it."

The two of them headed back out to the deck just as a horrible shrieking erupted from somewhere below, causing everybody to jump. Farley came hurtling up the stairs and sprinted past everyone, screaming as he went. Rooney appeared at the top of the stairs, out of breath. His eyes were wide and his expression grim.

"Captain," he puffed, "you're going to want to see this."

Sean followed Rooney down the stairs. Out of sheer curiosity, so did most of the crew, including Emery. Like the rest of the ship, the hallway below was streaked with scorch marks and the walls were painted with crimson blood. It smelled horrible, like burnt hair and rotting flesh. Emery had to cover her nose with her tunic to keep from gagging.

The smell only intensified the deeper into the ship they went, and as the group rounded the last corner, they all halted so fast that the people in the back crashed into the people in the front. Terrified gasps escaped everyone's mouths, and Aleksy even screamed as they laid their eyes upon something straight from Emery's nightmare.

They were human bodies. They had to be. Only they didn't look human anymore. There was at least a dozen of them. Their skin was black and waxy, and flaking in some places. Their bones stuck out of their charred flesh and their limbs were stuck in odd positions, as if they had all been flailing about moments before their deaths. Their eyes were gone, leaving only hollow holes behind, and their mouths were propped open, as if they all died screaming.

Sean whipped around, looking as sick as Emery felt. "Everybody, back aboard the *Audacity*, now! Drop everything!"

No one needed telling twice. The crew stampeded in a terrified turmoil back along the hallway and up the stairs.

Emery flung herself at the railing so she could throw up over the side of the ship. She was quickly joined by Seadar, and then Cam. When she was finished, she ran to help the crew as they scurried about in a panicked flurry.

Chapter Seven

The *Audacity* floated on a dark and silent sea. All was quiet upon her decks, save for the creaking of wood and the whispering of wind. All slept soundly below her decks, save for a few skittering mice and her very awake captain.

Sean sat alone in the crow's nest at some point during the ungodly hours between midnight and dawn. It wasn't an uncommon occurrence, though, lately, he'd been sleeping better. Or, at least, he'd been fleeing from his quarters less then he used to. But that night, after the ghastly sight aboard the ghost ship—as his crew decided to call it—Sean knew sleep would be either elusive or horrifying or both. So, he decided to take the worst shift of watch and avoid attempting to sleep altogether.

Bile rose in his throat every time he thought of the charred bodies, with their hollowed-out eyes and their silently screaming mouths, of the stench of burnt hair and roasted flesh. Forbiddens were responsible for the heinous scene, he was certain. But why they did such a thing, he couldn't fathom.

At least his crew had stopped worrying about it. The mood aboard the *Audacity* after finding the ship had been somber. But, with Emery's permission, Sean had called for a crew meeting, informing everybody of their possible new plan to search for Emery's treasure.

He'd allowed a vote to make sure everyone was onboard with chasing a random riddle, and it turned out the chance of treasure and the possibility of never having to raid again was appealing to everyone—except Cam.

She had merely crossed her arms and glared at Emery. When the vote came back in Emery's favour, Cam had scraped her chair back and left. Sean had frowned as he watched her stomp from the galley, but then read the riddle to everyone a second time, so the crew could work on solving it together.

No one agreed on what it meant. After a confusing hour of quarrels and sighs, of head scratching and shoulder shrugs, the crew broke apart to get some other work done, but they'd parted in a much better mood.

"Sean?"

He startled before realizing it was only Emery. She clung to the rigging, at eye level with the crow's nest. Her dark blue eyes were round and shimmered in the moonlight.

"I'm sorry. I didn't mean..." She sounded breathless, her words all coming out in a rush. "I couldn't sleep. Can I join you?"

Sean eased back against the mast and patted the spot beside him. The warmth of her shoulder pressed against his own as she climbed up and sat. He wondered if it was intentional or because there was so little space on the platform. Then he inwardly shook himself because it didn't matter. It *shouldn't* matter.

"Are you alright?" he asked.

Emery placed her hand on her lap, palm up. The 'F' branded into her skin was still pink and shiny, but healing. She opened and closed her fist, tears sparkling in her eyes. "I dream about him," she whispered. "A lot."

She didn't have to say his name. Sean knew.

Tavor.

The sight of tears in her eyes wrenched his heart, and he confessed, "Me too."

"But," she choked.

"Em?" Sean raised his hand, but wasn't sure what to do with it, what to say. He wasn't even sure what was causing her so much distress. "He won't ever hurt you again, Emery. I promise. I'll never let that happen."

She squeezed her eyes shut, a tear finally escaping. He wiped it away with a thumb, and she flinched. He froze, his stomach dropping. He'd gotten so good at comforting her, and it had been so very long since she'd flinched away from him. He thought they'd gotten past this. What had he done wrong?

He moved to pull away, but she rested a hand on his arm. He went perfectly still. She opened her eyes but didn't meet his gaze. "Sean, I don't think he *can* hurt me again. I think I killed him."

For a moment, Sean just sat there. That had not been what he expected to hear. Images of that moment flooded in his head, of the way Emery's elemental abilities had exploded around them, blasting the ship apart and flooding the hold. The way the flames warped to Emery's fear and fury, wrapping around Tavor's body in a fiery vortex. The way Tavor screamed as he vanished in a twister of red and gold. Sean imagined Tavor's skin melting, his hair burning away, his bones charring.

And he realized why Emery was so distraught. She'd probably been torturing herself over that moment for the past month, and the bodies they'd found earlier... That's what Tavor might look like now. Because of her. And seeing the gruesome sight had finally yanked lose the careful self-control she'd kept on her emotions since then.

Sean swallowed, knowing full well what carrying a weight like that was like. But the guilt he carried? That was founded. Hers was not. He thought of a dozen things he could say to comfort her, but he settled on the stark truth. "If you killed him, then good riddance."

She didn't respond. Another tear escaped.

"Emery. Please look at me." When she finally did, the guilt and horror shining in her eyes nearly killed him. "Emery, if you did kill him, then you made the world a better place. A safe place. You've probably saved hundreds, if not thousands, of lives." When she still didn't look convinced, he added drily, "But he's probably still alive. He's hard to kill. Trust me, I know."

He meant it as a half joke, and it half worked.

She bit her lip. "I should have let you kill him that day."

The day they'd met. The day he'd finally hit rock bottom and was ready to throw it all away to get his revenge and die in the process. The day a strange girl had thrown hot tea in his face, knocked him unconscious, and unwittingly saved not only his life, but his soul too.

"I am so grateful you stopped me that day," he said.

"Why?"

So many reasons, but mostly...

"I never would have met you otherwise."

She blinked, and heat rose to his cheeks as he realized he shouldn't have said that. He shouldn't say things like that to her at all, even if they were true. *Especially* if they were true.

She lapsed into silence again, her expression so lost and haunted, he couldn't stand it.

"Tell me about your sister," he blurted, desperate to get her talking and thinking about something else.

A ghost of a smile traced her mouth. "She's kind. Courageous. And stubborn."

"A family trait?"

She casted him a look but that ghostly smile remained. "She loves flowers, plants. She made her room into a garden. And she likes to mother me and Liam."

"Just the two siblings then?" he asked.

"Yeah." She looked up at the sky again, her face finally clearing, her eyes less glassy. She hesitated. "Was Lily your only sibling?"

The sound of his sister's name made him flinch. It had been so long since anyone had said the name out loud in his presence. He even avoided thinking her name in his head.

He cleared his throat. "I had an older brother."

"Had?"

In truth, this pain was so old, he barely felt it anymore. "He died when I was a toddler, along with my parents."

"Gods," Emery breathed, obviously realizing this meant Sean was the last of his entire family. "I'm sorry... What were they like?"

"I don't remember my brother. I was too young when Thomas died. Lily..." He choked off, his throat closing as if his body physically could not talk about her. How could he tell her that Lily had been his only family, his best friend, and he had let her down in the worst way? That he'd... Gods, but he had to tell her. He needed to tell her everything. "She..." he tried again, but he couldn't get anything else out.

Emery took pity on him. "Do you remember your parents?"

He took a breath. "Not really. Do you?"

"Not really," she echoed. "Too young."

Silence settled over them again, but it wasn't uncomfortable. Sean closed his eyes, trying to force down the nausea-inducing mess of emotions that always followed any thought or talk of Lily.

"Sometimes," she said, "I wonder if my parents left because they never wanted us at all. Because they never wanted *me* at all."

Even though he suspected this confession had been long buried, he couldn't help but laugh.

She stared at him, her ocean eyes wide.

"Emery, that is absurd." He took her hand, turning to face her as fully as possible. "Who in their right mind wouldn't want you?"

He immediately flushed again, realizing how very forward that sounded. Why did his mouth have to say such things before his brain could stop it? Emery just stared at him, pinning him in place with those eyes, her hand impossibly warm and soft in his own.

Let go of her hand, the rational part of his brain urged.

But he couldn't, and his gaze finally dipped to where he'd avoided looking during their entire conversation: her lips.

By the gods, he wanted to kiss those lips again. The first

time she kissed him, he'd been so shocked—so shocked his mind had gone blissfully blank and his body had barely responded at all before she'd shoved him off the ship. The second time, he'd been just as surprised, but his body had been ready. He'd been convinced he was about to die, that he'd never get the chance to do it again. So he kissed her back. But he hadn't died. And neither had she. And by some miraculous twist of fate, she became part of his crew. He got to see her every day. And he'd realized he couldn't let it happen again, no matter how much he wanted it. Because she didn't know what he truly was.

Sea-wolf. Scum. Scourge of the Sea.

She'd told him he wasn't these things, but he knew the truth. He was all these things and far worse. She didn't know what he'd done. Even his crew didn't know the worst of it. How could he tell them? How could he tell her? He couldn't handle the thought of her looking at him like she did when they first met. With horror. With disgust. With hatred.

So he refrained from kissing her again, because it wasn't fair to her. And luckily, she'd made no move either.

Until that morning in his cabin. Gods, he didn't even know what happened. Suddenly, she'd been in his lap, her lips a breath from his. And he'd lost his restraint. Thank the gods Ranit had interrupted. Sean might not have been able to stop if Emery had allowed it.

Now, staring into those unfairly beautiful blue eyes, holding her warm hand, the heat of her body so close...he felt all his reasons slipping from his mind again, his restraint dissolving like sugar in the rain. Especially when she leaned closer, her lips parting. His mind went blissfully blank again.

"Captain!"

The sound of his title caused the world to come crashing back in, nearly giving him a heart attack. They both jumped, and he released her hand as Rooney's big beaming face popped up. Sean wasn't sure if he wanted to throttle or hug the man for his timing. Rooney spotted Emery, and his smile turned a little sheepish. He, of all people, knew how difficult finding private time on a ship could be.

"We did it!" Rooney exclaimed, his booming voice startling loud in the silent night. "We solved the riddle!"

SEAN FOLLOWED Rooney down to the galley in a daze, Emery just behind him. He could still feel her heat, hear the tinkling of the beads in her hair as she moved. And he tried his best to ignore it all, to block out the moment they'd nearly shared just minutes ago.

When they entered the galley, a few oil lamps cast the space in golden light. Aleksy sat at one of the long wooden tables, a map spread out before her and a quill in hand. She looked up as they approached, and the flickering light caused the spiralling scars on the side of her face to shift. Her dark eyes shone with excitement.

Rooney plopped in a chair next to his wife, propping his booted feet on the table and leaning back, the chair groaning under his weight. "The riddle was bothering us, so we stayed up to solve it."

"I think you mean *I* solved it," Aleksy teased. Sean couldn't stop his small grin. Aleksy was such a silent, serious women. He liked seeing Rooney bring out her playful side.

Rooney waved a big hand. "Alright, yes. My brilliant wife solved the riddle while I sat here, so she had something pretty to look at."

Indeed, Rooney was shirtless for some reason, his sculpted muscles on full display. He was a huge man and had once told Sean the reason he got into cooking was because he got bored trying to keep himself full with bland food.

"Anyway," Aleksy said, tapping the map with a finger, "I know where to find the treasure."

Sean and Emery sat at the table across from her.

Emery peered at the map, her face awash with hope. "Where?"

"'*The next clue is hidden under a stony memory,*'" Aleksy quoted one of the lines from the riddle. "I'm pretty sure this is referring to a tombstone. And the line, *'the year of 1507 takes love s key'*? I don't think it's referring to a key at all. I think Love S. Key was a person, and they died in fifteen-oh-seven."

Sean sat forward, pulling the map towards him. "'*The isle of the god will bring you said charms'...* " he whispered. "Vespera's Isle."

Aleksy nodded earnestly. "Yes! That was my thought too."

"I guess it's as safe a place as any to bury a treasure..." Sean said, his voice a little hesitant.

"Aye," Rooney said. "A bit awkward, that."

Sean looked at Emery. "I'll have to check with the others too, but...would you be alright going there?"

Emery looked up at him, her brows creasing with obvious confusion. "Why wouldn't I be?"

"Because," he said, "Vespera's Isle is a giant cemetery."

Chapter Eight

Liam was really dying this time.

Honest to gods dying.

He lay flat on his back, the wooden deck of their little boat pressing into his aching spine. A scrap of canvas covered his face, so the sun couldn't scorch his already red and peeling skin. His lips cracked and bled. His stomach cramped, like he was being crushed from the inside out, and gods, his throat...dry like tree bark.

They ran out of water last night, food three days before that. Not that it had been very nourishing near the end anyway.

Thirty nicks on the mast, at least. They hadn't bothered counting for days. Too much energy. Too depressing.

Liam groaned, his throat on fire, and when Caelin did not groan back, Liam uncovered his face and cracked an eye. The glare of the sun immediately caused his eyes to run with tears, wasting the precious water he had left in his body. He blinked them away and squinted.

Caelin sat slumped on his bench, his head resting on the railing. He still gripped the oar in his blistered hands, even though they hadn't rowed in days. He didn't move. He didn't open his eyes.

Liam lifted a foot, his muscles burning, and nudged him.

"Uhg," Caelin mumbled.

"Just making sure you're still alive," Liam croaked.

"I am. Unfortunately."

"If I die first," Liam said. "You have permission to eat me."

Caelin gagged. "Well, you can't eat me."

"Rude."

Liam's stomach churned with both guilt and hunger as he thought of their last meal, a bony little fish they had shared. The first animal either of them had ever eaten. So disgusting, so delicious.

The fish had been sent by the gods, he was certain. It had leapt right into their boat, and flopped around, gasping for air, until Caelin whacked it with the hilt of his dagger. They tried to catch another afterwards, their hunger outweighing their guilt. But they had no bait, no equipment, no knowledge.

They had no energy.

Liam licked his tears from his cracked lips, desperate for any kind of moisture. Gods, if only he had more control of his abilities. He'd seen his family pull water right out of the air back home. And yet, he couldn't even move the ocean spray that gathered on the railing. He couldn't do anything.

He gazed at the blue, blue sky. Empty but for the blinding yellow sun. If he tilted his head a little, he could see the blue, blue ocean. Empty, but for them.

Never a ship. Never an island. Never a dolphin or a bird or even a breeze. It was like they'd found the edge of the world where nothing existed.

As he stared at the horizon, the blues swirled together, and he closed his eyes to keep from throwing up the nothingness in his stomach. But he was hot, so hot. Rolling onto his side, Liam retched. Nothing came up but burning yellow bile.

He retched again, nearly vomiting right on Caelin. His friend lay on the deck beside him now, his eyes closed. Had time somehow passed? Liam gazed at his friend's red face. It blurred so he couldn't even make out his features. With shaking fingers, he reached out and poked Caelin. Caelin did not respond. He didn't even twitch.

"Caelin?" Liam croaked.

Nothing.

A rush of fear tightened his guts further. "You aren't allowed to die first, you selfish ass." He shook his friend's shoulders, but still, Caelin lay unmoving.

His energy spent, he flopped back to the deck.

They had to get home. They had to warn their friends, their family. They had to live.

Emery would be so mad if he died right now.

"You're almost home, child."

Liam jerked his head up so fast the world spun again, and his vision swam with shadows. Not Caelin's voice. But who?

Empty sky. Empty sea.

The wind tickled his ear, ruffled the hair on his forehead.

The *wind.*

Yes, a breeze. A glorious, cool breeze that felt like gentle fingers running along his burned cheeks. So glorious, he could cry. The boat rocked, spun in a slow circle.

"We will bring you home," the wind whispered, the voice both familiar and strange.

Liam stared up at the blue sky, listening to water slapping against the ship's hull, feeling the bobbing of the ship as she rode the waves.

Because they were *moving.*

Or his brain had finally melted.

That seemed more likely.

With shaking arms, he pulled himself up just high enough to peer over the side of the ship. Turquoise ocean rushed by, spitting up salty sea spray.

He dropped back to the deck, curled into himself. Fought the urge to vomit again. Shadows swirled in his vision. His eyes slid shut.

"Liam." A soft voice. Hands shaking his shoulders.

He forced his eyes open, squinting against a setting sun.

Caelin, slumped against the railing, looked down at him. Not dead, thank the gods.

"Look," his friend rasped. He didn't point, but stared towards the horizon.

Liam followed his gaze. Through the gaps in the railing, he spotted a tiny blob of grey breaking up the blue.

His heart flipped. But he couldn't form the words. *Is that…?*

"Home," Caelin whispered.

As Liam stared, his vision blurred and darkened. He slipped in and out of consciousness, catching only a few images and sensations every time he woke for a few moments.

The grey blob grew. An island.

Steep, sharp cliff faces. Waves crashed against the rock, threatening to smash their little boat.

A gap between the cliffs, swallowing them whole.

A bay, round and quiet. A bay he'd seen a hundred thousand times.

Distant yelling. The crunch of the hull against sand.

"Teralyn's Teeth! It's the children!"

"Look at them!"

Hands holding him, hands lifting him.

"Where's Tavor?"

Faces. Red hair, freckles. Horrified.

Fia.

"Oh my gods, what happened to them?"

Golden skin. Long dark hair. Tears.

Grandmother.

"My boy! Oh my boy—where's Emery?"

Home.

Darkness.

Chapter Nine

Vespera's Isle was tiny, even smaller then Orabel, an unassuming green oval amongst the quiet black sea. And yet, the crew stood aboard the *Audacity*, gazing at the little island with unease and trepidation. A hush fell over the ship as they weighed anchor a few leagues out so they wouldn't draw the attention of the island's residents. They'd already doused their lanterns, allowing the night to mask their presence under the half moon.

"The people living on the island are protective of their charges," Sean had told Emery. "They will not be happy to catch us snooping about."

Emery stood amongst the crew, studying the island herself. Her stomach was a mess of knots, though not because of the island itself. To her, Vespera's Isle appeared silent and serene. But the quiet island also potentially held the answers she'd been searching for her entire life. Tonight could be the night she finally learned what became of her parents. Tonight, maybe she'd even *meet* her parents.

Emery wanted to vomit at the thought, though she wasn't sure why. Anxiety? Excitement? A noxious mixture of both?

She nearly jumped when Sean asked, "Are you ready?"

Inhaling deeply, she nodded.

"You're certain you're alright with what we're about to do?"

Emery surveyed Sean from the corner of her eye. He watched her with a frown.

"Sure." She shrugged and tried to keep her face from turning red as Sean's frown only deepened before he schooled his features.

In truth, Emery had no idea why Sean and the crew were so put off by this island, why the thought of going there seemed to fill them all with dread and disquiet. She didn't know what awaited them on the island at all, save for her answers. But she had pretended, because everyone else seemed to know what a cemetery was, and she'd already given away just how little she knew about the world too many times before. Though he rarely said anything on the subject, she knew Sean grew more and more suspicious by the day.

She guessed a shrug was not quite the attitude Sean had been expecting from her.

"If it means finding my parents, I'm willing to do just about anything," Emery amended, lifting her chin.

Sean gazed at her for a moment longer, then nodded, turned to his crew, and began giving orders.

Within minutes, Sean, Rooney, Cam, Ranit, Farley and Emery sat crammed in a longboat. Billy, Smythee and Aleksy opted to stay aboard the *Audacity* to keep watch, though Emery had overheard Aleksy say to Sean that she didn't feel comfortable disturbing the dead.

A chill skittered up Emery's spine at the confusing words. It only strengthened when Sean ordered Seadar to stay behind too, much to the younger boy's frustration.

"Our souls may already be damned," Sean said. "But there's hope for you yet."

Again, Emery wondered what exactly they were about to do.

Nobody spoke as they rowed towards the island under the half-moon's light. From the boat, the island's silver limned shore appeared empty and still. The calm, dark water lapped at the hull, and reeds scraped against the wood like so many hushed whispers. The crunching of sand and rocks as the longboat speared into the shore was deafening, as was the sound of splashing as Sean, and Rooney jumped into the shallow waters and pulled the boat up to hide it amongst the reeds and seagrass.

As Emery leapt from the boat and her feet sank into the cool mud, she finally sensed the strangeness of the place. The atmosphere felt heavy, hallowed, as if to speak louder than a whisper would bring doom upon them all. Like they shouldn't be there, and not just because the people living there wouldn't be pleased.

Emery eyed the wall of scraggly oak trees that rose before them. The trees blocked any view of what dwelled farther inland. Nothing moved beyond those trees. Nothing made noise, save for a few crickets. The feeling of foreboding only grew worse, and she fought the urge to reach for her lim.

Beside her, Sean scanned the trees as well, one hand gripping a shovel while the other rested on the pommel of his sword. "Right." His voice was quiet, but it seemed to shatter the silence of the place. "Cam and Farley, you search the North. Rooney and Ranit, search the South. Emery and I will search the West."

"What about the East?" Emery asked.

"The caretakers live in the East," Sean said. "We avoid the East. Whether or not you find anything, we meet back here in two hours."

Farley whimpered, his white-blonde hair bright in the moon light. "Why'd we have to come in the dark?"

Frankly, Emery was surprised he came at all. Though Farley and Cam looked alike with their icy-blonde hair and blue eyes, they could not have more opposite dispositions. Cam was fierce, brave, and confident, while Farley was none of these things.

Rooney slapped Farley on the shoulder with a huge hand, causing him to wince. "Relax, kid."

"Aye," Ranit added. "It's not like the dead will rise tonight."

The pairs split up, each heading in their assigned direction.

The ground shifted from mud to dirt to grass as Emery and

Sean pushed further inland. They crossed the threshold of trees and halted, surveying the land sprawling before them. The half-moon cast just enough light to illuminate the gently rolling fields of grass, the sparse collections of gnarled trees, and the hundreds —if not thousands—of stone slabs wedged vertically into the earth. Emery had no idea what they were, nor did she know what to make of the jutting marble statues and the compact marble buildings randomly dotting the land. The moonlight gilded the stonework in silver, and cast everything else in strange, warped shadows.

The feeling of disquiet only intensified, and Emery wondered for the umpteenth time, what was this place?

Sean sighed. "This is going to be a *long* night." He led the way to the closest cluster of vertical stones. "You remember the name?"

"Love S. Key," Emery said, and recited each letter, because Sean had made sure she knew how to read it before they'd left.

"If we can find the right dates, this will go faster," Sean mused. "Then we'll at least know if we're in the right area."

"Dates for what?" Emery asked as she approached the first stone slab. Like most of them, it was arched and smooth, but worn around the edges. Clearly man-made but beaten by the weather.

When Sean didn't respond right away, she glanced up to find him watching her with a barely veiled expression of suspicion. He brushed away a patch of moss on the stone slab, revealing etchings underneath. In the moonlight, Emery could just make out two sets of dates.

"The date of Love S Key's birthday," Sean said, watching her again, "and of her death."

Emery stared at the stone for a moment, and then backed away, a chill creeping along her skin. She eyed the hundreds of other stones just like it. She couldn't help it anymore; she had to ask, "Sean, what are these things?"

His lips tightened, as if he didn't want to answer. "Tombstones."

"And this place?"

Sean chewed his lip, as if again, he didn't wish to break the news to her. "This is a cemetery, Emery. Do they not have cemeteries where you're from?"

Again, she couldn't help it. So what if it was suspicious? She had to know what she'd accidentally gotten them into.

"No," she breathed.

Sean's face softened and he let out a sigh. "That explains why you were so...untroubled about this whole thing." When she said nothing, he cringed a little. "A cemetery is where the dead are laid to rest. Each tombstone, each monument, each crypt, is the burial spot of at least one dead person."

"Oh my gods." Emery froze, suddenly afraid to take another step lest she tread on a corpse. "I didn't know."

Nausea crept up her throat as she observed the hundreds and hundreds of tombstones, and the hundreds and hundreds of dead people underneath each one. Suddenly the anxiety of the crew became clear.

"We have to dig up a dead body to find the treasure, don't we?"

"Not necessarily," Sean assured. "There might not be a body under Love S. Key's tombstone. It could be a cover. It's as good a hiding spot as any."

"I'm sorry," she said. "I didn't realize what I was asking you to do."

His words to Seadar echoed in her head: *Our souls are already damned.*

"You may not have known," Sean said. "But we all did, and we all agreed to be here." When she still didn't look convinced, he added, "Frankly, most of us have done worse things. And if there is a body, we'll be as respectful as possible."

Emery didn't answer, her mind still processing the fact that the outside world buried their loved ones in the dirt, left them in a hole in the ground to rot away and be eaten by creepy crawlies. That did not seem respectful to her.

"What do you do with the dead where you're from?" Sean asked.

Emery hesitated. "We burn them."

It was mostly true. They did burn them, at least at first. Once someone's body was reduced to ashes on a pyre, they had four choices, picked sometimes by the dead before they died, or by their family members afterwards. One's ashes could be placed amongst the always burning fire upon the Sacra, to be nestled amidst the warm flames forever more. Or the ashes could be strewn into the island's bay waters, where the tide would eventually take them out to sea. Some chose for their ashes to be scattered off the cliff's edge, so the wind could carry them off into the world that denied them while they lived. Or the ashes could be set into a seed, which would then be grown into a beautiful tree that supported life on Orabel. Emery supposed the closest thing they had to a cemetery back home was the group of these trees. But they were beautiful. This place... This place set her on edge.

"Are you still alright continuing?" Sean asked.

She swallowed her shock, her discomfort. "Yes."

She meant what she said to Sean earlier. She'd do just about anything to learn what happened to her parents, even if it involved corpses.

And so, they searched. Slowly, painstakingly. They read every tombstone, and every plaque on every crypt by moonlight. The dates seemed to be random, in no order at all. Sometimes Sean got her to read the names out loud, if only for the practice. But mostly, they were quiet, that inexplicable urge to stay discreet heavy in the air.

After almost an hour of searching, they seemed no closer to finding Love S. Key. Emery's eyes were sore from straining to read in the half-moon's silvery light. Every once in a while, a thin cloud drifted in front of the moon, casting them into shadows and making it nearly impossible to read at all.

When they crested a hill to find another field of tombstones,

Emery's heart sank. "How are there so many dead people on such a small island?"

"The dead don't come from this island," Sean explained, crouching to read yet another name. "The only people who ever lived here are the caretakers."

"Where do they come from then?"

"Mostly from the continent. We're not far from its coast."

Emery cringed, remembering the one and only time she'd been to the continent. When Tavor had tortured Liam and herself, had nearly killed Sean. She resisted the urge to look at the 'F' burned into her palm.

Sean paused, absently rubbing his leg as if also remembering the bullet that had pierced his thigh. "This island was unused and uninhabited until the Elemental War. There were so many casualties they created a whole new cemetery just to hold the dead."

Shuddering, Emery scanned the astonishing number of tombstones once again, unable to imagine the carnage that would have caused so much death. "Gods, why would my parents send me here?" She gasped and grabbed Sean's arm. "What if they're *buried* here?"

Sean cast her a small but sad smile. "Well, the good news is, that's unlikely..."

"Why?"

"Because elemists are not allowed to be buried here. We're not allowed to be buried in any cemetery. Just walking around in here alive is offensive to the Ungifted and to Roark."

Sean had mentioned Roark before, the one god people on the continent worshipped. A false god, perhaps, because Emery had always been told there were four gods. And none of them were named Roark.

Despite the further proof of how much the world hated her kind, Emery's fraught nerves relaxed a little in knowing her parents most likely weren't rotting away beneath her feet. "That's...harsh."

"Just as well," Sean said, leaves crunching under his boots as he moved to read the plaque on a crypt. "I'd prefer to be tossed in the sea anyway. Become part of the ocean forever."

"Good choice," Emery said. When contemplating her own mortality, she always chose being scattered into the wind so she could finally see the world one way or another. Liam had liked that idea too, but Ayana always wanted to be placed in a seed so she could grow into a 'spectacular tree'. These were her actual words, and she made this very clear when she became ill. Sorrow pierced Emery's heart at the thought of Ayana. What if her sister had already gotten that wish? What if she was gone and Emery had missed it?

She had to clear her throat before she asked, "What if the sharks just eat your corpse?"

Sean waved his hand, as if brushing off the thought. "I eat fish, they eat me. Circle of life and all that."

"Then you'd spend the afterlife as fish poop," Emery said, and Sean laughed out loud before catching himself and lowering his voice.

"But think of the things I'd see down there," he said, but then froze, snapping his gaze to the left and peering into the shadows.

They stood in silence for a moment, and then Emery heard it too. Whispers on the wind.

"Did you hear that?" someone said.

"Hear what?" answered another.

They were far enough away that Emery had to strain to hear them but close enough that Sean's hand wandered to his sword.

"Laughter. I swear, I heard laughter," said the first voice.

The second voice scoffed. "The dead aren't laughing at you, moron. They're dead."

The voices faded, only to be replaced by a strange rumbling instead.

Sean raised a finger to his lips, rather unnecessarily, and beckoned her over. Crouching, they crept up a grassy knoll. When they reached its peak, they dropped to their bellies in the cool grass and crawled beneath a bush, pulling aside the foliage so they could gaze down the other side of the hill.

An orange circle of flickering lantern light illuminated yet another cluster of tombstones. Two figures moved within the light, though it was difficult to discern any features. One stood before a tombstone, their hand hovering over the space before it. The rumbling noise intensified, and when Emery angled her head to see better, she realized the earth itself was vibrating, the dirt shaking itself lose and skittering off to the side, until there was no dirt left at all before the tombstone. Just a rectangular hole with a box inside.

"Elemists," Emery murmured.

"Gravediggers," Sean corrected, disgust in his voice.

The second figure stood off to the side, leaning against a tree and flipping a coin over their knuckles. "Captain will be pissed that we're taking so long." A man, judging by the voice. He sounded more bored then worried.

"The Captain doesn't need to know about this," said the first figure, and though the voice was deep, it was unmistakably female. She dropped into the hole to stand upon the wooden box and released a hatchet from the tool belt around her waist. Without preamble, she drove the hatchet into the box.

The cracking of the wood was so loud in the otherwise silent night, Emery nearly jumped.

"Do you think that's Love S. Key's grave?" she asked.

"Doubtful," Sean whispered. "That would have to be quite a coincidence."

The woman crouched and poked around in the box. With a snap, she ripped out an entire skeletal arm. The woman snapped the wrist clean off the arm and held up a sparkling golden bracelet.

"That will fetch a pretty penny," she said, sliding the bracelet onto her own wrist where it jangled against several others.

As the woman tossed the skeletal arm back in the box and stood up, Emery noticed several rings glinting on her fingers in the lantern's light, and more than one shiny bauble hanging around her neck.

"Disgusting," Emery hissed, and then gasped as something sharp pricked her back.

Still laying on her belly, Emery craned her neck backwards to find a huge man standing behind them, the tip of his sword pressed into her spine.

Chapter Ten

The darkness felt like mud, sucking Liam down while he tried to crawl his way up into the light. He could hear murmured voices, muffled as if he were underwater. With enormous effort, he forced his eyes open, blinking away the darkness still clinging to his vision.

"Liam! Thank the gods." A blurred face hovered over him, the familiar voice still slightly muffled. "He's awake!"

"The fluids are helping," said a less familiar voice. "His heartbeat is strengthening. But he'll still need plenty of rest."

"Thank you, Aran."

Liam dredged the name up through the mud.

Aran. One of Orabel's healers.

He was home.

"I'll give you some time alone, Elma." Footsteps faded away.

A cool hand pressed to his forehead. "Liam, my love?"

Liam blinked again to clear away the haziness, refraining from shaking his head due to a dull pounding behind his eyes. "Grandmother?" he choked, his tongue sticky and heavy, his throat scorched as a desert.

"Drink this." He was helped into a sitting position, his grandmother fluffing a goose down pillow behind his back and pushing a clay mug into his hand.

His muscles shook as he lifted the mug and sipped the hot chamomile tea. He nearly sighed at the apple and honey taste, and the way it coated his throat like a balm.

Leaning back against his pillow, his vision finally cleared enough for him to see he was indeed inside Orabel's infirmary. Sunlight spilled in through lightly vine-veiled holes high up near the ceiling, and the redwood walls curved away from him in both directions, as the infirmary was a circular room set inside one of the many giant redwoods on the island. He couldn't see much more though; a curtain of woven grasses cut him off from the rest of the infirmary, granting him a semi-private space.

Inside this space sat two cots, one he currently occupied, and the other taken by Caelin. He lay there, perfectly still, his skin red and blistered, his hair matted, his face gaunt.

"Is he alright?" Liam asked, his voice still hoarse despite the tea.

"He'll be alright," Grandmother assured. "He hasn't woken up yet. But you're both getting stronger by the hour."

When Liam went to take another sip of his tea, he finally felt a tugging on his arm. Blinking down, he noticed a hollowed bone needle sticking out of his arm, an equally hollowed vine snaking its way from its end and up into a round, glass sphere hanging from a wooden pole. The sphere contained a mixture of liquid and nutrients that drained into his veins, and he couldn't help but stare at it. He'd been in the infirmary plenty of times as a child: after he fell from a tree and broke his arm, after he dove into the lake and cracked his head on a rock, after he and Caelin got too rowdy with their lims, and Caelin hit Liam so hard in the face he cracked a tooth... But he'd never needed to be hooked up to nutrients before.

"How long..." he tried to ask, but coughed before he could finish. He sipped more tea.

Grandmother's eyes swam. "You've been home for a few days. But you were gone for months."

She pushed his messy curls from his forehead and tucked his blanket tighter around his legs. If he had the strength, he would have thrown his arms around her shoulders, both to stop her from fussing and because he'd missed her so much. Instead, he took her hand and squeezed. She closed her eyes, wrapped his hand in both of her own, and then raised it to press against her soft cheek. He swore she'd aged years in the months he'd been away.

"Where's Grandfather?" Liam asked. "And Ayana?"

He was also surprised not to see Grace or her parents standing vigil at Caelin's cot. And, he had to admit, he was shocked and a little wounded not to see Fia.

Grandmother visibly swallowed, her voice quivering. "We've been taking turns keeping watch. The infirmary has been... crowded lately."

Liam blinked. The infirmary was never crowded.

"Liam, where is your sister?" Grandmother blurted. "Where is Tavor? What *happened* to you?"

Before he could answer, a noticeable hush fell over the infirmary. It hadn't been loud before, but now it was dead silent, as if no one dared breathe.

Grandmother dropped his hand and stood, her breath catching as the curtain of grasses was pushed aside and two elderly beings glided towards Liam's cot. Both wore identical robes woven of leaves, and crowns of twisted wood.

"Arch-Elemists," Grandmother breathed, bowing and smoothing out her disheveled braid and plain cotton gown.

Liam grimaced as he attempted to swing his weak legs over the side of the cot to stand for his leaders.

Celosia, the Arch-Elemist with short white hair, waved a hand dismissively. "That's not necessary, Liam. Please remain abed." She turned to Grandmother, a pleasant smile appearing in the ancient lines of her face. "Elma, could we have a moment alone with your grandson?"

"Of course, of course." Liam's grandmother puffed his pillow one last time and planted a kiss upon his curls. "I'll let everyone know you're awake."

She bustled off, leaving Liam alone with two of the four leaders of his home island. He absently wondered where Dyzek and Aeolius, the third and fourth Arch-Elemists, were. It was strange enough seeing the Arch-Elemists outside of their home, let alone inside of the infirmary. Stranger still to see only two of them. It was always all of them or none of them when it came to making appearances.

"We trust you are feeling better?" Nyneve asked, her long silver hair glistening in a beam of sunlight. Her voice was as calm as a placid pond.

"It was a trick!" Liam blurted, unable to help himself. He'd travelled so far, for one goal. He'd left his sister behind and nearly died getting back for one purpose. One moment. And this was it. "Tavor lied. He never had a cure. He never wanted peace. He tortured—"

"Yes," Celosia said, her voice still serene though her eyes held pity. "We are aware."

All the breath rushed out of Liam in one word. "*What?*"

The two Arch-Elemists gazed at him with blank expressions, as if they were simply talking about the weather he'd experienced on his trip.

"We are aware of Tavor's true nature," Nyneve said. "We knew what he planned. We know what he plans yet."

Her words hung like a crack of thunder in the silence, echoing around Liam's skull. A silence amplified, he suddenly realized, because he could hear absolutely nothing from the infirmary behind the curtain of grasses, as if the Arch-Elemists had created a wall of solid air blocking any sound from getting in. Or out.

His words came out flat with shock. "You knew he lied? You knew he planned to *torture* us, and yet, you still sent us out there?"

"The gods showed us what must come to pass to save our people," Celosia said. "We listen, and we follow."

Anger, hot and fierce, bubbled in Liam's gut. "The gods told you to send children to get tortured. And you just obliged?"

He tried to stand again, ignoring the quake in his knees and the dizziness in his head, but a soft breeze nudged him back against the pillows.

"Everyone has a part they must play," Celosia continued. "You were meant to leave the island, to sail with Tavor, to set certain events into motion. Just as you were meant to return."

His anger flared. "Emery—"

"Your sister is where she is meant to be."

The breath left Liam again as conflicting emotions crashed together in his chest. His fury still roiled, but to hear Emery was where she was meant to be, as decreed by the very gods themselves, meant Liam hadn't abandoned her on her fool's errand for no reason. The notion banked the anger, just a little. But then the fear settled in. Because if the Arch-Elemists where to be believed, the gods had also decreed their torture. That meant Emery wasn't safe, whether watched by the gods or not. Which meant she could be in danger. Right now.

"Is she safe?" he choked.

"She is where she is meant to be," Nyneve echoed calmly.

Liam gritted his teeth. "But is she *safe?*"

"For now."

Liam sucked in a deep breath. His thoughts reeled, his emotions about to explode.

For now. What did that mean?

He never should have left her. Gods and their wills be damned.

Before he could lash out, Caelin's scratchy voice cut him off. "You know of Tavor's plans to invade the island. To turn it into another prison."

Liam's heart leapt at the sound of his best friend's voice, even if it sounded like he'd just swallowed hot coals, at the sight of him glaring with glassy eyes at the Arch-Elemists from within the nest of his cot. Awake. Alive.

"Yes," Celosia replied, seemingly unsurprised to find Caelin suddenly conscious and part of their conversation. "We know he plans to turn Orabel into another Abyssus. If we heed the gods, his plans will not come to fruition."

"We must warn our people," Caelin said, and though his voice remained calm, the tendons straining in his neck told Liam he was barely restraining his own rage. "Get them ready for a fight."

"We must do no such thing," Aeolius said.

Liam and Caelin stared at their leaders.

"They need to know the truth." Liam barely managed not to scream.

"They do not," Nyneve said, voice as calm as ever. "The truth is too upsetting."

"I'd say!" Liam snapped and immediately bit his lip to shut himself up. One did not speak to the Arch-Elemists like that, even if they truly deserved it.

But Nyneve carried on as if he hadn't spoken. "Our people do not need to know the extent of our danger, not yet."

"They deserve to know," Caelin growled. "Just like we deserved to know what we were being thrown into."

"The truth can disrupt what must come to pass. The truth will be revealed when the time is correct." Caelin opened his mouth to argue but Nyneve spoke over him. "That time is not now." Her calm façade finally cracked, like a frozen pond fracturing at the edge. "You have not been home for some time. Orabel is not how you left it."

Liam and Caelin exchanged wary glances.

"What does that mean?" Liam asked, trepidation smothering the remainder of his anger.

"The Withering has gotten worse. It strikes more of our people. It crumbles more of our land," Celosia said. "Worrying about outside dangers is not helpful now. Saving ourselves from within, is."

Liam swallowed his dread. "So we just...say nothing? If people ask, we lie?"

"Yes."

There was a beat of silence.

"We can't do that," Caelin said.

"You must," Nyneve said. "Say nothing. If people ask, Emery is still seeking peace, is still acquiring the cure. And you two were separated from her in a storm."

"That seems...flimsy," Liam muttered.

"And yet, it's all true."

Liam opened his mouth to argue, but he supposed it *was* all true. Technically. Emery was still searching for a cure, and perhaps a way to find peace. He and Caelin had lost her in a storm, just not as recently as the Arch-Elemists would have everyone believe. But gods, how was he supposed to hide the horrors they faced from his friends and family? How was he supposed to stay quiet about the possible horrors to come?

"We will leave you to rest." The two Arch-Elemists headed back through the curtain of grasses. Nyneve peered over her shoulder before she stepped through. "The leaves and the breezes speak. And we listen. We will know if you speak too."

And then she was gone.

Liam and Caelin stared after their leaders, at the very people who had vowed to keep their island, their people, safe. The thinly veiled threat settled upon them like chains.

Chapter Eleven

With the point of his sword still digging into Emery's back, the huge man jerked his chin up, as if ordering them to stand.

Gods, he was even bigger than Rooney.

Emery glanced at Sean, and he nodded, his mouth pressed into a firm line. They slowly pushed to their feet. Although Emery itched to grab her lim, she followed Sean's lead when he raised his hands in the air, keeping them well away from his various weapons. He had also discreetly left their shovel in the bushes.

"We don't want any trouble," Sean said, adopting a new accent Emery had never heard before.

The man said nothing but jerked his chin once again. Emery sucked in a breath as he dug his blade harder into her back, forcing her to march forward lest he break the skin.

Sean's expression turned lethal, but he still made no move for his weapons. They stumbled down the knoll into the lantern's light.

"What's this, Jaro?" asked the woman mildly when she noticed them, toying with her new stolen bracelet.

Up close, Emery could see her high cheekbones and her jet-black hair, cut at the chin, the slight angle of her eyes reminding her of Ranit's, though her eyes held none of Ranit's kindness.

"Little spies?" asked the woman.

The man with the sword nodded. The slanting lantern light somehow made him appear more massive, with bulging muscles that were on display because he wore nothing but a vest over his torso.

"We saw nothing," Sean said, his voice uncharacteristically fearful. His eyes darted about as if searching for an escape route. "Let us go and we'll tell no one. We swear."

The woman smirked, as if unconcerned she'd just been caught stealing. "And why, dare I say, were you two frolicking in a cemetery in the *dead* of night." She elbowed the other man who had been watching her rob the grave. "See what I did there, Ace?"

"Really, Torra?" The man rolled coal-rimmed eyes. He also had dark hair, with a matching short beard and moustache. Once again looking bored, he crossed his arms and leaned back against a tree, the leather of his long coat creaking with the movement.

"I was taking my fiancé for a stroll," Sean said, wrapping an arm around Emery's waist and successfully knocking the sword away from her spine. Again, Sean's voice wavered, as if truly terrified. The huge man holding the sword let it drop, as unconcerned as the other two seemed.

The woman—Torra —swept her dark gaze up Sean's body, and then down Emery's, noting the grass stains and dirt smears on their clothes, the twigs caught in Emery's hair from laying in the bush. Her smirk deepened. "Ah, I see. Dead people turn you on. Were you screwing in the grave dirt? Maybe on a tombstone?"

Emery did not have to fake the blush staining her cheeks. "Please don't tell on us!" she whined, attempting to match Sean's new accent.. "It's just so boring here."

Torra nudged the man again. "I told you the locals are freaks, Ace."

The dark-haired man—Ace—slid his gaze the length of Emery's body too. "I like a little freak."

Emery suppressed a shudder, and Sean's arm tightened around her waist.

"As do I," Torra said, leering at Sean.

"As fun as that sounds, Captain will throw a fit if we take much longer," Ace said. "We should just kill them and get it over with."

"I like that idea too," Torra said, hefting the hatchet she used to smash open the box, the sharp edge gleaming in the moonlight. Her other hand rested on the whip coiled at her belt.

Sean tightened his hold again, but this time, it was not in a protective way. It was a signal. Emery met his gaze from the corner of her eye. His gaze flickered to her lim, then the man behind them, and he nodded almost imperceptibly. She nodded back, her fingers tingling with adrenaline.

Sean's fingers tapped on her waist. Once. Twice. On the third tap, Emery ripped her lim from its sheath and drove it backwards, straight into the groin of the muscled man. All his breath escaped in a high wheeze, and he pitched sideways, dropping his sword to cup himself. Emery grabbed the sword and hurled it into the darkness.

At the same time, Sean threw up his hands, sending a blast of hard air at Torra and Ace. They both stumbled backwards, and the lantern sputtered out, casting them into the blue and silvery shadows of night. As Torra windmilled her arms to keep from falling, Sean's blade caught the head of her hatchet and flung it out of her grasp. It followed Jaro's sword into the darkness. Sean darted behind Torra, looping an elbow around her throat and pressing his blade to her cheek.

"Let us go," Sean demanded, dropping his fake accent. "And nobody has to get hurt." He glanced at Jaro, who was still wheezing on the ground, and smirked. "Nobody *else* has to get hurt."

Ace, somehow, still looked bored, even as he drew his cutlass. He stepped sideways, forcing Emery to do the same so they slowly circled each other, waiting to see which party would cede first.

"Nice trick." Torra grinned and the subtle movement was enough to cause Sean's blade to nick her skin. "But I have a better one."

A groaning, creaking sound split the silence, and the air rushed out of Emery's lungs as her leg was pulled out from under her and she slammed into the ground. She barely held on to her lim as she was dragged across the dirt, and then dropped it when she was suddenly yanked into the air. A tree branch wrapped around her ankle, grinding her bones together, and she dangled upside down. Her heart hammering, she pried at the wood, but to no avail.

Sean remained with his elbow locked around Torra's throat, his blade still resting on her cheek. He growled, "Let her down."

"I don't think I will, thank you," said Torra.

Ace walked up to the tree, his coal-rimmed gaze now level with Emery's. He twined her hair around a finger, clanking together the beads woven within. "Oh dear. A stalemate. Whatever shall we do?" His breath smelled of rum.

Emery tried to punch his hand away, but he grabbed her wrist with his other hand and squeezed, grinding the bones there like the tree branch had done to her ankle.

"I will kill you if you don't put her down," Sean said, pressing his blade into Torra's cheek, drawing more blood.

The massive man—Jaro—had finally picked himself off the ground and limped to the tree where Emery hung. He reached for her throat, his callused fingers scraping over her skin. Emery flailed, trying to punch him with her free hand, but Ace grabbed that one too. Jaro smiled wide, revealing the reason he had yet to speak: his tongue was gone.

"*Don't touch her!*" Sean shouted. He moved his blade to Tora's throat instead, pressing hard enough for more blood to bloom. Emery knew he'd never intentionally killed anyone before. But would he now, for her?

She couldn't let him do that. She wouldn't—

An unnaturally cold breeze washed across the little clearing, smelling of dirt and leaves and something else Emery couldn't name, something sweet and cloying.

"None of that now," Ace commanded.

Jaro's huge fingers tightened around Emery's throat, enough to block her breath. She couldn't even tell him it hadn't been her calling the wind, as much as she wished it had been.

"What is that?" Ace asked, and everyone, including Emery, with difficulty, turned to follow his gaze. A thick, yellowish fog rolled down the hill towards them. Tendrils flowed between trees and slithered across the ground like smoky snakes, swallowing everything they passed.

"It's not me," Torra said, raising her hands as much as she could with Sean's blade in the way.

Jaro squeezed Emery's throat tighter, her bones bending under the pressure. She tried to shake her head but couldn't.

"It's not us!" Sean said. He spun so Torra was between him and the fog, and backed away slowly, though he had nowhere to go. Not unless he wanted to leave Emery behind.

Still in Sean's grip, Torra raised one hand again, and sent a blast of wind into the fog. It did nothing. The fog hurtled towards them, devouring the cemetery, the trees, the tombstones. And then it washed over them like a yellow wave. Sounds became muffled, like they were underwater.

Jaro released Emery's throat, and she sucked in a desperate breath, nearly choking on the fog's thickness. It flowed into her mouth, her nostrils, tasting like mold and decay. Ace released her hands. Emery couldn't see anything but the two men standing right next to her, who both turned to peer into the fog with their weapons drawn. It was like they were the only three people on earth.

Screams flooded the fog, at once close and distant. The sound of metal clanking punctuated the screams, and the hairs on her arms stood up as she recognized Sean's voice. But his shouting didn't sound like pain. It was terror.

"What the...?" Ace said, his coal-rimmed eyes wide as he

tried to peer through the yellow wall of fog. Then he, too, screamed as something yanked him into the mist. A moment later, Jaro vanished as well.

And Emery was alone, surrounded by screams, trapped upside down with no weapons. Fear flooded her veins.

"Sean?" she called. "Sean!"

She nearly yelped as something materialized out of the fog, right in front of her. For a gleeful moment, she though it was Sean. But then her heart stopped.

It wasn't Sean at all.

A skeleton stood before her. An honest to gods human body comprised of nothing but bones. Its hollow gaze was levelled with her own. A beetle crawled from its empty eye socket. It opened its mouth as if to scream, but its jaw fell off instead.

So it was Emery who did the screaming.

Chapter Twelve

The yellow fog swirled around the skeleton, weaving between its empty ribs, as it stared at Emery with its fathomless eyes. Maggots squirmed in its nostrils. Bits of rotting flesh still clung to its bones and decaying cloth hung from its frame.

Though the thick fog clogged her mouth, her throat, her lungs, Emery screamed again.

The undead thing reached for her with fleshless fingers, and she kicked at it with her free foot. The head flew off its boney neck, vanishing into the fog. But the body remained upright, its fingers curled around her tunic, and Emery punched at its torso again and again, until its ribcage caved in. She grabbed its wrist and twisted it until it snapped, freeing her from its grip. She kicked once more, and the thing crumpled to the ground in a pile of bones.

Almost immediately, a second walking corpse emerged from the fog, this one nothing but white bone.

Emery clawed at the tree branch still crushing her ankle and holding her suspended in the air. It wouldn't budge, her ankle still locked helplessly in its grasp. Her muscles straining, she held onto the branch anyway, since it at least kept her out of the skeleton's reach.

Muffled shouts echoed in the fog, as if coming from everywhere and nowhere at once.

"Sean!" Emery shouted, panic making her voice shrill.

Gods, was he alright? Did the thieves have him? Did the skeletons? How many of each were there?

A yelp escaped her as something tangled in her hair and yanked. Tears sprang to her eyes, but she dared not let go of the tree branch. Three corpses, all in various states of decay, converged under the tree now. They climbed onto each other in attempts to reach her, the highest one still gripping her hair. It pulled again, so hard Emery's hold on the tree branch slipped and she was left to dangle again.

Fear, pain, and now outrage raced through her. All she'd wanted was to find out what had happened to her parents. Why did undead skeletons have to be involved?

She reigned in her emotions enough to concentrate, reaching for the wind spirit with her own, and it came rushing to her faster then it had in a month, like a beast heeding its master's call. With another scream, she unleashed it.

Bones scattered into the fog in all directions as the skeletons flew apart. But the fog itself never wavered. It was completely unaffected by the wind.

Even so, elation filled Emery's heart. The wind had finally listened to her again. She'd barely been able to do any elemental manipulation since escaping Tavor.

Her relief was short-lived. More skeletons emerged from the fog, bones clacking, fingers outstretched. Two, three, four of them at least.

She grasped the wind again, gathered it to her in anticipation of releasing it in a blast, but before she could, another figure flew out of the fog, its sword catching one of the corpses in the chest. The corpse imploded into shards of bone, but the figure and its sword had already moved on to the next skeleton.

"Sean!" Emery cried with relief, still mentally clinging to the wind. She couldn't let it go now, in fear of hurting Sean. "Are you alright?"

"I've been better," he panted, glancing at her long enough for her to note new bloody scratches on his cheek. "You?"

He turned to kick a second corpse in the back and took a third out by its knees with another swing of his blade. The fourth lunged at him, but Emery managed to release her wind then, scattering its bones again.

"I'm alright." She assessed her sore scalp. "I think one of the buggers tore out some hair though."

Sean tossed her a dagger as more skeletons appeared. He dodged the reaching fingers of one corpse, then lopped off the head of another. The hoard was relentless, never ending. "Cut yourself free!"

Emery pulled herself up to the branch, growing dizzy from the blood rushing to and from her head so many times. She sawed and hacked frantically at the wood holding her hostage, resisting the urge to look back at Sean and the army of dead things.

But then his shout drew her attention.

She looked just in time to watch him become overwhelmed by the sheer number of corpses. They yanked him off his feet, dozens of hands grasping at his arms and legs and clothes. He fought with everything he had, using his blade and the wind and his bare hands. But there were just too many.

"Em!" he shouted, the fear in his voice palpable.

They dragged him away, the fog swallowing him whole.

Emery was left alone, her ears ringing with the sudden suffocating silence. "Sean!"

She hacked and hacked at the wood and then—

"To Pyralis's Flames with this!" Rage rushed through her again and she closed her eyes, reaching out to the tree with her mind, entangling her angry and terrified soul with that of the tree's steady and calm spirit.

"Let go!" she commanded. "LET GO!"

With an almost reluctant grown, the wood encasing her

ankle loosened, and she fell to the grassy ground, barely twisting in time to avoid snapping her neck.

She leapt to her feet, kicked around in the pile of bones under the tree until she found her lim and, ignoring the pain in her ankle, sprinted into the fog after Sean.

She tried to stay in a straight line while dodging the tombstones and trees continually looming out of the fog. "Sean!" she shouted. "Where are you?"

As if from a hundred leagues away, she heard him calling, "Emery!"

She veered right, nearly colliding with another walking corpse but dodged it at the last moment.

"Sean!" she cried. "Keep yelling!"

"Em!" came his voice, closer but still muffled by the fog.

And then she nearly tripped over him. She leapt over him instead, to avoid trampling him, and then nearly fell in her hurry to turn back. She gasped at the scene before her, one straight out of a nightmare.

Sean clung to a crumbling tombstone with all his strength, his muscles straining as dozens of skeletal hands clung to every part of him, attempting to drag him into a yawning pit of a grave. Sweat, blood, and mud glistened on his face, but even through all that, Emery could see the sheer terror in his expression.

"I'm losing my grip," he shouted. Indeed, his fingers were starting to slip as the skeletons pulled and pulled on him. And the tombstone was crumbling under his arms, the old stone and Sean's only anchor to life about to break apart from the ground.

Emery swung her lim at the skeletons, bashing in skulls, crushing wrists, snapping arms. But it wasn't enough. When one skeleton released Sean, another took its place. The tombstone Sean clung to shuddered and finally disintegrated in his grasp, and Sean clawed at the ground as he was pulled further into the pit of corpses.

Abandoning her attack, Emery dropped to her knees and thrust her hands into the cold grave dirt. A skeleton turned to her, reached for her, clawing at her face hard enough to draw blood, but she ignored it. She reached for the calm, steady presence of the earth beneath her.

"Help us!" she begged in her head, in her soul. The dirt beneath her fingers began to roil. From all sides of the grave, the dirt began to pour into the pit like a waterfall, burying the corpses in the earth from which they'd risen. The dirt poured and poured until only a few corpses were left, their arms or heads poking out from the earth. Emery bashed them to bits with her lim until, finally, Sean was able to pull himself free.

He rose on shaky legs. Emery ran to him and threw her arms around him. "Are you alright?"

He embraced her back, his entire body trembling against hers. He didn't reply, as if beyond words. She felt him nod once, his heavy breaths ruffling her hair.

Emery untangled herself from his arms, grabbed his sword from where it lay half buried in mud a few paces away, and thrust its pommel into his shaking fingers. She grabbed his other hand and yanked him into the fog, away from the pit and the skeletons that were already attempting to climb back out of the earth.

They ran blindly, hand in hand, any thoughts of her parents or a treasure long gone. She didn't care anymore. She just ran, trying to keep their trajectory as straight as possible, knowing they'd eventually reach the edge of the island, that the nightmare would have to end once they reached the water. More skeletons leapt out of the fog as they ran, but they dodged them all, swinging their weapons if any got too close.

"How is this possible?" Emery cried, ducking under an outstretched arm.

"Necromancy?" Sean shouted as he severed the spine of a skeleton.

"What is that?"

"A dark magic meant to raise the dead."

Emery tried to process this as they continued their sprint. "There are other magics?"

She'd never heard of magic outside of elemental manipulation.

"In theory," Sean panted. "There's many. I've only read about them."

Indeed, Emery recalled reading about all kinds of other magics in Sean's books, including stories about curses so cruel and objects imbued with powers. Could those things be real too?

A scream pierced the fog.

"Farley!" Sean shouted, pivoting directions and yanking Emery along with him.

Another scream, and then shouting. They sprinted for those screams, lungs heaving and legs burning until, finally, the fog spat them out.

But it wasn't the beach that lay before them. It was just more cemetery, clear of the fog, more tombstones and—

"Captain!" Ranit shouted. "Thank the gods! We found her!"

It took Emery a moment to realize what Ranit was talking about.

Ranit, Cam, Farley, and Rooney were all there, in various states of disarray, covered in mud and blood and the gods only knew what else. Bones littered the ground around them as Farley dug with a shovel and Ranit dug with just one hand in front of a tombstone—Love S. Key's tombstone, presumably—while Cam and Rooney fended off any skeletons that dared to lurch out of the fog.

Sean immediately joined Cam and Rooney in their defence of the clearing, and Emery sprinted for the grave, diving into the hole they'd already created, and began scooping away dirt with her hands. She didn't have the time or the energy to worry about what they might find. She just wanted to find it and get out of there. A part of her wanted to tell them all to forget about it, to just run. But she was so close now, so close...

Farley's shovel clanked against something hard, and for a moment, all fell silent and still as everyone looked towards the grave. Even the skeletons seem to pause their attack. Then Emery, Ranit, and Farley renewed their digging with vigor until, finally, a chest emerged from the earth. It was wood, and it was big enough that Emery certainly couldn't lift it on her own.

The corpses attacked again, this time with more vitriol, as if enraged the chest was uncovered, pushing Sean, Cam, and Rooney closer and closer to the grave as they struggled to hold back the attack. Sean alternated between slicing them down with his sword and blasting them apart with the wind. Cam tore into them with her two axes, and Rooney, presumably having lost his blade, took them down with his bare hands.

But one darted past them all, grabbed Farley's arm, and twisted it.

An awful crack split the air, followed by an even more awful scream from Farley as his arm snapped. Cam flew at the corpse, demolishing it with a kick to the ribs, an axe to the head and a roar of pure rage. She dropped next to her brother, examined his clearly broken arm as Farley let out a sob.

"It's alright. You'll be alright," she said soothingly, smoothing his hair, and then glared at Emery. "This is your fault."

Emery's heart hammered but she didn't have time to say anything before Cam had to turn to fend off another undead. Farley whimpered at the edge of the grave.

Ranit heaved on the chest, managing to pull it out of the dirt, though just barely. "It's heavy."

Panic reared in Emery's chest. How were they going to get the chest back to the ship? They couldn't fight and run and carry it all at the same time.

Ranit frowned as he examined the chest. "There's no way to open it."

As Emery scrutinized the chest herself, she realized he was right. There was no keyhole, no visible opening of any kind. Just a bunch of swirling designs etched into the wood. Just like the small box currently sitting in her pocket.

And she knew what to do. She hoped.

Emery reached out with a hand bloodied from her fights with the corpses and pressed her palm against the worn wood.

A series of clicks sounded, and the chest's lid sprang partially open. At the same time, every single skeleton left standing collapsed into heaps of bone and rags and flesh. The fog that still lingered at the edges of the clearing dissolved into nothing, as if it had never been there at all.

All at once, it was silent. Calm. Save for the pounding of all their hearts. In the confused stillness, Rooney bent down and examined one of the piles of bones that used to be a walking dead man.

"It's wood," he said, astonished.

"What?" Sean asked, turning sharply in his direction.

"They weren't...real." Rooney picked up a few pieces of the skeletons. "This isn't bone. It's wood and moss and leaves."

Cam scattered a pile with her boot. "How? *Why?*"

Indeed, as Emery gazed at the closet pile of crushed skeleton, she realized the bones were in fact bleached wood, the flesh just moss and leaves. Between the fog and the adrenaline and the panic, it had been impossible to tell otherwise.

"It doesn't matter now," Sean said, kicking a skull out of his way as he stalked towards Love's grave. "Let's get whatever's in that chest and get out of here. Farley needs to see Aleksy."

Emery turned back to the half-opened chest, her heart suddenly in her throat. This could be it. This could be the moment she finally got the answers she'd been seeking her entire life.

With a deep breath, she flipped open the lid. She blinked. Once. Twice. Disbelief and confusion washed over her, for what lay inside was almost more unbelievable than the walking dead.

The chest was full of rocks.

Chapter Thirteen

Sean watched Emery's hopeful face go blank as she flipped open the chest's lid. She didn't say anything, just stared at the chest's contents. In unison, Sean and his crew leaned forward to see what lay inside.

Sean's stomach dropped.

Oh no.

"Rocks?" Cam growled. "We came all this way and fought those *things* for rocks?"

Emery shook her head, her expression still blank. She picked up a rock from the chest, examined it, and then set it aside. She did it again, and again, as if intent on scrutinizing every single rock until the chest was empty.

Sean kneeled in the dirt beside her. He picked up a few rocks himself, turned them over in his filth-encrusted hands. They were just ordinary rocks. Heavy. Solid. Greyish. His stomach sank even lower with every rock they removed from the chest until, finally, they reached the bottom.

Emery released a little gasp, making him jump and survey the clearing, certain the bones—or wood, apparently—had risen again. His blood was still pumping, adrenaline still coursing through his system.

But Emery reached into the bottom of the chest and pulled out a scroll, tied with a crimson ribbon. Her eyes shone with hope as she pulled the ribbon loose and carefully unrolled the parchment with her bloodied fingers. The light in her eyes guttered once again. She sat back on her heels, a breath whooshing out of her as if someone had punched her in the stomach.

She crumbled the paper into a ball and hurled it into the grave.

She stood. "Let's get out of here."

Sean wanted nothing more than to do just that, but he hesitated, waited until her back was turned before he snatched the crumpled scroll from the dirt. He scanned its front and back. Both sides were blank.

THE TREK back to the longboat was uneventful, but fraught with tension. Sean could tell everyone had questions, wanting to know what on earth they had just experienced and why. Cam seethed with fury, and Farley barely suppressed his sobs of pain as he walked holding his broken arm to his chest. But no one seemed willing to speak as they tiptoed through the cemetery, not when their voices could catch the attention of the caretakers or raise the skeleton things again.

Sean wasn't sure what became of the graverobbers either. When the yellow fog had first rolled in, it had swallowed him and the woman he'd been holding hostage like the maw of a monster. The entire world had vanished, and all Sean had been able to think about was getting back to where Emery had been hanging in that tree. Then the first skeleton had reared out of the fog and yanked the woman from his grasp.

He didn't see any of the graverobbers after that. He assumed —if they still lived—they must have fled. But he didn't fancy running into them again if they were still around, even with back up this time.

No one spoke until they were back aboard the *Audacity*, and the sun was peeking over the horizon as if hesitant to arrive for the day. It cast the sky in a crimson hue.

"Egads," Billy gasped as their group hauled themselves over the ship's railing and onto the deck, all of them sporting mud and blood and ripped clothing. "What happened out there?"

"That's what I'd like to know!" Cam shouted, her anger finally snapping now that they were safe. "What did she get us into back there?"

Cam jabbed a finger into Emery's chest. Sean expected Emery to bat Cam's hand away with irritation. But Emery just stared blankly.

"What happened?" Billy asked again, his worried eyes raking over Sean's disheveled appearance.

None of them looked great, but Sean looked distinctly worse than the rest of them. His trousers were torn to ribbons and one of his sleeves had been ripped off. Scratches marred his legs and arms and face. They stung now as the adrenaline wore off.

Aleksy took one look at Farley and ushered him belowdecks to the infirmary.

"The dead...rose," Ranit said, his face still pale under streaks of dirt.

"But they weren't dead," Rooney corrected. "They were made of wood and moss."

"Who cares what they were!" Cam screeched. "They attacked us because of some stupid rocks!"

"Do we know that's why they attacked?" Sean asked. Honestly, he couldn't think of any other reason, save for sheer coincidence. But he'd been through enough in his life to never believe in coincidence.

"Fairly sure," Ranit said. "As soon as we found Love S. Key's grave, that yellow fog came rolling in out of nowhere. And then those things appeared. Like they were trying to keep us away."

"And then we almost died for nothing!" Cam shouted.

Sean's temper flared. "We all knew there was potential danger, Cam. We voted to look for the treasure anyway."

"I didn't."

"You didn't have to come with us," Sean snapped.

She glared at him. "Yes, I did. Someone has to protect you dullards."

Sean's anger faltered because he knew that was the root of her outburst. Her fear for them and her anger that her brother was hurt. "I'm sorry, Cam."

She shook her head. "I just want to know why we just about died for nothing. Why was the chest full of rocks?"

That was the question, wasn't it? Why would Emery's great aunt give her a clue that led to a chest full of rocks and a blank piece of paper? And why had it been guarded so heavily by the strangest use of elemental magic he'd ever seen?

"Someone beat us to it," he mused out loud. That was the only explanation. But who? And why? And why bother leaving the chest there? The whole thing made Sean's already overloaded and exhausted brain hurt.

He turned to Emery but found she was no longer standing there.

"She went to your cabin a few minutes ago," Ranit said quietly. He then took Cam's elbow and led her towards the stairs. "Come on, let's go visit Farley. I'm sure Aleksy will have him right as rain."

Sean watched them go, eternally grateful for Ranit and his unshakable calmness. But he nearly jumped when Billy touched his shoulder. "Are you alright, my boy? You look terrible."

He felt terrible. And he had the sudden urge to turn into his adoptive father for one of his bear hugs like he used to when he was a child. But he didn't allow himself to do that. He'd lost the privilege to do so long ago.

Instead, he patted Billy's hand. "I'm alright. Just some scratches."

Billy canted his head to the side, examining him with his bright blue eyes. "Are you sure?"

"I just need to clean up and sleep. Can you get us out of here?"

Billy squeezed his shoulder and headed for the helm. Sean glanced between his cabin door and the stairs leading below deck, caught between checking on Emery and checking on Farley. In the end, he figured Cam was with Farley and probably needed some space away from him, so he headed for his cabin.

He knocked lightly on the door. "Emery? It's me."

When there was no answer, he cracked the door open.

Emery stood in the center of the cabin, staring at the bed.

Sean slowly approached. "Are you alright?"

She blinked and looked up. Dark circles underscored her glassy eyes. "I wanted to sleep, but..."—she looked down at her soiled clothes—"I'm filthy."

"Well, that's a problem easily solved. Wait here."

She did. In the minutes it took for Sean to boil water in the galley and then lug up two large buckets full, she hadn't moved at all. She just stared out the window at the small island growing ever smaller as they left it behind.

Her silence, her stillness—it told him exactly how she was feeling. But still, he asked again, "Emery, are you alright?"

She sighed, dragged her gaze away from the window to look at him. "I'm just...tired," she said.

I'm disappointed and devastated and angry, she didn't say, but he heard it in her voice. She clearly didn't want to talk about it yet, so he didn't push. Instead, he took the buckets of water into the washing room attached to his cabin and poured the steaming contents into the small tub. He set out a bar of soap, and then returned to the cabin to search his wardrobe for a towel.

As he rummaged, he heard Emery ask, "Are *you* alright?"

Quite frankly, he wasn't sure. And he didn't think he was ready to talk about what had just happened either. The memory of the skeletal fingers dragging him into the earth... He shuddered and focused on trying to make her feel better. "I'm sad."

"What? Why?"

"I really liked these pants." He gestured to his tattered trousers as he continued his search for a towel.

She laughed softly behind him, exactly what he'd hoped to hear. Finally locating a towel, he turned and said, "There's no saving them now…"

He forgot how to speak.

Emery still faced away from him, but she was now naked from the waist up, her soiled tunic a heap on the floor. Her shoulder blades shifted under her smooth skin as she fiddled with the laces of her pants. The rising sun gilded her curves in gold. Sean's mouth went wholly dry.

She turned to face him, and he lost the ability to move, to speak, to think.

Holy gods.

Now the sun gilded a whole new set of curves, and set her dark hair aglow, lighting her up like some sort of celestial being. Even with the blood and mud and tangled hair, she was the most beautiful thing he had ever seen.

He cursed the heat creeping up his neck. And frankly, everywhere else.

"Definitely beyond saving," she said.

Sean blinked. "What?"

"Your pants."

"Oh, right, my…"

He tore his gaze up to her face. She wasn't even looking at him. She was still toying with the laces of her trousers, which were slung low on her hips because they were slightly too big for her. Her tongue poked out as she struggled to undo the knot.

Was she…trying to *kill* him?

Gods, he wanted to help with that knot. His body even leaned forward, his mouth opening to slyly offer a hand before his brain caught up.

No. You cannot.

He slammed his mouth shut, forced his feet to stay planted on the floor. It took all his willpower, all his strength, to stay put. Which meant no willpower left for his eyes. His weak, treacherous eyes. He tried to look away, to look at anything else. But he couldn't.

Until Emery's laces finally loosened, and she began shimmying out of her pants.

"Whoa, Em!" Finally, he tore his gaze away, looking everywhere that wasn't her. When he heard her pants hit the floor, he thought his thundering heart would explode.

"Sean?" She sounded wholly innocent, like she truly had no idea what she was doing to him.

"Here you go!" He threw the towel in her direction, not allowing himself to check if he aimed properly. "Enjoy your bath."

He bolted for the door, fumbled with the handle, and slammed it shut behind him, pressing his back against it. Ranit stood right there, his eyes wide with the sight of his captain in such a frantic state.

"What happened?" he asked. "You look like you just saw another walking corpse."

"She... She took off her clothes." It was all he could manage.

Ranit blinked once. Twice. And then burst out laughing.

⚓

SEAN SCRUBBED HIMSELF RAW, his cold bath water already brown. He didn't mind the cold water. In fact, he'd drawn himself a frigid bath in the ship's communal bathing room on purpose, needing to shut down any lingering thoughts of Emery and her state of undress.

The cold had somewhat helped.

But when he'd begun washing the cemetery dirt from his skin, he found he couldn't stop scrubbing, even when his various cuts stung and bled. He had to get that night off him, had to wash away the memories of the skeletal fingers gripping his hair, ripping his clothes, crushing his limbs, and scraping his skin as they dragged him through the tombstones.

Nausea clawed up his throat as the memories rose and he scrubbed harder.

It had been a scene straight out of his nightmares. He literally had dreams just like it. He dreamt the souls of all those he'd let down in this life came back to drag him into the deepest pits of the underworld, like he deserved.

This had been so terrifyingly similar, it had almost been surprising not to see his sister's corpse at the forefront, demanding her vengeance and damning him forever.

Sean scrubbed and scrubbed and scrubbed.

When he finally finished, he borrowed a fresh set of clothes from Billy, claiming he didn't want to go back to his cabin and wake Emery. In truth, he didn't want to face her quite yet, and he didn't want to imagine what she might be doing in there, if she was still in the bathtub...

He poked his head into the infirmary to find Cam slumped over, asleep on Farley's cot, and Farley himself equally as passed out, his arm in a sling. Not wanting to wake them, he slipped back out.

He managed to avoid everyone else as he retreated to the bowsprit. As he sat, he noticed something in the pocket of the trousers he'd borrowed and dug it out. It was an envelope. His heart sank at his name written in familiar handwriting on its front and he had a feeling Billy probably put it in the pocket on purpose, hoping Sean would find it.

The envelope was already open, the letter already read. Billy had taken it upon himself to read and reply to the letters anytime they were in Brimlad, because Sean had stopped doing it himself after Lily died. He'd read them, but that was it. Replying felt...wrong now.

Taking a deep breath, he took the letter from the envelope, carefully unfolded it, and began to read.

Dear Sean,

Hope all is well. I hope the crew is also doing well. Billy has informed me you have a new crew member. He seems fond of her.

Sean shook his head. Of course, Billy would tell him about Emery. He told him everything.

I'm doing well myself. I found some lovely roommates, and school is going well. It's tough, but you know me. I can handle tough. I grew up with you, after all.

Sean tried to smile at his old friend's attempt at humor, but it wouldn't come. The rest of the letter talked about fascinating new scientific discoveries constantly happening at his school, none of which Sean understood.

Sean read the letter several times, hearing his friend's voice in his mind, imagining a life where they were together and nothing at all had changed.

But everything had changed.

He leaned back against the mast, thinking about his friend's letter while simultaneously allowing himself to wonder what Emery was doing in his cabin now, and whether the bath had cheered her up a bit. And he suddenly realized how he could help her, and where they needed to go next. Even if it was the last place he wanted to be.

Chapter Fourteen

Emery lay curled in a ball on Sean's bed. Even though her skin was scrubbed clean, she wore fresh clothes, and her hair was no longer a tangled mess, she still felt...gross.

She still felt like she was covered in grave dirt, still had the touch of corpses on her skin. Even though they turned out not to be corpses at all, which she didn't understand.

But they'd seemed real enough at the time, and the injuries they'd inflicted had been real enough too. Her stomach clenched at the thought of Farley, that she'd been the reason yet another one of Sean's crew was hurt. Ranit lost his arm saving her life and now Farley had broken his.

All day, she'd stayed in the cabin, her exhausted mind a jumble of tattered thoughts, her emotions somehow both raw and numb. She'd sat in the bath until the warm water had grown cold, and even then, she sat an hour more. Eventually, she'd moved to the bed, and though she was so tired she couldn't move, she barely slept. She dozed, here and there, only to jerk awake from a nightmare. She had not needed more nightmare fuel, but alas, that's what she got.

Awake, her thoughts ran rampant. Why was the chest empty? Had there ever been anything in there worth finding?

Why was the chest guarded by wooden undead? It had to have been elemental magic, so had someone been watching them, ready to raise their monstrosities when the time came? If so, who? Her parents? If so, why would they attack her? If it hadn't been her parents, then why would a clue from them lead to an empty chest guarded by elemental magic?

She had hoped her questions would be answered on that island. Instead, she had a hundred new ones, and no way to answer them.

So, she lay there in the silence with her thoughts, disappointment and guilt and anger weighing her down like a heavy blanket.

At some point, Rooney had brought in a meal, but otherwise, she'd seen no one else. The sun was sinking in the sky when the cabin door eventually opened again. Emery faced the wall and couldn't see who entered the room, but assumed it was either Cam or Sean. Since a few moments passed and there was no ax buried in her spine, she figured it must be Sean.

After drawing her a bath, then throwing a towel at her and sprinting from the room, he hadn't returned. On top of everything else, that had kept her awake too. Why had he done that? Was he angry with her?

His footsteps were soft as he crossed the room and quietly placed a plate on the side table near the bed. He didn't speak, probably assuming she was asleep. And for a moment, she thought about keeping up that charade. She wasn't sure if she could face him yet. Wasn't sure if she could handle the look of anger or disappointment on his face if she'd been the cause of it. But as his footsteps moved across the room, she couldn't help it. While she was afraid to see the look on his face, she couldn't deny his face was also the only thing she wanted to see just then. She wanted one of his hesitant smiles.

Bracing herself, Emery rolled over. He froze halfway through unrolling a blanket on the floor. They made eye contact, just for a moment, and then he averted his gaze.

Her stomach sank. He *was* angry with her. He couldn't even look at her.

She wanted to ask how Farley was, but she was afraid. Before she could work up the courage, Sean spoke.

"Did you sleep?" He kept his eyes on the bed he was carefully making.

"Not really," she admitted. "Did you?"

Stupid question, since he'd been gone all day. But she supposed he could have slept in the crew's quarters or even the infirmary in his desperation to stay away from her. But judging by the circles under his eyes, she didn't think so.

"No," he confirmed, fluffing out a pillow.

An awkward silence fell between them, and her stomach sank further. She'd never felt awkward around him before. Not even back when they barely knew each other and were actively trying to hate each other. He continued to pile blankets on the floor, still not looking up. She watched him, noting that he must have bathed and changed clothes at some point, because there wasn't a speck of dirt on him anymore.

He glanced sidelong at her, probably sensing her probing gaze.

"Are you alright?" They blurted at the same time.

Another silence ensued as they both waited for the other to answer.

Finally, Emery replied, "I'm just tired."

It was partially true. She was so exhausted, she didn't think she had the energy to get into how she was really feeling right then.

"Me too," Sean said, flapping out the last blanket.

"How's Farley?" she blurted.

He finally looked up at her again, his expression softening. "Aleksy was able to set the arm fine. He's been sleeping most of the day. He won't be drawing any time soon, but he'll be alright."

Thank the gods.

"Cam is going to hate me even more now," she said.

"Cam doesn't hate you," Sean said, and Emery cast him a

look. He winced. "She's just...protective. Especially when it comes to Farley. They're the only family each other has."

Emery's heart panged. She hadn't known that. Despite being part of the crew for over a month now, she really didn't know much about any of them. She wanted to, but she couldn't ask many questions because, when she did, they'd ask questions back, ones she usually couldn't answer without either revealing her home or lying to them. And she hated lying to them.

"Are they orphans too?" she asked.

"No. But they were both disowned by their family, so they might as well be."

"That's horrible." Emery couldn't imagine how awful being disowned by your own parents would feel. Or maybe she could. Maybe she had been disowned and didn't even know it.

Thoughts of her parents and skeletons and the stupid chest full of stupid rocks filled her with more rage and sorrow. And when Sean pushed up his sleeves, exposing a few new nasty scratches along his arms, guilt flooded in too.

Gods, if he'd been killed—if any of them had been killed... Panic sluiced through her at the memory of watching Sean being dragged away by the corpses. She gripped the sheets with white knuckles, trying to control her breathing.

"Sean, don't sleep on the floor tonight," she whispered.

His gaze snapped up. "What?"

Emery scooted over and patted the mattress beside her. "Sleep on the bed tonight. Look, there's plenty of room for two of us."

Sean's brows rose with uncertainty, his eyes wide, almost like he was afraid. "I don't think—"

"Please" she blurted, barely able to control the quiver in her voice. "I don't want to sleep alone tonight."

Sean hesitated, and it almost looked like panic flashing across his face.

"Please," she said again. "I just... I can't."

Silently, he grabbed his pillow from the floor and headed for the bed. The bed was narrow, built in the wall between two bookshelves, hardly big enough for two people. He lay on his back on the very edge of the bed, as far away from her as he could get, and made sure no part of him was touching her.

Emery's heart panged again. She'd made a mistake. She shouldn't have asked him to share the bed because it was now so obvious how much he didn't want to be there with her.

Her chest felt like it was cracking. She'd been so terrified she was going to lose him to those corpses. Now it looked like she lost him anyway.

This realization was the final blow of a day full of punches, and tears welled up behind her eyes. She whispered, "Sean, I'm so sorry."

Genuine shock crossed his features as he finally looked at her. "What?"

"I never meant for anyone to get hurt. I'm sorry. Farley—"

"Farley will be alright," he said. "None of this is your fault."

"It is. And now you're so angry with me..."

"What? Em." His voice was firm, but soft, if a bit surprised. "I'm not angry with you."

Emery blinked, partly to rid herself of the tears still building and partly out of bewilderment. "You're not?"

"Of course not. Why would you think that?" He looked genuinely confused, and now, she was becoming puzzled herself.

"You literally ran away from me earlier. You've avoided me all day. And now you can barely look at me."

It was Sean's turn to blink. And then he laughed. A full-throated laugh that was both so surprising and beautiful to hear that any of Emery's residual tears immediately dried up.

He scrubbed a hand down his face. "Emery, I am not *mad* at you."

Emery hesitated, more confused than ever. "I wouldn't blame you if you were..."

"I'm not. I promise." Yet, he still avoided her gaze, his cheeks tinged slightly pink. "I...uh... This is...hmm."

Emery waited for him to finish, but when he just trailed off, she pressed, "What's the problem then?"

"Alright... When you took off your clothes earlier..." He tripped over his words, his blush deepening from pink to crimson.

"Wait, what? That's what this is about?" Though she was still confused, she felt heat rushing into her own cheeks when she remembered the way he'd literally sprinted from the room at the sight of her. "Am I that disgusting to you?"

"Oh god, no!" Finally, he turned on his side to face her, his expression horrified. "No, you are anything but *disgusting*. You are..." He trailed off, cleared his thought. "Not disgusting."

"I don't understand."

A look of wonder passed over his face, the same one that usually appeared when she accidentally let slip how ignorant of the world she was. "Undressing in front of others means nothing where you're from, does it?"

She slowly shook her head, her stomach sinking once again with dread. "What do you mean?"

He nodded to himself, like this explained a lot, even though Emery still felt clueless herself.

"Well, generally, women do not undress in front of men if they are not married to them."

The heat in Emery's cheeks deepened with a sort of slow horror, and she resisted the urge to hide her body under the sheets even though she was now fully clothed. Thinking back, she realized she'd always changed clothes or bathed in the mornings, when Sean was already gone. "Why?"

"It's seen as...indecent?" He seemed to be struggling for the words, cringing a little as he said them. "Lewd?"

"Lewd?" she blurted, her embarrassment sparking for a moment into ire. Why did this world have so many stupid rules? She suddenly felt extremely homesick. "It's just a body. We all have them. Back home, everyone bathes in the same lake. No one cares if you're naked or clothed or somewhere in between."

"Ah, well, where I'm from, removing one's clothes in front of another can be seen as...an invitation."

She'd never seen Sean look so uncomfortable and it made her

own embarrassment flare. And now, she felt even worse. Sean had thought she was inviting him to be romantic with her, and his response was to *run*? Then it dawned on her...

"Asking you to sleep in the bed with me...?"

He cringed. "Men and women don't share beds unless wed. It's...scandalous."

"Why?" she burst, her humiliation boiling into anger once again. Everything was so much easier back home. She shared beds with her grandparents, her sister, her brother—even Caelin —all the time back home.

"I don't know." Sean looked mildly amused now. "I didn't make the rules."

"Who did?"

"I guess she did." He pointed to the ceiling.

Right. His god. Roark, or whatever her name was. "She's a prude."

Sean laughed again, the sound easing her mortification a little. "You're not wrong."

But again, Emery was struck by the realization that Sean had thought she'd invited him into bed with her twice and, both times, he'd looked almost sick at the thought.

She rolled onto her back, her heart fragmenting a little. It was all too much. "I'm sorry I made you uncomfortable."

Sean said nothing. After what felt like an eternity but was probably just a few seconds, she snuck a glance at him. He looked stricken, and his hand hovered over her arm as if wanted to touch her. But after a moment, he tucked his hand against his chest. "Em..."

"I'm tired." She closed her eyes against the pain of her heart cracking a little more. She had not been expecting to be so thoroughly rejected today on top of everything else. "You can go back to the floor if you'd like. Or stay. It doesn't matter..."

Silence followed.

"I think I know where to look for a cure for your sister." His words came out in a rush, as if he hadn't planned them. And it was such a jarring turn in the conversation it took Emery a moment to even register them.

Her eyes snapped open. "What?"

"There's a place called Audrye. It's full of universities and scholars. Medical miracles and scientific breakthroughs are always coming out of that place. If there's a cure, or someone who can make one, it would be in Audrye."

Emery was so shocked, she didn't reply.

"I know you're disappointed about your parents. And we can keep looking for them. But we can go to Audrye first, while we search for another lead."

Tears sprung to Emery's eyes again, her emotions now truly overloaded. "You'll take me to Audrye?"

"Of course." He said it without hesitation.

A cure. A way to save her sister, her home. She hadn't let herself think about Ayana much lately, terrified that she may have already succumbed to her illness while Emery was away. She'd been stuck, unsure how to even start looking for a cure.

Her bruised and beaten heart lightened at the thought of this new plan. They'd search for a cure and continue looking for her parents later.

She smiled, "Thank you."

And finally, exhaustion washed over her, so heavily she couldn't keep her eyes open any longer. She reached out blindly and grabbed Sean's wrist.

"Sean?" she whispered.

"Hmm?" He sounded on the verge of sleep himself.

"I'm really glad you're alright."

He wrapped his strong fingers around her wrist, the warmth of his palm pleasant through her sleeve. "I'm glad you're alright too."

Neither of them let go of the other, and for once, they both slept like the dead.

Chapter Fifteen

Three days and three nights passed, and no one else came to visit Liam and Caelin in the infirmary. As if no one had been allowed.

They'd both slept most of the time anyway, slowly healing and gaining energy after their perilous journey. When they did wake, there was usually a healer in the room, slathering their burnt skin with aloe, filling their veins with nutrients, and forcing them to eat vegetable broth the first day, and then allowing them to eat heartier food the next.

Because they were rarely alone during their waking hours, Liam had not been able to discuss what the Arch-Elemists had revealed with Caelin—what they had demanded of them.

But what was there to say? Liam didn't quite know what they'd actually do if he and Caelin were to blab the truth about Tavor, but their threat had been clear enough.

On the fourth day, the medic, a kindly older woman by the name of Maple, finally deemed them well enough to go home.

"I'll escort you to your homes," Maple said, already stripping their cots and tossing their used sheets into a wicker basket. She had to be around eighty but moved with the grace and efficiency of someone in their twenties, her black hair pulled up in a knot on the top of her head.

"That's not necessary," Caelin began.

But Maple waved him off. "The Arch-Elemists insist," she said, and though her words did not sound like a threat, Liam could hear an echo of the threat nonetheless. "And you are to stay home and rest for a few more days at least."

Liam and Caelin exchanged glances but didn't resist as they were ushered past the vine curtain blocking them from the rest of the infirmary. Liam stopped in his tracks, his breath whooshing out of him in shock.

"Gods," Caelin breathed beside him.

The infirmary was full, more crowded than he'd ever seen it in his entire life. It was so full in fact, they must've enlarged the hollowed portion of the redwood tree the infirmary was set inside just to make more room. Dozens of people lay in rows of cots, all of them with streaks of silver shooting through their brittle hair, their faces gaunt, their bodies in various states of frailty.

It seemed the Arch-Elemists had been telling the truth about one thing: The infirmary was at full capacity. The Withering had run rampant in their absence. It was hard to tell, but Liam was certain most of the affected were elderly, but he recognized a few younger faces. No Fia or Grace, thank the gods. And no Ayana either, but he wasn't sure if that was a good thing. Suddenly, all he wanted to do was get home and see his sister's face.

One of the medics, a man named Aran, was tending to an older gentleman. He'd glanced up when Liam and Caelin left their private area, and he'd been watching them ever since. Liam made eye contact, and Aran held it, his gaze full of suspicion. What he was suspicious of, Liam could only guess, but he hadn't forgotten the way Aran had tried to kill Tavor all those months ago, or how he'd been willing to go through Emery to do it. While he had ultimately been right about Tavor, Liam couldn't forgive him for nearly murdering Emery to get his way.

He was vaguely aware of Maple being called to a different patient, leaving them alone for a moment.

"Dray?" Caelin asked.

Liam tore his glare from Aran to follow Caelin's gaze. Dray was standing by a cot, fluffing a pillow for one of the patients. He turned at the sound of his name and Liam almost gasped. They'd known Dray their entire lives. He was a year older than Liam, the same age as Grace. He'd courted Emery for a few months a while back, and he was one of Aran's sons.

And he looked like he'd aged ten years in the short months Liam was gone. He did look sick from the Withering, though. Had stress done that to him?

"So, you are back," Dray said without preamble. "Why?"

"We...umm..." Liam didn't know what to say, and blurted, "Gods, Dray. You look awful."

Dray flashed a smile that used to drive all the girls wild. Now it was a sad shadow of itself. "Surprisingly, I feel awful," he quipped. "That's what no sleep will do to you."

"Are you a healer now?" Caelin asked.

"I've been helping in the infirmary, yes. My father has been training me. But it's been...tough," Dray said.

Liam swept his eyes across the full infirmary again. No doubt, Dray and the other healers had been run off their feet lately."

"Did you do it?" Dray's voice drew Liam's attention again. His face was lit up with hope. "Are you back with a cure?"

Liam swallowed, unable to answer.

"No," Caelin said, his voice small. "I'm sorry, Dray."

Dray's face fell. "Oh. Then why are you back?"

"Emery is still looking for the cure," Liam blurted again. "She'll find it."

Gods, he hoped that was true.

It took all of Liam's courage to ask, "Dray, your brother...?"

Dray frowned and looked down at the patient he stood beside. Liam followed his gaze and barely contained a gasp again. They'd been standing by Dray's nine-year-old brother the entire conversation and Liam hadn't recognized him. Fynn's once dark hair was nearly all silver, his cheek bones jutting out under pale skin. He looked asleep, save for the faint movement of his chest with every shallow breath.

Liam's stomach clenched with an escalating horror. It had taken years for Ayana to be ravaged by the Withering, and she hadn't even been this bad when he'd left. In only months, Fynn looked like he had one foot in the afterlife already.

Liam scanned the infirmary again, double and triple checking that Ayana was not there. And again, when he didn't spot her, he wasn't sure if that should make him feel better or worse.

"I'm so sorry," Liam and Caelin said at the same time.

"We need a cure," Dray whispered, a tear sliding down his haggard face.

"Emery will find a cure," Liam said. "She *will.*"

He wasn't sure if he was trying to convince Dray or himself. He suddenly couldn't breathe, couldn't stand to be in the infirmary anymore. He had to find Ayana right now.

"I'm sorry," he said again, before bolting for the exit.

He had to see Ayana's face, had to know she was still alive.

Liam burst outside, blinking in the bright sunlight. Caelin was right behind him.

"Liam—" Caelin started.

"No," Liam panted, panic strangling him. For once, he didn't know what Caelin was going to say, but he didn't want to hear it. He started running down the dirt path that led to the village, winding between redwoods and oak trees. The familiar scent of the pine needles and blossoms engulfed him, the familiar sounds of birdsong and distant crashing waves washed over him.

Home. He was home.

There had been so many moments in the last few months when he truly believed he'd never see this island again, when all he had wanted was to be home again, in the safety and simplicity of the place where he'd spent his entire life.

Now he was here, and he was numb to it all. Panic and dread and guilt sluiced through him instead.

"Liam? Caelin?" An elderly woman with a crooked spine stepped out of their way. Liam had barely noticed her, almost ran right over her.

"Hally," he said, blinking at her familiar face. A fleeting relief swept through him. At least she, so far, had been spared from the Withering. For now.

"I hear you had a harrowing encounter with a storm," she said. "Glad you boys are alright."

So, the rumors—the half lies—had already begun to spread.

"Thanks, Hally," Caelin said. He sounded far more composed than Liam felt. "It's good to see you too."

Before they could sidestep Hally, Aran came up behind them, apparently having left his post in the infirmary to follow them. He spared no time for niceties. "Why did you come back? Where's Tavor?"

To warn you, Liam desperately wanted to shout. *Tavor's coming to destroy us all!*

"I—we..." Liam stammered instead, but more and more people were noticing them, were approaching from all sides, crowding them in and blocking the path home.

With each familiar face he spotted, relief shot through him. But dread followed soon after, because so many faces were missing. And because they relentlessly began hurling questions at Liam and Caelin.

"Where's Tavor?"

"Where's Emery?"

"How'd you survive the storm?"

"How'd you get home?"

"Did you find a cure?"

"Did you help Tavor?"

Question after question came at them, and though none of them were malicious or suspicious in nature, Liam's head spun, having no idea which to answer first, or how, or even if he was allowed. Beside him, the usually unflappable Caelin was looking overwhelmed too. But he at least managed to answer some of the questions, and mostly with honesty.

"We don't know where Tavor is."

"We don't have a cure yet."

"We were separated from Emery."

"She's looking for a cure."

Liam backed up, trying to get space from the crowd. He tripped over something—a stone, a root, a foot, he didn't know —and shot a hand out to catch himself on a tree trunk. But his hand sank right through the wood as if it were soggy bread. He fell sideways into it, his arm sinking up to its shoulder. When he pulled his arm out, it was covered in a brownish sludge.

"Uhg, what the...?" He stared at the sludge on his arm, and then the oak tree from which it came. Its trunk seemed to be rotting from the inside out, and its few remaining leaves were shriveled and grey.

Before he could properly process what he was seeing, a familiar voice rang over the crowd. "Let them breathe. Back off!"

There was a flash of red hair and then someone was heaving Liam to his feet, dragging him through the crowd, and grabbing Caelin too.

"Fia!" he exclaimed, relief and joy washing over him with such force he was momentarily dizzy. "Thank the gods you're not all withered too."

"Not yet," she said, but when she saw the stricken look on his face, she amended. "I'm not sick. But the Withering has been spreading like crazy since you've been gone."

"We've noticed," Caelin mumbled.

"I see you also noticed it's hitting the island itself pretty hard," she said, indicating Liam's sludge covered arm. Before he could reply, someone else tried to approach them. "Nope, back away," Fia commanded, neither breaking her stride nor releasing Liam and Caelin. "I've got strict orders from the Arch-Elemists to get these two home to bed. No more questions."

Liam and Caelin exchanged glances. But Liam could only feel relief in that moment. He was sure the ire would come later.

Familiar faces and homes blurred past as Fia marched them through the village, until finally, Liam's gaze landed on—

"Home," he breathed.

A giant redwood tree that looked like all the others. But this one was his.

They pushed through the curtain of vines that acted like a door, and Liam was instantly engulfed in a hug. Fia released his hand, and he immediately missed the contact, even as a familiar cinnamon scent washed over him as his grandmother squeezed him tight. A second pair of arms wrapped around them both, smelling of mint and woodsmoke.

"Grandfather," Liam choked, nearly sobbing. He'd been so worried about him too. So worried...

He pulled away, scanned the familiar living quarters: the hearth, the wooden table and chairs growing from the floor, the crowd of people near the door, including Caelin's parents.

Ayana wasn't there.

"Where's Aya?" he asked.

A terrible silence settled in the room.

Caelin pulled away from his parents' embrace, also scanning the room. "And Grace?"

Liam's grandparents exchanged glances, and Fia shuffled her feet behind them, staring at the ground.

"Where's Ayana?" he asked again, nausea climbing up his throat.

His grandmother visibly swallowed. "Liam, listen—"

No.

No. No. No.

Liam raced for the stairs, taking them two at a time. When he burst into Ayana's room, he fell to his knees. She wasn't there, and her room... Her room was once alive with an array of flowers and plants and the insects that loved them. Now, what plants remained where shriveled and dead.

Liam's grandparents stepped into the room after him, tears glinting in both their eyes. His grandmother's voice cracked as she said, "Ayana is gone."

Part Two

A Past Life

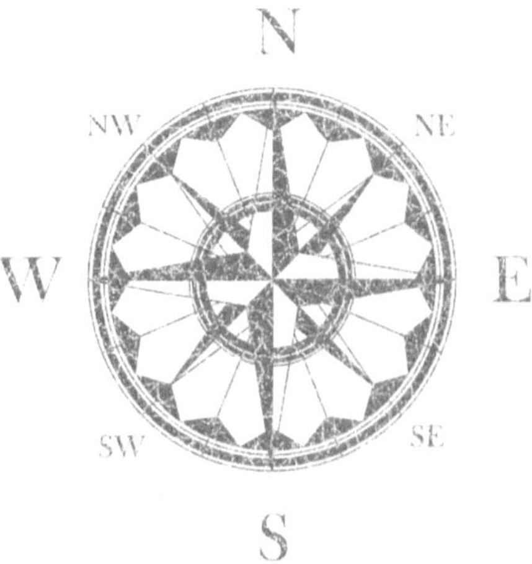

Chapter Sixteen

Emery had only been to the continent once, and though she spent most of that time locked in a dark, dank dungeon, what she remembered of the city Dornwell was grey. Everything, from the buildings, to the landscape, to the sky, had been grey.

Audrye, an island city just off the coast of the continent, was not grey.

The city exploded with colour and noise, and Emery was so eager to explore she bounced on her toes. But she had to wait a little longer.

"We're here with a shipment for the Cheeky Monkey," Sean was saying to the harbor master, his voice lazy and unconcerned. Once again, he'd adopted a different accent, this one closer to the one Serdar spoke with. He barely looked at the harbor master, instead gazing at the city as if it contained his wildest dreams. "And of course, we'll stay for the festivities."

"Papers?" asked the harbormaster. He was a middle-aged man with a scroll and quill, and he looked rather harried as he attempted to keep track of all the ships coming and going.

It was precisely why they'd chosen this day to arrive in Audrye.

"Ah, yes." Sean's attention briefly snapped back to the

harbormaster as he began rummaging through the various pockets of his large coat, a coat Emery had never once seen him wear before.

Indeed, Sean looked nothing like himself in that moment. His overcoat hung to his knees, with shiny copper buttons and trimming that gleamed in the afternoon sunlight. The high collar of his coat was upturned, nearly touching the short beard he'd managed to grow in the two weeks it took them to reach Audrye. His beard was dark, almost black from the gunpowder they'd rubbed into it minutes before. They'd done the same to his hair, though it was mostly hidden by his tricorne hat. He looked every inch the reputable merchant he was pretending to be, who he—Emery realized—used to be, before Tavor had taken it all away from him.

"Here we are," Sean said, finally locating the papers. He absently unwrinkled a stack of folded parchment and handed them to the harbormaster before turning his attention back to the city.

Emery swallowed and tried to keep from staring at the harbormaster as he scrutinized the documents, which, Sean had told her, contained a fake merchant license and a shipping order. They always made sure to keep a few handy for when they needed to make port somewhere that was unwelcoming to infamous Forbiddens, which was most places.

The harbormaster's gaze flicked to the *Audacity* bobbing in the slip behind them, specifically to the name the *Serendipity* that had been newly painted on her keel. The ship was just as disguised as her captain. They'd even replaced her recognizable crimson sails with plain canvas for the time being.

"Cocoa beans, coffee beans, and cinnamon?" the harbormaster confirmed.

"Yes, sir. Straight from Brazilli," Billy replied from Sean's other side. He looked the same as usual, with his bushy salt and pepper beard and his mane of hair to match. Apparently, his face wasn't as recognizable as everyone else's aboard the *Audacity*.

Nor was Emery's, which was why she also looked like herself. No one should look twice at her face, because no one knew it.

"Anything else in the hull?" the harbormaster asked.

"Excluding our supplies, no sir," Billy replied.

The harbormaster glanced at the papers again and gave each of them another probing gaze. Emery tried not to squirm under his scrutiny. He stamped the documents and handed them back to Sean. "You came at the right time," he said, breaking into a smile. "Enjoy the festivities."

"Believe me, I intend to," Sean said, casting the man a wink before leading the way across the docks towards the city proper, Emery and Billy following at his heels.

Now that they'd made it into the city without issue, Sean's air of nonchalance fell away, and his face tightened into a frown.

Emery knew he'd been anxious about coming here. He hadn't outright said it, but she'd been able to tell by the way he'd meticulously planned everything. They'd spent the past two weeks putting together their papers and backstories and disguises. They planned to show up during one of Audrye's busiest weeks, and decided only the three of them would disembark, so the chances of discovery were minimal. Rooney had been upset to miss out on the great food, and Ranit groped about missing the music, but ultimately, everyone agreed it was for the best. But the closer they got to Audrye, the more anxiety radiated off Sean. Emery could tell, even with all their planning, he was worried something would go wrong. But she was also certain there was something more to it, something he wasn't telling her.

They'd continued sharing the bed, but he'd been sleeping less with each passing day, his nightmares getting worse every night. And that morning, he'd been quiet, that blank expression creeping on to his face and not leaving until the moment they stepped onto the dock and had to interact with the harbormaster.

She'd been startled and impressed by how quickly he could turn on a different façade, how he could become someone else with such little effort. She snuck a glance at him now that he wasn't playing his role to find the blankness had returned.

Emery probably should have been apprehensive as well. She certainly didn't want anything else to happen to Sean's crew for her sake, and she was glad Sean had decided only three of them would risk venturing into Audrye to keep the chances of recognition low. But, mostly, her excitement about finally being able to properly explore the world, her eagerness to find a cure for her sister, and the sheer beauty of the place eclipsed her anxiety.

The turquoise water shimmered under the hot sun, and the gentle waves rolled onto sugar white sand. Palm trees dotted the shoreline, casting pockets of shade where people gathered to take refuge from the heat.

A neat cobblestone path led them into a bustling market square, and though Sean tried to lead them straight through without stopping, Emery couldn't help it. She slowed, gawking at the various stalls and their many wares. The stalls themselves were beautiful, made of bamboo and striped awnings in yellows, pinks, and greens. They sported trinkets made from seashells, coconuts husks and leather bits, stands of straw hats, and colourful woven blankets, piles of leather-bound books and rolls of parchments, jars of guava jelly and pineapple jam, bottles of white rum, cigars, paper masks, and figurines carved from wood.

Emery stopped to stare at the wooden figurines, which reminded her of the ones her grandfather had made for her with every birthday she reached. But Sean caught her elbow and guided her onwards.

"We can't stop and risk getting split up," he said, scanning the crowd and barely glancing at the stalls, as if he didn't notice them.

But a stall of stringed instruments caught her eye, and she stopped again, unable to stop herself from examining the delicate designs the creator had painted on them. Sean hovered, allowed her to look for a few seconds, and then tugged her onwards again.

"Relax, Sean," Billy said, patting Sean on the back, which

only made him startle. "We're in. We're fine. No one is going to notice us. Take a breath."

Sean did take a deep breath, but he didn't appear any less anxious afterwards. Billy disappeared for a moment, only to return with a baggy full of colourful sweets.

He grinned. "Eat one. It will help."

Sean looked dubious but he was too busy keeping an eye on their surroundings to protest as he took a yellow sweet and popped it in his mouth. He made a face, glancing back at Billy. "What was that?"

"Sour lemon," Billy said, grinning even bigger. He offered the baggy to Emery next. "Have you had one of these before?"

"What is it?" she asked.

"Are you telling me you've never had candy before?" Sean asked, his face a mask of mock horror.

Emery shook her head and tried a green candy. Her mouth was instantly filled with a sour citric flavor so powerful she couldn't stop her whole face from pinching. "What was *that?*" she asked.

"Lime." Billy chuckled, and to her surprise, so did Sean.

The act seemed to help him shed some of his anxiety, and Emery ate another candy, partly because they were delicious and partly to allow her face to pinch so Sean would laugh again.

"This might be the best thing I've ever eaten," she moaned.

"Don't let Rooney hear you say that," Billy said.

Sean's eyes lit up with mischief. "Wait right here." He vanished into the crowd and returned a few minutes later with some sort of bread with a yellow jelly on it. "Try this."

Emery bit into the bread, the citrus flavor of the jelly coating her tongue. Her eyes almost rolled back into her head with pleasure and Sean laughed again.

"Alright, this wins," she said, stuffing more into her face.

"What about the rum cake?" Billy asked, raising a brow at Sean.

"Oh, yes! Rum cake will haunt your dreams." Sean vanished again, returning this time with three paper plates each sporting a small slice of brown cake on it. He divided the plates between them. The cake didn't look like much, but its syrupy flavor had Emery moaning with ecstasy, and even Sean basically crammed his entire piece into his mouth at once.

Momentarily forgetting his unease, Sean darted off several more times as they continued to make their way through the market, always returning with something new to show Emery. Usually, it was food, but once he returned with something else.

"Hold out your arm," he ordered.

She obeyed, curious. Gently, he tied a new bracelet made of hemp and seashells around her wrist, his fingers lightly grazing her skin and sending currents of electricity up her arm. Emery kept her face down so he couldn't see the heat pooling in her cheeks.

"You can start a collection, like mine," Sean said as he finished tying the knot and let go of her wrist.

Indeed, the new bracelet settled on her wrist next to the bracelet of braided rope Sean had made her as a goodbye gift months ago. It was her favourite possession, followed closely by the compass he'd also given her.

Her heart swelled in her chest, and she looked up. "Thank you, Sean. I love it."

He held her gaze, a satisfied smile on his lips, the contrast of his dark beard causing his emerald eyes to appear more striking than usual.

Billy nudged his shoulder. "Varens. Two points east."

Sean's smile vanished as he followed Billy's gaze. Indeed, four varens stood a few stalls down, all of them laughing at something the stall owner had said. They appeared relaxed, peaceful, and yet, the sight of their black and indigo jackets caused Emery's stomach to drop.

"Time to go," Sean said.

The three of them discreetly ducked into the closest alley, which led them to an adjacent street, the cobblestones neat and clean. Though the crowd wasn't nearly as thick here, the street was still bustling with people. Mostly young.

Emery's gaze wandered upwards, taking in the tall buildings lining both sides of the street. They were unlike anything she'd ever seen, stunning with their pastel paint jobs, carved stone pillars, and arcing windows. Through some of these windows, Emery spotted more products being sold, such as dresses, trousers, and shoes. She slowed again, marveling at the colours and strange fashions she'd never seen before.

They turned down another street, and the buildings where somehow larger, and more spread out, with stretches of green lawn between them. Young adults wandered in and out of the open doors, most of them wearing shoulder sacks or carrying armloads of books.

Sean must have noticed her staring, because he explained, "These are the universities I told you about,"

"They're wonderful," she said, gawking at a building with an image of a quill and ink embossed in the stone above its door.

Answering her question before she had a chance to ask, Sean explained, "That one is a school for scribes." When she pointed to a building with a symbol of a hammer and anvil, he said, "Metalworks, I believe. That one over there is mathematics. Beside it is history."

Emery marveled at each in turn, wondering at all the knowledge this town contained, wondering if she'd be able to learn everything in one lifetime. She didn't think she could, but maybe Grace could have, if given the opportunity.

Her stomach twisted a little with homesickness.

"At the end of the street, there's a medical school too," Sean continued.

Emery's ears perked up. "Is that where your friend learns?"

"Yes." Sean did not elaborate, which seemed to happen every time she tried to ask him about his childhood friend over the last few weeks. All Emery knew about him was that his name was Kess, he and Sean had grown up together, he now attended a prestigious medical school in Audrye, and Sean hadn't seen him in almost a year. And he was the reason they were in Audrye. Sean reasoned if there was anybody they could safely ask about a possible cure for the Withering, it would be his old friend.

They turned onto another new street, the buildings casting them in blessed shade. The buildings here were smaller but still beautiful, with pastel colours and overflowing flower boxes. It wasn't as busy either, though there were still plenty of people ambling about. Emery locked eyes with a few of them, noticing the way some smiled warmly, while others scrutinized the beads and feathers in her hair.

The sugary aroma of baked goods and sweet scents of teas and fruity drinks mingled with the sea breeze, making Emery's mouth water.

Billy whistled merrily along, his hands in his pockets, but Sean slowed, eyeing the open doorways of the buildings, where people sat around tables both inside and out, enjoying food and drink.

"What was the café called?" Billy asked. "Funny ape?"

"Cheeky Monkey," Sean said. "I'm sure it's around here somewhere."

His friend had mentioned in a letter that he liked to study at this café, and they hoped to find him there now.

Emery's spine tingled and she glanced over her shoulder. Two restaurant patrons sat at an outside table. They whispered behind their hands, looking directly at her. Were they laughing at her? While Sean led them farther down the street, their eyes tracked her. People physically turned in their seats so their gazes could follow her. Emery fought the urge to cower under their stares, knowing that would make her look guilty. But she wasn't sure what it was about her that was catching their attention. She'd never been around so many people before and the anxiety that had been so far eclipsed by excitement was rearing its head.

"Sean..."

"I see them," he responded. Of course, he had. He missed nothing. Raising his voice to a normal volume, Sean took the tricorn hat from his head and popped it on hers instead. "You're looking hot, love. Let's hide you from the sun for a bit."

He adjusted the hat so it fell low over her face.

"Why is everyone looking at me?"

"Maybe you're just hard to look away from," he said, winking. Though the comment made her belly swoop, she took it for what it was: a way to hide his own growing unease.

"Oh no…" Billy gasped, immediately drawing their attention. He gazed at a sky-blue wall, the brick façade covered in papers. Emery stepped closer, realizing that each paper had a different face on it, rendered in ink. Most she didn't recognize, but some she did. There was Ranit's face, and Cam's. Farley, Smythee, Rooney, and Aleksy. Even little Seadar. All of them stared down at the street with the words "Wanted, Dead or Alive" printed underneath.

And there was Sean's face, etched with even more detail than all the others. His simply read, 'Wanted Alive,' with an outrageous reward under it. Beside Sean's poster was that of a girl. Emery had never met her before, but she knew the name, saw the family resemblance in the eyes and the cheekbones.

Lily.

Sean stared at the poster, at his sister, his face draining of colour. He reached up, as if to touch the poster, but then his gaze shifted to the next poster over, and he swore, his face growing paler still.

Because that was Liam's face looking down at her, and Caelin's.

And her own.

Emery stared at the depiction of her face, stared into her own eyes. The drawing was startlingly accurate. And underneath, the reward for her was even larger than Sean's.

"Well," she said, her mouth dry. "It seems I got you beat for popularity."

Sean did not laugh. Didn't even crack a smile. He looked at her. "He's alive."

For a blessed moment, Emery didn't understand what he was talking about. And then it clicked.

Tavor. Tavor was alive.

Because he was arguably the only person who knew her face well enough to be able to have it drawn with such accuracy. No one else knew she existed, and the few varens who had seen her never got close enough to memorize such detail.

"Oh no," Billy repeated, and Emery followed his rattled gaze again. Two varens stood not far down the street, deep in conversation with two women. One of the women pointed directly at Emery. She ducked under her hat, but it was too late. The varens immediately headed their way, already reaching for their weapons.

Panic broke across Sean's face seconds before he hissed, "Run!"

Chapter Seventeen

Sean grabbed Emery's hand and yanked her down the nearest alley. Billy sprinted after them. The varens gave chase and shouted for them to stop, their footsteps echoing off the stone buildings in time with Sean's pounding heart.

The alley led to an adjacent street. Sean veered left, taking Emery with him, all but shoving people out of his way. He flung his cumbersome jacket off and glanced over his shoulder in time to see the two varens race onto the street, spot them, and charge after them.

"Billy, they don't know your face. Get out of here!" Sean demanded.

Billy looked torn for a moment, but the older man was already puffing from the exertion and, ultimately, he probably knew he'd do nothing but slow them down. He swerved into a crowd of people watching some sort of puppet show, while Sean pulled Emery in the opposite direction. They plunged into a café and women shrieked in startled outrage as Sean bumped them as they passed, causing them to spill their drinks down their bodices. Sean vaulted over the serving counter, Emery close behind, and they raced through the little kitchen in the back until they slammed through another door leading to another small alley.

Two barrels were stacked outside the door and, together, Sean and Emery pushed them over to block the door, the red wine from within spilling over the cobblestones like blood. The sight mixed with his adrenaline almost made Sean dizzy.

His heart hammered, from fear, from adrenaline, from the knowledge that Tavor was still out there somewhere, looking for them. Was he here, in Audrye? Would the varens take them straight to him?

This was too much like last time. He knew they shouldn't have come here. He knew something like this would happen again. He knew it, and yet, he'd come anyway, like an idiot.

He swore as the alley turned into a dead end, and they were forced to skid to a halt. Together, they turned to find their exit blocked by varens. Four of them approached now. One drew a gun and fired. They were still far enough away that the paralyzing dart missed, ricocheting off the stone wall behind them. But they'd be close enough in moments.

Terror flooded Sean's veins, causing his vision to blur. He remembered another time, another alley, where he'd been trapped with a different girl by his side. They hadn't gotten out that time. And his sister...

He refused to let that happen again.

He reached for his sword, but Emery's voice drew his attention. She was scrutinizing the wall behind them. "Can you climb this?"

He wasn't sure, but it didn't matter, as long as she could climb it. As long as she got away. "I can certainly try."

Emery launched herself at the wall. Sean faced the varens again, mentally grasping the wind and pouring all his emotions into it until a small twister formed. He threw it at the varens, forcing them back, giving himself and Emery a few more precious seconds.

"Sean, come on!"

Sean glanced up to find Emery had already made it onto the

roof, and he absently wondered how and why she had learned to climb so quickly. "Go! I'll hold them off!"

"Absolutely not! If you stay, I'm climbing back down." She even swung her foot back over the eave to prove her point.

With no other choice, Sean leapt for the wall, finding the tiny footholds in the brick façade and working his way up. But, despite years of climbing the rigging of his ship, he was not as quick or nimble as Emery at climbing walls. He sensed the twister he'd made had died, and the varens were nearly upon him.

The only reason he wasn't dead right now was because Tavor wanted them both alive.

He felt a stinging in his leg and reached down to pull the dart from his calf, costing him precious seconds. Immediately his leg began to go numb, followed by the other.

"Sean, hurry up!" Emery cried. She lay on her stomach, trying to reach him.

Something grabbed his boot, yanking him from the wall. He hit the ground hard and was immediately surrounded by three varens. The fourth still glared up at Emery, aiming his dart gun at her. Emery didn't even glance at the varen. She stared at Sean with dismay.

Sean couldn't feel his legs at all anymore and tried not to let the claustrophobic sensation of being trapped by his own body distract him. At least he could still use his arms, possibly because he pulled the dart out so fast. But he knew he'd never get away now.

"RUN!" he roared at Emery before yanking a dagger from his boot and slamming it into the thigh of the closest varen.

The varen screamed and fell back, blood pouring from the wound with the dagger still stuck in it. Before the other two varens guarding him could react, he yanked the air from their lungs. They both clawed at their throats, desperate for oxygen. Sean wouldn't give them any.

"That's enough!" The varen who'd been aiming his dart gun at Emery demanded. Now he aimed a pistol at Sean's head. "Commissioner Thantos may want you alive, but I'd be happy to see you dead, especially by my hand."

Sean did not relent. He kept pulling the air from the other varens' lungs. Their faces slowly turned purple.

"And you—if you don't come down, I'll blow a hole through his skull," the varen said.

Sean realized he was talking to Emery.

She hadn't run.

Why hadn't she run?

"I'll come down."

Emery's words ripped his attention from the suffocating varens.

"Emery, no!" he shouted. "Run!"

If he died so she could get away, so be it.

"I can't do that." She stood, raising her hands in the air. She looked at the varen. "I'm climbing down."

Horror rushed through him. "NO!"

But then Emery leapt off the roof, landing on the varen with the gun and tackling him to the ground. They rolled together across the cobblestones in a tangle of limbs.

Sean made to drag himself towards them, but an arm banded across his throat, yanking him back and squeezing so tightly he couldn't draw a breath.

"Payback time," one of the varens he'd been suffocating wheezed into his ear.

Sean wrenched at the arm but couldn't pry it loose. He flung an elbow back, catching the varen in the stomach. The varen wheezed again, but still didn't let go. Sean's chest burned, and his vision darkened at the edges.

This was it. Either he was going to die here and now, or he'd wake up in a cell to Tavor torturing him. His tunneling vision locked on to where Emery and the varen still grappled, wishing he could help her, protect her, ensure she got away. He wished he had been brave enough to tell her everything. He wished he had kissed her one last time when he'd had the chance.

His heart thundered in his ears and his vision darkened to

the point that he couldn't see anything. All he could do was cling to consciousness and pray for some sort of miracle.

The varen's arm released him so suddenly, he slumped to the ground, gasping for air. As his vision slowly cleared, he glanced behind him. The varen had dropped to the ground, a dart sticking out of his neck. The other two varens lay on the ground too, darts poking from their bodies as well.

Panicked and confused, Sean spun towards Emery and the last varen. A hooded stranger stood over them, dart gun at the ready. He fired, hitting the varen in the spine and the varen slumped, his dead weight pinning Emery to the cobblestones.

The stranger heaved the body off her, and Emery immediately rolled to her feet, blood streaming down her face. Obviously panicked and not realizing the stranger had saved them, she swung her lim into the side of the figure's head, causing him to stagger sideways.

She darted for Sean, crouching beside him. "Are you alright?"

"Your...head," he croaked, his throat sore from being crushed.

A nasty cut ran along her forehead near her hairline.

"I can fix that for you," a voice said from behind her.

His heart seized.

He knew that voice.

Emery spun to face the stranger, who stood there, holding the side of his head. He still had his hood up, but now, Sean could at least see his face. Sean sucked in a breath.

Emery held her lim at the ready. "Who are you?"

The man removed his hand from his head and held it out to her, as if offering a handshake. He cast his voice low, probably not wanting the paralyzed varens still laying on the ground to hear him. "My name is Kess. Can't say it's been nice to meet you."

Chapter Eighteen

"I'm sorry I spooked you," Sean's oldest friend said to Emery. "I was trying to help you."

Kess's hand remained extended, but Emery did not take it. She stared at his hand, at his face, and then turned to stare at Sean, her blue eyes still wide with adrenaline, still dazed from the chase, or maybe the brief tussle she'd had with the varen.

Sean could only nod because his own mind had turned to mud.

Slowly, Emery lowered her lim. Sean remained on the ground, his legs still not working properly. But honestly, he wasn't sure if it was from the curare still coursing through his veins, the relief of knowing Emery was alright, or from the sheer number of emotions that floored him at the sight of his friend again after so long.

He looked the same but different, with the same dark skin and dark hair, but his haircut was new, short around the ears with a few longer dreadlocks spilling over his forehead. The same spectacles were perched on his nose, but there was a crack running through one of the lenses, and Sean had the suspicion Emery was the cause of that. His expression was the same concern mixed with amusement that he'd often worn when they'd been kids and one of them had hurt themselves doing something stupid. But this time, his look was directed at Emery and the blood leaking from her hairline.

"May I see?" Kess asked. "I'm an almost doctor."

Emery nodded, as if still unable to speak. Sean noted the way she swayed on her feet, and the way she leaned her weight on her lim, using it like a cane. He wished he could get up and go to her.

"Is she alright?" he asked.

Kess carefully parted Emery's hair and she sucked in a sharp breath. He tilted her face so it was in the sun, then moved her face back into the shadows, watching her eyes.

"It looks worse than it is. Pupils are dilating properly. She needs stitches and she may have a bit of a concussion, but otherwise, she should be fine." He took a handkerchief from his pocket. "For now, keep pressure on the wound."

"I'm sorry I broke your..." Emery said, pressing the handkerchief to her forehead and pointing at his spectacles. "Those."

If Kess thought it was odd she didn't seem to know what glasses were, he didn't say it. "Your accent, it sounds like...never mind. That can wait. Don't worry about the glasses. I have another pair. I'm more impressed than anything." Kess stepped back and looked Emery up and down, assessing. "Are you injured anywhere else?"

"I don't think so." Emery turned abruptly to Sean, her eyes wide again. "But Sean was paralyzed!"

"Not to worry," Kess said, grinning. "I can help with that too." He crouched in front of Sean and pulled a syringe from his other pocket. "Hello, old friend. Sorry about this."

He stabbed the syringe into Sean's thigh. Sean didn't feel it, thankfully, but soon enough, his feet began to tingle, as if waking up.

"Is that the antidote?" Emery frowned. "You just happen to have that on you?"

"Always," Kess said, still pitching his voice low and patting his pocket. "We figured out how to make it at school. You never know when you might need it. But to be honest, I haven't actually had to use it until now. I also carry a dart gun, as you can see."

He swept his arms out, indicating the four paralyzed varens laying on the ground around them.

"Speaking of, we should get out of here," Kess whispered. "I can't have them recognizing me."

The feeling had mostly returned to Sean's legs, and he hauled himself to his feet. Together, the three of them stepped over the fallen varens, and Kess led them to an adjacent alley.

"The *Audactiy* is waiting at the docks," Sean started. "If we can keep to the back alleys—"

"Absolutely not," Kess cut him off. "You're coming home with me. Both of you."

Now that Sean's own adrenaline was wearing off, his anxiety was quickly taking its place. "No. It was a mistake coming here. They're looking for us."

"All the more reason to hide out at my place for a while," Kess argued.

"I can't risk leading the varens to your doorstep, Kess," Sean said.

He refused to be the reason his friend's peaceful life and bright future got upended. Again. He refused to cause Kess any more pain.

"Too late for that, Sean," Kess said brightly. "They already know where I live." At Sean's horrified look, he clarified, "I'm friends with most of the varens in this city. I'm hiding in plain sight."

Sean was not sure how he felt about that. "Regardless, I'm sure that...*friendship* wouldn't last much longer if they discovered two wanted fugitives in your house."

"That won't happen" Kess said.

His friend shot Emery an amused, knowing sort of smirk, the same one he used to wear whenever he and Lily ganged up on him about something in their youth. Sorrow shot through Sean at the memories. So many memories, all of them tainted now.

"He still likes to play the hero, huh?" Kess said to Emery.

Emery smiled back. "Constantly."

"Kess—"

"Sean, she needs stiches," Kess urged, cutting him off once again. "Come back to my place until things die down. Let her get cleaned up. And then you can leave whenever you want."

Sean glanced at Emery, noting the way she was squinting as she watched their conversation, as if in pain. And she was unusually quiet. Kess was right. Emery needed somewhere to rest sooner than later. Sean nodded at Kess, conceding. "We need to find Billy."

"Ol' Bill is fine," Kess said. "I already sent him to my place. He's safe. It's just a few blocks down."

Relief flooded Sean's veins once again.

Kess shrugged off his hooded jacket and tossed it to Sean. "Here, best to hide your pretty face for a bit."

Sean immediately donned the jacket and flipped the hood up.

Instead of stepping onto the street, Kess led them further into the shadows of the alley. Emery still wobbled on her feet, and though Sean's balance wasn't fairing much better, he placed a hand on the small of her back in case he needed to catch her. And he couldn't deny that her solid presence under his palm, the physical proof that she was still here with him, helped calm his nerves. He was aware Kess noted the action and was both relieved and disappointed when he said nothing about it.

Once upon a time, Kess would have teased Sean. But now... now a slightly awkward silence followed them down the alley and out onto a tight side street. There were very few people here, thankfully, and only a few noticed the handkerchief pressed to Emery's forehead.

Sean must have opened his mouth a hundred times to speak, but he didn't know what to say, where to start. His thoughts reeled in too many directions; his heart hammered with too many emotions.

He was still on high alert.

Tavor was alive. He was looking for them—both of them. He could be here, in Audrye, right now. He could be around any corner. Keeping his head down, Sean scrutinized every face that passed them, searching for the Viper. Every fleck of blue caught his attention, made his heart stutter, until he confirmed it wasn't a varen uniform.

They'd been lucky. They'd been so lucky to escape. Emery had been lucky to walk away from the fight with only a mild injury. And they'd been lucky Kess had spotted them from the Cheeky Monkey while they'd sprinted from the varens.

When would their luck run out?

When Sean wasn't searching the streets for danger or eyeing Emery for any signs that she was hurt more then she'd let on, he watched the back of his best friend's head. Could Sean even call him his best friend anymore? He'd avoided Kess for an entire year, dreading the moment he'd have to face him again—the moment he'd have to tell his friend what he'd done.

The same dread pooled in his stomach now, like acid, and his blood pounded so loudly in his ears, it made him dizzy. So loudly, he only just realized Kess had been talking for the past few minutes, and he hadn't heard a single word.

"...this section of city is old," he was saying to Emery. "It's far away from the city's center and doesn't get a lot of love."

Sean hadn't noticed they were in the slums either, hadn't noticed the way the bright paint chipped off the sagging stone buildings here, or the way that several foundations were cracked. But if these were Audrye's slums, they were the nicest slums he'd ever seen. In fact, this street was probably nicer than the nicest street in Brimlad. For a moment, Sean allowed himself to feel glad he was able to give this life to his friend. A safe and fruitful life. Even if the life was once meant to be his. And even if the life was incomplete because of something he'd done.

"Are you alright?" Emery whispered, soft enough that Kess probably couldn't hear.

Sean forced his face blank. "I'm fine."

She didn't look convinced, but she didn't pry further.

Kess was still prattling about the city. "This section was destroyed during the Elemental War and they haven't managed to build it back up yet. The Elemental University is just down the street. It's abandoned now."

"Elemental University?" Emery asked. "What's that?"

"Back before the war, when elemists were free, it was a place we could go to learn how to hone our abilities," Kess explained.

"You're an elemist?" Emery asked, her voice low but shocked.

Kess raised a brow, glancing at Sean. "Yes. He didn't mention that?"

"No," Emery said, and Sean was thankful she didn't say anything about how little Sean mentioned Kess at all, so little Emery hadn't known he existed until a few weeks ago. "Can we go to the school?"

"No," Sean and Kess said in unison, though Sean's tone was more forceful. He tried to turn it into a more teasing tone instead. "Have you forgotten we're supposed to be hiding?"

"I didn't mean right this second," Emery said, though he suspected that might have been a fib.

Kess added, "It's not safe to go there at all. Varens are always watching the place."

"Why?" Emery asked. "I thought you said it was abandoned."

"It is, but they watch it just the same, in case an elemist shows up to explore. So elemists never go there."

"Why would elemists want to explore it?"

"There are rumors of a lost library in the ruins, full of forbidden books about elemental manipulation and elemists in general," Kess said, his voice full of wonder.

"But those are just rumors." Sean shook his head. "The varens would have destroyed such a thing."

"Well, according to the rumors," Kess continued, "they left some of the library intact as bait to lure elemists in. But no elemist is stupid enough to risk going near the place, let alone go inside. So, the rumors remain rumors."

Kess cut through another alley, which led them onto another street that appeared less dilapidated than the last. There were still no signs of varens, which only set Sean more on edge. Where had they gone?

This street was much busier than the previous one as well, as if they'd wandered back into the heart of the city. Young people from all corners of the realm wandered past them and Sean noted the way Emery watched them with wide eyes, the way she took in the tall man with ice-blonde hair who was clearly from Jokul, and the way she stared at the strawberry-blonde woman playing a violin in the corner.

Though Emery watched everyone, no one watched them. They didn't stand out at all here. Nobody cared.

"We're in the living quarter now," Kess explained. "We're right in the middle of the schools, where most of the students live. Varens rarely come here."

Though Sean believed him, and trusted Kess with his life, he still couldn't ease his anxiety, couldn't stop himself from scanning every face they passed.

"So," Kess said. "What did you want to talk to me about? Billy mentioned you came to ask me something."

Emery glanced at Sean before looking back at Kess. She kept her voice low. "I don't know if it's safe to talk about out here."

"Oh, it's fine," Kess said, hands in his pockets as if he didn't have a care in the world. "One of the best parts of this city is that you can talk about anything, and no one cares. Everything is studied here. Every question is asked."

"Alright, well," Emery began, "we were wondering if, in your studies, you came across an illness that only strikes elemists. One that basically sucks the life out of them until there's nothing left."

Kess stopped walking so abruptly, Sean nearly ran straight into him. He was already reaching for his cutlass, scanning the crowd for a threat, when he realized Kess was simply gazing at Emery with open curiosity.

"You are not the first person to ask me that."

Emery's face filled with surprise and hope. "Really?"

Kess examined Emery's face more closely for a moment. "Where are you from?"

Emery shifted on her feet. "Just a tiny island no one has ever heard of."

Her standard answer.

Kess tilted his head, his curiosity only seeming to grow. "Maybe we should wait to talk about this until we're home after all. We're almost there."

Indeed, only a few more minutes passed before they came upon a sunshine yellow building with ivy crawling up its walls. Flowers of every kind and colour spilled from the window pots.

Kess led them towards the door but, before opening it, said, "I suppose I should warn you: I have roommates."

Alarm flared inside Sean. "Kess—"

"They're trustworthy, I promise. They're like *us*..."

Sean clenched his jaw, understanding his meaning.

His roommates were elemists too. While he understood why Kess might think that would reassure Sean, it didn't. It only meant if varens found them, even more lives would be ruined or lost. And even if these people shared the same abilities as them, it didn't make them on the same side. Years of dealing with other Forbiddens on the sea had taught him that.

But they were here, and they didn't have much of a choice. Sean did not want to be out in the open anymore, and Emery was growing paler every minute.

Kess swung the door open, and they stepped into the humble abode. The first thing Sean noticed was the abundance of plants taking over the small apartment. He felt like he'd just stumbled into a tiny jungle. The second thing he noticed was Billy siting at a small, round dining table in the middle of the room. Safe and sound. Sean had just a moment for the relief to wash over him before he noticed the third thing. A young woman stood at a counter with her back towards them. Her hair fell in golden waves down her back, and for a moment, Sean was hit with a disorienting mixture of past, present, and future. How many times had he and Kess walked into a room together to find Lily and her golden locks waiting for them? If things had not gone so dreadfully wrong, he would have been walking into *this* room to find her too, living the life she and Kess had always talked about. This *should* have been their life. This *should* have been their future.

But then the girl turned and she looked nothing like Lily, and the spell broke.

Beside him, Emery had gone completely still. She stared at the blonde girl with huge eyes and when the blonde girl noticed Emery, she gasped and dropped the tea she'd been preparing.

Another woman appeared from a door, her silver-streaked curls bouncing as she moved. The woman stopped dead when her dark eyes landed on Emery, and in that moment, everything grew silent and still.

Sean had just enough time to realize the woman wasn't as old as she first appeared, before Emery sucked in a breath, and burst into tears.

Chapter Nineteen

"Ayana!" Emery cried as she launched across the room. "Grace!"

Her sister and her best friend met her in the middle of the room, and they crashed together in a tangled embrace of tears and limbs. Emery buried her face into her sister's curly hair, inhaling the familiar scent of blossoming flowers and life-giving soil.

She was *alive*. Her sister was alive. Emery squeezed her tighter, just to make sure she was real and wasn't a hallucination brought on by her head injury. She *felt* real.

She was here and she was alive and the joy that coursed through Emery was so intense, she felt like she was floating.

"What are you doing here?" Emery asked through a sob, remembering the last time she saw both Ayana and Grace. They'd been standing on the cliffs of Orabel, waving goodbye, as Emery, Liam, and (unbeknownst to everyone at the time) Caelin sailed away on Tavor's ship so many months ago.

"What are *you* doing here?" Ayana countered, her own voice thick.

"And why are you bleeding?" Grace added.

Emery realized she was probably bleeding all over both of them and pulled back.

"I'm fine," she began but then swayed dangerously backwards. The only thing keeping her from toppling over was the press of a warm hand appearing against her spine as Sean caught her.

"You need to sit down," Sean murmured into her ear.

"She needs stitches," Kess said.

Before either of those things could happen, Billy swept both Emery and Sean into a giant hug. "Thank the gods you're both alright!"

Emery hardly noticed. She watched Ayana as she rushed from the room, moving faster than Emery had seen her move in years—and without using her lim as a cane like she used to—and returned quickly with clean towels and a little leather case she handed to Kess. Kess cleared the table and pulled out a chair, gesturing for Emery to sit. Sean reapplied the handkerchief she'd dropped upon seeing her sister to her forehead and led her to the chair, taking the seat beside it. Billy had vacated that one to hug them and now helped Grace quickly clean up the broken bits of teacups.

"What happened?" Ayana asked, setting a bowl of purified water on the table.

"I'm not sure," Emery said. Kess removed the handkerchief from her head and instead dabbed the wound with a dampened towel. "It happened during a fight with some varens."

"Of course." Grace sighed as she reentered the room with a new tea set. For the first time, Emery noticed she wore a lovely blue dress, the rich colour and style nothing like the boring clothing they had back home.

Ayana took the seat next to Kess and peered over his shoulder as he worked, her dark eyes shining with concern. "Will she be alright?"

Ayana's clothes were less bright, but still a style uncommon in Orabel, with a billowy start white shirt and tight black pants.

"Yes, but this is going to hurt." Kess opened his leather case and produced thread and a sharp metal needle that glinted in the light.

The blood rushed from Emery's head at the sight. "Oh gods."

She instinctively reached for Sean's hand, and he intertwined their fingers without hesitation, giving her a reassuring squeeze.

"This should help," Ayana said. She produced a vial with some sort of clear tincture inside. She gently dabbed the contents on Emery's forehead. A cooling sensation immediately spread around her wound as if someone was pressing ice over it, and the pain subsided a little.

Kess finished threading his needle. "Are you ready?"

Emery's stomach dipped with nerves. She'd never had stitches before. But she nodded, clutching Sean's hand so hard, it probably hurt. But he said, "Squeeze as hard as you need. Break my fingers if you need to."

"Distract her," Kess suggested.

"Tell her how you got here," Sean said, addressing Ayana and Grace for the first time.

"We left about a month after you," Grace rushed to say as Kess lifted the needle to Emery's forehead.

Pain flared as the needle pierced her skin and the thread was pulled through, but it wasn't as bad as she'd feared. Whatever Aya had put on her skin seemed to be working. But still, Emery couldn't contain her flinch and squeezed Sean's hand even harder.

"I got worse," Ayana continued. "And I decided I'd rather die searching for a cure and having an adventure than wilt away at home."

"We built a boat," Grace said.

"*Grace* built a boat," Ayana interjected, casting Grace an admiring smile. "From scratch. Fia helped. I mostly watched and cheered them on. Fia was supposed to come with us, but her mother got sick a few days before we left, and she decided to stay."

Emery's heart clenched for Fia. Her mother had always been so kind, and she was the only parent Fia had left. Her father had passed away years ago. And Fia had no siblings. If her mother died, she'd have no immediate family left.

"The Withering?" Emery asked as Kess continued to sew up her wound.

"Yes," Aya said sadly.

Gods, the cure couldn't be found soon enough. And she'd wasted so much time selfishly looking for her parents.

"We didn't tell anyone we were leaving," Grace said.

Guilt flashed across Ayana's face. "I knew Grandmother and Grandfather would never let me go."

Emery's heart twisted again, imagining her grandparents discovering Ayana's empty bed in the morning, imagining the fear and heartbreak and betrayal they must have felt when they realized their granddaughter ran away just like their daughter had. Now their daughter and all three grandchildren were gone, leaving them alone. Unless Liam had made it home.

But even if Ayana had said goodbye to her grandparents and they let her go, the rest of the villagers may not have. It was, after all, forbidden to leave the island.

"Where did you go?" Emery asked.

"We floated around the sea for a bit," Grace said. "I was able to direct us by the stars at night and the sun during the day. Mostly tried to stay in a straight line until we found land. Thank the gods we stocked up on a lot of provisions before we left."

Emery imagined Grace rowing their tiny makeshift boat through the Barren Sea, since Ayana likely wouldn't have been strong enough to help, the sheer determination to keep the girl she loved alive the only thing keeping her going as the days stacked on top of each other.

Emery also noted the way they didn't mention the Barren Sea and kept everything vague as to not give any hints to Orabel or its location. This told Emery that they likely hadn't told Kess anything about their home. Orabel remained a secret in this room.

Ayana continued to watch Kess stich. "We eventually came across a fishing vessel. The captain was a kind old man who was happy to bring us back home to his pretty little coastal village. While there, Grace worked for a bit until we were able to find passage to Dornwell to look for you."

Emery stared at her sister. That was the most words she'd heard her sister speak without losing her breath in a long time.

"But when we got to Dornwell," Aya continued, "we couldn't find any of you, or Tavor."

A palpable silence and stillness slammed into the room. Billy grew pale, his teacup halfway to his mouth. Kess's fingers paused their work on Emery's forehead, and Sean's fingers tightened in Emery's.

"We know now that Tavor isn't who he said he was," Ayana said. "Kess has told us about him."

Grace's eyes scrutinized their faces curiously as she continued the story. "We couldn't find you. We asked around but no one had heard of you. No one seemed to know where Tavor was either."

"According to the varens around here, no one has seen him for a while," Kess added.

"We stayed in Dornwell until it became apparent that you weren't there. We decided to look elsewhere," Grace continued. "We figured you might be searching for a cure, and when we heard about Audrye, we headed here."

"How did you end up as roommates?" Emery asked, waving her free hand between Kess and Ayana.

"Well, after we got here, we got in a bit of an altercation with some varens," Ayana said, grinning guiltily at Grace.

Grace shook her head in mock exasperation, and Emery wondered exactly what Ayana did. But Grace said, "Luckily, Kess overheard everything and talked us out of trouble."

"Sounds like Sean isn't the only one who likes to play hero," Emery teased as Kess sat back to admire his work.

He shrugged. "What can I say? I suppose that's what made us such great friends."

Emery didn't miss the way he said 'made' instead of 'makes.'

Apparently, neither did Sean. His jaw tightened, but he said nothing.

"We saw your wanted posters, and that at least told us you were likely still alive," Grace said. "We figured we'd find the cure, and then continue to search for you."

Kess snipped the thread. "You might have a little scar, but that just adds intrigue to the face."

Emery clenched her right hand, the F branded into her palm tugging uncomfortably at her skin. She'd take the tiny forehead scar over that monstrosity any day. But she supposed she was stuck with both.

As Ayana cleared the soiled towels, Kess cleaned and put away his medical supplies, and Grace finally sat down with a tray clattering with pretty floral teacups and a steaming teapot.

"Alright, your turn," Grace said when everyone was seated around the table. She poured six cups of steaming tea. "Where's your brother? Where's *my* brother? And where's...Tavor?" She hesitated before saying his name again, as if unsure if she should even speak about him.

Emery's pulse raced at the sound of his name, and the fact that she'd confirmed she hadn't killed him like she'd feared. But now, knowing he was out there somewhere, looking for them... She wondered why she'd ever been afraid of such a thing. This was worse.

Emery finally released Sean's hand, her fingers stiff from grasping his so hard, and wrapped her hands around the warm teacup. But then she let go, her stomach clenching as she remembered the last time she'd had tea. With Tavor, in his cabin, when he was busy spinning lies and she was falling for each one.

"Liam and Caelin are safe. I think. They headed home, and hopefully are there now. Tavor, he..." She took a breath, not even sure where to begin. Sean's knee pressed against hers under the table, bolstering her courage.

"He's a monster. He lied about everything. He never had a cure. And he certainly didn't want peace." She faltered again, unsure of how much to say. Sean, of course, didn't know about Orabel, and she never did tell him why she was really with Tavor, because doing so would have revealed her home.

But Ayana and Grace had both gone pale, her vague story more than enough.

"That bastard," Ayana spat.

She didn't know the half of it.

"What did he actually want?" Grace asked.

Emery chose her words carefully. "He wants to build a new prison for elemists."

What she didn't say was that he wanted to do that on Orabel.

A heavy silence passed as Ayana and Grace blanched further. Kess and Billy looked equally horrified. Beside her, Sean had gone completely still, and she felt his questioning gaze on her face. She'd never told him that part either. For the most part, she'd avoided talking about Tavor altogether. She couldn't return his gaze, and instead took a sip of her tea just to give herself something to do.

Emery knew the curiosity must be killing Grace and that she probably had a thousand questions that she couldn't voice in front of Sean, Billy, and Kess. But she directed her next query to Sean: "How did you to wind up together? How did you meet?"

"Umm, well..." Emery sensed his gaze on her again, and this time, she looked back. He was flushed, his bottom lip trapped between his teeth as if he didn't know what to say.

No doubt he didn't wish to tell the story of his lowest moment, the moment when he almost threw everything away for revenge—including his own life. Which also happened to be the moment they met.

"I threw scalding hot tea into his face," Emery said, smirking. "And then I knocked him unconscious."

Sean cast her a quick, grateful look as Ayana, Grace, and Kess gaped at her. Billy, of course, already knew the story and looked mildly amused.

"Then he saved me from a sea monster," Emery said, not

going into detail that this only happened because she thought he'd kidnapped her and had been trying to escape.

"And then she saved me from some varens and a few angry drunks," Sean added, a ghost of a smile flitting across his lips.

"And then we saved each other from Tavor," Emery finished. This time she barely felt the fear of uttering his name, because her eyes had locked with Sean's, and he gazed steadily back.

Their story sounded simple and easy spelled out this way. It had been anything but.

Ayana, Grace, and Kess gaped again, and then Ayana turned to Grace. "I wish we had an interesting story of how we met. I don't even remember meeting you."

"We have plenty of other firsts to remember," Grace said with a wicked smile. Ayana returned the look and leaned over to kiss Grace on the lips. Grace whispered something into Ayana's ear and Ayana giggled.

Emery noticed the way Sean blinked in surprise, and then seemed to relax a fraction in his seat. What caused the initial tension, she had no idea.

Kess let out a long-suffering sigh. "Always with these two."

"You have no idea," Emery said. Truly, she could barely remember a time when Ayana and Grace weren't disgustingly in love with each other. Emery had missed seeing it. Ayana also had a spark in her eye that had been missing for a long time.

"So," Ayana said, leaning away from Grace again, her face a little flushed. "Why are you in Audrye now?"

"We had the same idea as you," Emery explained. "Sean thought if there was a cure to be found anywhere, it would be here."

"So, Sean thought to come speak to the smartest person he knows," Kess said, grinning.

Sean's lips twitched. "Actually, that would probably be Aleksy."

"You wound me," Kess said, clutching his chest.

"You're an almost doctor now," Sean said, his tone teasing. "I'm sure you'll be fine."

Kess chuckled, and Sean held his gaze for only a moment before his ghost of a smile faded, and he looked down at the table instead. Kess's smile slipped too.

"Actually, now that we've met, I'm the smartest person you know," Grace said matter-of-factly.

"True," Emery, Ayana, and Kess agreed in unison.

Sean raised a brow, studying Grace with more interest.

"Regardless, there doesn't seem to be a cure here," Grace said, setting her chin in her hand. "Here or anywhere."

Emery's heart sank.

"We can't seem to find any mention of an illness like the Withering," Ayana said. "And we've spent months searching. We've talked to everyone we can think of and have scoured every library on campus. Nothing."

"Well, not every library," Grace mused, her eyes glinting with mischief.

"Indeed, you two showed up at an interesting time," Kess said, sitting back in his seat and folding his arms.

"Oh?" Emery said, interest peaked.

"There's one last place we haven't tried," Ayana said. "And it's the most likely place we might find information about a disease that only hits elemists."

Sean went still in his seat. "I don't like where this is going."

"We have to look," Grace said. "We can't have come all this way and not look. What if the cure is there?"

"Where?" Emery asked, lost. "What if it's where?"

"They guard the place day and night," Sean said, his voice growing so calm Emery knew it was masking a growing anxiety. "Watching specifically for elemists."

"We're aware," Grace admitted.

"And we have a plan," Ayana added.

Emery finally realized where they spoke of. "The old Elemental University? But you literally just told me no elemist would be stupid enough to go near the place."

"Yeah," Kess said, wearing a mischievous grin that reminded

her so much of Liam her heart ached. "I guess we're not that bright."

"Speak for yourself," Grace said.

"What's your plan?" Emery asked. Her stomach was beginning to tie itself in knots, but she couldn't tell if it was from anxiety or anticipation or both.

"As you well know, All Gods Day is in two days," Kess said.

They had known this. Or at least, Sean had known this, and Emery had learned it from him. All Gods Day was an old holiday during which everyone celebrated ancient, half-forgotten gods. There were festivals, and everyone dressed up as random gods. Sean told her Audrye was a city of students, meaning young people who desperately needed to blow off steam, so All Gods Day became an all-day chaotic festival every year. People came in from all over the realm to celebrate, so the harbor and city were always packed, which had made it easier for them to sneak in. They had also hoped it would make it easier for them to stay anonymous amongst the crowd, but that hadn't gone as planned.

"We're going to use the chaos as a distraction," Grace said. "The guards will be stretched thin, and they'll be overwhelmed. We're going to sneak in around midnight when the festivities reach a crescendo. We'll attend the party, do our sneaking about, and then return to the party with no one the wiser."

A silence fell as Emery and Sean took in the words.

Sean broke it first. "This is not a good idea."

"Good thing we didn't ask for your opinion," Ayana said.

Before Sean could retort further, Emery said, "I'm in."

"Em—" Sean began, his eyes flaring wide.

"I know it's dangerous," she said, cutting him off. "But they're right. We've come this far. What if the cure is right there? What if it can save our people?"

"We're going to do it with or without you," Grace added. "We already had this planned. We don't need your help."

"I'm helping," Emery said immediately. She had to. She had to try for her sister and for all her friends and family back home, who were currently dying or already dead because of this mysterious illness. She turned to Sean, her heart suddenly in her mouth. "I understand if you don't want any part of this. You've already done so much for me. You've upheld your end of our bargain, and then some. You can go back to the *Audacity* and get out of here if that's what you want to do. It's alright."

She hated the words as they came out of her mouth, but she had to say them, even if the thought of saying goodbye to him now tore something essential in her chest.

He gazed back at her, searching her eyes as if for an answer, his expression softening a fraction at whatever he saw in them. "I have not held up my end of the bargain. You haven't found your parents yet."

"You've been looking?" Ayana interrupted.

"With little luck," she said, giving her attention to her sister for just a moment. "That's a whole other wild story." She turned back to Sean. "What are you saying?"

Sean held her gaze for another moment and then sighed. "I've been part of so many stupid plans in my life. What's one more?"

Chapter Twenty

"How's she doing?" Liam asked.

Fia sighed as she descended the staircase of branches leading from the second level of their home back down to the first. Purple smudges underscored her glassy brown eyes, and her red hair was up in a haphazard bun. She plopped onto the wooden chair at her kitchen table beside Liam, propping her chin with her hand.

"No worse than yesterday, but no better either," she said.

Liam gazed up the staircase, as if he could see all the way into the room where Fia's mother lay bedridden. "I'm sorry."

"Why? It's not like you brought the Withering here," Fia said, her voice heavy with exhaustion.

No, but he had been chosen to find the cure. And even if all that had been a lie, he still felt like he failed. Failed his sister, failed Fia's mother, failed everyone who has suffered from or succumbed to the Withering. For that, he was eternally sorry.

Not knowing how to put any of that into words, he pushed a mug of steaming tea towards Fia. He'd made it while she'd tended to her mother. He pointed a thumb over his shoulder at the heaps of dishes and half-chopped vegetables in the kitchen area and the cauldron of bubbling soup boiling in the hearth that was certainly too much for just Fia and her mother. "So, what's all that?"

"Oh." Fia wrapped her hands around the mug and inhaled the scent gratefully. "I've been cooking meals for anyone who needs them right now. Everyone is either so busy helping at the infirmary or dealing with their own ill family members... I wanted to help somehow."

"You're doing this all by yourself?" Liam asked.

"People come to help me from time to time. Dray, Hally..." Fia smiled ruefully. "But then they get too busy and stop coming. Really, I think they get tired of me. You know I like things done a certain way..."

"Nope, certainly never noticed that," Liam teased, glancing pointedly at the perfectly arranged bowls waiting to be filled with the soup.

Fia laughed but then it turned into a sigh. "Maybe Emery will return soon with a cure, and this will all be over."

"Maybe," he mumbled. He was sorry for that too. For feeding Fia's hopes with lies. "How long has your mother been bedridden?"

"A couple of weeks." Fia sipped her blackberry tea, and it seemed to bring a little more life into her expression. "She'd been sick for months. Fell ill a few days before I was supposed to leave with Ayana and Grace. I couldn't bear to go after that."

Liam sipped his own tea, the hot liquid searing away some of the cold shock that settled in his gut every time he was reminded Ayana was gone, that she just left in the dead of night, exactly like his mother had.

"Why isn't she at the infirmary?" he asked.

Fia shrugged. "She doesn't want to be there. She... She said she'd rather die comfortably in her own bed."

Tears glistened in her eyes; she tried to hide them by taking another drink of tea and blinking them away. But Liam had seen them. A lump formed in his throat, and he raised a hand to reach for her, to comfort her, but dropped it before she looked back up. What could he do? What could he say?

Her tears were already gone as she added, "The infirmary is full anyway. Aran comes to check on her though, as much as he can."

Liam was certain some of the other islanders came to check in sometimes too. But that meant the rest of the time, her mother's care fell mostly on Fia. Her father had passed away years ago and she was an only child. It had been just her and her mother for most of her life.

Liam clenched his jaw, and stared at the black depths of his tea, cursing Tavor for his false hope and lies, and cursing the Arch-Elemists for forcing him to continue these lies. Did Fia not deserve to know the truth? Did she not deserve to know that there was no cure and possibly never would be? Or was it kinder to allow her to hope?

It didn't feel kind. It felt cruel.

"Tell me a tale from the outside world," Fia said.

Liam swallowed, his throat suddenly dry despite the tea. "It wasn't very exciting," he lied some more. "I spent most of my time on a ship or boat with nothing but blue skies and blue water to look at."

Fia gazed at him, disappointment clear in her tired eyes. And something else too. Something like suspicion. "Surely *something* exciting must have happened."

"I did almost blow up a ship with gun power," he said, offering her a mischievous smirk and a kernel of truth. He *had* almost blown up a ship. On more than one occasion.

This earned him another little laugh that made his insides flutter.

"Of course, you did." Fia grinned. "What's gun powder?"

Liam told her all about the explosive powder and the many experiments he conducted. He just failed to mention that a lot of these experiments occurred while he was grieving Emery after he thought she'd drowned in a shipwreck, that the experiments were the only thing that made him feel anything during those awful weeks. He wanted so badly to tell her about that time, but he couldn't, because that story didn't line up with the lie they'd been telling.

But gods, he wanted to tell her. He wanted to tell her what it was like to watch the ship sink into the dark depths of the ocean with his sister still inside it. He wanted to tell her about being locked in a dungeon and listening to his sister scream as she was branded, screaming himself as his own flesh burned. He wanted to tell her Tavor was a monster, that there was no cure, that the whole island could be in more danger than she realized. She deserved to know.

To Pyralis's Flames with the Arch-Elemists. To Pyralis's Flames with being their submissive lackey. To Pyralis's Flames with it all.

He wanted to tell her, and he would.

They just needed somewhere secluded.

"Come for a walk with me," he said abruptly.

"But my mother—"

"It will be quick, I promise!" Now that he'd made the decision, it felt urgent, like if he didn't get it out now, he'd explode. He grabbed her hand, pulling her from her seat and towards the door.

"Liam?" Fia questioned. She didn't fight, only looked over her shoulder at the staircase as they rushed out the door.

Instead of following the dirt path that led deeper into the village, Liam pulled Fia around the giant redwood she lived in and darted into the woods, away from prying eyes and ears. He hoped. He didn't know exactly how the Arch-Elemists kept tabs on them. Did they listen through the wind? Watch through the trees?

It was late enough in the evening that no one was at the Gardens. The setting sun gilded the fruit trees gold, set the berry bushes aglow. The neat lines of vegetables glistened from the rain that had fallen that afternoon, the water droplets reflecting the sunset like little pricks of flame. The effect was almost enough to mask the fact that half the fruit trees stood barren, that many of the berry bushes had turned brittle, and that, though the vegetables still grew, a lot of them came out stunted and misshaped. The Gardens were dying. Just like the island. Just like the islanders.

Liam tried to ignore it all and pulled Fia between rows of corn, going so deep that the sun ceased flowing through the leaves. He hoped if anyone saw them enter the Gardens, they'd assume he and Fia were simply two young adults searching for a place to be alone. The thought caused his cheeks to burn when he finally stopped and turned to face her.

She looked up at him, eyes wide. "Liam, are you alright?"

Nerves rattled in his belly. They'd never been alone quite like this before. And suddenly, it was difficult to remember the real reason he brought her here.

"Liam?" she prompted.

When Liam did remember why they were there, his nerves only worsened. He wet his dry lips. "I must tell you something, but you can't tell anyone. You *can't*."

"Alright..."

Liam glanced around, making sure they were truly and utterly alone. All he could see were corn stalks all around them, stretching so high they hid the sky. The wind shouldn't be able to hear them over the buzzing of bees and the chirping of cicadas, the rustle of the stalks. The trees couldn't see them. But still, he hesitated. Were the Arch-Elemists still watching somehow? Still listening? Could they really do that or was it a scare tactic? Could they really silence anyone from anywhere?

Liam had never seen any evidence that they could. Perhaps it was just a ruse.

He opened his mouth, then closed it, unsure where to even start. "Emery is not with Tavor."

This seemed safer, somehow, to start with.

"Alright..." Fia repeated, and when Liam didn't continue right away, she asked, "Then where is she?"

"Aboard a Forbidden's ship. Captain Denzel." At the look of horror on her face, Liam quickly added. "She's safe with him. Gods, I hope she's safe."

"But why?"

Liam paused again, eyes darting around. The words were coming out and still, he was breathing, unharmed. Not silenced. Gaining confidence, Liam spoke quickly. "She's looking for our parents. And she *is* searching for a cure. She's just not with Tavor."

Fia shook her head. "I don't understand."

"Because Tavor is—"

A monster. He tried to say it, but no sound came out of his mouth. He chocked, gasped for air. But there was no air. It was like he was suddenly underwater, drowning.

"Liam?" Fia's eyes widened further. "Tavor is what?"

A monster. A murderer. A manipulative psychopath. He tried to say it all, tried to scream it.

But he couldn't breathe. He clawed at his throat, as if that would do any good.

His chest ached. His vision darkened at the edges.

His knees hit the dirt.

"Liam, what's happening?" Fia knelt with him, grabbed his face, but he could barely feel her touch. Could barely feel anything but terror.

The Arch-Elemists, he tried to shout, tried to think loud enough that she'd somehow, impossibly, hear him. *They're killing me!*

Dizziness tore through him, and his vision tunneled further, until all he could see was Fia's confused, horrified expression. He faintly registered that she was screaming for help, before he slumped sideways into the dirt, and the world faded.

Chapter Twenty-One

"That absolute bastard," Ayana seethed, grabbing Emery's hand and glaring at the F seared into her palm. Her sister shook with barely contained rage. "If I ever see him again, I will kill him myself."

Emery's stomach clenched with a mixture of her own fear and fury. "Let's just hope we never see him again."

She lay squished between Grace and Ayana in their small but comfortable bed, in their small but comfortable bedroom, which was just as full of plants as the living room, her hair still damp from her bath and her head still sore from her fall.

After tea and a meal, Emery and Sean had taken turns cleaning up in Kess's tiny washing room. It contained a basin of rose scented water, and a tub so small, Emery barely fit inside. She couldn't imagine how Sean had bathed properly in it but when she thought of that, her face heated and she had to push the images out of her mind immediately. She'd been covered in dirt and blood, while Sean still had gun powder masking the colour of his hair and beard, and so, tiny tub or not, they both had needed to bathe.

During Emery's turn, Grace and Ayana had wedged themselves into the small room too, as if unable to bear having Emery out of their sights again. When Emery stripped her ruined clothes and folded herself into the steaming water, she couldn't help but remember the another time she'd had a bath, when she'd removed her clothes in front of Sean, and he'd fled the room.

"Have you two noticed how scared of nudity outsiders are?" Emery had asked.

Grace and Ayana both cackled with laughter.

Ayana said, "Oh my gods, we went for a swim in the ocean with Kess not long after arriving and he almost fainted when we started taking our clothes off."

"To be fair, so did most of the people on the beach at the time," Grace added. "A lesson learned for us at any rate."

After they had finished marveling over outsiders and their prudish ways, Emery told them her entire story all over again. Without Sean and Kess listening, she didn't have to be careful. She began her tale with the moment she and Liam had sailed away on Tavor's ship and Caelin had been discovered stowing away below deck. And she continued the tale, with every detail she could remember until the moment Tavor had her branded like an animal.

She'd talked so long, her bath grew cold, and they'd eventually vacated to the bedroom. Emery had no idea how late into the evening it might have been, though it was certainly dark outside now, and her eyes where growing heavier and heavier.

"I just don't understand how the Arch-Elemists made such a mistake," Ayana nearly growled, running her thumb over Emery's brand.

"They didn't," Grace said and Ayana and Emery both stared at her. "Well, they supposedly know everything, don't they? The Gods supposedly give them council. So, either the Gods lied to them, or the Arch-Elemists knew the truth the entire time. Which means the question isn't how they made the mistake, but why they allowed this to happen, knowing what was to come."

Emery shook her head, laying her head back on the pillow. "I don't know, but Liam and Caelin should be back by now. If The

Arch-Elemists didn't know, they certainly do now. And, hopefully, so does everyone else."

"So, what happened after Sean showed up to save you?" Ayana asked, and there was a devious little smirk on her lips that made Emery's cheeks warm.

Ignoring the look, she launched into the next tale, recounting how Sean had been shot and they'd both been recaptured and tortured, only to escape again when Emery's abilities surged. Then how she had parted ways with Liam and Caelin so they could go home and warn their people, and she could continue searching for a cure and her parents. She'd already told them about meeting her alleged aunt Lilith.

"What are the odds of that?" Ayana had asked.

"Much better than the five of us all finding each other, separately and then together." Grace shook her head. "Honestly, I keep going over the numbers in my head and the statistics are staggeringly against us. It makes no sense."

"Not everything has to make sense, Grace," Ayana said.

Grace made a face, as if truly baffled by her words. "Of course, it does."

"Perhaps the gods just pointed us all in the right direction," Emery suggested.

Soon, she was describing the undead who turned out not to be undead at all, and the treasure chest full of nothing but rocks and disappointment.

"I'm at a dead end now," Emery said.

"You've gotten closer than we have," Ayana said, "We've asked around about a Kathleen Aalokin everywhere we've been, but so far, we've gotten nothing."

"And I've got a pile of rocks and a blank piece of parchment." Emery sighed.

"Where is the parchment now?" Grace asked. "I'd like to examine it."

Emery shrugged. "I saw Sean pick it up. It's probably in his cabin somewhere. But there was nothing on it, Grace."

"Nothing we can see, maybe," she pondered.

"What do you mean?" Emery asked.

"Perhaps there's some sort of clue hidden on the parchment somewhere. Or maybe the parchment is the clue."

Emery was too dubious and too tired to even think about it. "It was just parchment."

"We'll see about that," Grace mused.

Emery leaned further into her pillow, snug under the blankets and amongst the family she had feared she'd never see again. She was cozy, comfortable, and yet, something was off. It took her a moment to realize that the bed was too still. After sleeping on a ship for so long, Emery missed the gentle rocking of the sea and the gentle lapping of the water against the hull, the creaking of the ship as she swayed. And if she was being totally honest with herself, there was a certain presence she was missing too.

She glanced at the door, as if she could see through the yellow painted wood to the small living room and the lumpy couch Sean was sleeping on. She wondered if he was already asleep, and hoped no nightmares plagued him when she wasn't there to shoo them away.

"Kess will take good care of him tonight, you know," Ayana said.

Emery's gaze snapped back to her sister. "Huh?"

"That's like the hundredth time you've looked at the door since we've come in here," Ayana said, that grin back on her face.

"Actually, it's been fifty-six times," Grace said.

Emery's cheeks flamed again.

"Kess has talked about Sean a lot," Ayana continued.

"Really?" Emery asked, surprised considering Sean barely mentioned Kess at all.

"Mhm. Did you know Sean paid for all of Kess's schooling?" Ayana said. "Apparently, Sean had saved up for himself, but when he had to run, he gave it to Kess, so he could go to school instead."

Emery gaped at her sister. She had absolutely not known that.

"But Kess somehow failed to describe how utterly dashing he is," Ayana added. "You're a lucky girl."

"I—what?" Emery sputtered.

"You can go sleep with him, if you want," Ayana said. "We won't be offended. We know how difficult it is to sleep without your significant other."

Emery wanted the bed to swallow her whole. "Oh. Uh, no. We aren't *together*. Like that."

"You're not?" Ayana said at the same time Grace asked, "Why not?"

"I mean, we've slept together a few times—" At the look on Ayana's face, Emery hurried to correct herself. "Not like that! I mean, we've shared a room and a bed a few times. That's it!"

She'd told them everything that had happened to her since leaving Orabel, excluding all her little moments with Sean. She had not felt ready to take them out and examine them yet, to share them. But, apparently, that had been the wrong move.

"Why not?" Grace asked again. "He's so pretty."

"And he clearly wants you," Ayana added.

Emery blinked, because that had not been clear to her at all, not after a month of barely anything happening between them and then him running from the room when she stripped in front of him. "What makes you say that?"

"Umm..." Ayana held up her fingers and began ticking them off. "He saved your life like a hundred times. He's been chauffeuring you around the world. Since you've been here, he's always had one eye on you. He keeps finding reasons to touch you. Need I go on?"

"We had a deal..." Emery said lamely.

Ayana rolled her eyes. "Honestly, Emery, you've always been so dense when it comes to love. You're as bad as Grace."

Grace frowned at Ayana. "What's that supposed to mean?"

Aya cast her a look. "I flirted with you for months and you never noticed. When I finally just kissed you, you still asked why I did it. I had to tell you I liked you before you got it."

Grace grinned. "But then, if you remember, I kissed you back."

"Oh, I remember." Ayana and Grace leaned over Emery for a quick kiss.

But Emery barely noticed. Her mind had spun out after Ayana said the word love. Was that what this was? Did she love Sean? She'd never allowed herself to even think the word, not when she was keeping so many secrets from him and not when, sooner or later, they'd have to go their separate ways. And she certainly never considered, or at least never let herself hope, that he might love her back.

"I don't... I don't think he feels that way," Emery said, the words shooting pain through her chest.

"Oh, Em," Ayana pulled her into a hug and patted her head. "I missed you and your obliviousness."

Chapter Twenty-Two

Sean groaned as he stretched his back, his muscles stiff after sleeping on Kess's lumpy couch all night. Or at least, some of the night. In truth, he hadn't done much sleeping.

After they had finished dinner and Sean sent Billy back to the *Audacity* to relay their new plan to the crew and tell them to leave and wait for them at a different island, Kess had offered them the use of his washing room to clean up. Sean had been thankful to retreat to the silent solitude of the cramped room for a few blessed minutes. His nerves were still on edge, even though the varens didn't know where he was, even though Kess's roommates turned out to be more than trustworthy, even though, for the time being, they were safe. He could not shake his queasy dread, even as he climbed into the too small tub and washed the itchy gunpowder from his hair and beard.

After he'd cleaned up, Emery had taken her turn and, to his surprise, Grace and Ayana had followed her into the washing room, leaving Sean and Kess alone for the first time since Lily's death.

Dread, guilt, and anxiety had washed over Sean so strongly, it left him dizzy.

"Feeling better?" Kess asked.

Sean had panicked. "I'm tired."

Kess had offered him the couch, grabbed him a pillow and blanket, and then they said an awkward goodnight. At least, it felt awkward to Sean, but he didn't know if it was all in his head. Guilt knifed through him again at the brief look of disappointment Kess hadn't been able to hide before he retreated to his bedroom.

For a moment, Sean had wanted to call him back, to spill his guts and tell his best friend everything, to get down on his knees and beg his forgiveness. But he had done none of those things. Like a coward, he had lain on the couch amongst the forest of plants crowding the room and watched stars prick to life through the window.

He had hoped Emery might reemerge, but she never did. For most of the evening, he heard the girls giggling and chatting and swearing, but the words were muffled.

He was happy Emery had found her family, glad her sister was not only alive, but seemed to be thriving. But a small, terrible part of him was also envious, envious that he wasn't enjoying the same kind of reunion with his own sister and best friend. And he couldn't help but wonder if this meant that Emery didn't need him anymore. He agreed to help them sneak into the old Elemental University against his better judgment. It was a stupid plan, a stupid risk. But the alternative was to leave Emery behind and head back for the *Audacity*. Something akin to panic had risen inside him at the thought. So, he'd agreed to help. At least this way, he could protect her, protect all of them. At least this way, she still needed him for a little longer.

As Sean lay there all night, listening to the girls chatter, it helped push back the onslaught of old memories that constantly threatened to drown him, helped the deep loneliness from swallowing him whole. He both yearned for, and dreaded, sleep. As he did most nights. When he finally had drifted off, the nightmares struck and struck hard.

In the morning, Sean rose with the sun as he always did, running from the nightmares into the gold dawn as usual. He was exhausted and still full of that deep dread that had stayed with him all night, like an old companion in the shadows.

The small house was quiet as the others slept. He suspected the girls would sleep late into the day since they'd stayed up so late. But he was wrong. Perhaps an hour after the sun rose, they burst from their bedroom and into the living room like a whirlwind. Well, the whirlwind was mostly Grace. Emery and Ayana were caught in her wake.

Emery and her sister both rubbed their eyes in the exact same way and yawned in unison. They had the same wild hair, though Ayana's was a little curlier and streaked with silver from the Withering. But otherwise, they didn't look that much alike, not like Emery and Liam did. Ayana's skin was a little lighter, and her eyes brown instead of blue.

Emery's sleepy gaze found his and she smiled. As usual, Sean's stomach swooped. Before he could say anything, Grace whisked back into the room. He didn't even realize she'd left.

"Let's go, let's go! We're wasting daylight!"

"Where are we going?" Sean asked.

"Us ladies are going shopping," Grace announced, linking arms with both Emery and Ayana and all but dragging them to the door. "We need to prepare costumes for the festival tomorrow, not to mention, this poor girl needs some new clothes that actually fit her."

Indeed, Emery had to toss the clothes she'd arrived in—a pair of pants she'd borrowed from Seadar and a tunic from Sean—and now wore a floppy hat that hid her hair and part of her face and a loose dress that he assumed belonged to her sister. He'd never seen her in a dress before and it seemed he wasn't going to see much of it that day either, because Emery shot him one last overwhelmed look before she was whisked out the door by Grace, leaving Sean alone once again.

Or almost alone.

"That girl has never-ending energy," Kess said.

Sean turned to find him leaning against the kitchen doorway, still in his pajamas, shaking his head after Grace, with obvious affection.

Guilt slammed into Sean again. Last night, while he'd still been trying to figure out who everyone was, Sean had wondered if something romantic was happening between Kess and Grace. To his shame, the thought of Kess already moving on from Lily had made him nauseous. Then it became clear that Grace and Ayana were together, and Sean felt relieved, then immediately guilty that he'd been nauseated over his friend's possible happiness.

Now they were alone. Again. Anxiety wedged itself up Sean's throat, making it impossible to speak. They stood in an uncomfortable silence until Kess asked, "Coffee?"

"Yes, please," Sean managed to say. He'd need ten cups of coffee to make it through the day. They didn't have much coffee aboard the *Audacity*. It was too expensive to buy and if they found some during a raid, they'd usually sell most of it so they could buy food instead.

Sean followed Kess into the small kitchen, noticing two long sticks much like the weapon Emery constantly carried leaning against a wall. He could only assume they belonged to Grace and Ayana and that they hadn't bothered grabbing them that morning because they felt safe enough without them. Or maybe they were armed with other weapons instead. Kess puttered around until he produced two steaming mugs of coffee and offered one to Sean. "We'll have to head into town ourselves. We'll need costumes for tomorrow too."

The thought of wandering the streets filled Sean with more dread and he nearly scalded his tongue in his hurry to get some coffee in his belly.

His trepidation must have been evident on his face, because Kess's expression softened. "You can stay here if you want. But I have some clothes and a hat you can wear while we're out, and I promise, if you're with me, the varens won't look at you twice. They all know me. And love me, in fact."

"That's a dangerous game, befriending varens," Sean said, though he had to admire Kess's audacity.

"You know what they say, keep your enemies closer," Kess said, waving a hand. "Truly, if I tell them you're my cousin or something, they won't think twice about it. And besides, it's so packed out there today, it's unlikely we'll see any varens anyway. I'd like you to come with me."

"Alright," Sean said, not sure what else to say. The last thing he desired was to stroll these streets, but he wanted to make his friend happy, even in this small way. He owed him so much more.

Sean borrowed a long jacket and a hat from Kess, and though his hair was back to its regular colour, his short beard and new clothes seemed to be enough to keep the general public from recognizing him. Though to be fair, no one looked twice at him.

Kess had been right. The streets were even busier than they'd been the day before, packed with both tourists and locals alike as they got ready for tomorrow's festivities. Some people were already donned in costumes, too excited to wait one more day to put them on. Sean did not stand out at all.

They spotted a few varens marching about, but for the most part, they were too busy with the early partiers to pay any attention to Kess and Sean. If they did glance their direction, they'd make brief eye contact with Kess, give him a small wave, and then be on their way.

And yet, as Sean followed Kess from clothing store to clothing store, his dread only intensified. Most of the stores were picked clean this close to the holiday, and so the day's tasks took a lot longer than anticipated. Kess kept up a steady stream of chatter, as if determined not to allow another awkward silence to fall. But fall it did, because every once in a while Kess would run out of things to say, and Sean couldn't find any words of his own, as if he'd forgotten how to even speak.

All day, every time he looked at Kess, the only words his mind could conjure were, *it was my fault, I destroyed your happiness, I'm sorry*. Sometimes the words would bubble up his throat, the confession on the tip of his tongue, as if his body finally just wanted to expel the guilt. But he'd seal his mouth shut, stuff the words back down. He could not tell Kess in the middle of a crowded street. He couldn't have all these strangers bear witness to the moment his best friend disowned him forever.

He'd known coming back here, seeing Kess again, would be hard. He'd known it, and it was why he'd put it off for nearly a year. But it was so much worse than he'd anticipated.

All day, his anxiety rose, squeezing his chest harder and harder until it was becoming difficult to breath, blurring his mind until it was challenging to concentrate, to think. Half his brain was focused on the task at hand, at helping Kess pick out costumes for the two of them, but the other half was busy constantly scanning the crowds for any sign of varens, or Tavor, or indications that someone out there recognized him, or noting the best escape routes from each building they entered and each street they strolled down. He couldn't stop.

And sometimes, he'd catch a glimpse of long golden hair in the crowd and his heart would stutter and he'd nearly trip as memories crashed into him all at once. But then he'd look again, and she wouldn't be there. Of course, she wouldn't be there. She was gone forever.

It was nearing sunset when they spotted another trio of varens marching along the street. This time, one of them spotted Kess and broke off from the others, heading straight for them.

Sean immediately, and discreetly, reached for his blade hidden under his long coat, his body already primed for fight or flight.

Kess obviously noticed the varen approaching, and Sean's reaction, because he placed a hand on Sean's arm. "It's fine, Sean. I promise. I know her."

But Kess's face looked vaguely panicked, which did nothing to ease Sean's nerves.

The varen walked right up to them, not even glancing at Sean, and kissed Kess right on the lips.

Chapter Twenty-Three

Sean's grip on his blade only tightened as the varen kissed Kess. She stepped back, giving him an adoring smile.

Kess shot Sean a nervous look before returning her smile. "Hi, Melina."

"Hello, handsome," the varen said, only then glancing at Sean. "Who's this?"

"Just an old friend," Kess said. "We're getting last minute costumes..."

Kess and the varen—Melina—exchanged a few more words, but a dull roaring had filled Sean's ears, and he heard no more of them.

She'd just *kissed* him. A *varen* just *kissed* his best friend. On the lips.

A flurry of confusing emotions stormed in his gut. Kess *had* moved on from Lily after all. He'd found happiness with someone else... Sean should have been happy for him. He knew that...but he just felt sick again. And there was a little kernel of anger burning underneath the nausea. If Kess had to move on, why did it have to be with a varen, a member of a group that actively tried to kill him and his family every day?

"Sean?"

Sean blinked, realizing that the varen had wandered off and Kess stood alone before him. Kess winced. "I'm sorry. I didn't mean for you to find out that way..."

Sean didn't know what to say. He had so many questions. How long had they been together? Was she trustworthy? How much did she know about Kess?

"Does she know what you are, Kess?" he asked.

Kess pressed his lips into a line and shook his head.

"This can only end badly..." Sean said, fear now rearing its head amongst everything else.

"She's a good woman," Kess said.

Sean didn't know what to say to that, so he didn't say anything.

The walk back home was even more silent and awkward than before.

When they stepped through the door, it was to find the girls already there. Grace was perched on the lumpy couch with heaps of fabric surrounding her. A needle and thread flashed in her nimble fingers, and she barely looked up from whatever she was creating.

"Oh, good!" Ayana said. "We brought home dinner." She stood next to the couch with what looked like a tangle of vines and flowers draped over her arms.

Emery walked out of the kitchen with a fistful of cutlery. Sean nearly dropped his new costume at the sight of her. Gone were the baggy tunic and too big trousers she'd been wearing since he met her. Gone, too, was the loose dress from that morning. Now, black tights clung to the curves of her legs. A fitted white blouse with slightly billowy sleeves left her shoulders bare, and an indigo bodice matching the precise blue of her eyes outlined the hills and valleys of her chest and waist.

For a few seconds, the anxiety building to a crescendo inside him seemed to fade away. For a few seconds, all he could think about was walking up to her and slowly releasing the ties of her bodice.

He cleared his throat. "You look like a pirate queen."

Emery looked both surprised and pleased, but then ducked her head. "Perfect. That's what Grace was aiming for."

As she moved around the table to set out the cutlery, Sean noticed that she remained barefoot. For some reason, the sight of that familiar quirk only eased his anxiety further, and it coaxed the first smile out of him all day.

Giggling caught his attention and he glanced to the sofa to find Ayana whispering in Grace's ear. Grace smiled, looked straight at Sean, and said at full volume, "I know." She then looked pointedly at Emery, who ignored her completely.

"Food's ready," Emery said, sitting down at the table.

Everyone else gathered around the table too, except for Grace.

"Too much to do before tomorrow," she said from under her pile of fabrics, feathers, and flowers on the couch. "I'll eat later."

"The food here is unreal," Ayana said through a mouthful.

Finally, Sean tore his gaze from Emery and looked down at their meal. His stomach shriveled in on itself.

"What is it?" Emery asked, lifting a forkful of rice and vegetables to her mouth.

"Paella," Ayana said through another mouthful.

Emery took a bite and moaned.

Sean stared at his plate, at the rice and the peppers and tomatoes and zucchini. He'd been hungry when he'd walked in the door. He wasn't now. And whatever peace he'd momentarily achieved was instantly gone.

Paella had been Lily's favourite food. He couldn't even begin to count the times he, Lily, and Kess had sat around the table just like this, stuffing their faces and telling each other about their days.

Fiddling with the timepiece hanging around his neck, Sean risked glancing at Kess. He was looking back, his face slightly stricken, as if he remembered too.

His chest ached. His body flashed hot, and then cold. His fingers began to tingle.

He forced his face neutral, forced his hand to pick up the

fork, to raise it to his mouth. Forced his mouth to chew and swallow one mouthful of paella. It tasted like ash.

"Sean?"

He lifted his gaze to find Emery watching him. Had she asked him a question? Her eyes filled with concern, and it only made him feel worse. He didn't deserve her concern. He didn't deserve to be sitting there with her and Kess. He didn't deserve to be there at all.

His breaths turned shallow. His vision tunneled. A flash of golden hair caught his attention. He looked and his whole body went numb. The seat between him and Kess had been empty, meant for Grace. But it wasn't empty anymore.

Lily sat there now, with a face that so resembled his own and a sheet of golden hair, with her accusing stare and the gaping hole through her head where her right eye should have been.

The one bite of food Sean had managed to get down now fought its way back up as he stared at the ghost of his dead sister. It had been months since he'd seen her. Months since her ghost materialized to torment him, months since his brain conjured her to taunt him with the images of her blasted apart eye socket.

His throat closed. He couldn't breathe.

"Sean?"

He didn't know who said his name this time.

"Sean, are you alright?"

He shouldn't be here. He couldn't be here.

His chair screeched loudly as he shoved it back and stood. Lily stared at him with her one good eye, her mouth twisting into a sneer. He bolted for the door, desperate for air, desperate to be anywhere but in that room.

His vision tunneled further, his body starved for oxygen. But still, he couldn't breathe.

He fled, running blindly down a random street, shoving people out of his way.

He had no plan, no destination. He just ran.

He stopped only briefly, contemplating the seedy tavern at

the end of the street, considering the sharp burn of the rum that would make everything go away for a few precious hours. But then he turned and kept running. Soon the cobblestones turned to dirt and the buildings turned to palm trees and ferns. He pushed through the foliage blindly, still desperate for air, until the jungle spat him onto a little beach. He waded waist deep into the chilly ocean. And finally stopped fleeing.

The cold water embraced him, and he closed his eyes, frantically trying to suck in a breath. But his chest had caved in, leaving no room for air.

Soft hands cupped his cheeks and his eyes jerked open. Emery stood before him, the sea nearly up to her belly. For a moment, he wondered if his oxygen starved brain was hallucinating again. But he reached for her wrists, and they were warm and solid and real under his fingers, his only lifeline in this storm.

"I can't breathe," he gasped, squeezing his eyes shut again.

"Look at me," Emery demanded, her palms pressing hard into the sides of his face.

He looked into her eyes, which were the same deep blue as the twilit sea all around them. They gazed back at him unflinchingly.

"Breathe through your nose," she commanded, demonstrating for him. "And out through your mouth, slowly."

He sucked in a shaky breath through his nose, forced it back out through his mouth.

"Again," she said. "Breathe with me."

He pulled in another breath. Another. Another. Each breath came easier than the last. All the while, Emery stayed with him, breathed with him, her gaze never leaving his. Gradually, the blackness around the edges of his vision receded, and the dizziness lost some of its grip on him.

Emery rose to her tiptoes and pressed her forehead against his. "I'm here."

Sean closed his eyes again and tried to piece himself back together, but something inside him had finally crumbled and his whole body ached with the emotions he'd been suppressing for so, so long. A fierce burning built behind his eyes and when he opened them, the tears he had never let fall finally escaped. They leaked down his cheeks, dripped from his jaw, mixed with the seawater swirling around them.

The breath he'd been fighting so hard to maintain hitched as Emery kissed a tear away, and then another, her lips so soft and warm against his cheeks, his jaw, his chin. When a tear trickled to the corner of his mouth, she kissed there too.

She pulled away slightly, gazing up at him from beneath her dark lashes.

His self-control shattered.

He released her wrists to tangle his fingers in her hair, to splay his other hand against the small of her back and press her closer. Her lips were so warm against his, her body a fiery contrast to the cold waves swelling around them as she rose up to meet him in the kiss.

His wild mind went blissfully blank, his rampaging emotions narrowing into something else, until all that remained in the world was Emery and the swells of her curves under his hands and the taste of her tongue in his mouth and the burning, swelling feeling in his chest that was always there when she was around and that was now exploding with heat inside him. He couldn't breathe again, but for an entirely different reason.

Emery pulled away, breathless herself. "You don't have to talk about it. But I'm here if you want to."

Just like that, the empty serenity in his head splintered, the tight ache in his chest returned. Gods, what was he doing? He couldn't let this happen.

He released her and backed away until he stood on the sandy shore. She remained in the water, watching him with a carefully calm expression.

He did not deserve this. She did not deserve this. She deserved so much better.

He backed up one more step and then his legs gave out, dread and despair driving him to his knees. The tightness in his chest squeezed the breath out of him again. The back of his throat burned with the truth he'd been hiding, the words rising like bile. He had to tell someone. He had to tell *her*.

She stood right in front of him now, just out of reach of the waves, her clothes dripping wet. The moonlight gilded her bare shoulders, caught on the beads in her hair. She looked like some sort of ocean goddess, here to witness his moment of reckoning.

She looked at him with so much concern, so much warmth and patience and compassion. He couldn't bear it. He couldn't bear to watch her expression shift to horror or disgust or hatred. So, he looked down at the sand when he finally told her what he had never confessed to anyone else.

"I killed Lily."

Chapter Twenty-Four

"I killed my sister." Sean's voice cracked as he said it, staring at the sand between them.

Emery froze. A moment ago, her entire body had been alight with fire, but now it felt like the waves behind her had reared up and crashed their cool waters over her skin.

"You—what?" she blurted before she could catch herself.

Sean looked up, and the anguish in his expression, the silver once again lining his eyes, nearly stole her breath. He choked out the words. "I killed her."

Emery forced her expression blank, swallowed her rising horror. He'd talked about his sister's death exactly two times. And he'd given very few details. "You said Tavor killed her."

"It's my fault she's dead." His voice splintered again. "I killed her."

Carefully, as if approaching a spooked animal, Emery knelt in front of him. She gently gripped both his hands and gazed unflinchingly into his anguished eyes. "Tell me what happened."

Sean stared as her fingers curled around his limp ones, and then looked back up at her, as if surprised she was still there. His breathing quickened, turned raspy. "I...can't."

"Breathe, Sean," she instructed, squeezing his hands gently. He squeezed back, hard, and sucked in breath after breath. "Tell me what happened."

He shook his head, squeezing his eyes shut. "I killed her."

"I don't believe you," she said. It was true. She didn't believe it for a second. Sean was not a killer.

His eyes snapped opened, surprise momentarily focusing his attention. He opened his mouth, closed it. "It happened the last time we went home to visit Kess, before he moved here." As Sean concentrated on his words, his breathing grew steadier. "The three of us grew up together. Kess was my best friend but he and Lily, they courted on and off for years. They had a... complicated love. Lily was... She was not an easy person to love."

Emery wanted to know why, wanted to learn more about this sister who had been so important to Sean. But she dared not speak, not when he was finally talking.

"After I was forced to go on the run, my adoptive parents had to hide, and Lily, I thought I could keep her safe with me. I thought...I thought I could keep her safe." His voice broke and a piece of Emery's heart broke with it. "She lived aboard the *Audacity* with us for a while, but this meant she didn't get to see Kess much. He was home in Ruhette, working towards the future they'd always talked about." Sean stopped, swallowing several times as if trying to make his throat work again. It took almost a full minute before he spoke again. "We went to visit him one day. I thought we'd been careful. It was only Lily and me. I didn't realize back then just how many eyes he had. That he had been watching Kess because he knew... He knew we'd show up eventually."

Sean didn't have to say his name. A chill snaked down Emery's spine at just the suggestion of his name, and in anticipation of what Sean was going to say next.

"I was so stupid," Sean said. "I didn't see it coming. We'd barely been home ten minutes before a swarm of varens surrounded us. We tried to fight, tried to run. But there were too many."

The more Sean spoke, the sicker Emery felt. The more she understood Sean's growing anxiety over the last few days. He had been so terrified the past would repeat itself. And it almost did.

"They brought us to a ship and Tavor was waiting." Sean swallowed again. He turned her right hand over, and his left hand, so both their brands where visible. "He tortured us."

Now Emery really thought she might be sick. She knew what Tavor did to them back in Dornwell had been similar to what he'd done to Sean and his sister. He'd hinted as much while he'd been doing it. But this... Tavor had forced Sean to relive that moment on purpose; there was no doubt about it.

Fury rose like flames in her chest, and she almost wished Tavor was watching them right now, that he'd step out of the shadows so she could set him on fire all over again.

"He kept asking me where my crew was," Sean continued. "I refused to tell him. He would have killed them, or worse... He burned me, cut me...but when he realized it wasn't working, he turned his sights on Lily. But no matter what he did to her, she kept screaming at me not to tell him anything. Keeping my mouth shut while watching Tavor torture my little sister was the hardest thing I ever had to do. But she told me not to tell, she told me not to..." A sob cracked his voice then and Emery became aware that her own cheeks were wet. "Even when he branded her face, she screamed for me not to tell."

Sean ducked his head, more tears trickling down his cheeks. His shoulders shook with sobs, but he didn't make a sound, as if he wouldn't let himself fully release the pain. Emery realized that's exactly what he'd been doing ever since his sister's death. He'd been drowning himself in the pain and the guilt because that's what he believed he deserved.

"The worst part," Sean managed to say, "is that I don't think he really cared where my crew was. I think he was just playing with us. He was *enjoying* himself. So, when he brought out the gun, I thought he was bluffing. I didn't think he'd end his fun. I didn't think he'd pull the trigger."

Emery hated everything about this story. She hated hearing

it. She hated hearing the raw anguish in Sean's voice. She hated that she could do nothing to erase the words Sean said next, that she couldn't make it so it never happened.

"He held the gun to Lily's eye. Pressed so hard it bled. Gave me one last chance to tell him where my crew was. Lily kept screaming at me, demanding I say nothing. Still, I almost did. It was on the tip of my tongue. But I didn't say it. I chose my crew over my sister that day. I killed her."

"Sean..."

Emery squeezed his hands again, but this time, he pulled away, folding into himself. When he spoke next, his voice was monotone, his eyes dry. Like he'd exhausted all his emotions, wrung himself dry. Like he had nothing left. "He shot her. Right in the eye. Right through the head. Sometimes, I can still feel her blood all over my face, taste it in my mouth. I—I think I blacked out, then. I don't remember how, but I ended up with Tavor's gun. I shot him in the knee. I think guards must have come in. I don't know."

Emery remembered back when she didn't know who Tavor really was, back when he'd told her Sean was the monster, the reason he needed to walk with a cane. At the time, she hadn't known what to think, who to believe. But now, she wished she could go back to that moment, swipe Tavor's gun, and shoot him in the other knee.

"It could have been immediately after, or it could have been days—I truly can't remember—but my crew eventually found us. They blasted the ship apart. I don't remember any of it. They got me out somehow, got us away. But we never retrieved Lily's body. We had to leave her behind. She never even got a proper burial."

Too many emotions twisted in Emery's body like a tornado. Horror and rage and despair. It was too much, and she didn't have any words. She had so much she wanted to say but she didn't know how to say any of it.

Sean gazed at her, his expression empty, almost cold. "I killed her."

Emery knelt forward, taking his hands once again. He didn't pull away this time, just watched her with an almost detached shock.

"No, you didn't."

"It was my fault—"

"Sean, listen to me." Her voice came out sterner than she intended but it had the desired effect. He blinked at her, falling quiet. "You did *not* kill your sister."

"How can you say that after what I just told you?"

"What you told me was that Tavor killed her. You did not pull the trigger. You were put in a terrible position. You had to make a terrible choice that no one should ever have to make. There was no right answer. But you did not kill her. Tavor did."

Sean blinked a few more times, and tears welled in his eyes again. This time, his expression was different. They weren't tears of grief or rage. They were of hope.

"Sean, you need to say it."

"I..."

"I did not pull the trigger."

"I... I did not pull the trigger."

"I did not kill my sister."

"I did not kill my sister." He repeated the words, but he did not sound sincere.

"I need you to believe this, Sean," Emery urged. "You need to forgive yourself for this thing that wasn't your fault. This thing that's been killing you."

His voice was a whisper. "I don't know how."

She matched it. "I'll help you."

He shook his head, his eyes bright. "How do you not hate me?"

"I know you don't believe it, Sean. But you are not a monster."

"But I've done so many terrible things. How do you know?"

"I know, because..." Honestly, she didn't know how to tell him in words. But she could show him. "Because I don't kiss monsters."

She leaned forward and kissed him lightly on the lips. He didn't kiss her back like he had before. He didn't even move, as if too shocked to react. But when she went to pull away, he wrapped his arms around her, keeping her perched in his lap. He hugged her hard, burying his face in her neck. His shoulders shook again, and Emery wrapped her own arms around his torso, pressing her cheek into his hair, and she stayed there, letting him feel whatever he needed to feel, letting him expel whatever emotions he still needed to get rid of.

"I know," she continued. "Because you're kind and caring, and sometimes, you're even a little funny."

After a time, he murmured, "You throwing that tea in my face was the best thing that ever happened to me."

"I'll throw tea in your face any time you need me to."

His chest rumbled against hers as he chuckled, and her heart somersaulted.

"Sean, have you ever told that story to anyone before?"

"No."

Emery raised her head to look at him, but his forehead was still pressed into her shoulder, as if he lacked the energy or the will to lift it. "I think you need to."

Finally, he lifted his head high enough to meet her gaze. Their faces were so close, they shared breath. "How can I do that? How can I tell Billy I'm the reason he lost his daughter? How can I tell Kess I'm the reason he'll never have the future he was supposed to have with her?"

"First of all, say it again."

When Sean looked momentarily confused, she sent him a flat glare.

"I... I didn't pull the trigger."

"That's right. You didn't," she said. "Billy and Kess will see that."

"But what if they don't? What if they hate me?"

"They won't, Sean. They love you. They'll see it wasn't your fault. You need to believe you aren't a monster."

"Right. Because you don't kiss monsters." Though he still looked empty, exhausted, the tiniest spark of mischief glittered in his eyes.

"That's right." To emphasize, she closed the tiny distance between them and kissed him again. This time, he leaned into it, and though it was nothing like the frenzied, lustful kiss they'd shared moments ago in the ocean, it was somehow deeper, full of something Emery was afraid to name.

"What if something is wrong with *you?*" Sean teased when they pulled apart.

She placed a hand on her chest in mock offence. "Impossible! I'm perfect."

Sean did not laugh. He didn't even smile. "You are."

Heat blossomed across her whole body. Before she could think of anything to say, he rested his head back on her shoulder, as if suddenly exhausted again. She felt him trembling, and for a moment, she thought his sobs were back. But then she realized he was shivering. And so was she. She'd nearly forgotten they were both soaked from the cool ocean, and a brisk breeze now rustled the palm fronds along the beach, chilling them both.

Without a word, she climbed from Sean's lap and pulled him to his feet. She'd never seen him look so utterly drained.

She kept hold of his hand and led them through the jungle, back towards the city. Once they were amongst the buildings again, Sean wordlessly took the lead since she didn't know how to get back to the house. No one noticed nor cared about them as they wandered through the streets silently, beyond words at that point.

When they reached the house, it was to find it quiet and dark. Emery had no idea how long they'd been gone but it felt like no one had been awake in the house for a while, like it was just her and Sean.

They took turns changing out of their wet clothes in the bathroom. When Emery came back out, she glanced at her sister's bedroom door briefly, knowing they might be waiting for her. She turned to the pillows and blankets Sean had already arranged on the floor. He lay down in the makeshift bed and lifted one corner in silent invitation. She crawled under the blanket without hesitation, pressing herself against his warm chest. His arms wrapped around her, and he planted a kiss on the top of her head, causing butterflies to erupt in her stomach, before resting his chin on her hair.

He fell asleep almost immediately, but Emery lay awake. She was exhausted, warm, comfortable...but guilt chased sleep away.

Sean had just laid himself bare to her, had confessed his deepest demon. He'd trusted her with a secret he'd told no one else, and something between them had shifted because of it. She could feel it. And yet, she still hid the biggest part of who she was from him. He still knew nothing about where she came from, about her life, about the real reasons Tavor had wanted her in the first place.

She felt like she knew all of him, but he knew nothing of her.

And it wasn't fair. She hated hiding herself from him. She wanted him to know her—all of her.

But she was scared to tell him. Not because she worried he'd judge her for any of it. She knew he wouldn't. But because telling Sean about Orabel could bring death upon them both. Growing up in Orabel, she'd always heard rumors that the Arch-Elemists could stop someone from speaking about Orabel even oceans away, that they could steal the breath from one's lungs so they physically couldn't speak the name. That they would kill them for even trying.

But Emery's mother had left, and surely, she'd told her father about Orabel. She'd brought him to the island the night they'd left Emery and her siblings with her grandparents, so he must have known. But after that, they'd never come back. And now Emery wondered if that been their choice? Or the Arch-Elemists'?

And who knew how many people Tavor had told about Orabel? Maybe the Arch-Elemists didn't care whether Orabel remained a secret anymore? Maybe she could tell Sean every-thing and it would be fine?

But the question remained, was she willing to risk his life to find out?

Chapter Twenty-Five

Liam sat curled on his bed, staring out the window. He hadn't left his room in days, and he was slowly going crazy with boredom once again. But this time, the boredom was better than the alternative.

After he'd tried to confess everything to Fia, after the Arch-Elemists had forced the air from his lungs to stop him, he'd woken up in the infirmary, with Fia and his grandparents standing over him worriedly. Aran had been there too, taking his vitals.

"He seems to have fainted," Aran had said, his fingers at Liam's pulse point on his wrist. "Perhaps he's still unwell from his adventures."

But even as Aran said it, his eyes narrowed on Liam's face, as if he didn't quite believe this, but also had no idea what else to think.

Fia had also looked suspicious, and worried of course, but she was wise enough to say nothing in front of everyone.

Liam hadn't seen Fia, or Aran, or anyone but his grandparents since then. He'd been whisked home, and told to remain in bed, which suited him fine. It was the perfect excuse to wallow in his misery alone, to not have to lie to anyone else and fear asphyxiating again because he'd said the wrong thing.

He looked down at the cup of water in his hands. He closed his eyes, and focused on his anxiety, his loneliness, the cold betrayal that stung in his heart. And then he channeled it into the water. When he opened his eyes, the water was frozen solid.

All elemist children could manipulate the elements in small ways, like freezing a cup of water, but it wasn't until they were older, and their abilities grew more powerful, that they began their lessons. Liam should have been at lessons with the other seventeen-year-olds whose abilities had surged, learning how to properly harness and control them. He'd waited his whole life for these lessons. But now he couldn't attend; it was one more thing the Arch-Elemists had taken from him. Not that he particularly wanted to be in a group of people right now, and it felt wrong to go to lessons without Emery... But still...

He glanced to where his lim leaned against his bedroom wall, hidden in the shadows of his room that seemed darker than usual. He hadn't bothered practicing that either. Didn't feel like there was a point with the threat of Tavor and his outsider weapons looming on the horizon. What would a stick really do?

A soft tapping at his door drew his attention. His grandmother stood there, pulling back the vines and holding a steaming bowl of soup.

"May I come in?" she asked.

Liam nodded.

She placed the bowl of soup on the wooden bedside table, which grew out of the wooden floor, and instead of leaving right away like usual, she perched on the edge of the bed, her long dark braid swinging over a shoulder.

"Thank you for the soup," Liam said, not meeting her gaze and hoping it was enough to signal that he'd rather be alone.

Besides bringing him food and water and peeking in on him from time to time, his grandparents had left him largely alone, because that's what he'd asked. But Grandmother didn't rise to leave this time.

"How are you feeling?" she asked.

"Tired," he mumbled.

Bored, scared, angry, useless, helpless.

Too many things.

Grandmother cleared her throat and glanced out the window, at the breeze shifting the redwood branches outside. "You're not feeling...faint?"

She said the word 'faint' as if she meant something different, but Liam wasn't sure what.

"No."

Grandmother crossed her legs, her leaf woven dress rustling, and tossed her braid back over her shoulder. "Liam, I need to ask you something."

Liam's body tensed. "Alright."

"Is Emery with Tavor?"

Liam wasn't sure what he'd been expecting, but it wasn't a direct question like that. His first instinct was to tell her the truth. But he remembered what it was like to suffocate on nothing. He didn't want to do it again.

"Yes," he lied.

"So, she's not currently with someone named Sean Denzel?" Grandmother asked, watching his face carefully.

Liam couldn't keep the shock from leaping onto his expression. "How do you know that?" he whispered, as if that could save him if the Arch-Elemists decided to silence him again.

Grandmother uncrossed and re-crossed her legs. "I need to tell you something, Liam. But it does not leave this room."

"Alright," Liam said again, not having a clue what she was about to say.

"I've been practicing wind watching. For years. I started after your mother left the first time..." Grandmother said.

"You did?"

"Yes. I wanted to try to find her. But it's a difficult skill. I've only caught glimpses of her a few times. And not for years." She frowned, her shoulders slumping a little. "I never told you children because I didn't want to get your hopes up."

"Why are you telling me this now?" Liam asked, reeling. Wind watching *was* a difficult skill. An elemist had to become one with the wind, to allow their souls to mingle enough that one could see what the wind saw, hear what it heard. As far as he knew, only the Arch-Elemists were powerful enough to do that, at least for long distances.

"Because after you children left with Tavor, I watched for a while," Grandmother said. "I saw the storm happen. I saw you three get separated. I saw you reunite again in Brimlad. But that's as far as I can see and hear. After that, you were too far away, and I lost track of you for a time. Until you showed up in Brimlad again and you left your sister behind."

"I didn't leave her behind!" Liam burst, needing his grandmother to know he never abandoned his twin.

She held up a hand. "I know. It was her choice to stay with Sean Denzel. But what I don't understand is what happened to Tavor? What happened when I couldn't see you? Why are you and Caelin lying to everyone?"

Liam's breaths turned shallow with panic. She knew so much. He could tell her everything. And yet, he couldn't risk it. What if they stole her breath next? He whispered, "Please don't ask me that."

Grandmother's expression shifted, as if something had been confirmed for her. "You didn't pass out in the cornfield, did you?"

Liam slowly shook his head, too afraid to say anything out loud.

Grandmother swallowed hard, as if clinging to calmness. She stood up, smoothed her dress. "Don't try to speak about it again. They may not take mercy on you a second time. I'll try to find…a solution."

Speechless, Liam stared after his grandmother as she headed for the door. Her hands shook by her sides, and she balled them into fists, furious but trying her best to hide it.

A thought struck Liam. "If you can see all the way to Brimlad…how far can the Arch-Elemists see?"

Grandmother lingered in the doorway. "Far. And they can do more than see..."

"So, Emery...?" Liam asked.

Grandmother swallowed again. "Emery needs to be careful what she says."

192

Chapter Twenty-Six

The fire dancer twirled his flaming baton between his legs, tossed it into the air, and caught it mid-cartwheel, all while his bare chest glistened in the flickering firelight.

As the crowd cheered, a woman dressed in what looked like snakeskin bent herself backwards until Emery was certain her spine would snap. The woman grasped her own ankles and then rolled onto her stomach before nimbly uncoiling back to her feet. The crowd whooped for her too.

"Liam would have loved this," Ayana said wistfully from their spot amongst the crowd.

Emery nodded, a sharp pain wedging behind her breastbone at the thought of her twin.

The parade winding down the street continued, the fire dancer and the contortionist disappearing only to be replaced by a group of dancers dressed as birds. The dancers flipped each other into the air to the beat of a steel drum.

The festivities had started at noon, though Grace had woken them up long before then. Ayana, however, had personally been the one to wake Emery. She'd nudged Emery's foot with her own, grinning down at where Emery still lay on the floor wrapped in Sean's arms. He'd slept as soundly as Emery had ever seen him, even sleeping past dawn for once. Her sleep, on the other hand, had been fretful.

Ayana's grin had said, *I told you so.*

Emery answered with a scowl that said, *shut up.*

Grace had whirled into the room then, fabrics, feathers, and flowers already in hand. "The festival starts in six hours, and we still have so much to do!" She paused beside Ayana, also peering down at Emery and Sean. She glanced at Ayana, as if unsure. When Aya wiggled her eyebrows suggestively, Grace looked back down at Emery and Sean and let out a long, "Awwww!" before slipping into the kitchen. "Up and at it! I'll make coffee."

"Does Grace have an off button?" Sean had mumbled into Emery's hair. His eyes were still closed, and she suspected he had faked still being asleep when Ayana had entered the room.

Emery laughed. "If she does, we've never found it."

But after that brief interaction, she hadn't seen much of Sean for the rest of the day. Grace had split the girls and boys up, helping each group with final touches on their costumes. Apparently, part of the All Gods Day's tradition was for couples to not know each other's costumes beforehand, so they could find each other in the crowd later. If someone was single, they were supposed to find someone whose costume matched them, if they wanted.

Emery had tried to point out that she and Sean were not a couple, but Ayana and Grace levelled her with flat stares. Luckily, Grace didn't have time to make further comment about Emery's sleeping arrangements the night before while she'd been fretting with Emery's costume. Once she was finished, she flitted off to help the boys and to dress in her own costume, leaving Emery to help Ayana with hers.

But Ayana hadn't needed Emery's help after all. Ayana stood amongst a lattice wall of flowers hanging on her bedroom wall, and in seconds, she willed the flowers to twine around her body. Lilacs and bluebells dripped from her hips, settling into the shape of a skirt. Pink carnations made up the bodice. Baby's breath and buttercups wound through her curls. A mask of vines and pink geraniums settled over her face, covering the entire top portion, save for her glittering eyes.

Emery had gaped, her heart thundering with surprise and hope. Partly because Ayana looked magnificent, but mostly because… "Aya, your abilities are back?"

"This didn't tip you off?" Ayana asked, indicating the dozens of plants growing in her bedroom, and indeed, the rest of their home.

"Well, I hoped they'd come back a little, but this…" Emery had never seen Ayana manipulate flowers to this degree, even before she was sick.

"I know," Ayana said, and in her glittering eyes, Emery saw something she hadn't seen in them for years: hope.

Even now, as Emery watched her older sister take in the festival while dressed as an old Aedion goddess, Emery noted the way she stood straighter, the way she moved easier, as if the weight of her illness was no longer pulling her down. She wasn't even using a cane.

"Aya," Emery said. Ayana turned away from the man dressed as a fox playing the flute to look at her. "I thought when I'd see you again, you'd be…" She trailed off, unable to voice what she'd been imagining, dreading. *Bedridden. Broken. Dead.* "But you seem better."

Ayana smiled, tilting her face to the stars. "I am better. At least, I feel better."

"How?" Emery asked. People rarely lived long once the Withering took hold of their bodies. And if they did, their abilities to manipulate the elements vanished.

"I don't know. I mean, there are medicines out here that help with the pain and exhaustion. But they aren't cures. And honestly, I thought all the travelling was going to be hard. But the longer I'm away from home, the better I feel. Maybe my body just needed a change."

Gods, Emery hoped it was that simple. She hoped she'd never again have to see her sister struggle to walk, to breathe.

"So," Ayana said, "are we going to talk about this morning or not?"

"What about it?"

Ayana raised a brow and Emery pretended to watch a drummer. She waited for the teasing, but her sister surprised her by asking, "Is he alright?"

Emery had nearly forgotten that the others had been there to watch Sean break. She didn't know how to answer the question. *Was* he alright? She wasn't sure. Regardless, his story wasn't hers to share. Especially since she was the only one who knew it. She felt sick all over again, thinking of the things Sean had told her last night. "It's hard for him to be here."

"Lily," Ayana said softly.

"Kess told you?"

"Yes, he's mentioned her a few times. He gets sad and we talk. I don't know the whole story. Just that Tavor was involved."

Fresh fury flashed inside Emery's chest. "He did it."

Ayana looked down for a moment, then reached for Emery's hand. Emery went still. Her sister was not a touchy person, not with anyone but Grace. "If he had killed you or Liam, I would have hunted him down and killed him myself. Perhaps I still might for what he did to you."

Emery figured it was all emotional talk. She was literally a walking and talking flower right now. But when Ayana looked up and her dark eyes flashed, Emery saw the truth there, and fear spilled into her belly.

"Don't," she choked. "It wouldn't be worth the risk."

Ayana squeezed her hand. "I was so scared I would never see you again."

Emery pulled her into a hug. "Me too."

"Let's never part again." Ayana sniffed, surprising Emery again. She couldn't remember the last time she saw her sister cry, not even when her illness was at its worst and she couldn't get out of bed for days, not even when her bones had grown so brittle she fell and snapped her wrist.

"Alright," Emery promised.

Ayana pulled away, wiping furiously at her cheeks. "Alright, enough of this. We're at a festival. We should be having fun!"

Emery didn't bother reminding her that fun was only their secondary goal of the evening. As if on cue, a trumpet player dressed like a storm cloud followed by a lutist robed as a golden sun blasted a melody at them as they marched past in the parade.

"So, again, are we not going to talk about this morning, Miss 'I'm not in love'?" Ayana asked.

Emery sighed. "I never said that." Aya's eyes lit with delighted surprised, but then she frowned when Emery asked, "Have you told Kess about...home?"

"No. He has no idea where we're from. Have you told Sean?"

Emery shook her head. "I feel like I should. But I also feel like I shouldn't."

"We haven't told Kess. Not because we don't trust him, but because it's not important that he knows. It's not worth the risk," Ayana said.

"What are you saying?"

"Is Sean knowing worth the risk? Do you trust him?"

"With my life." But did she trust him with the lives of her friends and family?

Ayana shrugged. "The worst person who could have possibly found us did. And he's still out there. At this point, I don't see how it could hurt to tell one more person. But..."

"But..." Emery agreed, sighing.

"The rumors might just be rumors. We have no proof they can hear us this far away, that they can reach us."

"But we have no proof that they can't. And I don't know if I can risk *that*." She'd already accidentally put Sean in danger countless times. She didn't want to do it again.

Ayana nodded pensively. Her mischievous smirk returned. "We could tell a random stranger. See what happens. If they don't immediately stop breathing, we're probably good to go."

Emery stared at her.

"I'm *kidding*." She winked. When Emery didn't look amused,

she added, "Alright, I get it. I don't have an answer, Em. Mother told Father, didn't she? She even brought him home and left again, breaking just about every rule we have. And the Arch-Elemists did nothing."

"That we know of," Emery said. "What if that's why they didn't come back?"

"Seems unlikely," Ayana said. "Why would they wait until after Father had been told, had kids, dumped said kids on the island, and then left again just to finally silence him?"

Emery flinched. She'd nearly forgotten how blunt Ayana could be.

"Gods, here we go again. Why are our conversations so dark? Let's have fun tonight." Ayana grabbed Emery's arm and dragged her deeper into the festivities. Emery did not resist.

They made their way to the city center, where they were supposed to meet up with the other half of their party near sunset. Along the way, they gasped at dancers, cheered on the musicians, devoured tamales and dumplings and doughnuts.

Every once and a while, Emery would catch their reflections in a window and she gaped, barely recognizing herself. Grace had created many magical outfits for them back home, but with an entire new world of fabrics and paints and whatever else at her fingertips, she'd truly outdone herself this time.

Emery's hair had been left wild and wavy, but she wore a crown dripping with seashells, tiny starfish, and pearls. Her bodice was tight, and truthfully, barely there. A white clamshell covered one breast, a large white starfish hid the other, and the white fabric between dipped so low it exposed her sternum all the way to her belly button. Strings of pearls adorned the back, keeping the whole thing on. Emery didn't know what fabric the skirt was made of, but it resembled pale blue scales. It was tight over her thighs before flaring out past her knees to resemble a fish tale.

Grace called her a siren goddess, and quite frankly, she felt like one.

Eventually, the streets all merged into a circle of cobblestones with a large, bubbling fountain at its center. A statue of a man reading a book, another holding a quill, and a third lifting a set of scales was set in the middle of the fountain, and the water poured from each instrument. The water was dyed bright blue, and each statue had beaded necklaces tossed around its neck.

Next to the fountain was a swatch of green grass, full to bursting with musicians and dancers. It was a blur of music and laughter and bright colours.

As the sun gilded the square in gold, a woman dressed as a white owl swooped for Ayana. Emery tensed. But the owl woman wrapped her arms around Ayana's middle and pecked a kiss on her cheek.

"I found you," Grace said.

"Who are you supposed to be?" Emery asked.

"*Who* indeed?" Grace chuckled at her own joke and Ayana lovingly rolled her eyes. "I'm the owl queen, of course."

She looked it, with her headdress of white and gold feathers, and her white mask with its gold beak. Her dress matched, also made up of white and gold feathers, and sprouting from her back was a pair of enormous wings. Emery had no idea how Grace had created them. They even flapped.

"I should have known," Ayana teased, plucking at one of Grace's feathers, which earned her a little swat from Grace. "Grace read about her in one of the libraries and now she's obsessed with her."

"She's the goddess of knowledge! She knows everything!" Grace explained. "Who wouldn't want to be her?"

As it turned out, Grace had learned to read quickly due to her perfect memory, and once she learned of the existence of books, she couldn't get enough. At first, she read all of Kess's medical textbooks. After that, she made her way through the various libraries throughout Audrye, absorbing knowledge about any and every subject she came across. Grace had always been in pursuit of knowledge back home, but of course, she'd also been limited. Out here, with Grace's beautiful mind, Emery couldn't imagine what she'd be able to do.

"Where are Sean and Kess?" Emery asked.

"*Who* knows?" Grace chuckled again. "You must find each other, remember? That's part of the fun. Come, my flower," she whispered to Ayana. "Dance with me."

And they were gone, melting into the sea of bodies, leaving Emery alone. But she wasn't alone for long.

As the music reached a crescendo, and then rolled into a new song, someone tapped her on her shoulder. "May I have this dance?"

Chapter Twenty-Seven

Emery's stomach fluttered at the voice, and when she turned, the fluttering turned into more of a frenzy. Sean grinned at her, bowing at the waist with his ankles crossed and his palm extended towards her. But she didn't take his hand right away. She was too busy staring.

His costume was strikingly similar to her own, which meant that he, too, was wearing very little. While he had a few seashells and starfish somehow adhered to his skin, he didn't seem to be wearing a shirt at all. Instead, faint shimmering silver and blue scales were painted all over his chest, torso and arms. They even crept up his neck and onto his jaw, which was cleanly shaven for once. His sleeve of tattoos was on full display. On his head perched a crown of shells and pearls, which was attached to a mask that hid only his eyes. His pants were tight, also adorned with shimmering silver and blue scales. They only flared slightly at the bottom, giving the impression of fins on the sides of each of his legs. The only thing truly recognizable about him, was the timepiece still hanging around his neck.

"You found me," she stammered, her mouth dry.

"Always."

"You look..." Words would not come to her. She'd seen him

shirtless before but this... The way the painted scales seemed to flow with the movement of his muscles, the way the fabric of his pants hugged the shape of his legs, the way the pearlescent sheen of the mask brought out the mischievous glint in his green eyes... He truly looked like some sort of ocean god.

Now she was beginning to understand why outsiders didn't undress in front of each other. It was rather...distracting.

"Dashing? Devastating? Devilishly handsome?"

She grinned mischievously herself. "I suppose you clean up well." She tilted her head and gave him a brazen once over. "Although I kind of miss the scruff."

His grin only deepened. "Lucky for you, I don't clean up often."

Emery tried to think up another witty retort, but her mind went utterly blank as Sean's eyes roamed along her own costume, lingering on all the places where her costume wasn't. The heat of his gaze lingered like a physical touch.

"You look..." But he, too, seemed lost for words now.

"Dashing? Devastating? Devilishly handsome?" she finished for him.

"Yes," he said and offered his hand again. She took it.

He pulled her into the crowd of dancers, one hand still gripping her fingers while the other splayed at the small of her back, his touch hot against her bare skin as he pulled her so close, their chests almost touched.

A moment of panic overtook her. "I don't know how to dance like this."

"Just follow my lead," Sean said.

"I thought you said you couldn't dance?" Emery questioned as he expertly twirled them in time with the beat of the drums and the trill of the flutes.

"I never said that."

Emery allowed him to guide her body to the rhythm, but honestly, it was hard to pay attention to her feet when she was distracted by the way his muscles constantly shifted under the paint. "When did you learn to dance?"

"Billy and Luana made sure to educate us as much as possible with whatever money they could spare. I'm learned in a great many random subjects and sometimes, like now, they even come in useful."

"Like what?"

He swept her into a spin and, when he caught her again, he held her so close their chests pressed together. His grin widened. "You'll have to wait and find out."

Emery couldn't stop her answering smile. The thought of a future where she *could* find out, where she could learn everything there was to know about him, filled her with a dizzying warmth. And the fact that he hadn't stopped smiling once so far had her heart soaring. She'd never seen him smile for so long and so bright. He even moved differently, lighter and more carefree, as if the weight of a thousand worlds had been lifted from his shoulders.

Even as she thought it, his smile faded just a little, his expression shifting into seriousness. "I'm going to tell them. Billy. And Kess. When this is over. I'm going to tell them both everything."

She squeezed his hand. "I'll be here if you need me."

Sean's eyes brightened and his expression flickered with the same disbelief as the night before when she'd said something similar, as if he truly couldn't believe his luck. As if he truly didn't understand why she didn't run away screaming from him after his confession.

"They won't blame you, Sean," she said. "Like me, they know you are not a monster. I wished you believed it too."

"Perhaps I simply need more kisses to convince me."

Without a moment of hesitation, as if her body had been waiting and primed, Emery surged onto her toes and brushed her lips against his. He released her hand to cup her jaw, deepening the kiss until she was completely lost in it. He tasted like lemons, as if he'd eaten one of those citrus candies not long ago. The music around them rose to a crescendo again, and without warning, he twirled her into a dip, and he planted a kiss on her throat, and then below her ear, the sensation of his lips on such sensitive skin turning her insides molten.

He whispered into her ear, "If you keep kissing me like that, I'm not going to be able to resist plucking every one of those shells off you, and we are in a very public place."

He pulled her back up, so they were chest to chest again, and Emery wasn't sure if the blood rushing to her head was from suddenly being upright again or from Sean's words. He'd never said something so brazen to her before, had never been so free and honest with his words. And she loved it.

She met his intense gaze. "I told you before, I don't care about public nudity..." The utter shock on his face made her cackle, but then the hunger that replaced it made her bite her lip, and she rose on her toes again, so she could whisper, "Alas, we have a job to do tonight. Trying to sneak into a forbidden university while utterly naked will probably get us caught."

Sean closed his eyes and took a visible breath. "I've never hated our society more."

An echoing bang split the sky, the sound so similar to cannon fire that Emery ducked before she even realized what she was doing. Sean chuckled and pointed skyward. "Look."

Colours exploded above them, creating shapes of flickering light that lit up the entire city. The colourful lights slowly fell towards the ground before fading altogether, only for more to shoot into the heavens, exploding with more colours.

Emery felt each boom in her chest, so loud, they almost masked the ooohs and aaahs of the crowd. "What is that?"

"The first round of fireworks," Sean said, watching her face instead of the sky. "It means it's almost time."

Almost, but not quite. They still had half an hour before they had to leave, and neither of them seemed inclined to cut their time short. Emery backed into Sean's chest, and he wrapped an arm around her collarbone, his other hand resting on her hip, and together, they watched the sky explode.

When the last of the fireworks faded into the night and the music picked back up, Sean turned Emery around for one last dance. This time, there was no space left between them. She wrapped her arms around his middle, pressed her cheek to his bare chest. His chin rested on the top of her head. They swayed slowly to the music, completely off tempo from the upbeat melody, but neither of them seemed to care.

"Lily used to love fireworks," Sean murmured. "She liked the loud chaos of it all."

"What was she like?" Emery asked.

His chest expanded under her cheek as he took a deep breath and then let it all out. "Hot headed. Quick to anger. Loved fiercely. Protective. She had this dry sense of humour." He laughed quietly, as if amused by a memory. "She used to love pulling pranks with Kess and I when we were kids. And she knew the exact puppy eye expression to use to get herself out of trouble."

Emery smiled to herself. "You used to pull pranks?"

"Aye. We were little hooligans."

"That's Liam's favourite pastime too. I wish the two of you had more time to get to know each other."

"Maybe we still can one day," he said, his voice full of optimism.

"I hope so," Emery said, but her heart deflated a little bit. Would it be possible? If Liam made it home, what were the chances he'd ever leave again? And it's not like Emery could just take Sean home with her...could she? Gods, he still didn't even know Orabel existed.

"Em," Sean began, and then hesitated. His heartbeat under her cheek quickened, as if he was nervous. "If you find a cure tonight, will you go home?"

Honestly, she hadn't thought that far ahead but she assumed Grace and Ayana would probably be the ones to bring the cure home.

"No. I can't go home until I find out what happened to my parents."

Sean's arms relaxed around her by just a fraction. "And after that? When you have your answers, will you go home?"

This time, she didn't know what to say. Did she want to go home? She missed her grandparents terribly. And Liam, Caelin, and Fia, of course. But the thought of going home did not fill her with joy. It filled her with a peculiar dread instead. She'd barely gotten to know Sean's crew, but the thought of leaving them behind...the thought of leaving *him* behind...

"I don't know," she answered honestly.

"You can stay with me—us," Sean said. "You can stay aboard the *Audacity* for as long as you want."

You can stay with me. She did not miss this slip of the tongue. He wanted her to stay with *him*.

She pulled away far enough that she could look up into his face. They stopped dancing and stood perfectly still in a sea of swaying bodies, watching each other. Sean's face was so open, so full of hope, and all at once, guilt flooded her system.

Something had undeniably changed for him after he'd confessed his darkest secret to her. He wasn't holding anything back anymore. And yet, he still knew nothing about her. He still didn't know where she came from, and that was a huge part of who she was. It wasn't fair to him that she was hiding so much of herself. She couldn't do it anymore.

Ayana was probably right. Tavor knew about Orabel. The king did too. So why should the Arch-Elemists care if another random boy also learned about their home?

She took a deep breath. "Sean, I need to tell you something."

Sean's hopefulness seemed to shutter a little, as if he was preparing himself for some sort of blow.

She opened her mouth to speak, but one of the dancers bumped her, sending her flying into Sean. He caught her, saving her from hitting the ground, but her ankle twisted painfully in the process.

"Are you alright?"

"I can walk but I think I need to sit down for a moment," Emery said, testing her weight on her foot and wincing as pain flashed through her ankle.

Sean helped her to the edge of the fountain where she took a seat. "Don't move. I'll fetch you a drink and some ice."

He disappeared into the crowd and Emery massaged her ankle, thanking the gods that the pain was already starting to wane. The last thing they needed that night was for her to not be able to walk. They only had a few more minutes until they had to head to the university.

While she was looking down at her ankle, someone tapped her on the shoulder. "May I have this dance?"

Before she could refuse or even look up, the person grabbed her hand and roughly hauled her back to the grass. Her ankle throbbed and she bit back a curse. She looked up into pine green eyes and for a perplexing moment, she thought Sean had come back. But then she took in the rest of the man. He was dressed like a viper, in a tuxedo of black scales. Half his face was covered by a vertical mask, also of scales, but the other half was bare.

It was a face that had haunted her nightmares for months.

The world tilted beneath her as his name rasped from her mouth. "Tavor."

Chapter Twenty-Eight

A frigid shock coursed through Emery's body, freezing her bones in place, turning her thoughts into slush.

The ground beneath her seemed to vanish, as if she was falling, falling into a nightmare. But in her nightmares, Tavor was always on fire. This Tavor, the one gripping her hand and waist too hard, the one sweeping her around the dancefloor despite her locked limbs, was perfectly fine, even bordering on handsome in his viper costume.

Finally, Emery's instincts kicked in and she tried to yank her hand from Tavor's grasp, but he held fast, his grip so tight, her bones ached. The fingers that gripped her bare waist dug into her flesh and they felt like thorns, his venom seeping under her skin.

"Having a lovely evening?" he asked. Despite his familiar accent, his voice sounded different. Rougher. Raspier.

Sour fear lodged in her throat, coated her tongue, making it impossible to form words. Her lim hung heavy against her spine, disguised as the trident the sea goddess she was dressed as used as a weapon. But she didn't reach for it. She couldn't attack him in the middle of this crowd. Dozens of varens would swarm in seconds and she'd never escape.

But would he attack first?

Her eyes darted amongst the dancers, searching desperately for Sean, if only to warn him to stay away. Her stomach twisted more and more with every moment she couldn't find him.

"Oh, he's fine," Tavor drawled. "For now."

He spun Emery so she faced the opposite direction, and through the crowd, she finally spotted him. He was *smiling*. And laughing at something one of the food vendors said as he reached for two glasses of some sort of pink drink, completely oblivious to Emery's predicament.

Run! Emery silently urged, begged, screamed, as if he could possibly hear her increasingly frantic thoughts from across the crowd.

"I hate that smile and I hate that laugh," Tavor said nonchalantly, as if commenting on a dish he didn't care for.

He spun them around again and Emery's pulse stuttered as she lost track of Sean again. She glared at Tavor with as much hatred as she could muster, summoning as much rage as she could to overshadow her fear. This was the man who had taken everything from Sean, and who had tried to take everything from her too.

She continued to glare and asked something she'd wondered for so long: "Why do you hate him so much?"

Tavor's green eyes flashed behind his mask. "That's like asking why the snake dislikes the mouse."

Emery had no idea what that meant.

"But I guess I should thank you for putting that smile back on his face," Tavor said.

Emery knew she probably shouldn't take the bait, but she asked, "Why?"

"I'll very much enjoy ripping it from his face again."

Fear and rage burned in Emery's stomach like acid, and it took everything in her not to strike him, not to grab a dagger and stab him through the eye.

"But all in due time. He's not the blonde you should be

worrying about tonight," Tavor said. "You should be more concerned about the blonde who isn't where she should be."

Emery's heart plummeted to her feet.

Grace.

"What do you want?" Emery growled through her teeth.

Tavor shrugged, casting her one of his awful, beautiful smiles. "Just to say hi."

He pulled Emery in close, and then shoved her away in a spin that sent her reeling. By the time Emery regained her balance and bearings, he was gone. Like he'd never been there at all.

Chapter Twenty-Nine

The cool drinks felt good in Sean's hands, his skin hot from the humid air and the lovely dancing and the constant proximity to Emery all evening. Just thinking of the way they danced, the way she'd kissed him, even the way she'd leaned against him as they'd watched the fireworks together, heated his blood and coaxed a smile onto his face.

Honestly, his face was starting to hurt from all the smiling he'd done already that night. He'd probably smiled more in these precious few hours then he had the whole previous year.

He dodged a man on stilts as he carried the drinks back to where he left Emery near the fountain, his steps light, his heart lighter. But she wasn't there. He scanned the crowd near the fountain, the anxiety that had been mercifully quiet for once that evening beginning to rear its head.

A breath of relief flowed out of him when he finally spotted her, back in the middle of the dancing crowd, as if she hadn't been able to resist getting up and dancing again, despite her sore ankle.

Joy shot through him like lightening as she fought her way through the crowd towards him, the way it had every time he'd seen her face that evening, the way it had every time he remembered he'd spilled his darkest secret to her, and she didn't hate him for it.

He still couldn't believe it.

But then he registered her blanched complexion and the distress in her expression. Alarm bells pealed in his head. She looked close to tears. She looked like she'd seen a ghost.

He met her halfway. "What happened?"

She immediately folded into his chest, peering over her shoulder before looking up at him with too bright eyes. "We have to go. Now."

"What happened?" he repeated.

She took a deep breath. "He's here."

Sean felt every drop of blood drain from his face, as if the magic of the night was bleeding away too. The shattering of glass told him he dropped their drinks. He didn't care.

He wrapped his arms around her, holding her tight and scrutinizing every person in their immediate vicinity. Which was a lot of people. "Where?"

"I don't know where he went."

"Where was he?"

"Right here. He made me dance with him."

"*What?*" A rush of dizzying horror washed over him, followed closely by rage. Rage at himself for foolishly letting his guard down, rage at Tavor for daring to lay hands on Emery again while Sean still lived. He held Emery slightly away from him so he could examine her. "Did he hurt you?"

"No." She shook her head vehemently, as if trying to convince herself too. "But we must find the others. I think he knows what we're planning to do tonight."

Sean listened to her while also scanning the multitude of people surrounding them, all of them dancing and singing and laughing, and none of them glancing at the pair of them.

Nobody seemed out of place. But Tabor was out there, somewhere. Waiting. Just like last time.

Panic sliced through him like a knife.

"Keep calm," he said as much to himself as to her. "We shouldn't bring attention to ourselves, even if he's here."

But even as he said it, he couldn't force his body to move, couldn't decide which direction to go, what to do next. Last time, none of it mattered. Last time—

"Sean." He blinked and realized Emery was holding his face. He was breathing hard, fast. Panicked. "Breathe."

He tried, but it was so difficult. Taking charge, Emery gripped his hand and pulled him away from the fountain and the music and the dancers, away from the city center and the festivities. They moved as fast as they could without running, blending in with the other strolling revelers as just another young couple searching for a quiet, private spot.

It took everything Sean had not to grab Emery and flee for the harbor. Not that that would have done any good. His ship was no longer there, but rather, waiting for them at a neighboring island.

"I think he has varens waiting for us at the university," Emery whispered. "We have to catch Grace before it's too late."

The plan had been simple. Sean, Emery, and Grace were supposed to meet up at a rendezvous point, and then sneak into the university together. But if any of them got hung up and didn't make it to the point, the others were to go in anyway. This meant if Sean and Emery were late, or didn't show up at all, Grace would still go inside without them.

They had to hurry.

Just as they'd hoped, the streets were still full of festivities, even at such a late hour; it wasn't difficult for them to reach the designated street without raising suspicions. But they hadn't quite reached the rendezvous point when booms echoed against the stone buildings and lights exploded in the sky again. This was just one of many rounds of fireworks set to go off throughout the evening, but these fireworks were distinct. Somehow, the explosions of light formed the shapes of blossoms. Sean had no idea how Grace made that happen, and at any other time, he might have marveled at the beauty and wonder.

Relief and fear clashed in his chest instead. Relief because Ayana was supposed to set the fireworks off, which meant she was likely still safe for now, at least. Fear, because—

"It's almost time!" Emery cried over the echoing booms.

This round of fireworks was meant to be the signal to be in position. The next round was meant to be a distraction to help them get into the university.

Sean and Emery raced as inconspicuously as possible to the rendezvous point, which was an abandoned building of dormitories across the street from the ruins of the Elemental University. They slipped into the building and Emery bolted up the stairs.

"Wait!" Sean hissed, trying to grab her arm but missing. He rushed after her, his blade drawn, ready for a trap. But when he reached the dormitory, it was to find Emery alone.

"She's not here," Emery said tearfully. She moved to a grimy window, wiped a patch clean, and peered through.

"Could she have gone ahead of schedule?" Sean asked, circling the room to make sure no one was hiding in the shadows.

"She would have stuck to the plan," Emery said.

Which meant something had to have gone wrong.

When Sean finished assessing the room, he stopped next to Emery and followed her gaze.

Another small wave of relief washed over him, momentarily dulling his ever-rising panic.

Across the street, Kess, wearing a wolf mask, stood with two young uniformed varens. The three of them watched the waning fireworks. As the last few flares flicked out, leaving nothing but smoke behind, Kess turned, grinning. He slapped one varen on the back, tipped his head to the other, and then walked away, hands casually in his pockets.

The next round of fireworks exploded in the sky.

Sean and Emery rushed back outside, catching Kess just as he turned down a back alley.

His eyes widened at the sight of them. "What are you—?"

"Where's Grace?" Emery burst.

"Heading inside, I'm guessing," Kess said, frowning. "Where the two of you are also supposed to be."

Emery turned her horrified gaze on Sean, and he tried to swallow down his panic. "Tavor is here. You said he wasn't here."

He hadn't meant to say that last part out loud.

"I said I didn't *think* he was here. No varen I spoke to knows where he's been," Kess said.

"But how trustworthy are your new *friends*?" He hadn't meant for the word to come out with so much vitriol either. But panic had a hold of his tongue now. "How much do you tell them, Kess?"

Kess looked both horrified and angry at the accusation. "Nothing! I don't tell them anything!"

"How did Tavor know we were here?" Sean demanded. "How did he know what we planned tonight?"

"Truly, I-I don't know!" Kess stammered.

"Stop!" Emery interrupted. "We don't have time for this. We need to get to Grace now."

Kess swore. "What do we do?"

Sean already knew what Emery wanted to do, what she was going to do, because there would be no dissuading her. And even though every cell in his body screamed at him to run, he'd be damned if he let her go alone.

"Go find Ayana and hide," he told Kess. "We're going in after Grace."

Emery stared at him with shock, then with an appreciation and adoration so fierce, it nearly made him change his mind.

"But what if it's a trap?" Kess asked.

"It's definitely a trap," Sean said.

"It doesn't matter," Emery said. "I'm not leaving Grace in Tavor's hands. Sean, you should go with Kess."

"No," he said simply.

"Sean—"

"*No.*" His voice was steel, brokering no room for argument.

"Wait," Kess interrupted. "How are you going to get inside now? I'll have to distract the varens again."

Emery grabbed Kess's hand. "You have to find Ayana!"

Kess brought her hand to his chest. "I promise I will. Right after I help you go after Grace."

Emery bit her lip, clearly trying to force down her panic, and nodded too many times.

As Kess slipped back onto the street, Emery wrapped her arms around herself. The sight of her blatant fear seemed to somehow help settle his own. She'd been strong for him when he'd shattered the night before. It was his turn to be strong for her.

"Em." When she kept staring after Kess as if she didn't hear him, he gently tilted her chin to look at him. Her ocean eyes were glassy and huge. "Kess will find Ayana and we'll find Grace, and everything will be alright."

He hoped she didn't hear the uncertainty in his voice, sense the fear coating his tongue. Because he learned long ago that when Tavor was around, nothing would be alright.

She walked into his chest, and he wrapped his arms around her, and they stood as they had while dancing less than an hour ago. It already felt like another lifetime.

They watched Kess stroll casually down the street towards the two varens still standing guard in front of the university. Somehow, he'd procured food, and as he reached the varens, they looked delighted. But Sean and Emery didn't wait around to see the rest of the interaction. They slipped back outside and, sticking to the shadows, crept to the crumbling brick wall encircling the university's expansive grounds. Even dressed as ocean gods, nobody noticed as they scaled the wall and dropped to the other side.

The grounds were quiet, save for the distant music and laughter from the festival. It was hard to believe they'd just been enjoying themselves like that too. Weeds, brambles. and overgrown trees choked the grounds, making their movements slow as they picked their way through.

Sean's fingers hovered over the pommel of his sword the entire time, and though Emery didn't reach for her lim, he knew she was ready. The grounds remained empty of people though, and soon enough, they reached the university itself without issues.

The sprawling building slumped towards the ground amongst more brambles and weeds, silent and still, like a slumbering beast. Sean scanned the arched doorway, which had fallen off its hinges, and the arched windows, many of which were broken. The university appeared empty, like no one had been stupid enough to venture here in years.

Emery glanced at Sean, and then tilted her head towards a broken window. He nodded. They might be walking into a trap, but they weren't about to make it easy for Tavor by strolling through the front door. After knocking the last shards of glass loose with a stick, Sean boosted Emery through the window and climbed in after her.

They stood in semi-darkness, the slivers of moonlight slipping through the windows and the holes in the roof the only source of light they had. Sean's heart hammered in his ears, the only sound he could hear in the otherwise silent hallways. The noises of the festival had faded away, as if it had been a dream.

"Do we go to the library?" Emery's voice was barely a whisper and yet it seemed to shatter the silence.

Sean dearly wished he could say no. Wished he could force her to leave, to run, to hide. Instead, he said, "That's where he'll be waiting. He won't ambush us right away. He'll want to take his time and make us squirm."

"Sean," Emery murmured, taking his hand. "You don't have to do this again."

"I'm not leaving you or Grace behind," Sean said.

"But—"

He leaned his forehead against hers. "Would you prefer I kiss you or stab you?"

A choked laugh escaped her. She'd given him that ultimatum once. "You'd never stab me."

"True." He brushed his lips against hers, praying to every god possible that he'd get the chance to do that again.

He drew his blade and Emery unsheathed her lim. Hands clasped, they ventured into the darkness. The buckled wooden floor creaked under their feet, making him wince. Most of the walls were cracked and many were collapsed, leaving rubble they had to carefully climb over. Vines crawled across the floor and clung to the walls.

Grace had memorized a blueprint of the university she'd found in one of the other university's libraries and had drawn them a map. Knowing they wouldn't have much light to see with until they were in the library, they'd taken their time to memorize the map too. But between the darkness and the fact that half the walls were missing, it was hard to tell where they were.

What's more, every shadow, every piece of broken furniture that loomed from the murky darkness, caused Sean's pulse to skitter.

A scream pierced the silence, startling them both. When the scream ended, it still reverberated throughout the university, echoing in his very skull.

"Grace," Emery gasped.

Without discussion, they abandoned all attempts at stealth. They sprinted and scrambled for the heart of the building, for the library, for Grace.

Chapter Thirty

Screams echoed in Sean's head, but they weren't Grace's. It was Lily's shrieks, as Tavor pressed the hot brand to her face, searing her flesh, as he pushed the barrel of the gun into her eye so hard it bled, right before—

Emery skidded to a halt, and he nearly crashed into her. Before them, the library's double oak doors stood open, one of them splintered down the middle and dangling by one stubborn hinge. Flickering orange light spilled from the room and into the hallway. Sean and Emery stood on the precipice of the shadows, just out of reach of the light.

It took a moment for Sean's eyes to adjust, but when they did, his heart sank. In the very center of the library, surrounded by boughed bookshelves and the corpses of brittle, yellowed tomes, crouched Grace. She was folded in on herself, her golden hair blocking her face, making it impossible to tell whether or where she was injured, making her look...just like Lily.

Sean's vision tunneled and bile crawled up his throat.

Behind Lily—Grace—in a chair backlit by a crackling fire of burning books in an otherwise decrepit hearth, sat Tavor. "It's about time you showed up."

That voice. The voice he hated above everything else. The

voice that taunted and tormented and tortured him in his night-mares. The voice of the man he had once tried to kill with his bare hands.

Instead of that voice filling him with fear, with dread, it filled him with fury. His tunneled vision turned so red he could barely see, so red he almost didn't notice Emery stepping into the library, into the flickering light.

Sean gripped his blade so hard, his hand ached as he followed right behind her.

Grace looked up as they approached, her golden hair falling away to reveal her tear-stained face. Not *Lily's* face. She cradled her hand, a blistering F forming in the center of her palm. A brand. The same one that marred his own palm, and Emery's, and each member of his crew.

His fury flared higher.

Tavor stood from his chair, and Sean's gaze narrowed to the branding iron he held, the F at the end still glowing faintly.

"Honestly, I wondered if you wouldn't come. If you were finally done playing the predictable idiot hero." Tavor spun the iron idly in his fingers, so the glowing F left an orange streak in the air. "I've been in Audrye for months, and imagine my delight to hear you both had been spotted here too. I figured you'd seek out this library. You creatures are nothing but predictable."

Sean fought to keep his rage in check, clenching his jaw so hard, it was a wonder his teeth didn't crack.

Emery took one step towards Grace, her own teeth bared. "What do you want?"

"You, obviously."

"Let her go," Emery demanded.

Still half-masked in shadows, Tavor shrugged. "Sure." He nudged Grace with his boot, but she didn't move. It was then Sean noticed the needle glinting on the floor beside her. She'd been partially paralyzed, unable to stand. "She's of no interest to me tonight. And I must confess, I found her to be another disappointing Orabelian. It seems the rumors of your strength are indeed incorrect."

Through his nearly blinding rage, Sean almost missed the nugget of information Tavor just dropped like a bomb. Nearly missed the way Emery sucked in a breath and glanced at him, eyes wide.

Orabelian. Was Tavor insinuating that Emery and her sisters were from...Orabel? But that was impossible. Orabel didn't exist...did it?

Sean wasn't able to mask his confusion fast enough, because Tavor said, "Ah, she didn't tell you? Not a surprise. You are deceitful creatures, are you not?"

"If you have the information you wanted from us, then what do you want?" Emery asked, her attention back on Tavor.

"Payback." Tavor stepped out of the shadows, finally letting the firelight wash over his face.

Emery gasped. Sean just stared.

On his cheek, below his right eye, just barely visible beneath other scarring, was an F. The one Sean had put there months ago. He didn't know where the other scarring came from—from Emery's attack on the ship, or an attempt to cover up the F perhaps?

He couldn't help it. He allowed a sadistic grin to twist his lips, one he usually faked when he was pretending to be The Scourge of the Sea. There was no pretending this time. "You deserve worse," he said.

Tavor's grip on the iron brand turned white knuckled, the only sign of his anger. Calmly, he said, "Do I? Did Lily?"

This time the fury flaring inside him was so great, Sean barely stopped himself from launching at Tavor, from reaching for his throat and squeezing the life out of him like he'd tried to do twice before. He'd failed both times. But maybe he wouldn't fail this time. The only thing holding his rage back was the fear of what might happen to Emery if he let it lose and left her side.

"Let Grace go," Emery demanded once again.

"I told you; you can have her." Tavor nudged her again. Grace didn't move. "But if you want her, you'll have to take her place."

Emery immediately stepped forward, but Sean grabbed her arm, fear momentarily frosting his fury. "Emery, no."

"I won't let Grace get any more hurt because of me," Emery urged, looking up at him with wide blue eyes.

But Sean couldn't do this again. He couldn't watch Tavor torture or kill someone else he cared about. "I can't let you do this."

"Awe, how cute that you two vermin found each other," Tavor mocked. "But I suppose even rats have to mate."

Emery tried to tug from Sean's grasp, but he held fast.

"Sean—"

"Please don't ask me to do this," he begged. He'd get down on his knees if he had to.

"Here, I'll make it easier for you." Tavor waved a hand and at least half a dozen varens emerged from the dark corners of the decrepit library. Tavor pointed a finger gun at Emery and when he pulled the imaginary trigger, the varens converged on them.

Emery stopped resisting Sean and instead stepped closer, raising her lim. Sean stepped partially in front of her, blade at the ready, trying to stamp down his rising panic.

Not again not again not again.

But just as the first varen reached Emery, a series of soft clicks and whistles sounded in the darkness. Darts whizzed out of nowhere, hitting three of the varens. Within moments, they were sagging to the ground, the curare paralyzing them quickly. Vines slithered across the library's rotted carpet, snagging the ankles of the three remaining varens, ripping them off their feet. The varens screamed as the vines pulled them against the water-stained walls and kept them fastened there.

Kess and Ayana strolled through the library doors, Kess with a dart gun in his hand, and Ayana with her arms raised, eyes focused on the vines ensnaring the varens. She truly looked like an ancient avenging goddess in her costume.

Sean had never been more relieved and horrified to see Kess. And judging by the look on Emery's face, she felt the same about seeing her sister.

"I told you to find her and run," she cried.

Kess sent her a sidelong, exasperated look. "Have you ever tried making your sister do anything? I'm only one man."

Ayana tore her gaze from the varens and froze when she beheld Grace. Sean followed her gaze and his stomach plummeted to the floor.

Tavor still stood calmly in the centre of the library, only now, he gripped a handful of Grace's hair, and held the barrel of his pistol to Grace's eye. Tavor cleared his throat. "Well, this is awkward."

"Let her go," Ayana snarled.

Tavor sighed, as if tired of explaining the same thing over and over to a group of toddlers. "How many times do I have to say it? You can have this one." He nodded at Grace and then jutted his chin towards Emery. "I want that one."

Sean instinctively grabbed for Emery again. So did Ayana. With her other hand, Ayana gestured to Tavor's face. "Was that your handiwork, dear sister?"

"I had help," Emery said.

"Very nice," Ayana said. "I think I'd like to have a go at the other side."

Out of the corner of his eye, Sean noticed Ayana slowly moving to place something in Emery's hand. Emery quickly palmed the item, keeping it hidden behind her back. Sean snapped his gaze back to Tavor as to not give her away.

Tavor appeared bored, but again, his knuckles where white from gripping the pistol so hard. Ayana's comment had hit its mark. His voice was calm as he said, "Emery takes this one's place. Or I smear her brain across the floor."

Sean's rage flagged, cold horror instead grasping him tighter and tighter with clammy, clawed hands. He couldn't feel his fingers gripping his blade, couldn't feel his fingers gripping Emery's arm. Flashes of the same conversation in a different room seared his mind like lightning. He smelled Lily's blood. Tasted it.

Not again not again not again.

When an excruciatingly long moment passed, and Emery didn't step forward, Tavor said, "I'm not bluffing. I don't bluff. Ask him." He pointed his pistol at Sean before placing it back against Grace's face. "Ask him how he let Lily die. Ask him how he listened to his own little sister beg for mercy and did nothing about it. Ask him how his sister's skull flew apart when the bullet ripped through her head."

Sean's vision went red again. But not with rage. This time, it was with the memory of his sister's blood misting across the room, across his face. He felt like Tavor had just reached inside his stomach and pulled out his guts, leaving him aching and hollow and exposed.

Somebody snarled with fury, and at first, he thought it had been himself. But he realized his one hand now only gripped air, that people were shouting Emery's name.

He blinked away the red mist to see Emery lunging across the room for Tavor.

But she never made it.

Fireworks boomed in the distance, and Sean belatedly realized it wasn't fireworks at all. It was cannon fire. A sound he'd always recognize.

The cannons crashed through the university, taking out walls and shelves and support beams. And then the library crashed down around them.

Chapter Thirty-One

Sean threw himself to the ground, shielding Ayana's body with his own and covering his head with his arms as debris rained down upon them. Another volley of cannons crashed into the university, blasting apart wood and rock and brick.

Splinters of wood and shards of stone ripped into his bare back, but luckily, nothing bigger hit him. As the world went quiet and the last of the debris fell, Sean carefully lifted his head. Plumes of dust swirled in the moonlight now filtering in through a newly collapsed portion of the ceiling. The fire had been snuffed out, leaving no other light.

"Teralyn's Teeth, what just happened?" Ayana cried, shoving at Sean to get him off her.

Dazed, Sean obliged, rising to his knees and wincing as pain rippled through his back. "I don't know."

Was this his crew coming to their rescue? They weren't usually so careless and reckless but perhaps panic had spurred them on. He peered through the gloom, fear lancing through him as he realized he couldn't see Emery. He couldn't see Kess or Grace or Tavor either.

"Where are they?" Ayana asked.

"I don't know," Sean repeated, his mind moving like mud. His body was numb and he wasn't sure if it was from the leftover rage, the new fear overtaking him, or if something had struck him on the head after all.

Ayana sucked in a pained breath, drawing his attention back to her.

"Are you alright?"

"No," she snapped, her voice filled not with pain but anger. "My leg is trapped."

Sean blinked into the dusty darkness, realizing that one of the heavy beams had fallen on Ayana's leg, despite his best efforts to protect her. Finally, his body allowed him to move. He heaved on the beam, over and over, while Ayana sucked in painful breaths. But the beam wouldn't budge.

Sean swore. "I need Kess."

He needed him to help move the beam. But mostly, he needed him to be alive, to be alright.

"Find him," Ayana demanded. "Find Emery and Grace."

Sean rose on shaking legs, thankful he was not the one giving orders for once. He swiped sweat and blood and dust out of his eyes. Why was his head bleeding?

"Sean," Ayana said, and Sean turned back. "If you find Tavor, kill him."

He nodded. But his fury was dead. The intense need to destroy Tavor had collapsed inside him as the university collapsed around him. All he wanted was to find the others and get out of there.

"Emery," he called, stumbling through the debris and choking on the dust. "Kess?"

He stopped, straining his ears. No one replied, although he may have heard distant voices. It was hard to tell over the ringing in his ears. He continued his search, and nearly tripped over Kess. His friend was half buried in rubble, covered in dust, silent and still.

"Kess!" Sean flung bits of stone and brick out of his way, digging his friend out of the rubble. He pulled him onto his lap, lightly slapping his face. "Wake up, Kess!"

He did not wake up.

No no no no.

With trembling fingers, he checked Kess's pulse and held his breath. Two of the longest seconds of his life ticked by, and then he felt it—the faintest flutter against his fingers.

The breath whooshed out of him. "Thank the gods."

Carefully, Sean heaved Kess over his shoulders and made his way back to Ayana.

"Oh my gods," Ayana gasped. "Is he—"

"He's alive," Sean panted, laying Kess next to Ayana. "Try to wake him up. I'll keep looking."

Sean made his way back to where he found Kess, only to find a gaping hole in the floor where he was certain Tavor and Grace had been standing. He peered into the hole but saw only darkness.

"Sean!" Ayana shouted, and he spun around.

Figures loomed in the darkness, barely visible in the dusty moonlight. They climbed through the gaping holes in the walls. For a moment, Sean's heart leapt, thinking his crew *had* come after all. But as the figures neared, his heart plummeted again. He didn't recognize any of their silhouettes. They were Tavor's men, not his.

He moved so he stood over Ayana and Kess. He reached for his sword but realized it wasn't there. He'd lost it during the collapse. He clenched his fists, ready for a fight anyway.

As the figures stepped through a ray of moonlight, confusion washed over him.

They certainly weren't his crew. But they weren't varens either.

"Excellent! We didn't kill them," the woman said, her angular eyes gleaming.

"You're lucky," a man said, fingering his dark beard. "Captain would have had your head."

Sean blinked once. Twice. Unable to place these familiar people. But they *were* familiar.

"Who in Pyralis's Fire are you?" Ayana spat, her voice surprisingly proud and mighty considering she was still trapped under a beam.

"Do you not remember us?" the woman asked, feigning offence.

Sean did remember. He just couldn't understand. He whispered, "The grave robbers?"

"The what?" Ayana asked.

But the woman—Torra, he thought her name was—clapped. "There he goes. A little slow, though, isn't he?"

She nudged the bearded man, who simply grunted. He wore a leather coat and had coal-rimmed eyes. Ace, Sean thought his name was. A third man emerged from the gloom, the huge one who lacked a tongue and had held his sword to Emery's back.

"What are you doing here?" Sean blurted.

"Retrieving what belongs to our captain," Ace said. "To get what you *stole* from our captain."

Now Sean was more confused than ever. Had he pirated from them before? It was certainly possible. Perhaps it was time to don the mask of the Scourge. Shoving his confusion and fear down, he forced his face passive, crossing his arms over his chest. "You'll have to excuse me. I can't remember the faces of everyone I've robbed."

Torra glared. "Give us the chest."

"What chest?" Ayana waved her hands, staring into the darkness with exaggeratedly large eyes. "We don't have a chest. Do you see a chest?"

Sean almost laughed. Ayana didn't seem to have a fearful bone in her body. She and Emery had bravery in their blood.

"Fine. Give us what was *inside* the chest."

Ayana dropped her hands and scowled. "What are you *talking* about?"

But Sean had made the connection. There couldn't have been *two* chests buried in that cemetery.

He kept his voice almost bored. "It was full of rocks. You're welcome to them. They're still in the cemetery."

"Liar!" Torra hissed. "Give us the contents of that chest, and we *might* let you live."

Sean tensed. "I think you might be the daft one." He slowed his words, as if speaking to a child. "There was nothing in the chest but rocks. We don't have anything."

"You're hiding it," she said.

Sean raised an annoyed brow and spread his arms, revealing the fact that he was still practically half-naked in ridiculous costume. What little clothing he did wear was certainly too tight to hide much. "Where would I hide anything?"

Instead of looking angry, Torra grinned and allowed her eyes to roam over his body. "Where, indeed?"

Ace rolled his eyes. "We don't have time for this. Grab them, Jaro. The captain can question them."

He flicked his hand and the big man stepped closer, wielding a cutlass and a pistol.

Ayana shoved in vain at the beam still pinning her in place. "We're not going anywhere with you. We're a little busy."

Sean's pulse raced. He didn't have any weapons, save for his body and the elements, if they cared to listen to him right then. He was outnumbered. He still didn't quite understand what was going on. And he refused to leave the university without Emery.

He swiped a metal rod from the ground, realizing belatedly that it was the branding iron Tavor had used on Grace. He called the wind, but they were so deep in the university that, despite the various holes in the building, he could barely sense it.

Jaro lunged.

Sean managed to shove him with a blast of hard air and blocked the swing of his sword with the iron rod. He kicked him right in the balls, not above fighting dirty just then. Jaro went down with a strangled cry.

"Again with the kick to the balls?" Ace sighed, drew his own cutlass, and rushed at Sean. Vines climbed up his legs, tripping him. He shouted, hacking at the vines with his blade, but they tangled around his body, and he vanished under their writhing mass.

Jaro lumbered to his feet, glaring at Sean. Sean raised the iron rod in defense, but something coiled around his wrist. At first, he thought one of the vines Ayana was manipulating had gone rogue, until he glanced back and realized it was Torra's whip wrapped around his arm.

"Enough of this," Torra's said, holding the whip with one hand and her pistol with the other. With a horrific crack, she smashed the butt of the pistol into Ayana's head. Ayana slumped. Torra then waved, smiling coyly. "Sweet dreams."

Pain lanced through Sean's skull, and darkness swallowed him.

Chapter Thirty-Two

Emery awoke in a void. The space around her was tight, black, and silent, as if the world had imploded and she was the only one left in it. Her bones ached, her arms and legs stung with tiny scrapes, but nothing felt broken. She got lucky.

Coughing dust from her lungs, she tried to sit up but bashed her head on something solid. Swearing at the pain, she carefully ran her hands along the solid thing, and determined it was wood. A bookshelf or a beam maybe? As she felt along the wood, it switched to stone. She poked around and managed to shift debris to make a small hole. The tiniest shaft of moonlight filtered through the hole, allowing Emery to see that the wood was indeed a bookshelf that had fallen at a slant and wedged itself between rubble in such a way that it likely had saved her from being crushed.

This realization did not thaw the cold panic leeching through her veins. Where were the others? What if they hadn't been so lucky?

She carefully shoved at the debris, making a larger hole until she was able to shimmy through.

Once she was out, Emery gazed into the hazy darkness surrounding her. A huge hole yawned in the library floor above her, and above that, another hole in the ceiling let in the moon-light. But the silverly glow barely cut through the thick shadows.

"Ayana?" she croaked, her throat thick with dust. "Sean?"

As if from a great distance, she swore she could hear Sean shouting her name. But maybe it was just her hopeful imagination. She paused to listen, and heard noises again, though much closer.

The scraping and clattering of falling rubble followed grunts of exertion and pain. Emery scrambled across fallen stone and ducked beneath a collapsed beam. Peering through the darkness, she could just see them.

Tavor dragged Grace by the hair and one of her arms, attempting to haul her through a pile of broken bricks. Grace feebly fought back as much as her half-paralyzed body allowed. She grabbed anything she could cling to with her free arm and dug in with her feet. When Tavor's hand strayed too close to her mouth, she bit him.

Tavor grabbed her hair again and smashed Grace's head against the rubble. "Stop fighting."

Even dazed and bleeding from her forehead, Grace did not stop struggling.

Emery scrambled over splintered bookshelves and littered books, checking the hidden pockets of her skirt to verify the two needles Ayana had given her just before the library collapsed were still there and intact. She released a breath of relief as she felt the cool metal of the glass vials, careful not to poke herself with the sharp needles. She thanked the gods she hadn't impaled herself in the fall. She'd also mercifully managed to hang on to her lim.

Her body vibrated with fury, still enraged by the way Tavor had taunted Sean, by the way Tavor had threatened Grace, by the way the bastard was still alive. The stagnant air shifted around her, and the cool earth trembled beneath her bare feet, both reacting to her rage. Somewhere far below, she could even sense the wrath of an underground river as it roared towards the freedom of the ocean. She'd never felt the elements so clearly. She'd never been so angry.

"Let. Her. Go," she snarled.

Tavor paused, glancing back at her with mild surprise. "Ah, so the rat lives as rats tend to do." He side-eyed Grace, as if considering a loaf of bread at the market. "I suppose my offer can still stand. You come with me, and I'll let this one go."

"I'd rather die than go anywhere with you," Emery said, not slowing down as she stormed towards them.

"But would you rather she dies?"

"You have no weapons," she pointed out. He didn't appear to have any, at least. The holster and the sheath on his belt were both empty. Even his cane was nowhere to be seen, which was, Emery realized, another reason he was making such slow progress through the rubble.

Tavor rolled his eyes, and then grabbed Grace by the throat, nearly lifting her off her feet. "I don't need weapons to kill."

Emery's fury flared and she sent it downward, past the cool earth beneath her feet towards the underground river. It answered. "Neither do I."

The ground's trembling intensified, and water seeped through the dirt, quickly pooling at their feet.

Tavor eyed the water as it steadily rose, licking at their ankles now. "Stop." It was only one word, and his face betrayed no emotion, but Emery heard the flicker of fear in his voice. Maybe she even liked it.

Emery stalked towards them, the water splashing with every step.

"Stop or she dies." Grace clawed feebly at Tavor's fingers, kicked at his legs. Her face was growing purple. When Emery didn't stop, Tavor's fingers dug in further.

Emery's heart lurched with cold fear, and she allowed the fear to mix with the fury she poured into the river. Tavor's gaze jerked down as the water, now at his calves, slowly solidified, freezing his feet in place. At first, he just watched it, as if fascinated. But as the ice climbed further up his legs, Emery saw the moment his fear finally won. He dropped Grace so he could bash at the ice.

Emery rushed forward to catch Grace before she could fall into the still rising water. Without wasting a moment, she pulled the antidote from her pocket and jammed the needle into Grace's thigh. Grace gasped, and then coughed from her bruised throat.

Emery pulled Grace away from Tavor, Grace half-floating in the now waist-high water. Emery could only pray the antidote worked quickly. She didn't know if she could keep them both afloat while also dealing with Tavor. And the water was still rising.

Wading through the water with Grace, Emery hauled them both atop a pile of rubble that wasn't yet submerged. Not far away, Tavor had managed to break free of the ice and had also climbed onto his own pile of debris. He stalked back and forth like a trapped animal, glaring at them all the while.

The water lapped at their feet.

"Emery, stop the water," Grace croaked. "We're going to drown."

"Not yet," Emery said. "We're not going to drown. I promise."

Emery glanced up. The yawning hole in the ceiling wasn't that far away now. If they could swim as the water rose, they could climb back out of the hole and hopefully lose Tavor.

"Do you think you'll be able to swim soon?" she asked.

Grace followed her gaze, her mouth forming a line of determination as she realized what Emery was planning. "Yes."

Across the span of water, Tavor's rubble island was swallowed, the water lapping at his calves. Emery focused on that point, pouring more of the cold fear from her soul into the water yet again. Ice formed around Tavor's boots.

"Are you ready?" Emery asked.

Grace stood, her stance a little wobbly but upright enough. "Yes."

Emery closed her eyes, willing the water to swell faster,

higher. The roiling river obliged, rearing up and lifting Emery and Grace from their feet, pushing them up towards the library. Emery lost track of Tavor. All her focus was on reaching the salvation above.

She clung to Grace just in case she wasn't quite able to swim on her own after all, and when they reached the edge of the collapsed floor, Emery shoved her up onto the moldy, damp carpet. Grace sputtered and reached to help Emery up after her.

She'd lost control of the water. It was already draining, sucking itself and Emery back from where it came from. Grace grabbed Emery's hand, hauling her up. But something grabbed Emery's ankle, yanking her violently. Her hand slipped from Grace's, and she barely had time to take a quick breath before she plunged back into the water. She kicked, opening her eyes and spinning to see what had her, though she already knew.

Tavor clung to her ankle so firmly, her bone ached. She kicked him with her free foot, but he held fast. As the water continued to drain, it formed a whirlpool, which sucked them down faster, away from light and air and life.

Tavor grabbed Emery's calf, and then hip, pulling her further down so he could band both arms tightly around her. Their faces were only inches from each other, and so, even in the dark water, she could see his expression. It clearly said, *if I die, you die with me.*

But she refused to die with him. Refused to die at all. She managed to wiggle her hand into her pocket, grabbed the last needle, and stabbed him. Bubbles erupted from Tavor's mouth, and his grip tightened for a moment. But gradually, as the whirlpool pulled them deeper and deeper, his fingers loosened their vicelike grip. She kicked away from him, and they both floated in the darkness, staring at each other. Tavor's limbs floated around him, unmoving, unable to save himself. But his eyes still promised her death.

Emery's lungs burned, her chest ready to explode. But she was so deep, the surface so far away. She would never make it back. So, she stared into those death-promising eyes, glad she'd at least get the satisfaction of watching him die first. She'd stay alive long enough to witness that, at least, to appreciate the fact that she was able to enact revenge for Sean and keep her people safe.

Something wrapped around her waist and yanked her up, away from Tavor's limp body. Sweet oxygen filled her lungs as she broke the surface. And still, she was pulled higher, until the vine around her waist deposited her on the moldy carpet of the library. Emery struggled to her hands and knees, spitting up water.

Grace slapped her back and moved her wet, wild hair out of her eyes. "Are you alright?"

Emery nodded, not able to form words quite yet, and carefully crawled to the edge of the hole. Grace kept hold of her ankle, as if afraid she'd slip over the edge again. Emery peered into the darkness. The water was gone, and she could just barely see Tavor laying in the mud at the bottom, unable to move. Helpless. Trapped

A wicked part of Emery wondered if she should go down there and end him...but now that her fear and anger were wearing off, she didn't think she could do it. Even after all the things Tavor had done to her and the people she cared about, she wasn't like Tavor. She wasn't a killer.

What mattered now was finding the others and then getting out of there.

On shaking legs, Emery and Grace pulled away from the collapsed portion of the library. They searched for Sean, Ayana, and Kess. They searched under rubble and debris, panic increasing with every passing moment. They searched until dawn broke across the sky in bloody colours. They searched until, finally, they had to admit that Sean, Ayana, and Kess were gone. And when Emery glanced back into the hole to check on Tavor, he was gone too.

Chapter Thirty-Three

Liam was done being home.

In fact, he wished he was just about anywhere else. Even bored to death and baking under the hot sun on their stupid little boat had been preferable to the never-ending days in Orabel. At least on that little boat, he didn't have to lie with every breath. At least on that boat, he only had to be worried about one sister instead of two.

He glanced at the empty seat beside him, the empty seat across from him. The seats where Emery and Ayana should have been sitting. Where they should have been talking and laughing and being silly. But it was just him and his grandparents, sitting down in their redwood home for another awkward meal.

Liam picked at his food, the silence stifling in their small home. Now that Liam had been inside true buildings, their hollowed-out redwood seemed almost claustrophobic. Or maybe it was just the company.

His grandparents sat across from him, both looking as if they'd aged decades in the months since he'd been gone. With every meal they'd eaten together since he'd been back, their conversations had grown more strained, the pauses growing longer and longer until they barely spoke at all. And after his grandmother's questions and revelations, it felt even more awkward, because they couldn't talk about any of it.

Liam also knew he wasn't the only one obsessively aware of the empty seats at the table. Some of those new lines on his grandparents' faces were from the constant concern for their granddaughters, he knew. But he could also see where Ayana's betrayal had left its mark. She'd left without an explanation or a goodbye, just like Liam's mother had so many years ago. Liam couldn't imagine what it must have felt like to have two generations flee from your care. And yet, his grandparents never spoke of it, as if, if they didn't acknowledge their granddaughters' absence, they wouldn't have to feel the ache.

So, Liam picked at his food, meal after meal, avoiding their sad eyes and speaking as little as possible. Eventually, when he could take it no more, he'd flee. This time, when he excused himself from the table and ducked out the vine curtain leading outside, they didn't even bother protesting.

He couldn't bear going back to his room either.

The familiar scent of pine needles and saltwater filled his lungs as he inhaled a fresh breath of air. The golden light of early evening pierced through the canopy of redwood and maple tree branches as Liam stepped out onto the dirt path winding through the village. But he didn't stick to the path. Instead, he darted to the outskirts of the village, to where the trees grew closer together and didn't have people living inside them, to where he could more easily avoid the islanders.

He just wanted to be alone, and not cooped up in his room. But he was never that lucky.

A man knelt at one of the creeks that flowed from the cliffs down to the lake in the middle of the island, filling up two large clay pots with fresh water. Liam recognized the back of his head immediately, and tried to backtrack before he was spotted. But a betraying trig snapped under his foot.

The man looked up and smiled. "Liam!"

Liam did not return the smile, a rush of anger flooding his veins. "Aran."

Aran, Dray's father and one of the best medics on Orabel. Aran, the man who hadn't trusted Tavor from the beginning and had launched an attack against him, hoping to kill him before he left with their island's secrets. Aran, who had been willing to go through Emery to get to Tavor, and while Aran had been right about everything in the end, Liam would never forget how little he cared about his sister's wellbeing that day, even if he'd been spending every moment he had in the infirmary attempting to help the ill since then.

Aran stood, lifting his pots of water. His dark hair was a mess, and his beard scruffier than usual. Exhaustion dulled his eyes. "Liam, I hope you're feeling better after your ordeal."

Liam managed to nod, already seeking a way to politely duck out of the conversation.

"Will you help me take this water to the infirmary?" Without waiting for an answer, Aran hefted one of the pots into Liam's arms.

Liam couldn't very well say no, so he fell into step beside Aran as they made their slow way through the trees.

"We haven't seen much of you or Caelin since you've come home," Aran observed. Though Aran didn't sound outright suspicious, there was something in his careful words that made Liam nervous.

"Being the chosen one is exhausting," Liam said, trying to muster up some of his old cockiness. "I've been doing a lot of napping."

"Yes, I'm sure whatever happened out there was tiring, indeed," Aran said, adjusting his pot. "How long were you out there before the storm hit?"

Liam blinked, caught off guard by the sudden question. He racked his brain for the details of the story they'd come up with. "I'm not sure. A month or two?"

"And the storm separated you from Tavor?" Aran's voice remained pleasant, his tired face placid, but Liam could see a hint of mistrust gleaming in his eyes now.

"Yes."

"How?"

Liam swallowed, the horrible memories of watching the sea swallow the ship he thought his sister was trapped in making him ill. "We were in separate long boats."

"But how did you get separated?"

His temper beginning to fray, Liam snapped. "We were in two bits of wood, bobbing in the sea in the middle of a storm. How do you think we got separated?"

Aran either didn't notice or didn't care about Liam's tone. "And Emery is still with Tavor? How did they not get separated?"

Liam stopped walking, forcing Aran to stop as well. Liam looked him dead in the eye. "Did something happen to you while I was gone, Aran? You used to be brilliant, but now you seem a little slow."

Aran didn't take the bait, just gazed at Liam patiently, waiting for an answer.

"Emery was in the *other* boat with Tavor," Liam said, speaking slowly, as if trying to explain something to a child for the tenth time. He'd hoped to make Aran angry, to distract him from his suspicions, but it wasn't working.

"And Emery is still with Tavor, searching for the cure?" Aran asked.

Liam gritted his teeth. "Yes."

"How do you know?"

"What do you mean?"

Aran's face grew stony, as if he was tired of playing their game as well. "How do you know she's with Tavor if you were separated from them during the storm? How do you know she's not dead? How do you know he's not dead?"

Liam's grip on the clay pot was so firm he was surprised it didn't implode. His anxiety about Emery's safety swelled in his chest, pushing painfully against his heart. And with it came more anger. How dare Aran question him like some sort of criminal? How dare Aran throw the possibility of his twin's death in his face just to try to get some answers? And the worst part was, Aran was right about all of it and Liam was forced to keep lying.

Liam tried a different tactic. He dropped all his bravado and allowed pain to lace his voice. "Why are you doing this?"

Aran studied Liam for a moment, his gaze narrowing. Purple circles underscored his dark eyes. "Because your story doesn't add up. You boys are lying about something, and I don't like being lied to."

Liam didn't flinch. "I'm not lying," he lied.

Aran took a step closer, the only thing separating them the two pots they carried. "Obviously, you know that, as the best healer on this island, I'm skilled with manipulating the water in blood. But did you know I can sense your blood running through your veins because of that?"

Liam blinked. He had never considered that before.

"I can tell when someone's pulse starts to race," Aran continued. "It's why I was, and still am, certain Tavor was lying about something too."

Lost for words, Liam gulped.

"I can feel your pulse racing, Liam. I know you're lying. I think Orabel is in danger, and I will protect our home however I need to, even if it's by prying answers out of you."

Shaking off the shock, Liam glared. "What are you going to do, torture me?" He barely refrained from adding, *'Been there, done that.'*

"I'll do what I have to, to protect my home."

Liam felt the blood rush from his face. Aran was not bluffing. And as a healer, he had the tools and means to torture anyone if he wanted to. Would the Arch-Elemists step in and stop him? Or would they allow Liam to be tortured once again?

Liam did not want to find out. He dropped the clay pot he was holding directly on Aran's foot. The man swore, dropping his own pot onto the first, causing them both to shatter, the water spilling everywhere.

"Oops, I guess my exhaustion got the better of me," Liam said. "I better be off for another nap."

He headed back home, walking as fast as he could without running.

Part Three

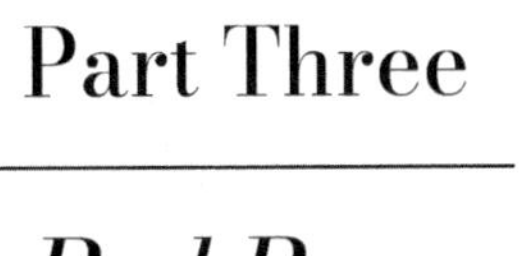

A Red Reaper

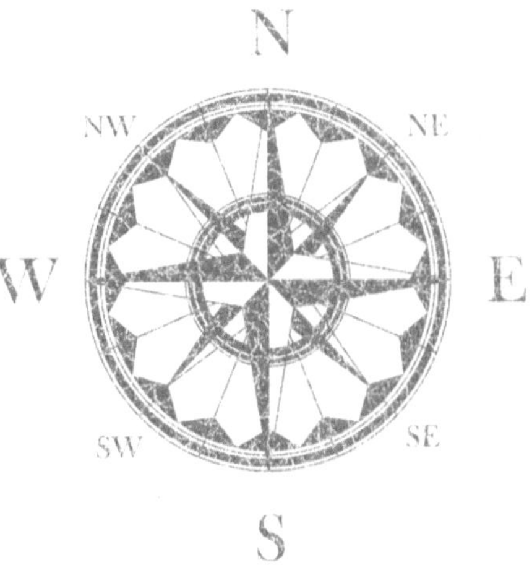

Chapter Thirty-Four

The familiar swaying of the ship, the creaking of the rigging, the water lapping against the hull and the scent of the briny sea was so comforting, it made it nearly impossible for Sean to drag himself back to consciousness.

But each throb of the increasingly sharp ache in his skull brought him closer and closer to wakefulness, and when he rolled over to bury his face in his pillow only to find cold hard wood beneath him, his eyes finally snapped open.

He blinked as he raised his head, taking in the dim, cramped space, and the iron bars right in front of his face. He was not in his beloved cabin aboard the *Audacity*. He was in the brig of some unknown ship.

The memories flooded into his mind like a river bursting a dam: Emery charging for Tavor, the library imploding around them, Kess's limp body.

The gravediggers looming out of the dust and darkness.

Surely that last part had been a dream.

Sean shoved himself up to his knees, wincing as the pain in his head reached a crescendo. He blinked away stars and felt the back of his head to find an aching lump and dried blood crusting his hair.

A moan in the shadows of his cell caught his attention, and Sean's heart leapt as he watched Kess attempt to rise. Sean was by his side in an instant, helping his friend slump against the ship's hull.

The relief Sean felt at seeing Kess awake nearly eclipsed his pounding headache.

"Are you alright?" he tried to say, but broke off to cough, his throat as dry as the Scorched Sea. How long had they been unconscious?

"I think so," Kess said, blinking a few times and touching his nose. "My head hurts. And I have no clue where my glasses are." He spoke slowly, his voice also raspy, as he took in their surroundings. "Where are we?"

Baffling images of the grave robbers flashed in Sean's head again. "I don't—"

"Thank the gods you two are finally awake!" Ayana's voice interrupted. She clung to the iron bars of a separate cell across the ship. Her wild curls wilted around her face, free from the vines and the blossoms that had tied them back at the festival. She wore nothing but a thin slip, and Sean realized her flowery costume had likely fallen apart as soon as she'd lost consciousness, no longer kept in place by her abilities.

Sean's immediate thought was to lend her his coat, or at least a tunic, only to realize he still wore the tight merman pants of his costume and nothing else, except for the layer of paint covering his bare torso. He'd also been stripped of his weapons.

"I've been shouting for you two to wake up for hours," Ayana continued. She sat back gingerly, as if suddenly exhausted now that her task was completed, and then winced.

"Your leg?" Sean asked.

"I think it might be broken." She said it matter-of-factly, almost angrily, as if it were more of an annoying inconvenience than a painful injury. But then her tone changed to that of distress. "Emery and Grace aren't here."

Relief and fear battled in Sean's gut. Relief because they weren't also imprisoned here, wherever *here* was. Fear because the last time he'd seen Emery and Grace was the moment before the world fell apart and the floor swallowed them whole, along with Tavor.

Gods, what if they were still down there? What if they were trapped and slowly dying and no one knew to look for them? Or worse, what if Tavor had them?

Ayana's voice snapped Sean from his spiraling thoughts. "Who are these people? Why did they take us?"

He shook his head, making his headache worse. "I don't know."

"Really?" Ayana snapped. "Because you spoke as if you knew each other."

"I don't know them," Sean snapped back, his nerves too frayed to stand being called a liar. He was many things, but he wasn't a liar. "Emery and I had one brief unpleasant interaction with them a few weeks back in which they tried to kill us because we caught them grave robbing."

Ayana blinked. "That makes no sense."

"I'm aware," Sean grumbled. He sat back on his heels, trying to remember the brief conversation he had with the grave robbers before they knocked him out. But it was hard to think past the pain in his head, his thoughts moving like slush.

Ayana said, "They asked for a chest. You said it was empty."

Sean kneaded his forehead. "Right. I think they might be after whatever was supposed to be in the chest we found in Love S. Key's grave."

"Why?" Ayana asked, her voice still accusing, like this was all somehow his fault.

"How should I know?" Sean's temper was rising.

"Folks, we're not alone down here..." Kess's voice broke the tension between them, cutting Sean's temper off at the knees.

He followed Kess's gaze to where the darkness fought back against the torchlight. A lump lay in the shadows, blending in so well Sean hadn't noticed it before. But then the lump moved, letting out a low grown.

"Emery?" Sean scrambled for the lump but when he got close

enough, his heart sank as he realized it was a man he'd never seen before.

The man whimpered as Sean approached, and scurried backwards until he was pressed into the corner, where the bars met the hull of the ship.

"He doesn't look very good," Kess murmured.

That was an understatement. The man's clothes were salt-encrusted and filthy. His hair and beard long and straggly. He reeked of piss.

"Sir, do you know where we are?" Sean asked, keeping his voice soft, calm.

The man trembled, the whites of his eyes bright in the shadows.

Sean tried again. "Whose ship is this?"

Another whimper escaped the man's lips. "It burns."

Sean exchanged a glance with Kess, who'd slowly approached as well. "What burns, sir? I'm a medic. Maybe I can help you?"

The man shook his head violently. "No help. So hot. Too hot."

"Do you have a fever?" Kess asked.

"My blood. It burns. She burns. Forever burning."

Silence fell, during which Sean and Kess exchanged another look. This man was not going to be any help.

Sean sat back on his heels again and turned back to Ayana. "Has anyone else come down here since you've been awake?"

"No. Just our sad little party."

Kess wandered to the cell door and shook it in vain, then examined the locked keyhole. "If anyone has some sort of pin, I might be able to pick this."

Sean had already considered this. He and Kess had learned how to pick locks as children, all the better to cause mischief, having no idea just how handy it would be in the future. But getting out of the cell was not the problem. Getting off the ship was. Sean was much more interested in figuring out who held them captive, and why, before they attempted to escape. If Sean had learned anything these last few years as a fugitive, it was to always know who you were playing against.

The thought had barely crossed his mind when the creak of hinges screeched in the silence, and multiple booted feet descended the steps leading into the brig.

"It looks like our new playthings are awake," Torra the graverobber said as she stepped into the torchlight.

It hadn't been a dream after all.

Trailing her was an ancient-looking man, with a long white beard. He wore a hat low over his face and appeared to be all skin and bones under his plain clothing. His appearance only made Sean more confused than ever.

Torra and the old man each stepped to the side, revealing the third and final member of their odd party: another woman, with waves of blood red hair spilling over her shoulders and a spattering of freckles across tanned skin. She wore a tricorne hat with feathers sticking out of it, and a long crimson coat with flashing brass buttons. A cutlass hung at one hip and a pistol at the other, and Sean could only assume she had other weapons too. She appeared young, maybe only a few years older than himself.

She was dressed like the captain, and though Sean knew—if not personally than from stories—most of the pirate and Forbidden captains in the area, he couldn't recall this one.

He pulled himself onto shaky feet. His head throbbed and his stomach lurched, but he refused to show any weakness to these people. Instead, he plastered on a look of intense irritation, as if he were angrier that they'd interrupted his reveries than worried about why. "My name is Captain Sean Denzel. I request parley and demand to know why you saw it fit to throw me in this cell like some common thief."

Freely giving his name was a gamble, but—

"Captain Sean Denzel!" The redheaded woman's whole face lit up, like she couldn't believe her luck, and her red painted lips split into a grin. She turned to Torra. "You didn't mention it was the Scourge of the Sea himself visiting my brig."

Sean forced himself to stand taller instead of wincing at the title he hated. His survival might depend on that title.

Torra, for her part, had paled, her eyes wide with obvious shock. Her voice was suddenly subdued. "I wasn't aware of his name. The Watcher just gave me a location."

So, they both knew of him then. He had been hoping for reactions like Torra's. He knew how to deal with people who feared him. That's how he'd survived for so long. But the captain's reaction was unsettling. He did not know how to deal with that.

"I have to admit," the captain said, her gaze running the length of Sean's bare torso. "After all the tales I've heard about you, you're a little disappointing to look at. Plus, by the sounds of it, you were easy to capture."

Sean resisted the urge to cross his arms over his chest. "Perhaps if you'd given me the courtesy of finishing my enjoyment of the festivities and offered a fair fight, instead of jumping me in the dark like a coward, you'd be more impressed." Sean adopted an almost bored expression as he took his turn appraising the woman. "And I fear I've heard no tales of you at all. I have no idea who I'm speaking to."

The captain grinned, not taking the bait, a gold tooth glinting in the torchlight. "Trust me, *Denzel*, you have heard of me."

She said his last name like it was poison on her tongue, which threw Sean for a moment. No one ever cared about his last name. It was always the Scourge whom they hated and feared.

Before Sean could answer, Ayana interrupted, "Enough with the niceties. Tell us who you are and why you've brought us onto your dump of a boat."

Sean forced himself not to grimace. If there was one sure way to piss off a ship captain, it was to insult their ship. And Sean didn't think angering this captain when they were at a huge disadvantage was the way to go.

The captain turned to appraise Ayana, her red hair catching

the torchlight. Ayana couldn't stand due to her injured leg, but Sean had to give her credit for still managing to look fierce and furious from the ground.

"What a tongue we have." The captain clicked her own tongue. "Perhaps your captain should cut that tongue out for speaking out of turn."

"Is that what happened to your ox of a henchman?" Sean mused, remembering the huge man and his lack of tongue.

The captain merely winked.

"He's not my captain," Ayana spat. "No man is my captain."

Torra spoke up again. "I believe she may be his paramour. They were rather friendly with each other in the cemetery."

Sean's gaze locked with Ayana's briefly as they had the same realization. These people, whoever they were, thought she was Emery.

He supposed most of their interactions so far had all been in the dark, where it could be easy to mix up the two.

"Ah, the lover of the Scourge," the captain said. "I suppose the lover of the second-most feared Forbidden of the seas would have to be a pain in the ass."

Sean fully expected Ayana to take insult, to snap back with venom. But instead, she played along. "You have it wrong. He's the *most* feared Forbidden of the seas."

The captain laughed, a lovely, high, tinkling sound that had no place in a dark brig. "Oh, my dear, I'm afraid it's you who is wrong. *I* am the most feared Forbidden of the seas."

A cold dread spread through Sean's chest. "Who are you?"

The captain locked eyes with Sean, her grin wicked. "You may know my ship, the *Crimson Vengeance*. And you may have heard what they call me: The Red Reaper. But my name is Captain Charlotte Ashborne."

The blood drained from Sean's face and nausea reared in his gut. Somewhere behind him, Kess sucked in a horrified breath.

Her grin widened. "Judging by your pallor, you *have* heard of me."

He had. He'd heard tales of this captain's bloody conquests, how they left no survivors. He'd heard the tales of their ruthlessness and their mercilessness.

And he'd heard the tales of how Captain Ashborne had slaughtered his parents.

Chapter Thirty-Five

S ean could barely hear the redheaded woman over the roaring in his ears.

The Red Reaper.

Ashborne.

Somewhere, the gods were laughing at him. Somehow, he had been rescued from his sister's murderer by being captured by his parents' murderer.

But when he really looked at Captain Charlotte Ashborne, he realized that couldn't be true. She didn't look older then twenty-five, which meant she couldn't have been older than nine when his parents died. She couldn't have done it. Which meant it was likely her father, the Ashborne that came before her. Or maybe even her grandfather. Still, hatred and rage sluiced through his veins like venom, and he barely refrained from stealing the air right from her lungs.

There was a small chance she wasn't as ruthless as her prede-cessors. He hadn't been lying before. He truly hadn't heard any stories of a redheaded female captain wreaking havoc across the seas. But was that because she wasn't wreaking havoc or because the stories left out the part about her being a woman? Or, worse, might it be because she left no survivors to tell the tales to begin with?

Was she truly the Red Reaper? Or was that all her father?

"Because I'm a woman of honour, I'll respect your request for parley, Captain Denzel," Captain Ashborne was saying, the sound of his own name dragging Sean back to the conversation. "You tell me what I want to know, and I won't kill you outright. Seem fair?"

Sean couldn't see any way through this but to play along for now. He clenched his jaw in an attempt to keep the hatred out of his voice. "What do you want to know?"

"Where is my chest?" Ashborne asked.

Sean fought not to roll his eyes this time. "We already told your incompetent lackeys; we don't have any chest."

Torra bristled behind her captain, but Ashborne didn't seem to care. "I want what was inside that chest."

"There was nothing in that chest but rocks. We went over this too."

Ashborne laid a hand on the pommel of her pistol. "I don't believe you. I believe you're hiding it."

Sean spread his arms, indicating his lack of clothing once again. "Where would I possibly hide anything?"

Ashborne arched a brow, her gaze scouring his body again, exactly as Torra had done. "Where, indeed? I never said I thought it was on your person. Perhaps it's back aboard your ship? Perhaps you buried it somewhere else?"

"Or perhaps there was nothing in the chest to hide or bury or otherwise?" Sean's curiosity was finally getting the better of him, and he couldn't help but ask. "What do you think was supposed to be in that chest? Why do you want it so badly?"

Ashborne held up a ringed finger. "Ah, ah, boy captain. I ask the questions. You only answer."

Sean scowled at being called a boy captain, unable to decide if he hated that or being called the Scourge more.

Ashborne sighed, as if suddenly bored. "In order to honor parley, I'm going to play fair. I'll give you time to think about the truth. And I'm going to show you an example of what happens when people on this ship don't speak the truth."

She snapped her fingers and Torra stepped forward to open the cell door. Sean braced himself for a fight, eyeing the whip coiled at her belt, but Torra stalked passed him, and instead yanked the strange man in the corner to his feet, all but dragging him back out of the cell.

"No, no, no," the man wailed, digging his heels in, to no avail. Torra wasn't a huge woman, but the poor man seemingly had no strength left in him to fight. "Too hot. So hot."

Sean resisted the urge to jump to the stranger's aid, and he made no move to escape while his cell door was open. He wouldn't get far if he tried, and he wasn't going to leave Kess and Ayana behind anyway.

Torra dragged the man in front of Ashborne and kicked his legs out from under him, driving him to his knees, where he trembled and wept.

"We've given this man plenty of chances to tell us the truth," Ashborne said, glaring down at the man. "But he's proven useless and fruitless, and I grow tired of his presence."

"I don't know, I don't know, I don't know..." the man wailed. "So hot."

"Watch carefully, boy captain, because this will be your fate if you lie to me again."

Ashborne knelt before the man and laid a hand on his cheek as if to comfort him. When he jerked back, she grabbed his jaw instead.

For a moment, silence fell. And then the man began screaming. He screamed and screamed, falling to the floor and flailing. He clawed at his clothes, his skin.

"Fire! Fire in my blood!" He screamed until his words became incoherent, until they were just the mangled cries of an animal in pain.

Sweat dripped from his brow, soaked his filthy clothes. And then his skin began to bubble, to blister, as if he was burning from the inside out. He flailed again, his face twisting in Sean's direction. And his eyes—his eyes were melting in their sockets.

Sean couldn't move, couldn't look away, as the man's skin began to liquify, to slough off. Where it remained attached to the bone, it charred, turning black. The man stopped moving, stopped screaming.

But his screams still echoed in Sean's skull. They probably always would.

"Think hard about your lies, *Denzel*." Again, the hatred when Ashborne said his last name was undeniable. She stood, not even glancing at the ruined body at her feet. She glared at Sean instead. "I'd hate for you to meet the same fate."

Chapter Thirty-Six

"Where is our Captain?" Camulus demanded, her hand settling on the head of the ax hanging from her belt.

"I told you," Emery said, keeping her own hands far away from her lim as she straddled the *Audacity's* starboard railing. She didn't want to spook Cam and risk her head being lopped off before she could get the words out. "They took him. And Kess, and my sister."

"Who?" Cam demanded again.

"We're not sure. We think varens."

Cam growled, taking a menacing step forward, but Ranit placed a hand on her shoulder. "Breathe, Cam. At least let her properly onto the ship."

"We should throw her off the ship into the sea like I'd said months ago."

Emery probably should have expected this less than welcome greeting. She'd been so focused on getting here, on not losing her mind to panic, that she hadn't thought about the crew's reactions at all.

Ranit, forever calm, said, "Tell us what happened."

Billy came up behind him, his blue eyes wide with fear. "Where is my son?"

Emery's heart stumbled. She'd never heard him refer to Sean as his son before. She swallowed, her throat suddenly dry, as the rest of the crew approached. She didn't know where to start.

"Tavor showed up. He tried to capture us. But then there was some sort of explosion or something and the building we were in collapsed. And we think they took him. Sean, Kess, and my sister —they were all just gone."

After searching the university for hours, Emery and Grace were forced to admit defeat when people finally showed up to investigate the explosion in the building. They had escaped through the back and fled into the grounds, taking cover under the overgrown foliage.

"Do you remember what happened before the floor collapsed?" Grace had asked, glancing back and studying the ruined exterior of the university.

Emery had shaken her head. All she remembered was Tavor's awful, taunting words and something snapping inside her. "One moment, I was running, the next, I was falling."

"I remember the sound of fireworks or thunder," Grace had said. "But now I don't think it was either."

"What do you mean?"

"I think it was cannons," Grace said, pointing at the rubble. "Those walls didn't just fall down. They were blown in."

The grounds of the university were perched on a cliff overlooking the sea, but there was a thin trail leading towards a sandy beach below. Grace's theory was bolstered further when they stepped upon the sand.

"Look," she'd said. "Someone's been here recently."

Footprints peppered the sand, along with one deep gauge, as if a boat had been wedged into the ground at some point. They could only assume it had been the varens lying in wait and that this was how they'd taken Sean, Kess, and Ayana.

If that was the case, they had been lucky in a way. They had initially considered entering the university grounds via the sea but had dismissed the idea because it had been too open. Had they come this way after all, things could have ended even worse.

Emery and Grace had crept along the beach until they found the edge of the stone wall encircling the grounds. They climbed over and joined the still celebrating city. Even covered in dust, they'd been able to blend in easily.

Grace had led them to a giant white building with white marble pillars, red roof tiles, and a giant clock tower, and then snuck them through a side door with a key she'd produced from her pocket. Apparently, Grace had spent so much time in this building, which had turned out to be a library, they'd given her a key. She'd also had the foresight to stash some of their belongings in the library if things went sideways and they weren't able to return to their home.

Then it took two days to track down the *Audacity*. The rest of that first day had been spent attempting to find passage off Audrye to the neighbouring island of Kann where the crew of the *Audacity* were laying low while their captain was gone. Finding a ship had proven difficult as the All Gods festival ended, and the docks became crowded with hungover and exhausted people trying to get home. But the crowds had proved useful when avoiding the varens, who were combing the streets, likely looking for them.

Eventually, Grace had managed to secure passage on a small ferry by offering the captain triple the coin to kick off two other passengers to make room for them.

Most of the second day had been spent on the ferry, anxiously wishing for the winds to pick up so they could sail faster. After nearly five hours of travel, Emery and Grace all but leapt off the ferry onto Kann's small docks. But the *Audacity* had not been at the docks, which Emery had known. They'd had to make their way through Kann's small but bustling village, passed the fields of sugarcane the island was known for, and onto a wide empty beach. Anchored just off the beach, the *Audacity* had bobbed in the turquoise water, as if waiting for them.

Emery and Grace hadn't even waited to see if anyone would spot them from the ship and send a longboat to fetch them. They'd thrown themselves into the surf and swam. When Emery climbed up the *Audacity's* hull and swung a leg over the guardrail, Cam, unfortunately, had been the first to spot her.

She'd been stuck halfway aboard the ship ever since, leg still slung over the guardrail, with poor Grace hanging onto the hull below. After she finished telling the story, a terrible silence fell across the ship.

Aleksy spoke first, her face a picture of horror. "Tavor has Sean?"

"I don't know." Water from her wet hair dripped into her eyes and she impatiently swiped the back of her hand across her forehead, trying to gather her words together properly. Now that she was finally here, standing on Sean's ship without him, the panic was finally sinking in. "When the building collapsed, Grace and I fell in a hole with Tavor. We...fought. We left him down there. When we climbed out, Sean and the others were just gone. And then Tavor disappeared too."

"This is your fault," Cam hissed, advancing one step. "We should never have allowed him to drag you out of that storm that day. We should have let you drown."

Emery swallowed, at a loss for words. Because Cam was right about one thing at least. This was her fault.

"Back off." Grace's furious voice made Emery jump. Grace must have clambered up beside Emery as she'd told the story, but now she hopped onto the deck, stepped between Emery and Cam, and shoved Cam backward.

Emery's heart nearly stopped. Cam stumbled back into Ranit, and Emery suspected the only reason Grace still had her head was because of Cam's pure shock.

"We came here because we want to get them back," Grace said, glaring at the entire crew as if they weren't Forbiddens with fearsome reputations. Emery knew these reputations were false, but still, she had to admire Grace's bravery. "We came here to ask for help. But if you don't want to help, that's fine. Let us go so we don't waste any more time getting our loved ones back."

"Who's this?" Cam asked, standing straight again.

"My sister," Emery said, because it was true enough.

"I thought you said Tavor took your sister," Ranit inquired.

"My other sister."

Cam opened her mouth again, no doubt to say something nasty, but Grace held up her hand. "We're done talking to you, thanks. Who's the first mate on this ship? We'd like to talk to them, please."

Again, Emery suspected only shock kept Cam from drawing her ax. The rest of the crew remained silent too, staring at Grace, at this slender, blonde girl in a soaking wet dress, glaring back at them all with no ounce of fear in her posture.

And then Ranit laughed, breaking the tension. "I like her."

"Ready the sails. We'll head north. If it is varens, they'll either be heading to Dornwell or straight to Abyssus. If we hurry, we can catch them," Billy ordered, and Farley, Seadar, Aleksy, and Rooney dispersed across the deck to do just that.

Emery let out a relieved breath and finally swung her other leg over the rail so she stood on the deck properly. It had never occurred to her until moments ago that they might not want to help. And she didn't know what she would have done had they said no.

As soon as both of Emery's feet hit the deck, Billy pulled her into a hug. "I'm glad you're safe!" He pulled back and rested his hands on her shoulders. "We'll get him back. He'll be alright."

Before she could respond, he was gone, presumably off to the helm.

Cam and Ranit remained standing before her. Grace stepped back now, so she was beside Emery instead of in front of her.

Though Cam didn't look nearly as furious as before, she crossed her arms and glared. "We should toss them in the brig."

"Cam." Ranit sighed. "Go ready the sails with the others."

Cam did no such thing, and pinned Emery with her acidic gaze. "This is the second time we've had to rescue Sean because of you."

"I know," Emery said, her voice pathetically small as her throat closed up, tears threatening as the panic really set it.

Cam leaned forward. "You better hope we get Sean back

unharmed and alive. If we don't, make no mistake. I *will* kill you."

Chapter Thirty-Seven

The brig smelled like burnt hair and cooked flesh.

Sean couldn't stop staring at the charred corpse, at the melted, blackened skin and the shining white bone peeking out from underneath. Ashborne had left the body where it fell, all the better for Sean to see what may become of him if he didn't come up with a way out of this situation soon.

In the cell across from his, Ayana retched in the corner.

Kess sat back against the hull, his expression oddly blank. Stunned. His voice was monotone as he asked, "How...did she... do that?"

Ayana sat back, wiping her mouth. "There's water in our blood. If you're skilled at water manipulation, you can manipulate the water in blood. She...made the water boil."

Sean had seen that blood manipulation many times. Aleksy used it to save them more often than he cared to remember. But this...

"I've seen this before," he said out loud as the memory slowly emerged through the shock. "We found a derelict ship with no one aboard. But in the bilge, there were bodies... They looked just like this."

"Gods," Kess breathed.

"Great," Ayana said. "So, we traded one psychopath for another."

In the silence that followed, a piece of skin sloughed off the carcass with a quiet squelch. Sean fought not to vomit too, and finally looked away.

"What do we do?" Ayana whispered.

Sean shook his head, trying to tug his fraying thoughts together. What *could* they do? Even if they somehow managed to escape the brig, they'd have to fight their way through the crew, who were probably just as ruthless as their captain, and then commandeer a boat, all while being outnumbered, out-skilled, and injured. Telling the truth about the chest hadn't worked. Could Sean lie? Make something up to buy them some time? But what did Ashborne want to hear? Sean had no idea what was supposed to be in that chest. He had no idea why Ashborne even wanted it.

A tiny spark of anger and hurt flickered with his next thought, because clearly, he hadn't been told everything.

Had Emery lied to him?

He watched Ayana's face carefully. "How does Ashborne know about a chest that belonged to *your* parents?"

She frowned. "How should I know?"

"Because they're *your* parents."

Her frown turned into a scowl. "Parents who are strangers. Excluding the fact that they dumped us when we were toddlers, I know exactly nothing about them. Especially my father."

Emery had told him as much. But was it true? He wanted to believe it.

"Do you have any idea what could have been in the chest?" he asked.

"No. Do you?" She spat the question at him.

"Of course not."

"Well, you were there. You actually saw the thing," she said.

"There were rocks. And a blank piece of paper," Sean

suddenly remembered. But, surely, that couldn't be what Ashborne was searching for.

Ayana tapped her cell bar with a finger, glaring at him. "How do I know you aren't lying?"

Sean's anger flared. "I'm assuming Emery told you everything. Do you not trust your own sister's word?" Ayana's scowl deflated slightly, but before she could reply, he continued, "How do I know *you're* not lying?"

What he really meant was, *'How do I know Emery didn't lie?'*

Because now that the shock of everything was finally wearing off, for some reason, the fear that Emery had lied to him, even used him, was beginning to overshadow everything else.

"Children, that's enough—" Kess tried to butt in.

"Why would we lie?" Ayana talked over him, and then, as if sensing Sean's thoughts, added, "Do you not trust your own *paramour's* word?"

She threw Ashborne's words for what Emery was to him in his face, and his anger flared higher, mixing with hurt. He didn't really know *what* Emery was to him, only that she was something, and he *had* trusted her. He'd trusted her with his deepest secret. And yet, she clearly hadn't trusted him.

Orabelian. The word had been creeping at the back of his thoughts ever since Tavor had said it, waiting to spring out at him like a monster when he finally had a moment to think clearly. But it was springing early, claws extended to tear into his heart.

His next words tasted like acid. "She lied to me about where she's from. She could have lied about anything."

Sean had hoped that maybe Tavor had been lying, playing one of his mind games to get them to turn on each other. But he remembered the look of shock on Emery's face when Tavor said the word. And as Ayana fell quiet, her scowl vanishing completely, he knew it was true. Emery was from Orabel, and she never trusted him enough to tell him.

Ayana had the grace to look chagrined. She opened her

mouth, her eyes darting around as if looking for something, and then closed her mouth again. She seemed to gulp. "That's...not her fault."

Sean didn't reply, trying to ignore the sting of Ayana's confirmation.

Orabel. Emery was from Orabel. A place of myth. A place of legend. It explained so much, and yet, revealed so little. Why would Emery hide this from him? Had she trusted him so little, even after everything they'd been through together?

"We're not supposed to leave...the island." Ayana's voice was hushed, and she glanced about the ship again, as if she feared the very ship could hear her. "Emery was a special circumstance."

Sean remembered Emery telling him that Tavor lied to her, to her people. That she hadn't known what he was at first. He had promised her people a cure, had promised them peace. But she hadn't mentioned who her people were. Once again, the sting of betrayal sparked his temper.

"Then why are *you* out here?" Sean snapped at Ayana because he had no one to lash out at but her.

Ayana visibly swallowed again. "It's forbidden to leave. The punishment is death." She paused, as if bracing herself for something. "Grace and I, we ran... I was dead if I stayed anyway. It was worth dying to try to leave."

"If you left, how would you be punished?" he asked.

She glanced around again, placing a hand on her throat. "Our leaders...are far reaching." Once again, she winced, as if bracing herself for impact. But nothing happened.

"Cryptic," Sean said.

"Talking about them is forbidden too." Ayana's scowl returned. "And you're not worth dying over, so I'm not saying anything else." Her face softened again. "But don't be angry with Emery. She was trying to protect you."

Sean sat back against the hull of the ship, the wood creaking behind him. He was done with this conversation, his anger slowly giving way to betrayal and hurt. He wondered how much he really knew about Emery. Or how little. He wondered about all the other possible secrets she'd kept from him. And he wondered how many more of those secrets Ayana knew.

There had to be a reason Ashborne wanted the chest that belonged to their parents. And he wasn't sure if he believed Ayana when she said she didn't know why. Sean was a pirate, after all. A fearsome Forbidden, even if only by reputation. And he'd learned long ago not to trust anyone.

ASHBORNE RETURNED HOURS LATER, leaving them to stew in their anxiety and argue over what to do and say next. If Ayana did know what Ashborne was looking for, she never admitted it. So they couldn't lie, couldn't make something up, because the risk of Ashborne knowing what was supposed to be in the chest was too high. It only left repeating the truth and hoping she believed them this time.

Sean jumped to his feet as soon as he heard the door creak open and boots descend the stairs. He stood tall, despite still being half-naked and dizzy from lack of food and drink. Sean had no idea how long they'd been in the brig, but no one had bothered to bring them food or water—likely another tactic to pry answers out of them.

The burned body remained though, and the smell coming off it grew fouler by the minute. Sean wasn't sure he even could eat, if given the opportunity.

Ashborne stepped down the stairs and into the brig, the ancient man and the woman named Torra following in her wake.

"So, Denzel," Ashborne said, nudging the melted corpse out of her way with the toe of her shiny boot. "Have you had a change of heart? Any new information to share?"

Sean swallowed, his throat dry from thirst and nerves. "We told you the truth before. The chest only contained rocks and a piece of blank parchment."

Ashborne cocked a red brow. "You never mentioned the parchment before."

Sean crossed his arms, feigning indifference. "Honestly, I'd forgotten about it. It seemed inconsequential. As I said, it was blank."

It had been a gamble mentioning the parchment at all. Would Ashborne believe he truly forgot about it? Or would she think he'd lied earlier and was keeping things from her now? Did she even care about the parchment?

Ashborne tsked. "You'll have to come up with a better lie."

Sean gritted his teeth. "I'm not lying."

"We'll see," Ashborne said nonchalantly. "Who should we start with, Watcher?"

It took Sean a moment to realize she was addressing the old man. After a pause, the man pointed a gnarled finger at Sean. "He was the only one to see the chest."

Torra spoke up and pointed at Ayana. "That's not right. She was there too."

The old man shook his head. "She was not there. You have the wrong girl."

Torra blanched and looked nervously at her captain, as if waiting for punishment. But Ashborne didn't even glance her way, which only seemed to make Torra more nervous.

Sean eyed the old man. He didn't understand who he was or how he possibly knew such information.

Ashborne's red lips twisted into a mock pout, her gaze still on Sean. "I suppose it's your unlucky day, Denzel."

She stepped up to the bars, so they stood nearly nose to nose. Or they would have, had Sean not been half a head taller than her. Still, Ashborne somehow made it seem like she was looking down at him. Sean refused to back down and glared back into her stormy grey eyes. They'd be interesting, stunning even, if they didn't belong to a ruthless killer.

Her gaze dipped to the timepiece still hanging around his neck. "Pretty trinket." Her breath was spicy, like rum. " Maybe I'll take that for myself when I'm done with you."

Sean resisted the urge to wrap his fingers around the time-piece. He wouldn't let her know how much it actually meant to him.

"I'll ask again," she said. "What was in the chest?"

"Rocks and paper."

"Where did you hide what was in the chest?"

"Nowhere. We took nothing from the chest."

Her gaze swept over his face, as if searching for clues of honesty or treachery. When her gaze snapped back to his, she narrowed her eyes. Her voice dropped to a whisper, so only he could hear it. "I've been waiting for this moment a long time, *Denzel.*"

Again, she spat his name like it was poison. He didn't understand what she meant. Sean didn't know what else to do but stare back, hoping if he didn't show any weakness, it might sway her. But then he felt it. At first, it was almost pleasant. Like he'd been the one to drink the rum. Warmth pooled in his gut, spread to his hands, his feet, his head. It was like a lovely buzz after an evening at the tavern. Then sweat broke across his brow, and his skin felt almost sunburnt. But on the inside. Fire flowed through his veins, as if he'd stepped into a flame and absorbed it.

He clenched his jaw to keep from groaning as his blood, his body, grew hotter and hotter. His vision began to swim and sweat poured from his skin, running blue with the paint still adorning his body.

And then the heat was gone. As if it had never been. The only evidence the sweat on his body.

He opened his eyes, not remembering squeezing them shut, and found he'd fallen to his knees. He didn't remember doing that either.

"Sean?" Kess stood beside him now and reached for his shoulder.

"Don't!" Sean tried to shout, but it came out as more of a pant. "Stay back."

"I'd listen to your captain," Ashborne said, "Or you'll be next."

"I don't care," Kess cried. He reached for Sean again, but the old man raised a hand and a blast of air knocked Kess back against the hull, pinning him there.

Ashborne just rolled her eyes. "Men are always so rash. And stupid. Now where is it?"

"Where's what?" Sean nearly shouted, fear cracking his feigned calm. "I don't know what you are looking for!"

This time, it didn't start pleasant at all. Fire raged in his blood all at once. Burning, boiling, scalding.

"Where is it!" Ashborne demanded, but Sean could barely hear her over the roaring of fire in his ears, over the sound of his own screams.

"I don't know!"

He burned and he burned and he burned.

"Tell me where it is." Ashborne's voice was cold, cruel.

"I hid it!"

All at once, the burning stopped. Sean blinked the blurriness from his eyes. He lay curled on the floor now, in a puddle of his own sweat. He grabbed at his arms, relieved and surprised to find he still had skin.

"Where did you hide it?" Ashborne asked, peering down at him through the cell door with a triumphant grin.

"I..." The lie wouldn't come, his brain too addled. The first one had just slipped out, a desperate gamble to make the hurt stop. "I climbed a tree and strung it up to keep it safe."

Did that even make sense? He couldn't tell.

"Where is this tree?" Ashborne questioned.

Sean said the first place that came to mind. "Back in Audrye."

Ashborne turned to the old man and raised a questioning brow.

After a while, the old man shook his head. "The wind sees nothing in the trees of Audrye."

Sean's racing heart plummeted.

Those stormy eyes stared down at him, and they seemed to

flash with lightning. There was no mercy in that stare, no kindness. Just a raging storm. Her voice dropped to a whisper again. "That first round was for me. This round is for my father."

And then Sean burned again.

He burned and burned and burned.

Chapter Thirty-Eight

Sean dreamt of fire and ash but woke choking on water.

"Oh, thank the gods," Kess said, and a hand gently touched Sean's back, trying to help him sit up.

Sean arched away from the touch, hissing as his skin stung as though someone had slapped a bad sun burn on his back.

"Sorry." Kess removed his hand and held out a wooden mug of water. "You should drink—"

Snatching the mug, Sean guzzled down water, the lukewarm liquid a balm on his scorched throat. He'd never been so thirsty in his entire life.

"Slow down!" Kess urged. "You're going to—"

Sean vomited, the bile mixing with the water burning his throat even more.

"...throw up." Kess finished.

While Sean finished retching on his hands and knees, Kess grabbed the fallen mug and moved to fill it up from a bucket of water on the floor.

As soon as Sean spotted the bucket, he crawled to it and dunked his entire head in the water, drinking slowly this time. Then he flopped back onto the ground, his wet hair sticking to his face. He lay still, finally allowing his mind to catch up to his frantic body.

"Is he...alright?" Ayana's voice drifted through the brig.

"I'd say no," Kess said. He crouched over Sean and gently peeled some wet hair out of Sean's eyes. "Sean?"

"Gods." Even the one word stung his throat, and he wasn't sure if it was from the blood boiling itself, or from screaming. "That...was unpleasant."

Kess's concerned face wavered in and out of Sean's blurred vision. "How are you feeling?"

"Bad," he rasped.

"I should have asked, *what* are you feeling?" Kess amended. "Is there anything I can do to help?"

Sean sat up gingerly, his head swimming and his entire body raw. With trembling hands, he took the mug from Kess again, dipped it in the bucket and slowly sipped the water. "Sunburned. On the inside. So thirsty."

Nausea also cramped his stomach and a headache pounded behind his eyes. All he wanted to do was lay back down and sleep for a month. But that was too much to say, and how could Kess really help him anyway?

"You're severally dehydrated," Kess said, but Sean didn't need medical training to have guessed that himself.

"I'm sorry," Ayana spoke up again.

She sat near her cell door, clinging to the bars. By the torch's light, he could see tears swimming in her eyes.

"I swear, I don't know why this is happening. I don't know what's in the chest or why this woman wants it. Up until a few days ago, I didn't even know about the chest."

Sean didn't have the strength to answer, but he believed her. He *had* to, had to believe that Emery's own sister hadn't betrayed them, that Emery herself hadn't betrayed him.

"She's telling the truth, Sean," Kess said gently.

Sean realized they'd both mistaken his silence for disbelief.

"Alright," he managed to say.

Ashborne's last words echoed in his head. *This round is for my father.*

He didn't understand what that meant. *Her* father had killed *his* parents. That's what Billy had always told him. But it sounded like Ashborne wanted revenge for her father. Why?

The longer he was awake, the worse he felt. His headache intensified with every minute. His stomach was twisting to the point he thought he may vomit again. And his body felt so weak, simply holding the mug and lifting it to his chapped lips was a tremendous chore.

"How did...that old man...know all that?" Sean managed to ask.

"Ashborne called him a Watcher," Ayana said. "Some elemists are skilled enough to be able to use the wind as eyes and watch things from far away. Perhaps he's one of them. Perhaps he was watching you at the cemetery."

Kess sat back on his heels, rubbed his hands over his face. "God, what do we do? How do we get out of this?"

Sean sipped more water and closed his eyes against the spinning world, so that he wouldn't puke the water right back up again. He didn't have any answers. If escaping had been difficult before, it would be impossible now in his state. Lying hadn't worked. Telling the truth hadn't worked. All they could really do was wait and pray to the gods someone would rescue them soon, before they all ended up like the corpse still rotting on the floor.

THEY CAME FOR AYANA NEXT. Though they tried a different tactic this time.

Sean woke to the thump of boots, the squeal of hinges, and shouting. He didn't remember passing out again, but he must have.

"Let go of me!" Ayana shrieked.

Ashborne stood outside the cells, watching as two of her

lackeys entered Ayana's cell and yanked her to her feet. Even with her injured leg, Ayana kicked and clawed and bit anything she could reach, but she was small and hurt and alone. The two lackeys barely noticed as they dragged her out of the cell towards the stairs leading to the brig.

"Leave her alone!" Kess shouted, reaching through the bars for Ayana's outstretched hand and missing by a hair as she was dragged past.

Sean crawled to the bars too, and managed to croak, "What are you doing? She doesn't know anything!"

Ashborne shrugged. "Perhaps. Perhaps not. But maybe you'll be more inclined to give me answers when you're imagining all the things I'm going to allow my crew to do to her. Perhaps Torra can have fun with her whip."

And with that, they were gone, leaving Sean and Kess alone in the brig to listen to Ayana's fading screams.

THEN SHE CAME for him again.

She came alone this time and crouched in front of the cell door. "Are you ready to tell the truth yet?"

"I *am* telling the truth," Sean snapped.

She smirked. "You know, you're making this more fun for me. I've been waiting to get my hands on you for years. How delightful this worked out for me so well."

Sean glared, because once again, he didn't understand. "What do I have to do with your father?"

Fury flared across her expression. "Your parents killed my father."

"Your father killed my parents!"

"Can't both be true?" she asked. And then she boiled his blood.

Again.

And again.

He burned and boiled and broiled from the inside out until he lost consciousness. He'd wake up sometime later, drenched in sweat, his entire body aching, with Kess worriedly fussing over him and Ayana still gone. And then she'd come for him again. Until one time, he woke not to Kess's concerned face, but to his sister's scowling one.

"Lily?" he rasped from where he lay curled on his side, his throat raw and shredded.

His sister crouched in front of him and pushed his damp hair from his eyes. Her hands where so cold, which may have felt nice on his fevered skin if the fact that he could feel her touching him wasn't extremely concerning.

"Look at the mess you've gotten yourself into," she said.

Sean blinked, wondering if he was somehow mistaking Grace for Lily again. Had they come to rescue them? Was Emery here too? But no amount of blinking or squinting would morph Lily's face into Grace's.

It was definitely his sister. But that was impossible.

"What are you doing here?" he choked out.

She sat back, shrugging, her golden braid falling over one shoulder as always. "You seem to be dying, big brother. And I'm already dead. Perhaps we're in Limbo."

Sean could only stare at her, at the tanned face that was shaped so much like his own. He'd seen her so many times since she'd died. Standing just behind the rigging aboard the *Audacity*. Lingering in the shadowy corner of his cabin. Standing at the edges of taverns. Always watching him, always condemning him. But she'd never spoken to him before, never touched him. And she'd never appeared without the hole blasted through her head.

He'd known she wasn't *really* there before. But now...

Too many words crowded Sean's tongue. There were so many things he wanted to say that he couldn't seem to get out. Finally, he managed a hoarse, "I'm sorry."

"Yeah, I know," she said, waving her hand as if to swat away his apology. "I've heard you say it a thousand times." She leaned forward, her green eyes flashing. "But Sean, if you're sorry, why are you letting this happen again?"

Sean shook his head with confusion but regretted it immediately as his skull throbbed. "What?"

She had been scowling before, but her expression twisted into something even angrier. "You need to leave Emery alone."

Sean went completely still, his stomach sinking.

"You already got me killed, big brother. And you're going to get her killed too," Lily said. "You *know* this. And yet, you're still holding on to her."

"I can protect her." His croaky voice held none of the conviction he tried for.

Lily laughed, a cruel, humorless sound that bounced around the brig. "Like you protected me? That worked out well, didn't it?"

His chest caved in, and he couldn't breathe. "I'm sorry, Lily. I've never forgiven myself. I never will—"

"Really?" she interrupted. "Because I seem to remember you laughing and smiling a lot at the festival, big brother. I was there, but you didn't even notice me this time. You were so *happy*." Her eyes flashed again, the coldness in them like nothing he'd ever seen on her face while she lived. "How can you be happy while I'm *dead*? You're forgetting about me."

Sean tried to dredge up any words of defence. But his chest was so tight, he couldn't draw a full breath to speak. She was right.

Lily stood up, towering over him. "You were happy. You let your guard down for five minutes, and look what happened? You nearly got her killed. Again. Maybe she is dead. We don't know, do we?"

Squeezing his eyes shut, Sean tried to block out her words, but each one hit his tight chest like a bullet. He'd been trying so hard not to imagine where Emery was, whether she'd been hurt or captured or killed. He'd been trying so hard not to let panic overwhelm him.

"It's only dumb luck that she's not above deck right now

instead of her sister. Only the gods know what's happening to her up there," Lily said.

"*Stop!*" Sean shouted, pain ripping through his throat. "I know all of this. I *know*."

When he opened his eyes again, Lily just stared down at him coldly. "Then make better choices, big brother. Don't be the cause of any more death."

"Lily—"

But Lily swept around, stepping straight through the cell bars. She glanced over her shoulder once, and Sean recoiled at the gruesome hole in her face where her eye should have been. She vanished into the hull, but not before saying one last thing, the words echoing around the brig: "Let her go, Sean. Let her go."

Chapter Thirty-Nine

Reminders of Sean were everywhere aboard the *Audacity*. The helm looked wrong without him standing next to it, the bowsprit empty without him sitting on its edge. His absence was like a heavy presence, a phantom intent on haunting the crew for every moment he was gone.

Nowhere was more haunted than his captain's quarters. Emery felt his absence there like a physical blow every time she set foot in his cabin, and yet, it was where she was forced to spend most of her time. It was the only place where she could hide from the glares and stares of the crew. They'd left her mostly alone since she'd returned without their captain, but whatever comradery she'd created with them seemed to have burned away like fog in the sun.

At first, she helped sail the *Audacity* just as she had this past month. But their gazes burned holes in the back of her head, and she could taste the bitter distrust in the air. They took over her jobs, so she had nothing to do, and soon, she felt like she was just in the way. Like an outsider.

She wasn't afraid of them. She knew they would never harm her, although Cam was a bit of a wild card. But Sean could be dead or dying and it was because of her, and she could feel the blame. After the first few days of silent glares, Emery found it harder and harder to keep her chin up, to keep her shoulders from sagging with guilt. Eventually, she couldn't bear it any longer, and retreated to the cabin.

Turning the compass Sean had given her over and over in her hands, she sat in the chair behind his desk, and it felt wrong. But it was better than lying in the bed where she still smelled his scent. Still felt his weight beside her like he was only a finger's breadth away, instead of only the gods knew how far away.

She tried not to look at the bed, or the bookshelves, or the spot on the floor where he'd been sleeping the past few months. It didn't leave many remaining places to look, and she found herself staring at a crinkled, blank piece of parchment sitting on the desk. Judging by the way it had been uncrunched, and the dirt smudges along its edges, Emery could guess it was the parchment from the chest. She couldn't fathom why Sean had bothered to keep it.

It seemed to taunt her, to flaunt her failures in her face. She'd asked Sean to sail all the way to that Isle, to face skeletal monsters and to desecrate a grave, all for nothing. She'd asked him to risk going to Audrye, to face varens and put himself in danger once again, all for nothing. And now...

She couldn't let herself imagine what he might be enduring at that very moment, what the varens might be doing to him. She'd seen him locked away in cells before, beaten bloody and barely conscious. It was too easy to conjure the images in her mind now. So, she stared at the parchment, willing her mind to go blank.

"That was some powerful elemental manipulation you did back there in the university," Grace mused, making Emery jump.

Grace was perched on the edge of the bed, sewing patches onto some of Sean's old clothes. She was no sailor and couldn't do much to help on deck even if she wanted to, so she'd been trying to stay out of the way. But she'd been so bored cooped up in the cabin that she'd been desperate for something to do. She'd wandered his cabin, perusing some of Sean's books and scouring his maps. Emery had to fight the urge to shout at her to leave his things alone. She knew this was Grace's way of stemming her own panic. This is why she also didn't protest when Grace had thrown open the wardrobe doors and stared into it.

She'd sighed and closed her eyes, standing still for so long, Emery had to ask, "What are you doing?"

"I'm having a moment of silence for all the beautiful clothes we left behind in Audrye," Grace said. Though her tone was airy, Emery knew her friend was truly grieving. She'd loved Audrye, and now she would likely never be able to go back.

And so, when Grace had pulled out some of Sean's frayed tunics to mend, Emery said nothing.

Now, Grace peered at Emery with her head canted to the side, as if Emery was a new problem to solve. "You said your abilities first surged when saving yourself and Sean from Tavor?"

Emery blinked, caught off guard by the random questions. "Yes."

"And then between then and your next encounter with Tavor, you hadn't been able to do much?"

"That's right," Emery said. "Why?"

Grace shrugged. "We've always been taught that the more we hewn our emotions, the easier it is to control our abilities. But you seem to have better control when you're feeling a lot of emotions, like fear."

Emery thought back to both moments when her abilities had really surged, and she was able to control the elements so easily. "I don't know if I had better control, but I could certainly do more. And my prominent emotion both times wasn't fear; it was anger."

And protectiveness maybe.

"Interesting," Grace said. "Think of what you could do if you really channeled that anger."

Emery just sighed. She truthfully didn't have the mental capacity to contemplate such things, especially her possible anger issues. She glared at the blank piece of paper again.

"What are you staring so hard at?" Grace hopped off the bed

to stand next to Emery. She quirked a brow at the blank parchment and flipped it over to its equally blank other side.

"Riveting stuff," she said, eyeing Emery with a hint of worry.

"It's the paper we found in the chest," Emery explained.

"Oh! May I?"

Without waiting for Emery's shrug of indifference, Grace snatched up the parchment and perched on the chair opposite the desk. She flipped the parchment over and over, inspecting its two blank sides, its four rumpled edges, its four curled corners.

"Interesting," Grace murmured, flattening the parchment on the desk and bringing her eyes level with it.

"What is possibly interesting?" Emery asked, leaning back in her chair. Her eyes were heavy but she didn't want to sleep. Not in Sean's bed. Not without him.

"Its mere existence is interesting," Grace said, carefully stroking the parchment with a dainty finger, then picking it up and folding it into squares.

Emery watched her with bemusement, not for the first time wishing she could see inside Grace's head to see how it worked.

Grace experimented with the parchment for hours with a single-minded concentration and determinedness only she possessed. It went on for so long, Emery eventually dozed off in the chair, but awoke when the cabin door burst open, slamming against the wall. She sat up so quickly, her neck cricked.

"Damn," Grace swore as her own flinch caused her to tear the parchment slightly in one corner. But then her eyebrows rose, and she began ripping the parchment a little more, inspecting its fibers. She didn't even glance at the door.

But Emery looked up with a hammering heart, certain it was either Ranit coming to tell her they'd found Sean or Cam coming to drive an ax into Emery's chest. But instead, Smythee skipped through the door with a wide smile on his weathered face.

Emery stood. "Smythee?"

She'd never seen him enter Sean's cabin before and wasn't sure what to do. Was he allowed in there? Should she shoo him away?

The old man did not seem to be in a lucid state, which was normal for him. He was usually seven pieces short of eight, or so Rooney liked to say.

Smythee sang, "He burns, he boils! He breaks and he broils!"

"What's that now?" Grace finally looked over her shoulder, squinting at the old man as if he was another puzzle.

Emery sighed. "It's just Smythee. He's not quite...all there."

"Hmm." Grace hummed and returned her attention back to the parchment.

Smythee smiled wide, his mismatched eyes full of mirth and insanity. "Burn it like he burns!" he sang again. "Lemons and flames, flames and lemons."

It was then Emery noticed Smythee had a wedge of lemon stuffed in one ear. He tottered over to the desk, yanked the lemon from his ear, and placed it directly on the parchment.

"Burn!" He screeched, and then laughed, heading back out the door and slamming it shut again, leaving Emery and Grace in a stunned silence.

Grace snatched the fruit from the parchment before it could do damage. She paused, blinked. "Could it be so simple?"

She swiped the parchment from the desk and turned to hold it over the landtern's flame.

"What are you doing?" Emery asked, alarmed, even though she should hardly care about the blank paper.

"Wait," Grace commanded. She slowly, carefully, lowered the parchment towards the flames, but not quite close enough for the parchment to catch fire. "Look!"

Emery leaned forward, her eyes widening as black marks began to appear on the parchment as if by magic.

A series of numbers.

"How?" Emery breathed.

"Lemon juice reacts to heat," Grace said distractedly as she removed the paper from the flame to read the numbers. "I need maps!"

Emery hurried to the drawer where Sean kept his maps and charts, and pulled them all out, not sure what Grace needed exactly. As soon as she placed them on the desk, Grace rummaged through them until she found what she was looking for. She scoured the map. Emery knew better then to ask her anything while she worked, so she waited until—

"Hah! I knew it. They're coordinates!" Grace pointed to a spot on the map. "And they lead here."

Emery followed Grace's finger to a tiny, unnamed island in the north.

"I knew it had to be a clue!" Grace cried, the high of solving a puzzle shining in her eyes.

"Well done, Grace." Emery's mind whirred.

Another puzzle. Another destination.

But where did it lead? And to what?

And most importantly, did Emery even care anymore?

Chapter Forty

It took all of Sean's strength just to open his eyes. His vision swam in and out of focus. Kess's worried face hovered over him as usual. But this time there was also the sensation of a cool, damp weight on his forehead, on his chest and arms. When Sean glanced down at his body, he realized Kess had laid wet cloths upon his fevered skin. Sean distantly wondered where Kess found cloths, until he realized his friend was now shirtless.

There was no sign of Lily.

Something else seemed off about Kess this time. As he wrung out another cloth in the water bucket to swap with the one on Sean's forehead, Kess wouldn't meet Sean's gaze. Not even when he handed Sean a mug of water.

Sean's stomach clenched with renewed fear. "Ayana?"

Kess shook his head, concern creasing his brow. "She hasn't returned."

"How long has it been?"

"I don't know. A day or two maybe?"

Sean sat up only far enough to sip his water, forcing himself to drink slow lest he vomit again. "What's wrong?"

"You mean excluding being locked in a brig while watching

my friend get tortured and wondering what is happening to my other friend?"

"Yes," Sean said simply, his throat too raw to utter anything further.

Finally, Kess looked at Sean properly and his eyes were dark with despair. "You... You were talking while you were unconscious. You sounded delirious. But...you said Lily's name. A lot."

His sister's name on Kess's lips felt like a gut punch to his already roiling stomach. "Oh."

Gods, what did he overhear?

How can you be happy while I'm dead?

Lily's words pierced his memories like blades.

Don't be the cause of any more death.

He scanned Kess's face, searching for hatred or disgust or horror, any sign that Kess had heard and now knew what Sean had done. But all he saw was grief and...guilt?

"Sean, I'm sorry. I'm so sorry," Kess blurted.

Sean could only blink at his friend for a moment. "What?"

"I know you hate me. And I get it. I understand." Silver lined Kess's eyes. "But you need to know how sorry I am. And I swear, I never betrayed you."

The words rolled through Sean's sluggish brain like slush, making about as much sense to him as the old language of Jokul. "Betrayed me?"

"I didn't! I swear, I didn't. I didn't know I was being watched in Ruhette. I had no idea!" Kess sounded frantic now, desperate for Sean to believe him. "And I have no idea how Tavor knew you were in Audrye."

Sean slowly shook his head, trying to clear it enough to understand. That thought had never occurred to him. Not once. He wished his throat wasn't so raw, so ruined. All he could manage was, "I know that."

But Kess couldn't seem to stop now. A tear slid down his cheek. "You can hate me forever. I deserve it. I hate myself for what happened. I—"

Sean rested aching fingers on Kess's wrist, the only way he could think to calm Kess down without raising his voice. "Kess," he said, the word full of disbelief. "I don't hate you."

Kess froze, staring at Sean's fingers on his wrist. "You don't?"

"No." Sean cleared his throat, wincing at the pain. "How could you think that?"

Kess looked panicked again. "You stopped writing. You don't visit. The whole time you were in Audrye, you barely looked at me, barely even spoke to me. Like you couldn't stand to be around me."

A lump formed in Sean's aching throat, making it even harder to speak. He hadn't realized that Kess was mistaking Sean's own guilt, his own inability to face his own demons, as hatred.

"Gods, Kess." Sean gently pinched the bridge of his nose, a new headache forming behind his eyes. He tried to choose his words carefully. "I didn't write or visit because I didn't know what to say. I can't look at you...because when I do, I'm reminded of everything you've lost and everything I took from you."

Kess's stared at him, frowning in bewilderment. "Sean, you've given me *everything*! If it weren't for you, I never would have been able to go to medical school. I'd never have the life I have now."

"Aye, a life without Lily. Because of me."

"Sean, I—"

Sean closed his eyes, not wanting to see Kess's expression. "It was my fault, Kess. I killed Lily."

There. He finally said it. After an entire year of fearing this moment, of dreading this moment when he would see the hatred clouding his best friend's eyes, he felt oddly numb. Even so, he kept his eyes shut. He still didn't want to see.

Emery had tried to tell him he was wrong, that it wasn't his fault. And for a little while, he'd even believed her. Long enough that he allowed happiness to trickle into his life, and then that life fell apart all over again.

After a moment of silence, Sean finally opened his eyes. Kess's face was horrified but there was no hatred in it, no anger. Not yet. "What happened?" he asked.

"Tavor forced me to choose between Lily and my crew." Sean tried to continue, to once again confess how he'd stayed silent and let Tavor shoot Lily through the eye. But his voice gave out. He tasted copper and ash, and when he coughed into his hand, specks of crimson dotted his palm.

Kess noticed, his eyes growing wide. "Sean, it wasn't—"

But whatever he was going to say was cut off by the brig door flying open once again. Ashborne was back.

Every other time she'd returned to torture him, the sight of her had sent his heart shuddering and his stomach shriveling. But this time, Sean felt nothing at all, like his body and soul were drained.

He just sat there and braced himself. Wondered if he'd even survive another round of blood boiling, or if this time, his body would finally give up.

"Alright, boys. This has been fun, but the party is over. Up you get," Ashborne ordered.

She opened their cell door and Jaro and Ace stepped inside.

"What is this?" Kess demanded, and to Sean's surprise, he stepped in front of Sean, as if intent on protecting him.

"I'm growing weary of our games," Ashborne drawled. "We're going to try something else now."

She snapped her fingers and Jaro lunged for Kess. Kess struggled, but he was not a fighter, and in the end, the huge man wrenched Kess's arms behind his back and marched him from the cell.

Sean didn't fight when Ace grabbed his bicep and hauled him to his feet. He couldn't. The skin under the man's tight grip screamed. The world lurched as he was dragged from the cell and up the stairs. He stumbled, fighting not to vomit. The only reason he didn't collapse was because the man hauling him was basically keeping him upright.

The sunlight pierced his eyes, making them water and lose

precious hydration his body couldn't stand to lose much more of. He blinked rapidly, everything too crisp and bright after so long in the darkness, a blur of colours he couldn't decipher. The man shoved him down, slamming his back against something hard. His arms were forced behind his back and his wrists bound in rope. He was being tied to the mizzenmast. Anywhere his skin made contact was agony.

"Fancy seeing you here."

Sean blinked harder, forcing his vision to clear faster, at least as much as it could. Ayana was tied to the mast next to him. Excluding a wicked sun burn on her face and chest, she looked mostly uninjured.

"Are you alright?" Sean choked.

"Yeah. She just left me to bake in the sun for a few days. But no one touched me." She squinted at him, as if also having a hard time focusing her vision. She was probably suffering from heat stroke. "Are you alright?"

Sean didn't answer, partly because the answer was definitely no, and partly because he realized Kess wasn't tied to the mast with them. He looked around frantically, finally locating Ashborne standing by the starboard railing. Jaro held Kess there too.

Ashborne was gazing at Sean, her head tilted almost admirably. "I must say, Denzel, perhaps your fierce reputation is warranted after all. You're tough. Lesser men would have folded already. But I'm afraid if we continue with our game any longer, you will die. A body can only take so much, no matter how tough you are. And I can't have you taking my information to your grave." She turned to eye Kess. "If your own torture doesn't warrant the spilling of secrets, perhaps watching the torture of a friend will."

Ashborne snapped her fingers and Torra stepped forward with a length of rope. Jaro held a squirming Kess in place as Torra bound Kess's wrists and ankles, smiling like a kid on her birthday. She even sang. "I just love a good keelhauling!"

Sean's fevered body suddenly turned to ice. "No!" he croaked.

Ashorne sent him a wicked grin. "Yes. We'll be dragging your friend under the ship, over and over, until you give me your answers. Or until he drowns, bleeds to death, or the sharks scent him out. Hard to say which will happen first."

"I don't understand," Ayana whispered.

Torra heard her. "You've never seen a keelhauling before? The barnacles on the hull will slice him to ribbons. If he can hold his breath long enough."

"Please," Sean begged. There was nothing left for him to do now. "I've told you everything, I swear."

"We'll see." Ashborne nodded at Jaro.

Jaro climbed onto the railing, pulling Kess along by the ropes bound to his wrists.

"Any last words?" Ashorne asked Kess.

Behind Ashborne, Lily appeared perched on the railing, her ruined eye on full display. She looked mournfully at Kess, and then glared at Sean.

No one else saw her.

Kess looked straight at Sean, his expression hard, determined. "Lily wasn't your fault. Neither is this."

"He's wrong. It's all your fault," Lily said.

No one else heard her.

The breath rushed from Sean's lungs, fear making it hard to draw it back in. "Ashborne, I don't know anything more. There must be another way I can prove it."

Ashborne simply shrugged and nodded at Jaro. The huge man moved to shove Kess into the water, but the old, bearded man—the Watcher—stepped towards Ashborne and whispered in her ear. She shot up a hand. "Wait!"

Jaro grabbed Kess's rope, stopping him from falling backwards into the water, Kess's heels hanging precariously over the railing.

"It seems we have guests arriving earlier to the party than I expected." Ashborne looked towards the east, and Sean followed her gaze.

The *Audacity*'s crimson sails fluttered on the horizon, the ship heading straight for them. And Sean didn't know whether to be relieved at the sight, or terrified.

291

Chapter Forty-One

Dawn had barely broken when Farley spotted the ship on the horizon. Emery and Grace heard the shouts from inside the cabin and raced outside, joining the rest of the crew as they gathered near the bow to watch the vessel grow as they drew closer.

The ship was anchored, its sails furled, and it bobbed languidly on the sea's surface as if waiting for them. The *Audacity* approached slowly and, eventually, the name painted on the hull became legible.

Crimson Vengeance.

"The Red Reaper?" Rooney sucked in a breath as he stared through his telescope.

Emery peered at the strange ship through her own telescope, her heart thundering somewhere in her throat, confusion roaring in her head.

"He's on deck," Farley shouted down from the crow's nest. "I can see him."

Cam rounded on Emery and Grace. "You said *varens* took Sean."

Emery refused to take a step back. "We thought they did."

"We told you; we didn't see who took them," Grace added,

obviously already tired of Cam. "But logically, varens made the most sense."

"True, because why would the Red Reaper take Sean from Audrye?" Rooney asked, accusation lacing his words as he glared down at Emery.

Her temper sparked, nerves already too on edge. "I don't know, Rooney. You are the Forbiddens; you tell me!"

The words tasted of regret even as they flew from her mouth, but to her surprise, Rooney simply cocked a brow, as if ceding to the point.

"Who even is the Red Reaper?" she asked.

"A ruthless Forbidden," Rooney said. "Ashborne."

Emery's stomach dropped to her feet,

Ashborne.

Some of the most notorious Forbiddens on the high seas.

One of the reason humans continued to hate elemists so much.

Murderer of so many, including Sean's own parents.

Suddenly, Rooney's anger and horror made more sense. Why *would* the Red Reaper take Sean, Ayana, and Kess?

"What do we do?" It was little Seadar who asked. He wrung his hands in front of him, staring at the ship with wide eyes.

"We attack, obviously," Cam said, yanking an ax from her belt.

"We don't, obviously," Ranit countered. "We can't attack blindly. Not until we know what we're up against and not until we know exactly where our captain and the others are on the ship."

So, they continued to approach slowly. Emery swept her telescope across the deck again, hoping to spot someone familiar. Farley had the best eyesight out of everyone and was always able to see things first. So far, Emery hadn't spotted anything. But then her gaze snagged on a woman with blood red hair, the colour like a beacon. Her posture was almost that of boredom as she leaned her elbows against the railing and watched the *Audacity* approach.

Next, Emery spotted Kess, bound by rope and standing on the ship's railing. The huge man gripping the other end of the rope seemed to be the only thing keeping him from plummeting into the ocean below. Relief and fear waged war in her belly at the sight of Kess like that. It was a precarious position indeed, but he was alive, and looked relatively unharmed, at least.

Emery's breath caught as she spotted her sister next. She sat against the mizzenmast, her curls wild and face aglow with what looked like a sunburn. She looked alert and alive and very, very angry. Emery's breath whooshed out of her completely when she finally spied Sean. He, too, was tied to the mizzenmast, only his whole body was slumped against it, as if he couldn't sit up straight. Emery couldn't spot any outward injuries on him, at least not from such a distance, but she knew in her heart that something was wrong.

After what felt like an eternity, the *Audacity* drifted up beside the *Crimson Vengeance*. A flurry of activity ensued as the crew furled the sails and threw grappling hooks to connect the ships and keep them from floating apart. And then all motion stopped.

"Welcome to the party," the redheaded woman waved and smiled, as if they had indeed just arrived at some sort of festivity and she was their host. "We were just about to enjoy a little keel-hauling. Glad you could join us."

"Kind of you to offer, but we'd prefer not to take part," Ranit replied. "We'd like our captain and people back, and we'll be on our way."

"Who is it I'm speaking to? Clearly, you aren't the captain, given he's currently"—she glanced over her shoulder at Sean—"tied up at the moment."

"My name is Ranit. I am the Scourge of the Sea's first mate. And whilst I always appreciate a good pun, we do not appreciate having our captain taken from us and held hostage for seemingly no reason," Ranit said. His voice and expression were hard, fierce even, completely at odds with the jovial version of Ranit that Emery was used too.

"Ah, believe me, I have my reasons," the woman said. "And don't you want to know my name?"

"You're the Red Reaper, I'm guessing," Ranit said. "And the only thing I want to know is why you kidnapped my people unprovoked."

Ashborne's smile remained, but the quality had changed. It seemed a predator's grin now. "It was not unprovoked. You stole from me, and I want what was taken back."

Ranit said nothing for a moment, clearly confused. But then he shrugged. "We're pirates. We steal from a lot of people. Perhaps if you tell us what you're missing, we can return it. That is, if we still have it."

"I want my chest," Ashborne demanded.

Ranit exchanged exaggerated glances and shrugs with the crew. "My apologies. There are no stolen chests here."

"That's her!" Someone suddenly shouted from the *Crimson Vengeance*. "She was the other one at the cemetery that night."

A woman with dark hair and angular eyes like Ranit's pointed straight at Emery. Emery fought not to shrink inward as both crews swiveled their heads to look at her. She stared at the woman pointing at her, and realized she'd seen her before.

The graverobber. And she realized what chest the woman was referring to. But how did this woman possibly know about it? And what did she want with it? Emery was tired of games. She just wanted answers. She turned her attention to Ashborne, who was already eyeing her with interest.

Emery's pulse raced.

Why on Teralyn's Teeth would an Ashborne want a chest hidden by her parents?

Emery swallowed down her fear. "There was nothing in the chest but rocks and a piece of parchment."

"Hmm, the same story your dear captain gave us." Ashborne turned to look at Sean, who was breathing quickly and shallowly. Was it from fear, Emery wondered, or something else? "My apologies, Denzel. Perhaps you weren't lying after all." She whipped back around, all but snarling at Emery. "Now, are you going to tell me the parchment is blank too?"

Emery considered whether she should lie, but in the end, she didn't see a reason to. If Ashborne wanted the parchment and whatever it led to, so be it. If it meant getting Sean, Ayana, and Kess back, Emery would wrap it up with a neat bow for her. "It was blank. It's not anymore."

"And what's on it?" Ashborne said, suddenly standing perfectly still.

"Coordinates. And I will give them to you in exchange for our people."

"I want the original parchment," Ashborne said.

"Fine." Emery glanced at Grace, who immediately rushed to the cabin. Moments later, she returned with the parchment rolled in her fist.

Ashborne eyed the parchment, eyes flashing eagerly. "That's the original?"

"Yes," Emery said.

"Are there copies?"

"No."

Ashborne swept a calculating gaze over Emery, as if assessing her honesty. Ashborne then turned to an ancient looking man standing next to her and whispered something in his ear. The man seemed to stare at absolutely nothing for a moment before nodding once.

"We have an accord. Give me the parchment," Ashborne said.

"Give us our people first," Ranit broke in once again.

Ashborne donned an exaggerated pout. "Don't you trust me?"

"Absolutely, I do not."

"Fine. Take them. They've served their purpose." She absently waved her hand. The man still clutching Kess's rope grumbled but pulled Kess off the railing and began untying him. Someone else released Ayana's and Sean's bindings from the mizzenmast. As soon as Kess was free, he rushed over to them.

He pulled Ayana to her feet, swinging one of her arms over his shoulders. Sean used the mast to climb to his feet, swaying dangerously. Kess tried to reach for him too, but Ashborne stepped between them.

"Please, allow me." Before Sean could pull away, she threaded her elbow through his, pulling him to her side, and began striding across the deck, as if she were helping an elderly person go for a stroll. She whispered into his ear.

Sean gritted his teeth but didn't struggle.

"I do apologize. I don't think your captain is feeling well," Ashborne remarked. "I may have a little to do with that."

Indeed, Sean's complexion was a peculiar mix of red, white, and green. He blinked rapidly as if trying to clear his vision.

Emery, Grace, and Ranit met them where the ships' hulls touched.

Kess helped Ayana over the railing onto the *Audacity's* deck. Grace took her from him and backed up, allowing Ranit to step up to help Kess over himself.

But Ashborne did not release Sean's elbow. "You have two parts of your trade back. You'll get the third when I get my parchment."

"Don't you trust me?" Ranit mocked, but he did not put on a pout. His face was still hard.

Ashborne smiled. "Absolutely, I do not."

Having already taken the parchment from Grace, Emery handed it over the railing. When Ashborne grabbed it, Emery's fingers hesitated to release their hold for only a moment. Not because she wanted the parchment. No amount of treasure was worth Sean's life. No number of answers either. She'd rather spend the rest of her life wondering what happened to her parents, then have his blood on her hands and his presence absent. But she couldn't help wondering what, exactly, she was handing over to this monster.

Ashborne carefully unrolled the parchment, her eyes scanning the coordinates and lighting up with success. "Fine. You can have him."

She shoved Sean forward. Emery and Ranit both lunged to catch him and help him clamber over the railing. He was still shirtless, and his skin was hot to the touch, almost feverish, and even when he was upright again and Ranit released him, he still clung to Emery. But she didn't think it was any kind of romantic embrace. She suspected it was so he wouldn't collapse.

"Pleasure doing business with you." Ashborne tucked the parchment safely away in her coat pocket and turned, walking across the deck of her ship. So softly, Emery wasn't sure if she heard correctly, she said, "Kill them."

The deafening sound of dozens of weapons unsheathing rang across both ships.

"We had a deal!" Ranit growled, his own sword drawn.

"Yes, and the deal is over now." Ashborne whirled to face them again, leaning casually against the main mast with her arms folded. "I've got what I wanted. No need to keep any of you alive to muck up my plans."

Emery's heart hammered. They were so outnumbered. They'd never win. Even so, she reached for her lim. But Sean snatched her wrist. "No." He stepped forward, one hand up in surrender and the other moving from Emery's wrist to her shoulder, as if he needed the physical support. "WAIT!" His voice sounded awful, ragged and torn. "We can make another deal. Our lives for whatever you want."

Ashborne raised an intrigued brow, stroked the feather in her hat. "What could you possibly have that I'd want?"

Sean swallowed once, hard, as if bracing himself. "My ship."

A collective gasp rose across the *Audacity*. Emery's own eyes widened in shock.

"Sean, no! We can fight," she urged.

The *Audacity* was his home. His everything.

"No, we can't." Raising his voice, he continued to shout across to Ashborne. "Take the *Audacity* and let us—*all* of us—leave unharmed."

"Sean..." Ranit started, his voice full of horror.

Sean ignored him.

"Interesting." Ashborne strolled back to the joined railings, stroked a finger along the polished mahogany wood of the *Audacity's*. "She is pretty."

"And fast. And she has a reputation to match yours," Sean said. It was hard to tell with his hoarse voice, but Emery could hear the fear lacing his words. He was desperate to get them away from this woman, as desperate as Emery had ever seen him, and it caused fear to coarse through her too. What had she done to him?

"Sails dripped in blood," Ashborne said, looking up to admired said sails. "I do like a good legend. Not to mention, she matches my hair."

Sean didn't reply this time, only waited. Emery didn't know what else to do but wait as well, placing a hand on Sean's back to steady him when he began to sway again. He flinched at her touch.

"Fine," Ashborne said. "You have ten seconds to get off my new ship before my crew starts killing yours."

"Let us release the longboats—"

"That wasn't part of the deal, and now, you have eight seconds."

For a moment, no one moved, everyone likely too shocked by the sudden turn of events. Ashborne's crew remained poised to attack, and the *Audacity's* crew were braced for the fight.

"Seven," Ashborne said.

"GO!" Sean shoved Emery and Kess backward towards the ship's opposite railing. "GO!"

In a flurry of panic, the *Audacity's* crew raced for the nearest railing and leapt for the water. Someone slashed at the lines of the nearest longboat, releasing the small vessel into the ocean. Emery stumbled across the deck, Sean still holding on to her, his extra weight throwing her off balance. They climbed onto the railing together, but before they jumped into the sea, they both glanced back.

"Cam, no!" Sean cried.

Cam still stood in the center of the *Audacity*, axes drawn, staring down Ashborne and her crew. She shouted, "This ship is our home, and I will not let you take it!"

"Five seconds," Ashborne drawled.

Sean leapt back to the deck but fell to his knees on impact.

"Sean, stop!" Emery called after him.

"Cam, abandon ship!" Sean shouted with his ruined voice. "That's an order!"

"Three seconds."

Cam looked back at Sean, furious tears shining in her eyes. "You gave up your ship. You're not my captain anymore."

"Two."

Ashborne's crew slowly inched forward in anticipation.

Sean tried to stand only to fall again. "You'll die, Cam!"

"One."

The Forbiddens rushed forward like one giant beast with dozens of razor-sharp teeth. Emery didn't remember making the decision, only that she was suddenly sprinting for Cam. Cam raised her axes, bellowing a warrior's cry, oblivious to anything but the fight before her.

Emery yanked Cam backwards by her tunic, causing her to lose her balance and flail towards the railing. Before Cam could regain her footing, Emery tackled her around the middle, flinging them both over the railing.

The last thing Emery heard before plummeting into the ocean was Cam's outraged cry—and the last thing she saw was an ax flying at her face.

Chapter Forty-Two

Liam perched on the branch of a redwood tree overlooking the ocean, his back against the trunk, knees pulled up to his chest, and blessedly alone. The sun was setting on yet another tedious and torturous day in Orabel. As the sky burst into hues of reds, pinks and golds, Liam stared at the otherwise empty horizon, and couldn't believe both his sisters were out there somewhere while he was here.

He wondered if they'd found each other. He wondered if they were alright. And every time he wondered these things—which was a lot, because he didn't have much else to do these days—he considered doing exactly what Ayana did. He wanted to sail away in the dead of night. But he knew, now more than ever, the Arch-Elemists would never let that happen.

Liam had thought that once he'd reached home and told the Arch-Elemists everything, he'd feel safer, lighter, free from the burden of knowing his people were in danger and the not knowing what to do about it. But he didn't feel any of those things now. There was always a stone of dread sitting in his gut, and since the Arch-Elemists had made good on their promise to silence him, the stone had only grown. He'd never been one to worry before, but now, it seemed it was all he did.

Especially now that Aran was onto him.

He stared at the ocean and wondered if today was the day he'd finally spot Tavor's ship on the horizon, full of varens and weapons and the thirst to kill or capture them all. And he wondered if the Arch-Elemists would do anything about it.

"Liam?" a voice called from below, a voice that always made his heart stumble with too many mixed emotions. "Can I come up?"

Half of Liam wanted to say yes, because he'd missed Fia, and he was lonely and scared and wanted to talk to someone. But the other half wanted to say no, because even if he felt all those things and more, he couldn't tell her. And now, she knew something was wrong, and he didn't know how to lie about it anymore.

He didn't know what to say, and so, he said nothing at all, hoping Fia would decide for him.

She did. She didn't wait for a response, and instead, scaled the tree branches easily until she sat on the same thick branch as Liam, her legs swinging in the air over the cliffs and the waves below. She quietly gazed at the sunset, and Liam gazed at her, marveling at the way the sun's golden light made her hair glow like flames.

"Wow," Fia breathed. "Did you see any sunsets like this while you were gone?"

The dread in Liam's gut expanded a fraction. It was such an innocent question, but who knew what other questions it may lead to?

"Sure, the sun sets out there too," he said vaguely.

He couldn't see her face properly since it was angled away from him, towards the ocean, but he was certain she rolled her eyes. When she looked back at him, her face was serious. "You've been avoiding me."

Cutting right to the chase, it seemed.

"I was put on bed rest," Liam said. "Hard to do much socializing from a bed."

"You've been avoiding everyone."

"Again, bed rest," he said. He suppressed a yawn but rubbed at his eyes. He'd been awoken too many times the night before by nightmares, and the exhaustion weighed on him, along with the dread.

As he lowered his hand, Fia caught his wrist. The warmth of her fingers on him made him freeze with surprise. He looked up at her, but she wasn't looking at his face. She stared at his palm. At his brand.

"What is that?" she asked, flipping his hand so she could get a better look.

Liam yanked his hand back, closing his fist and wrapping his arms around his knees again. "Nothing. I accidentally burnt myself with gunpowder."

Fia narrowed her eyes. "That's a precise looking burn."

"It was a precise accident." Liam cursed himself for not noticing the strip of cloth he'd been wrapping his hand in had fallen off. He'd known if someone saw the brand, they'd ask unwanted questions, like Fia was now.

Her voice was full of genuine concern. "Liam, please tell me what that is."

He hated this. Hated that he couldn't tell her anything. Hated that she was the one person he wished he could tell everything.

"I told you: I was experimenting with gun powder and accidentally set off an explosion. I burned myself." This was at least partially true. He had burned himself when playing with gun powder. It just hadn't given him this particular burn.

Fia gazed at him, and he knew she didn't believe him. She tried to keep her face impassive, but Liam knew her too well. Knew the tiny furrow between her brows was borne from worry, and that the slight flush in her cheeks was from suppressed irritation. And the little extra shine in her eyes? That was hurt.

Liam swallowed down the guilt and the truth that wanted so badly to erupt from his lips.

Glancing back at the sinking sun, Fia said, "Caelin's doing it again."

Relief flared inside him. It seemed Fia had decided to let it all go for now. But the dread remained at the thought of Caelin. He hadn't seen his friend in a while either. Caelin had come to see him in his bed, and Liam had told him what had happened, warned him that the Arch-Elemists' threats were real. Caelin had been like a silent storm cloud, taking in Liam's words without saying anything himself, anger radiating off him. He'd been like that a lot since returning home, though they hadn't seen much of each other. They were afraid to talk to one another, unsure whether it was allowed. They'd kept to themselves, feeling it was safer.

"We should go to him," Fia said now. "I think he needs us."

Liam sighed, again unsure of what to say. Fia already noticed so much, including the fact that Liam and Caelin had barely been speaking, which was odd unto itself. She never asked why, but he knew if he refused to see Caelin now, she would. Not sure what to do, he unfolded himself so he could stand. "Lead the way."

She did, climbing down the tree and then leading them along the outskirts of the village so they wouldn't run into anyone else. But Fia also made sure they didn't wander too close to the bordering cliffs. Lately, he'd been told, they'd started crumbling away in places.

Liam heard Caelin before he saw him, heard the singing of metal through the air and the thunk of said metal hitting its target, heard Caelin's heaving breathing and grunts of exertion with every swing of his weapon.

They found him in a small clearing with a dead oak tree in the center. The leafless branches twisted in the air as if begging for mercy, but Caelin didn't give any. He swung his sword at the tree's already battered trunk with a furious speed, chipping away more and more of its wood.

This was how Caelin spent a lot of his time these days. He practiced with his sword, the very one Tavor had given him, until he dripped sweat, pummeling the tree until splinters littered the ground.

"I think you've won," Liam said, tucking his hands in his pockets and circling his friend and his wooden foe.

Caelin didn't respond, didn't even glance at Liam or Fia. He just kept slashing at the tree.

Fia just shook her head at Liam, and he shrugged, as if asking, *what do you want me to do?* Because he truly didn't know.

She stepped forward and he froze as she whispered in his ear, "If neither of you will talk about what happened out there, with me or anyone else, you should at least talk to each other."

"What are you talking about?" Liam asked, his dread growing once again.

"You two are my best friends. I know when you aren't telling me something, and you are *definitely* not telling me *many* some-things." She didn't look angry though. She looked sad. "And it's killing you both. I've never seen either of you like this. I don't know what happened out there, obviously, but talk to each other at least. Please."

And then she marched off, disappearing into the woods and leaving Liam and Caelin alone in the clearing.

Caelin had finally stopped his slashing to watch her go. Liam stood awkwardly, his hands still in his pockets. He'd never, in his entire lifetime of friendship with Caelin, felt awkward around him. But he felt awkward and nervous now. He was never good at talking about his feelings, and clearly Caelin was having big feelings. Plus, what if they said the wrong things. Would the Arch-Elemists choke him out again, even if he was only talking to Caelin about what happened?

But...Fia was right. He felt like he was slowly dying from his anxiety, from the dread. If the Arch-Elemists didn't kill him from talking about it, his own body might just shut down from *not* talking about it.

Liam waved towards the tree. "What's going on, Caelin?"

Caelin glanced at Liam now. "Can't a man train without there being something going on?"

"Well, there's training, and then there's murdering an inno-cent tree."

"The tree was already dead."

This was true enough. It was one of several trees on the island that had died as the Withering continued to spread. "Alright then. There's a difference between training and butchering a tree's corpse while running yourself down too."

Finally, Caelin lowered his sword, sighing. "What are you getting at, Liam?"

"I think Fia is right. I think we need to talk."

Caelin's throat bobbed, a flash of fear flicking across his expression. "I don't think that's a good idea."

"I think we need to."

Caelin didn't say anything.

"I'm scared, too," Liam confessed. "I'm scared all the time. I worry all the time. I worry about Ayana and Grace. I hate that they're out there and we're not, and I'm sure you feel the same way."

"I'm not worried about them." At the look of surprise on Liam's face, Caelin amended. "I mean, of course I *worry*, and I miss them. But I also know those girls can take care of themselves. That's not why I'm angry."

"You're angry?" Liam wasn't sure why he asked it. Obviously, Caelin was angry. Liam was angry too.

"Of course, I'm angry!" Caelin suddenly exploded. "I'm angry that Tavor betrayed us. I'm angry that the one person like me, someone I was finally able to relate to, turned out to be a monster. I'm angry that the Arch-Elemists knew about this, let you get tortured, and yet, won't do anything about the fact that Tavor could show up at any minute to kill us all. I'm angry they almost killed *you*—"

"Did you say *tortured?*"

Liam and Caelin both whirled towards the trees. Fia stood there, her face white and aghast, her hands pressed against her mouth.

Liam's jaw fell open as realization dawned on him. Fia had orchestrated this conversation not only to try to help them—

because he was certain that was at least part of her motivation—but also to finally learn the truth.

"The Arch-Elemists tried to kill you?" She gasped as realization hit her too. "You were trying to tell me, weren't you? They stopped you..."

Liam didn't know what to do, what to say. She'd heard so much, and yet, no one was having the air sucked from their lungs yet. He swallowed hard, and nodded once, confirming both her questions.

Horror and rage chased each other across her expression. "Let me get this straight. Tavor's promises weren't true. He tortured you. You somehow escaped. But he's still out there somewhere, and he obviously knows how to find us..."

Again, Liam nodded just once, too scared to open his mouth. Caelin just stared at Fia, his expression a mix of dread and awe.

"Where is Emery, then?" A look of terror rushed over her. "Is she alive?"

Again, Liam nodded.

"Fia," Caelin finally said, his voice quiet. "Stop. The Arch-Elemists forbade us from telling the truth."

Fia's face hardened. "Since when do you two follow the rules?"

Liam and Caelin exchanged a glance. When *did* he start following the rules? Probably after thinking his sister dead multiple times and nearly dying himself more than once. Probably after the people who were supposed to protect him betrayed him.

"Tavor never had a cure, did he?" Fia asked.

This time, Caelin slowly shook his head.

"And we're in danger, aren't we?"

He nodded.

Fia's mouth thinned, and then she turned and stormed back into the woods.

Liam and Caelin exchanged another confused glance before chasing after her.

"What are you doing?" Liam asked.

Fia shoved through the brush, her fiery hair streaming behind her. "You might not be allowed to talk, but I can."

"Fai, wait—" Caelin began.

But she cut him off. "Our people deserve to know we're in danger. They deserve to know what the Arch-Elemists have done. And I'm going to tell everyone."

Chapter Forty-Three

Sean watched from his knees as Emery tackled Cam straight off the deck of the *Audacity*, and they plummeted into the sea below, saving her from the mass of Forbiddens storming the ship. Momentarily stunned, he stared at the spot where Emery and Cam had disappeared over the railing, until he realized he was the only one of his crew left on deck, and the Forbiddens were storming towards him now.

It took all his strength to haul himself to his feet and fling himself backwards over the rail. The sea embraced him with her cool waters, swallowing sound, enveloping everything in a calming turquoise. For a moment, he allowed himself to float in the serene silence of the sea, resting his weary muscles and bones, cooling his fevered skin.

But, all too soon, he ran out of breath, and he broke the surface to find chaos. Ashborne's crew stood upon the *Audacity*'s deck, shouting obscenities and brandishing weapons. But they didn't make any more moves to attack. His crew was busy clambering into two separate longboats that they'd somehow managed to release during their hurried retreat.

Sean swam for the nearest boat, but he struggled to draw breath and his limbs were so, so tired. The waves shoved him farther away and the current sucked at his feet, pulling him back under.

But then Aleksy was there, hauling him back to the surface by his arm and helping him swim the short distance to the longboat. Rooney heaved him into the boat, and he dropped onto a seat, dripping and panting, quickly surveying who else had made it onto the same boat. Rooney helped Aleksy up after Sean. Farley, Seadar, Kess, and Billy were already crammed into the rest of the narrow seats.

In the other boat, Smythee cackled beside Ayana while Grace and Ranit pulled Cam and Emery out of the water.

Momentary relief flooded Sean's veins. Everyone was accounted for. Everyone was safe. They'd managed to escape that mad woman.

He slowly turned to watch as the *Audacity's* crimson sails filled with wind, as his ship turned her stern to them and began sailing away.

Ashborne stood on the afterdeck, grinning. When her eyes locked with Sean's, she raised her hand and waved. He knew he should feel fury or hatred or anguish or something, but he felt nothing at all as he watched his father's ship, his home, grow smaller on the horizon, now captained by the very family who had murdered his own.

Ashborne pointed to something behind him, her grin growing sharper. Sean didn't want to know, didn't want to turn, but he did anyway, and his numbness gave way to frigid dread. Another ship sailed on the horizon, heading straight for their longboats. It was only a few leagues away already, and Sean could see it too clearly.

Indigo sails, serpentine hull.

"Bloody damn," Rooney cursed, spotting the varen ship as well. At his exclamation, everyone in their cramped, little boat tracked his gaze, followed by a series of horrified gasps and exclamations.

"Gods, we can't catch a break—"

"Is it *him?*"

"Captain, what do we do?"

It was those last words that echoed in Sean's head.

What do we do what do we do what do we do.

They always expected him to have the answer. But this time, he didn't know. He thought he'd bought them time by offering up his ship. He thought he'd ensured their safety. But Ashborne must have spotted the varens before. She had never intended to let them live. This way, she could let the varens finish them off while she made her own escape.

What do we do what do we do what do we do.

What was there to do but wait?

Again.

It seemed like only seconds and the varen ship was upon them.

Varens spread out across the deck of the ship in their black and blue uniforms, the silver trimming on their jackets glinting in the sunlight alongside the muzzles of their guns.

Sean's pulse raced as he searched for any sign of Tavor among them, but he didn't see him.

"Well, if it isn't the Scourge brought low," one of the varens said, watching the *Audacity* retreat into the distance and clearly recognizing the crimson sails.

Sean said nothing, his exhausted mind racing through scenarios. Whether Tavor was aboard that ship or not, they could not let themselves be taken. But if they tried to fight, they'd be shot at and either paralyzed or killed immediately. They were literally sitting targets. Even if they did fight and, by some miracle, they got away, they wouldn't get far in their little boats.

What do we do what do we do what do we do.

"Kess?" One of the varens stepped up to the railing, peering down at the longboat for a better look. She was a woman, with golden skin and a braid of golden-brown hair. She looked vaguely familiar, but Sean couldn't place her.

"Melina?" Kess's face shifted from shock, to horror, to guilt, and Sean suddenly realized it was the woman who'd kissed Kess back in Audrye.

Grace leapt to her feet, rocking the longboat violently. "Melina, thank the gods! You must help us!"

Everyone turned to stare at Grace, expressions ranging from confusion to betrayal.

"Grace? Ayana?" Melina asked. "What are you doing out here?"

"The Scourge kidnapped us!" Grace cried, pointing straight at Sean. "But then his ship was boarded and commandeered by Ashborne. They thought we were part of his crew. We barely escaped alive. Please, get us off these boats!"

A stunned silence rippled across the ship and the longboats.

Sean could see realization dawning on the faces of some of his crew as they realized what Grace was doing, that she had a plan. But some of them still looked confused, angry.

"Shut your mouth!" Cam screeched, launching herself across the longboat towards Grace. Ranit attempted to yank her back again.

But it was too late. Gunshots sounded and paralyzing darts flew. One struck Cam between the shoulders, another hit Ranit in his outstretched arm. Both of them slumped immediately.

And suddenly, Sean was starting down the barrels of a dozen pistols.

He leapt to his feet again, his hands raised. "STOP!" he shouted, at the varens, at his crew, at everyone.

He knew he wasn't exactly playing the part of the fearsome Scourge of the Sea. But he didn't care. He couldn't risk letting the situation dissolve any further. Couldn't risk anyone else getting hurt or dying, not when there was a chance he could get out of this, not when Grace had a plan. And if he understood correctly, it was a good one.

But he'd stood too quickly again. His body was done. Dizziness and nausea rushed over him.

"We cede!" he managed to shout before he passed out cold.

SEAN WAS tired of waking up in brigs. Tired of musty air, damp floors, and cold metal bars. Tired of being afraid. Tired of being tired.

He didn't want to open his eyes. He didn't want to move at all.

But he had to. Especially because he heard the jangle of keys, the creek of the cell door opening, and Kess's hurried voice saying, "Quick! We managed to knock several of them out. We took their pistols and keys. But we were outnumbered and thought it would be better to break you out first before we commandeer the ship completely."

Grace's voice cut in next. "Apparently the varens had been following Ashborne since the attack in Audrye, but they kept their distance as they waited for back up. But back up never came. When they saw the *Audacity* approach, and then us abandoning ship soon after, they decided to investigate. We just got lucky some of the varens knew us."

"Luck and your quick wit," somebody said, their voice farther away and too echoey to distinguish.

"If some of us had any wit at all, it would have gone smoother," Grace muttered.

"I had to sell it, didn't I?" Cam growled.

"We'll help deal with the rest of the varens," someone else— Ranit? —said, and then multiple footsteps sounded as some of Sean's crew crept up the stairs to finish commandeering the ship.

Sean should be going up there too. He should be helping them, should be leading them. But he was so tired.

"Sean?" Emery's soft voice finally motivated him to peel his eyes open. "We need you to wake up."

Her cool hand pressed gently against his forehead, his cheek, and he leaned his face into the touch. He blinked up at her, the blurry image of her worried face swimming in and out of focus. She chewed her bottom lip. Behind her, the brig was nearly empty. Seadar, Farley, Smythee, and Grace remained, presumably waiting for the signal that it was safe to venture above decks. Everyone else had gone up already.

"Is he alright?" Seadar asked, peering over Emery's shoulder with his big doleful eyes.

"He's burning up badly," Emery said, her hand still on his cheek. "Gods, Sean, what did Ashborne do to you?"

Instead of answering, Sean slowly sat up, allowed a wave of dizziness and nausea to sweep over him, and then used the wall to climb to his feet. His legs trembled, his whole-body aching. Emery rose with him, moving her hand from his face to his shoulder to keep him steady. His pride begged him to shake her off, to save whatever dignity he had left. But the rest of him savored the touch because he knew it would likely be one of the last times he'd get the chance to do so.

Shouting erupted overhead, along with the clash of steal and the boom of gunshots, the thuds of boots and bodies and whatever else hitting the deck.

"I need to help them," Sean rasped.

"I don't think they need your help," Emery said softly.

In the end, she was right. By the time they made it above decks, his crew had rounded up every varen on the ship. They were already loading the varens' limp, paralyzed bodies into multiple longboats.

Kess peered down into one of them, his expression full of regret and sorrow. "I'm sorry."

When Sean glanced into the boat himself, he realized Kess was talking to Melina.

She lay amongst her comrades, unable to move due to being shot by her own paralyzing weapon. She stared up at Kess with anger and betrayal shining in her eyes.

"Why are you helping them?" she managed to say, though the words were slow and slurred.

Kess set his jaw and stood up straight. "I *am* one of them."

Horror flashed in her eyes—horror, and...disgust.

Kess's voice turned cold. "You said Tavor wasn't in Audrye."

The mix of emotions swirling in Melina's eyes was momentarily overshadowed by confusion. "He," she managed to force out. "Wasn't."

Grace stepped forward, placing a hand on Kess's shoulder and gazing cooly down at Melina. "He was," she said. "And he did this."

She unwrapped the bandage around her hand, revealing the fresh, blistered brand on her palm.

Before Sean had a chance to see Melina's expression upon seeing the mark, the longboat dropped into the water and the varens disappeared from view. Kess turned, not watching as the long boat began floating out to sea.

Guilt burned Sean's blood as surely and thoroughly as Ashborne had. The varens would be fine, the paralyzing agent would wear off in an hour or two and they'd row themselves to the closest shore. But Kess was not only saying goodbye to a friend—seemingly someone who had been more than a friend— he was saying goodbye to the life he'd built for himself back in Audrye, goodbye to any future he once had there. Because Sean had done it again, just as he'd feared he would. He'd ripped away his friend's future.

As Kess walked by, Sean hesitantly touched his shoulder. He didn't know what to say, other than what he felt. "I'm sorry."

Kess paused for a moment. He didn't meet Sean's gaze, but Sean saw the way his eyes shimmered anyway.

"So am I," Kess said. He blinked a few times and when he looked up, his eyes were clear and dry. "But this wasn't your fault."

Sean said nothing, for he knew that was untrue. He glanced one last time at the longboat full of paralyzed varens floating out to sea, and then turned to find his crew gathered on the deck, looking at him, waiting.

"Orders, Captain?" Ranit asked.

Sean glanced wearily around at the unfamiliar ship they'd just taken, with its black hull and indigo sails and serpentine shape. And Cam's voice shouted in his head.

You gave up your ship. You're not my captain anymore.

He swallowed, his shredded throat aching with the small

motion. "The *Audacity* is gone. I'm no longer the captain of anything."

There was a short silence, until Ranit said, "With all due respect, Captain. That's the stupidest thing I've ever heard."

Sean blinked.

"Aye, it's not the *Audacity* we follow," Rooney said, "it's you."

"You know we'd all follow you to the underworld and back," Aleksy added.

To his utter surprise, Sean's eyes stung, especially when a series of ayes rang across the deck as the rest of the crew agreed. The only one who said nothing at all was Cam. She simply leaned against the main mast with her arms folded across her chest.

"So, what are your orders, Captain?" Ranit asked.

What do we do what do we do what do we do.

This time, at least he had an answer.

Sean blinked again and swallowed down his emotion. "We're getting the *Audacity* back."

A series of whoops rang across the deck this time.

Sean glanced at Grace, who perched on the steps leading to the afterdeck with Ayana and Emery. He tried to not look at Emery as he spoke to Grace. "I assume you memorized the coordinates you gave Ashborne, that you know exactly where she's heading?"

Grace nodded.

Sean turned back to his crew, his family. "Then I plan to follow her there. And we'll take back our ship, our home."

He'd planned this the moment he'd realized he was going to have to barter Ashborne for their lives. He never intended to let Ashborne have the *Audacity*, at least not for long. He'd known they'd never win a fight, not then. But if they caught Ashborne unawares while most of her crew was on some treasure hunt on an island somewhere, they should be able to take the *Audacity* back easily.

Still, there were risks.

"Ashborne and her crew are dangerous and merciless," Sean

said. "I won't force anyone on this mission. If you don't wish to fight, we can drop you off somewhere safe along the way."

Sean almost hoped most of them would take the offer, so he didn't have to put any of them at risk. But a series of scoffs sounded. And it was Cam who spoke up next. "Now *that's* the stupidest thing I've ever heard."

Another round of ayes followed.

"We want to help too!" Emery said. Sean locked eyes with her just long enough for his heart to skip a beat. He nodded and tore his gaze away. "Grace, what's our heading?"

"Northwest," Grace said immediately.

"Do we have any idea what's actually waiting at the coordinates?" Aleksy asked. "What is Ashborne looking for?"

"I truly have no idea," Sean said.

Grace held up a finger. "I have a theory."

Everyone looked at her, but she didn't seem to care about the attention.

"Of course, everyone remembers the first Ashborne," Grace said. "He started the Elemental War. But does anyone know how he was eventually defeated?"

There was a series of *no*s and headshakes from the crew.

"That's because the history books are undecided, unclear," Grace continued. "But I read one that says, in their desperation to stop him, other elemists called up the gods until they finally intervened and dragged Ashborne into Pyralis's fire."

"Pyralis?" Sean questioned, not recognizing the name.

"The fire god," Grace said.

"Alright... Even if this were true, what does it have to do with Ashborne and the treasure now?" Rooney asked.

"Well, this book also mentions that Pyralis placed a curse on Ashborne's bloodline to keep them in check. Something like, if they draw blood before a certain age, Pyralis will come for them too. But apparently, somewhere along the line, an Ashborne found or created objects to protect them from the curse."

Silence settled across the deck, most of Sean's crew staring at Grace as if she'd sprouted a new head.

"What were the objects?" Sean asked, curiosity getting the better of him.

"Not specified. Regardless," Grace said, "my theory is that this Ashborne is also cursed and searching for the objects."

"You think one of these objects was meant to be in the chest at the cemetery?" Emery asked.

"Perhaps?" Grace said. "But honestly, this is all a theory, and it doesn't really matter to us, does it? What matters is getting the *Audacity* back and then hopefully never interacting with that monster again."

Of course, she was right. Sean certainly didn't have the capacity to really care what Ashborne was up to. He just wanted to get his ship back.

"Well, you heard the lovely lady," Sean ordered. "Get us moving!"

His crew dispersed, readying the ship to sail.

Chapter Forty-Four

Sean hated these captain's quarters. He hated the black and indigo colours that adorned everything from the bedding to the curtains to the rug on the floor. He hated how the colours set him on edge, his body so used to seeing the varens' colours and then something terrible happening right after that it was difficult not to immediately turn and flee the room.

But most of all, he hated that these quarters weren't *his* quarters. That was not his bed in the corner nor was that his wardrobe on the opposite wall. This was not his desk, and these were not his things neatly arranged on its surface. This was not his home.

No, someone else was in his home now, possibly in his bed, or sitting at his desk. The thought made his stomach churn with violation and rage.

But he took a deep breath, and gingerly sat behind the foreign desk, weak sunlight filtering through the clouds and the windows at his back, illuminating the pile of charts and maps before him.

"What are the coordinates?" Sean questioned Grace. He'd asked her to accompany him to the captain's quarters along with Billy and Aleksy. All three of them were peering around the cabin as if they, too, felt uneasy in the room, though Grace's gaze was more clinical, as if she were cataloguing everything.

"It looks like Tavor in here," she said, and Sean did not miss the way Billy and Aleksy flinched at the name. But Grace's voice was calm, as if they were discussing the weather. She turned to Sean and recited the coordinates.

Sean was practiced enough at navigation to know the coordinates lay somewhere to the northwest of their current location, and he flipped through the charts, searching for the correct ones and trying to ignore the way even the soft edges of the parchment stung his raw fingers. He checked three different maps, pulled a few more out from inside the desk and checked those too. He frowned.

"There's nothing there. Just water," he said. Billy had moved to stand beside the desk, scanning the charts himself. Sean didn't know anyone who knew the sea as well as his adoptive father, which was why Billy was often in charge of navigating.

Billy's frown was nearly hidden by his salt and pepper beard. "I swear there should be an island around there. I think I've been to the area before, or close by."

"Why?" Sean asked, though he thought he knew the answer.

Billy grinned at Sean. "Exploring with your father."

"Actually," Grace spoke up. "On most maps, there's nothing there. But on one map, there is."

Sean looked up at her, lifting his brows, marveling—not for the first time—at that mind of hers. "Oh?"

She moved to the desk and plucked up a quill. "I hope you don't mind, but I got bored while we were trying to find you and I read all your charts and maps."

Sean swallowed down the sudden pinch of pain that came with thinking about his maps. He'd painstakingly drawn and labeled most of them, something he'd once taken great joy in doing—before Lily died. He wondered what Ashborne would do to those maps, to his things. All of his belongings where aboard the *Audacity*, including old things that belonged to his parents.

Thinking of his parents reminded him of Ashborne's claim

that they'd killed her father. As far as he knew, his parents had been merchants, and Ashborne had killed *them*. He couldn't begin to understand why Ashborne thought otherwise. He thought about asking Billy, but now was not the time.

Grace dipped the quill in ink, pulled a map towards her, and began outlining an island at the spot of the coordinates. "The island doesn't have a name—at least it didn't on the map—but it was there."

Sean watched the island take shape, frowning again. He couldn't remember ever recording that tiny spit of land, and he was usually good at remembering that sort of thing.

His puzzlement must have been apparent on his face because Grace glanced up and said, "This was not on a map you made. The map was drawn by a Jack Denzel. Your father, I assume?"

His father's name sent a little jolt through him as he nodded. It was so rare he heard anyone say it.

Grace snatched a fresh piece of parchment and began drawing the island bigger, adding beaches, hills, rivers, and anything else her extraordinary mind recalled.

"You sure are bloody convenient to have around, Grace," Sean said.

"I know."

Sean looked up at his adoptive father. "Billy, how long do you think it would take us to get there if we made no stops?"

Billy gazed at the chart, his brow furrowed in concentration. "A couple of weeks I'd say, if the weather holds."

Sean nodded, mostly to himself. He hoped a couple of weeks wasn't too long. "Could you chart us the fastest course? But first, can you have Rooney go through the supplies on this ship? We need to make sure we won't run out of provisions if we want to make a straight shot to this island."

"Aye, Captain," Billy said, his usual jovial smile on his face, probably relieved and glad that his son was not only back, but acting like himself.

As soon as Billy left, Sean wilted in his chair, dreading what came next.

Seconds later, as he expected, Kess stepped into the cabin, closing the door behind him. "We need to examine you. Now."

⚓

"THE DAMAGE IS...EXTENSIVE," Aleksy said, her dark eyes full of dismay.

Sean wasn't at all surprised to hear this, but the confirmation still caused his chest to tighten. He fought the urge to snatch his hand away as Aleksy gently pressed two fingers to the pulse point at his wrist and placed her other hand over his heart. Though her touch was feather light, the slight pressure caused Sean's skin to sting, her calluses abrasive. She sat on a chair in front of him, her eyes closed as she concentrated on Sean's boiled blood and whatever abnormalities she found there.

"Your organs are failing," Kess said softly. The stethoscope hanging around his neck caught the sunlight still streaming through the window as he sat down on the other chair beside Aleksy. He'd managed to find the stethoscope and other medical instruments in the small infirmary aboard the ship and had just finished using the instrument to listen to Sean's shallow breaths and irregular heartbeat.

"There's infection in your blood," Aleksy said, her eyes still closed and her frown deepening with every passing moment. "It's...everywhere."

"He's septic?" Kess asked.

"If septic means his blood is basically poisoning him as we speak, then yes," Aleksy said.

"Have you ever seen anything like this, Aleksy?" Sean asked.

Kess, of course, was in the room because he was a medical student, and of everyone aboard the ship, he was most likely to know of any modern medicine that could help. If such a thing existed. But Aleksy was here because of her training in blood healing.

Aleksy slowly shook her head, her braids swinging. "Not

exactly. When we heal, we manipulate the water in the blood. We cool blood to break fevers or heat blood to kill illnesses, but I've never seen anyone use it as a weapon before. I've never seen blood heat to such an extent that it did this much damage to a person."

Sean's chest tightened further, but it was Kess who asked the question, "There's nothing you can do?"

Opening her eyes, Aleksy finally removed her fingers from Sean's wrists and heart. "I fear I'm not skilled enough. I'm unsure what I can do, excluding a complete blood cleansing."

"Blood cleansing?" Kess asked.

"We would have to drain his blood so I could separate the infection out and then put his blood back."

"You mean a blood transfusion, essentially," Kess said.

"A blood transfusion would replace his blood with someone else's," Grace spoke up. She'd been watching quietly from behind Kess and Aleksy, looking more and more horrified as Kess had filled Aleksy in on what Ashborne had done to Sean, and then watching the diagnosis unfold. "But if she's putting his own blood back after removing the infection, then a cleansing is probably more accurate."

And this is the only reason he'd allowed Grace to stay in the room. She may not have any formal medical training or blood healing experience, but with her perfect memory and the sheer number of books she devoured in Audrye, Sean hoped she might be able to help in some way.

"Whatever you want to call it," Kess said to Aleksy. "Can you do it?"

Sean had never seen Aleksy's expression look so sad and defeated. "Not on my own. I would need help from others trained like myself. Someone more experienced, if possible."

"So, if we travelled to your old home, they could help him?" Kess asked.

"Possibly, but…" Aleksy trailed off and Sean waited for her to say what he'd been waiting for one of them to say this entire time.

But Grace was the one to say it, "He won't last that long."

Aleksy turned to stare at Grace.

Grace shrugged. "Judging by your facial scars, I'm guessing you came from one of the villages near the Scorched Sea? I read about your tribes. There's no way Sean will make such a trip. It's probably a month's voyage, plus a week or two on land."

Aleksy turned back around, struggling to make eye contact with Sean again.

"Is she right?" Sean asked.

Aleksy winced. "Yes."

"Grace and I could help!" Kess implored. "I've learned about blood transfusions."

Sean raised a brow. "Have you done one?"

"No but...we have to do something!" Kess leapt from his chair and began pacing.

"It wouldn't matter if you'd done one or not," Aleksy said. "I'd need help from someone who's done blood healing before. You two would likely just kill him."

Kess rounded on Grace. "Have you read anything at all about this? Anything that might help?"

Grace slowly shook her head. And Sean's last ray of hope diminished.

"Then what do we do?" Kess asked, his shoulders slumping.

"We go get the *Audacity*," Sean said.

Everyone stared at him.

"Sean, you don't have time. We have to get you—"

"Get me where, Kess?" Sean interrupted. "You heard Aleksy. The only people who can help me are a thousand leagues away and I'll die before I get there."

All three of them flinched when he said the word, but Sean did not. He'd known he was dying. But he'd wanted to know if he at least had a chance of living, even a slight one. Now that he knew he didn't, he was done with this conversation.

"We're going to get the *Audacity* back, as planned," Sean said. "There's no sense wasting our only chance to get her back."

Because if Sean was going to die, he'd make sure his family

was safe first. He'd get their home back, and then whatever became of him would be it.

"Captain..." Aleksy began.

But Sean cut her off. "Do not tell the crew of my...afflictions. As far as they need to know, I had a rough go with Ashborne but I'm on the mend."

The room fell silent again.

Sean looked directly at Aleksy. "Not even Rooney."

"You want me to hide something like this from my own husband?" Aleksy asked, her face stony.

"Please. It will only hurt everyone to know."

"Are you ordering me to say nothing as your captain?"

Sean closed his eyes briefly. "I'm asking you as my friend."

Aleksy stood up. "I won't say anything...but I'm not giving up either. I'll think of a way through this."

Sean heard her take a long, steadying breath as she crossed the cabin and left.

Kess stared at Sean, breathing hard, as if he wanted to argue but couldn't think of anything to say. In the end, Kess spun around and stormed for the door.

"Kess!" Sean called as Kess placed his hand on the handle. Kess paused but didn't look up. "Please don't tell *anyone* about this. Not even Billy."

Kess stared at the handle. "Billy deserves to know about this, Sean."

"You're right. He does. But not right away. I will tell him eventually." Sean swallowed a lump in his throat. He still hadn't gotten the chance to tell him about how Lilly really died. And now he had to also tell him that his other child was going to die soon too. He'd wait as long as possible, to not prolong Billy's misery. He'd have the rest of his life to mourn. There was no reason to make him fret when there was nothing to be done.

Kess stared a moment longer at the door before turning back to face him. "What happened to Lily wasn't your fault, Sean."

Sean went still. They hadn't been able to talk properly since

Sean confessed. He had not been expecting the conversation to happen now, nor was he ready for those words.

Kess...didn't hate him?

"Stop punishing yourself," Kess added, and then followed Aleksy outside.

Sean stared after him, stunned.

"You're going to ask me to lie to Emery." Grace remained standing in the middle of the cabin, arms crossed over her chest. He'd nearly forgotten she was there. She made no comment about what Kess said, or the bewildered look that had to be on Sean's face.

Sean swallowed, the movement causing his throat to ache. "It's better this way."

"Is it?" Grace asked.

"Please, Grace."

"She's practically my sister. I may not be great with emotions but I'm pretty sure I shouldn't keep something like this from her. And after everything you've been through together, she deserves to know."

"But what good would it do? Knowing will only hurt her," Sean urged.

Grace's eyes narrowed. "And you dying won't?"

Sean had to look away.

"Sean, I've been in love with a girl who's been dying most of our relationship. Knowing means I get to choose to be with her anyway, that I get to know that our time together may be fleeting, and that I need to savor every small moment. Emery deserves to know what she's getting into."

Sean forced himself to look back at Grace. "I won't let her get into anything."

Grace shook her head sadly. "She's already in, Sean. Deep."

Sean had to look away again. "I'll tell her, alright? All I'm asking for is a few days."

Grace scrutinized him for a moment. "Fine. But if you don't tell her, I will."

And with that, she left too, leaving Sean alone to stare at the door and contemplate his own death. He'd always expected to die young. Living to old age was nearly impossible with the life he'd led. But he'd always expected to go out on the end of a sword or at the hands of a storm. He never expected death to claim him so slowly.

But, fast or slow, death was coming for him all the same.

He watched the door another moment. He knew he should go out and help his crew man the ship. But the thought of being around everyone right now was too much...and there was only one more person he needed to talk to.

He stood and crossed to the small washing room attached to the cabin. He scrubbed himself the best he could with the cold water already in the basin, before heading for the doors that opened to the balcony behind the desk.

It had started to drizzle, and when he stepped out onto the balcony, the cool water spattering his skin eased the constant stinging just a little. He sat with his back against the railing, facing the cabin and the door leading to the deck beyond, and he waited, letting the rain wash over his feverish body.

Lily materialized out of the shadows and sat beside him. The rain did not touch her. Sean tried not to look at her, but Lily spoke to him anyway. "You're doing the right thing."

He knew he was. And he knew Emery would come find him soon. She always did. So, he'd wait, and give himself a brief respite before the moment came when he had to rip his own heart out.

Chapter Forty-Five

As soon as Sean finished giving his orders to get the *Audacity* back, the crew had dispersed. Aleksy, Billy, Grace, and Sean had disappeared into the captain's quarters, no doubt to finalize their heading and, Emery suspected, so Aleksy could give Sean a medical examination. Kess had taken Ayana down below to do his own examination of her leg.

Emery had been torn in two, desperately wanting to follow them both. But she knew she needed to give the medics space to do what they did best, and that she needed to help the crew get the *Audacity* back any way she could. So, she'd helped the crew get the ship on course, all the while keeping an eye below for any sign she could see either Ayana or Sean. As soon as she'd finished her work getting the topsails in place, she'd dropped to the deck to wait, pacing around the deck with her heart in her throat.

Finally, Kess had appeared, letting her know she could visit Ayana, and then he disappeared into Sean's cabin himself.

Emery raced belowdecks, finding this ship was laid out very similarly to *The New Dawn,* with long, narrow hallways and various rooms, instead of a wide-open space like aboard the *Audacity*. She headed straight for the room Kess had indicated, but the sound of her name caused her to stop short and turn.

Rooney was stepping out of the ship's galley, two plates in his large hands. His shoulders were so wide, they nearly brushed the narrow hallway's walls as he approached. He held out the plates, both ladened with steaming food. "For you and your sister. A peace offering."

Emery took the plates, stunned and a little confused.

Rooney tucked his hands in his pockets. "I'm sorry about how we've treated you these last few days."

"You are?" Emery blurted. Honestly, she deserved it. Especially now. "But you all just lost your home because of me."

Rooney shrugged. "We'll get her back. Besides, that ship is only home because of the people on it. You gave up your treasure to get our captain back. And you stopped Cam from getting herself killed. I don't know about the others, but for me, that makes up for the rest."

Emery didn't know what to say. Gratitude and hope swelled in her chest, even though she wasn't sure Rooney should forgive her so easily. The silence stretched until it grew awkward.

"Anyway…" Rooney cleared his throat and patted the top of Emery's head before turning to leave. "Oh," he said over his shoulder, "Aleksy wants to talk to your sister when she's up for it. She wants to try to help her with her illness."

And then he disappeared back into the galley, leaving Emery alone with her two steaming plates of food and a burning behind her eyes.

She pushed open the infirmary door and found Ayana laying on a small cot, her leg propped up on a pillow. Emery let the tears fall then, the relief that her sister was alive hitting her so hard, it was difficult to breath.

She placed the food on a table and carefully crawled into the cot with her sister. They hugged each other tightly.

"Are you alright?" Emery asked.

"Leg is broken," Ayana said. "My stupid bones are still weak. But it will heal. I'm a little malnourished and sunburnt, but otherwise, I'll be fine."

Emery took a deep breath, allowing more relief to flood her

system, before asking the question she so dreaded the answer to: "What happened?"

Ayana told Emery everything—how they'd been taken from the university, how Ashborne had boiled the man's blood to the point where he wasn't even recognizable anymore, and how she'd boiled Sean's blood too, over and over again, until Ashborne changed tactics and took Ayana away to bake in the sun.

"She was about to keelhaul Kess when you arrived," Ayana said, her voice a horrified whisper. "I think she would have done it too."

Emery sat in stunned silence, feeling more and more like she was going to vomit. Exhausted from the whole ordeal, Ayana eventually drifted off to sleep, leaving Emery alone to reel in a hurricane of guilt and confusion.

Ashborne, the descendent of the man who had started the Elemental War so many centuries ago, the daughter of the man who had killed Sean's parents, wanted Emery's parents' chest. Or whatever was in the chest. Perhaps it was a relic of old to save her from some curse, as Grace had suggested. Perhaps not. But the thought that her parents could have been in league with a woman like that made Emery's stomach coil with nausea. She could only hope that wasn't the case, that something else was going on, and that Ashborne knew about the chest some other way—knew what was *in it* some other way.

None of it made any sense to Emery, but in the end, Grace was right, it didn't really matter. Now Ashborne had the *Audacity*. Because of Emery, Sean and his crew lost their home and everything they owned. Because of her, Sean lost his father's ship and his last tie to his dead family.

She needed to talk to him. To apologize for everything and to beg for his forgiveness.

Finally, the door of the cabin squeaked open, and Grace slipped into the room. The only light was a lantern burning on the bedside table, but Emery could still see her devastated expression.

Emery sat up slowly, gently untangling herself from her sister so she didn't wake her up. "Grace?"

"You need to talk to him," Grace said.

Emery's already roiling stomach plummeted. "Is he alright?"

"You need to talk to him," she repeated.

Emery did not need to be told again. She flew out the door and up the stairs, nearly colliding with Smythee at the top. He sat on the steps, staring at nothing with his one blue and one milky white eye.

Emery paused. "Smythee, are you alright?"

The old man didn't so much as twitch in acknowledgment.

In all the craziness of the last day, she never got to question him about the parchment. "Smythee, how did you know about the lemon juice?"

Smythee slowly turned to look at her and then began to laugh maniacally. He stood up and teetered away. Emery sighed but didn't pursue him. She had more pressing matters to deal with.

She hesitated when she reached the door of the captain's quarters. She assumed he was still in there. After the insanity of the last few days, she knew Sean would seek isolation. Aboard the *Audacity*, there were two places he usually did that. She didn't think he was well enough to climb out to the bowsprit, so that only left the quarters. With her heart in her mouth, she knocked softly.

There was no answer, and briefly, Emery wondered if she was wrong, or if Sean didn't want to see her. Pushing down her anxiety, Emery opened the door and stepped inside.

The room made her entire body shudder. It was decorated almost exactly like Tavor's cabin aboard *The New Dawn*, all black and indigo, with silver trimming everywhere. It was even laid out the same, except for one difference: Instead of a big bay window at the back, there was a pair of glass doors leading to a balcony, which were currently swung wide open.

Sitting on the deck, as if waiting for her, was Sean. His back was pressed against the railing, his eyes closed, his face tilted up towards the sky. Dark clouds had rolled in, bringing with them a slight drizzle. His wet hair was pushed back off his forehead. The rain spilled across his face, dripped down his neck, and bare chest. The soft moonlight, fighting its way through the clouds, gilded him in silver.

Emery's throat constricted.

He was so beautiful.

Alive and here and beautiful.

With her heart racing with nerves, she quietly moved through the cabin until she stood just in front of the open doors, in front of Sean. She knew he heard her come in, or at the very least, sensed her presence, ever hyper aware of his surroundings. But he didn't speak, didn't move, didn't even open his eyes.

A part of her was grateful, because it gave her a moment to bask in the knowledge that they were both here and they were both safe, at least for now. But another part of her grew more and more nervous the longer the silence stretched. The fact that he hadn't leapt to his feet to make sure she was unharmed after their encounter with Tavor, or that he didn't even ask what had happened, was extremely uncharacteristic.

Something was wrong.

It took her several tries to speak. "Sean?"

He didn't react for a few seconds more, save for his throat bobbing once, and then he slowly lowered his face so he could look at her, his expression carefully blank, his eyes empty of all emotion.

Something in Emery's chest cracked. She knew that look, knew it was both a mask and a defense mechanism. He used it when he needed to hide his true feelings, when he was feeling too much, and when he shut down instead of letting it all to the surface.

He also used it as the Scourge of the Sea.

It had been so long since that expression had been directed at her, back when they barely knew each other, back when they hated each other.

Tears pricked the back of her eyes. "Sean, I'm so sorry. First, Tavor, and then...what Ashborne did to you. I can't—"

"How does she know about the chest?" His voice was quiet but it still somehow trampled her own.

She swallowed. "I have no idea."

"What was supposed to be in the chest?"

"I-I don't know." Emery stepped closer, so she was on the balcony too, the cold rain soaking her hair and clothes in seconds. "All the information I had was in that stupid riddle."

He just stared at her as if...he didn't believe her. The stare pierced like a blade into her chest. Did he think she was lying? How could he think that after everything they'd been through together?

She tried to ignore the pain. He was angry, and he had every right to be.

Slowly, she knelt in front of him, close enough that she could grab his hands. But as much as she wanted to, she didn't reach for him. "Sean, I swear. I told you everything. I don't—"

"Everything?" The calm in his voice broke.

"Yes."

He leaned closer but it wasn't an intimate move. He was taking up her space, able to tower over her even when they were sitting. It was something he used to do when trying to intimidate her while playing the role of the Scourge. It didn't intimidate her now, but it still caused her heart to race faster with fear. He was truly angry.

"Tell me, Emery," he said, his flat tone edged with suppressed emotion. "Where are you from?"

Emery was so caught off guard by the question, she just stared up at him. Her mouth opened, then closed, opened again. But she didn't know what to say. She was too afraid to risk saying anything at all.

Sean leaned back against the railing, his eyes shining with something like triumph. "Even now, after I told you my darkest secrets, after I withstood torture for you—*again*—after I lost my home because of you, you still don't trust me with anything."

Guilt, shame, and dismay curdled in her stomach. "No, that's not it! I trust you with *everything*. I trust you with my life."

"But not enough to tell me that you're from Orabel?"

Surprise and fear jolted through her like lightning. In all the chaos during and after their encounter with Tavor, she'd forgotten he'd said that. And of course, Sean had heard it. Her whole body stiffened as she waited for Sean's breath to be ripped from his lungs. Several seconds ticked by in strained silence. Sean watched her, his eyes narrowing at her reaction. But he didn't choke or claw at his throat or even cough.

Maybe the rumours had been wrong. Maybe the Arch-Elemists couldn't listen with the wind or otherwise manipulate the elements outside of Orabel. Maybe they were far enough away now to be out of reach. Maybe they had just been lucky, and the Arch-Elemists hadn't heard them this time. Or maybe they didn't care anymore, now that Tavor knew.

Trepidation still gnawed at Emery just the same. She cast furtive glances at the dark sky and the darker sea, as if she'd spot them eavesdropping. "Sean, don't—"

He cut her off. "I've dreamt of a place like Orabel my entire life. I told you that."

She winced when he said her home's name out loud again. It seemed thunderous in the silence of the night.

"A safe place for elemists to live, where you don't have to spend every moment hiding who you are and fearing for your life." Thankfully, Sean's breath remained his own as he kept talking. But his blank expression was cracking more, his tone growing edgier, with a mixture of anger and hurt. "I'd give anything to give that kind of freedom to my family. You *know* that. And yet, it never occurred to you to tell me it was real? That you *lived* there? Or maybe you just didn't want to tell me because, after you got what you wanted, you were going to leave us all behind to run back home?"

Each word was like another blade to her chest, slowly slicing her open. "I wanted to tell you, Sean. So badly." She glanced around again, unease still prickling her skin. "But it's forbidden. Our leaders have ways to silence us if we try to talk about it."

"And yet," he said slowly, "we're talking about it."

They were. The secret had been spilled, and yet, nothing was happening. Emery didn't know what to make of it, and while she was relieved that she seemingly could talk about her home without consequences, a whole new kind of panic was rushing through her veins now. It got worse with the ever-rising hurt and anger in Sean's voice, his expression. She had been expecting him to be angry about Tavor or Ashborne or the loss of the *Audacity* —or all of it. But she had not expected this, and somehow, it was worse.

Desperation made her scoot closer, and this time, she took his hands. Despite the cool rain soaking them both, his skin was hot. Too hot. And though he tried to hide it, she still noticed the way he winced as soon as she twined their fingers, as if it physically hurt him. But he didn't pull away, and she didn't let go either, afraid that if she did, that would be it. He'd be gone.

"I wanted to tell you about Orabel. So many times. That night you told me about Lily, I almost did. But we aren't allowed to tell, and I was afraid if I did, my leaders would permanently silence not only me, but you too." Her words came out in a rush, and she paused to gather herself, to take a deep breath. "Do you remember that night when we were dancing and watching the fireworks?" Of course he did. It had only been a few days ago. Gods, how had everything gone so wrong, so fast? "You asked me what I wanted to do after I found my parents and a cure..."

Sean said nothing.

"I had an answer, but I never got a chance to say it." She took another deep breath before plunging on. "I wanted to stay with you. I still do. When we get the *Audacity* back, I want to stay there with you. Or maybe...now that you know about Orabel, we could go there. With the whole crew. I don't care where we are, Sean. I just want to be with you."

Sean's whole body went completely still. He didn't even seem to be breathing. But he didn't say anything. He just stared at her with an expression that betrayed nothing.

"I want *you*," she said. Steeling her nerves, she leaned forward, closing the short distance between them, and kissed him. It was only a soft brush of her lips, partly because she didn't want to cause him more physical pain, and partly because she was terrified he'd pull away. He didn't. But he didn't kiss her back either. He remained perfectly still. She didn't think he'd even taken a breath.

With her heart shriveling in her chest, Emery began to pull away. This was it, then. He hated her. They were done.

But then finally—*finally*—Sean reacted. He leaned forward as she pulled away, so the kiss didn't end. He freed his hands from hers so he could cup her face, his palms so hot against her rain-slicked skin, and he deepened the kiss. She wrapped her arms around his neck, burying her fingers in his wet hair. And they both surged to their knees, so they were pressed chest to chest, with not a breath of space between them. Even through her soaked clothes, Emery felt every inch of where their bodies pressed together, felt the searing heat of his bare skin—the heat that was abnormally hot.

She almost pulled away, concern flickering at the edge of her awareness. But if any part of this was causing Sean pain, he didn't seem to care. He removed one hand from her face and his fingers skimmed down her ribs, leaving trails of fire in their wake. When his hand moved to the small of her back to press her closer still—if that was even possible—her awareness of anything that wasn't Sean and his mouth and his hands vanished.

Emotions flooded her system. She'd been so scared that she'd never see him again, that he wouldn't get off Ashborne's ship alive. Then she'd been certain he was furious with her, that he was back to hating her again, that she'd never again kiss him or even make him laugh. But this did not feel like anger, and it did not feel like hate. Relief and hope swelled in her chest to the point she thought she might burst. She tasted salt and wasn't sure if it was sea spray or her tears finally escaping.

When they finally needed air, they broke apart, resting their foreheads together.

"You know," Sean murmured breathlessly, "you can't just kiss me every time you want something."

Emery grinned at their familiar banter, almost giddy. "Because it bloody works?"

"Because I'm done being used."

Emery reeled back, his words like a blow, his flat tone finally registering through her giddy fog. "What?"

Sean released his hold on her, sitting back himself. His face was stone, but his eyes were glassy. "It's easy to say you want to stay aboard the *Audacity* when it's no longer an option. It's easy to say you wanted to tell me about Orabel when the secret has already been spilled. I'm not buying it this time. I've always just been a means to an end to you, and nothing has changed."

Emery gaped, his words so at odds with the moment they just shared that they were difficult to process. Confusion, and a spark of her own ire, flared to life. After everything, did he truly think so little of her? "How can you say that?"

"You don't care about getting the *Audacity* back. You just want a ride to whatever treasure is waiting for you at those coordinates. Were you actually planning to share that with us or was that bullshit too?"

Now his words were like bullets ripping through her chest, leaving her stunned and speechless. He couldn't really believe that, could he?

Her eyes burned, but she tried to reign in her whirling emotions—the hurt, the anger, the horrible realization that this really was it, that they were going to be nothing before they had a chance to be something.

But that kiss…Why had he kissed her like that? She couldn't let them end like this.

"I don't give Teralyn's Teeth about what's in that chest, or the coordinates, or any of that anymore. It's not worth it. It's not worth what Ashborne did to you, or the risk that she'll do it to someone else. And it wasn't worth losing the *Audacity* either. I'm so sorry for all of it, and I swear on Tadewin's Wind that I'll stop at nothing to get her back."

Sean simply glared at her, unmoved and unmoving.

"Sean," she tried one last time, her voice breaking, "I just want you."

A muscle feathered in his jaw, but otherwise, his expression didn't shift. And then he said, "I don't want you."

If his earlier words had been blades and bullets, this one short sentence was a cannonball, completely obliterating what was left of her chest. She was so stunned she couldn't form thoughts, let alone words, and didn't recover fast enough to react when Sean stood up.

"I don't want to talk to you until we reach our destination and then we're parting ways." Without a backward glance, he stormed from the balcony, through the cabin and out the other door, leaving Emery kneeling alone in the pouring rain, with a gaping hole where her heart used to be.

Now she understood the kiss for what it was: a goodbye.

Chapter Forty-Six

"Fia, wait!" Liam tried to catch Fia's wrist, to pull her back. But she snatched her arm from his reach and continued marching through the trees, twigs snapping beneath her feet. "Stop!"

Fia did no such thing. She didn't even glance at him. Her eyes were fixed forward, shining with rage and determination, her fiery hair flashing whenever she passed through a beam of sunlight streaming through the canopy.

"Fia!" Caelin called, also trailing her. "What if they silence you?"

"Then they'll have to do it in front of the entire village and give themselves away!" she cried.

Liam picked up speed and swung himself in front of her, forcing her to stop so she didn't slam into him. "Fia, please! I can't watch them steal the air from your lungs."

Fia gazed at him, breathing hard, her eyes still shining and her face still red with anger. She shook her head, and sadness settled across her features too. "Listen to yourself, Liam. What you went through... I'm sorry. But you never would have stopped me before. You were never afraid of anything. You'd be the one yelling the truth from the highest treetops."

Liam swallowed. She was right, of course. He missed the old Liam. The fearless Liam. He *hadn't* feared anything. Now he feared everything. "Yeah, well...torture changes a person."

Somehow Fia's gaze grew fiercer. "Exactly. And you shouldn't be forced to be silent about it. Our people need to know they're being lied to, and that they're in danger. If the Arch-Elemists steal my breath, well, at least I tried."

Liam swallowed again, searching Fia's face as if she held all the answers. Maybe she did.

Caelin stood silently off to the side, his own face contemplative. "She's right," he said.

"I know!" Liam snapped. He ran a hand through his curls, and with a lot less venom, repeated, "I know."

Of course, he knew. But it didn't stop the anxiety from attacking him now. Clenching his fists at his sides, he tore his feet from the ground and made way for her to proceed, praying to all the gods he wasn't about to watch her suffocate on her own voice.

Fia didn't hesitate. She continued her march for the center of the island, aiming for the clearing where the islanders held all their important gatherings and meetings. Liam and Caelin followed. Once they got close enough to see the clearing, she began shouting variations of, "WE'RE BEING LIED TO! WE ARE NOT SAFE!"

Islanders poked their heads out of their homes to see what the yelling was about, stopped in their tracks along the paths to stare in Fia's direction. And they began to follow. When Fia burst into the circle of lush green grass that was the clearing, Liam and Caelin still in tow, though a lot more sheepishly as the islanders trailed them, she strode straight for the wooden dais.

"THERE IS NO CURE. TAVOR IS A FRAUD!"

The islanders bathing in the lake at the center of the clearing glanced up and the ones practicing with their lims on the lake's bank ceased their movements. Liam's gaze jumped from them to the Sacra – a huge, round boulder that perched on a raised piece of land in the center of the lake with a fire burning atop it, and the most sacred area of the island – and his already racing heart tripped a beat. Liam had mostly avoided the clearing since being home, and so he hadn't really looked at the Sacra since the moment he'd been chosen to help Tavor. Back in that moment, when the Arch-Elemists had called upon the elemental gods to show the islanders their apparent savior, the symbols etched into the huge boulder had burst with colorful flowers. But now…half of those flowers were shriveled and brown.

Liam tore his gaze away from the further proof that his home was dying.

Fia stood in the center of the dais, and Liam and Caelin moved to hover just behind her. A crowd formed in front of the dais, at least half of Orabel's population pooling into the clearing to see what the ruckus was all about. This sort of thing did not happen on Orabel.

"What's going on, Fia?" Aran asked, standing near the front of the group.

"We've all been lied to," Fia replied, loud enough for the whole clearing to hear. "We are not safe and the Arch-Elemists have been hiding the truth from us for months. Maybe even longer!"

Liam couldn't help but flinch, bracing himself for the moment Fia choked. But it never happened. Fia was able to keep talking, to keep shouting the truths Liam had been forced to swallow for so long.

"Tavor is not who he said he was. He does not want peace, and he does not want to help us find a cure for the Withering. He wants to destroy us!"

A gust of furious whispers whipped through the crowd.

"What are you talking about?" It was Liam's grandmother, standing off to the side of the crowd, her face bleeding of colour. The sight of her horrified expression churned Liam's stomach.

Fia spotted her too, and finally, she seemed to lose a little steam, as if stealing herself to give terrible news. "Tavor never had a cure, nor did he know how to get one. And he never intended to help us in any way."

Though the expression on his grandmother's face was difficult to look at, especially because Liam knew she was about to hear even worse news, the fact that Fia was able to say any of this without choking bolstered his own courage. Perhaps Fia was able to speak freely because she'd made no promises to the Arch-Elemists. Or maybe they simply thought it was time.

"I knew something was off. But why are *you* telling us this?" Aran questioned, turning his glare from Fia to Liam. "Why has the Chosen One said nothing?"

Liam stepped up beside Fia. "Because as soon as Caelin and I arrived home, the Arch-Elemists threatened us, forcing us not to say anything. I tried once, but then..."

"They stole his breath, and he blacked out," Fia finished for him, grabbing his hand and squeezing. For a moment, Liam's total awareness zeroed in on the sensation of her fingers threading through his.

"We've been physically unable to say anything since we've been home," Caelin confirmed, moving to stand on Fia's other side, his arms crossed over his chest.

"What has changed?" Aran asked. "Why can you speak now?"

Caelin shrugged. "I don't know. Perhaps the secret has been spilled and they aren't bothering to cover it anymore."

"Liam." Liam's grandfather's voice was soft, but it seemed to cut through the crowd. He stood beside Liam's grandmother, his hand on her shoulder. "What happened out there? And where is Emery really?"

Liam swallowed the sudden lump in his throat. For all the long days he'd yearned to talk about what happened, now that he was facing his grandparents with the ability to speak, he almost didn't want to. And it seemed the entire population of Orabel had entered the clearing now, the eyes of all his friends and family fixed on him. Where could he even start? How was he supposed to tell them about all the awful things that happened? How—

Fia squeezed his hand again, and a fresh wave of courage flowed through him. He could do this. For the sake of his home, his people. They needed to hear the truth. And it was up to him to give it.

He took a deep breath and spun the tale, telling them how Tavor had kept up the façade for months, soaking up every ounce of information about Orabel that Liam, Caelin, and Emery willingly gave him, how he didn't show his true colours until they reached Downwell, when he threw Emery and Liam into the dungeons.

Here, Liam faltered, needing to swallow again. The memory of being trapped in his own body, of lying in the dark on the cold, stone floor, not knowing where his sister or his best friend were... He flexed his muscles to remind himself that he wasn't there anymore, that he could move. That he was safe. For now.

Caelin took over the story then, his voice eerily monotone, explaining how Tavor wanted Caelin to join him and how Caelin had pretended to do just that to save Liam and Emery. "But I wasn't able to get them out before..." It was his turn to trail off, his voice strained.

"Tavor tortured Emery and I," Liam said, looking down at his feet so he didn't have to look at his grandparents. "We think he was trying to draw our abilities out, to see how powerful we were. While he did that, he also gave us these." Liam untangled his fingers from Fia's, missing the contact immediately. He showed his palm to the crowd, and they all gasped as they saw the F branded into his flesh.

Caelin stared straight ahead, his face suddenly pale and a little green.

"He was going to move Emery and me to Abyssus to continue his...experiments. But, because of Caelin, we were able to escape," Liam continued. "Emery may have accidentally killed him. She wasn't sure. But if he is still out there, none of us are safe."

"Where is Emery now?" Aran asked.

Liam chose his words carefully. He didn't want to mentioned Captain Sean Denzel and his crew of Forbiddens. It was an unnecessary complication in the story they didn't need to know about. It might just cause more panic. "We split up. She stayed behind to keep searching for a cure. And we came back here to warn everyone...but as I said, when we got here, the Arch-Elemists forbade us."

The islanders began speaking over each other, flinging questions upon questions.

Aran's voice, as usual, rang louder than the others. "What did Tavor want with you? What was the purpose of his experiments?"

"He wants to take Orabel, to capture us all and turn it into another prison for elemists," Caelin said. "We think he lied his way onto the island because he wanted to learn about our weaknesses and our strengths. He wanted to experiment on us because there are rumors of Orabel's existence out there, and some of these rumors mention that we are more powerful than average elemists. He wanted to know what he was up against."

"And the Arch-Elemists knew of his plans the entire time?" Aran demanded.

"Yes," Liam said. "They told us when we got home that they knew what he was planning but—"

"This is outrageous!" someone shouted. "This cannot stand!"

"We must confront our leaders!" Aran hollered. "We must force them to explain their actions!"

Before Liam realized what was happening, the crowd before him turned like the tide and began flowing north, towards the Arch-Elemists' home. Liam, Fia, and Caelin stared at each other with a mixture of surprise and wariness, before the three of them hopped down from the dais and followed the angry mob.

As the islanders marched across the island, a furious wind tore through the branches above them, raining down pinecones and needles across their paths. The trees themselves bent and groaned, and the earth seemed to tremble. The collective anger of the islanders was affecting everything.

As they approached the gigantic red wood that served as the Arch-Elemists home, Liam braced himself for some sort of fight. Surely, the Arch-Elemists wouldn't let the islanders just burst into their home. Surely, they would use their abilities to stop the mob before things grew destructive. But nothing happened as the mob approached the giant redwood, and nothing happened when Aran and a few others banged on the trunk of the tree, demanding the Arch-Elemists come out and explain themselves.

When the elders did no such thing, Aran and a few others forced their way inside the tree, and the mob poured in after them.

Liam, Fia, and Caelin took up the rear, following the mob inside, ready to hear sounds of shouting or fighting from up ahead. But they heard no such thing. Instead, an eerie silence seemed to swallow everything. The islanders stood inside the tree, crowding around something in its center. The giant redwood the Arch-Elemists lived in was by far the largest on the entire island, and most of the islanders were able to pack inside. But the crowd wasn't moving, and Liam, Fia, and Caelin pushed their way to the center of the room to see why.

The Arch-Elemist Dyzek lay upon a stone slab. His skin was bone white, his gnarled hands clasped over his abdomen. He was utterly silent and still. He was, Liam realized with a start, very dead.

As Liam stared at the dead body in disbelief, much like the others standing around him, other islanders made their way down a set of stairs that snaked its way up the inside of the tree trunk, presumably having just searched the other levels.

"They're gone," Aran announced, slowly making his was down the steps. "They've abandoned us."

Part Four

A Dead Man

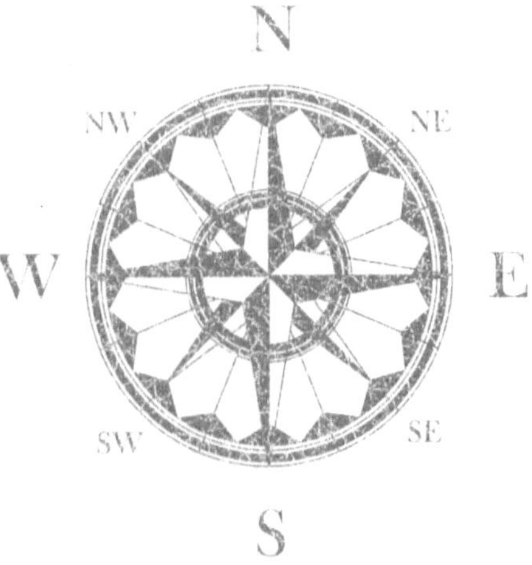

Chapter Forty-Seven

"**I** *don't want you.*"

Sean had been tortured on multiple occasions. He'd been shot, more than once, stabbed several times. He'd lost count of all the punches he'd taken. He'd been beaten to the brink of death. His very blood had been boiled in his veins.

And yet, nothing had ever been as painful as forcing those four words out of his mouth. The lie had carved its way up his throat, shredding him from the inside out. Nothing had ever hurt that much, but then he saw the look on Emery's face when the blow of his words landed. Somehow, that look had sliced him deeper than any wound.

When he watched his sister die, and through the grief and guilt-laden months that followed, it had been excruciating, but he'd also been mostly numb.

But in that moment, when he'd said those awful words to Emery, Sean had wanted the infection in his blood to just kill him then and there.

It had not. Nor had it killed him in the two miserable weeks since, as they raced across the sea after Ashborne and the *Audacity*. But he knew he didn't have much time left. His body grew weaker every day. He felt it every time it took a little more effort to stand up, or to open his eyes after each blink.

The only upside to the last few weeks was that they'd been so busy trying to keep the ship on course and at constant top speed, it had been relatively easy for Sean to avoid almost everyone. They worked in shifts, only stopping to eat and sleep before going back to work, which left next to no time for anything more than a quick conversation.

The varen ship was larger than the *Audacity*, and there were too few of them to sail it easily, even if they were allowing for longer breaks. He helped his crew as much as he could, shoving away the pain in his skin, his muscles, his very bones. Fighting back his ever-growing fatigue until he would quite literally pass out for a few blissed hours. He supposed that was another plus side. It had been a very long time since he'd been able to fall asleep immediately and not suffer from nightmares.

Frankly, he had no idea how he was still breathing.

The last few weeks were a blur of constant motion, but now, everything was silent and still, save for the pounding of Sean's heart as he peered through his telescope, ignoring the way the pressure of the metal against the sensitive skin around his eye ached.

The darkness of the night swallowed almost everything, save for three sets of lights in the distance. One set of lights marked the glowing lanterns aboard Ashborne's ship, the *Crimson Vengeance*, which bobbed languidly in the dark sea, her sails furled, and anchor let loose. The second set of lights marked the *Audacity*, which floated next to Ashborne's ship. Sean's throat tightened at the sight of his ship, and a quick scan told him that it didn't appear to be damaged at all, at least, not on the outside. The third set of lights, a few leagues further then the ships, marked the island. These lights moved, as if they were being carried, and Sean could only hope Ashborne and a good chunk of her crew were already on the island, looking for whatever the coordinates led to.

That's what they were relying on. They had a plan. A simple

one. But it should work, as long as Ashborne's crew was as split up as it appeared they were.

Sean lowered his telescope and glanced to his left. His entire crew, plus himself, Emery, Kess, Grace, and Ayana, all stood along the port railing, all of them gazing at the three clusters of lights with warring expressions of fear and hope. He couldn't actually see it on their faces—it was much too dark for that—but he felt it. And even though he could only see their silhouettes against the star-splattered night sky, and even though everyone wore an extra layer to ward off the cold, he could still tell who each one was. He could see Cam throwing an arm around Farley's shoulders, being mindful of his healing arm, in a reassuring farewell. He could see Rooney kissing the top of Aleksy's head, something he always did before a raid.

He could see *her*.

He allowed his gaze to linger on Emery longer than he'd allowed himself to look at her over the last few weeks. It hurt too much to do so, even more than the aching throughout his body. Especially when she would look back at him, her eyes full of so many emotions, he couldn't interpret them fast enough before he tore his gaze away again.

But now, as their stolen ship bobbed in the black sea, every lantern doused so they were hidden in the safety of the night, he allowed himself more than a fleeting glance. She wouldn't be able to see his face anyway, and soon, if all went well, they'd be parting ways and he'd never get to see her again.

And if things didn't go well...

He didn't let himself think about that.

Just like everyone else, Emery stood at the port railing, gazing through her telescope, separated from Sean by Billy and Ranit. She, like the others, wore an extra jacket to fend off the cold that had quickly settled around them the further north they sailed. Luckily, the varen ship had been well-stocked with jackets and coats and pants, but, of course, they were all varen colours. It had felt wrong watching his family wander around the varen ship wearing black, indigo, and silver. It had felt more wrong to wrap the coat around himself. He almost refused to put it on. He didn't notice the cold these days. His skin was always too fever-ish, too hot. But he didn't want to draw attention to himself, so he wore the jacket anyway, wincing at the colours and the weight of the thing on his skin.

He couldn't see the colours of Emery's jacket now, but he could make out the silhouette of her lim strapped to her back, and the way her long mass of hair was bound into a single braid. Sean watched as she lowered her telescope, and he was certain she shivered. From the cold or from fear, he couldn't tell, but he had to suppress the urge to go to her and wrap his arms around her just the same.

As if sensing his thoughts, she looked at him. He couldn't see her face properly, but he felt the pressure of her gaze. It was only because it was so dark and because she'd be gone soon that he allowed himself to gaze back. Even though it hurt just as much in the dark.

"Is it time?" Ranit asked quietly beside him, pulling Sean's attention away from Emery.

He swallowed, his throat still raw and aching. "Aye."

The steps leading up to the bow of the ship were to Sean's immediate right, and he climbed halfway up and faced his crew. He kept his voice low, knowing how sound carried easily over water. "You all know the plan, but it bears repeating anyway: Half of us will be taking the longboats to the *Audacity*. As we hoped, it looks like Ashborne's crew is split into three, which should make it relatively easy to board the *Audacity*, incapacitate the crew guarding her, and take her back. If all goes well, we'll be sailing away with our ship before anyone is the wiser. For those staying behind, as soon as you see the *Audacity* moving, you leave too. And if you see a flare?"

There was a strained silence. Sean knew they knew the answer, but nobody wanted to say it.

Always pragmatic, Grace spoke up. "If we see a flare, it means there's a problem and we're to prioritize saving ourselves."

"Aye," Sean said. "And this is your last chance. If anyone has changed their mind and wants to stay behind, there is no shame."

Nobody spoke up this time, as he knew they wouldn't. He'd just *hoped* maybe they would. If he could, he'd force them all to stay behind and he'd get the *Audacity* back himself or die trying. But he wasn't foolish enough to think he could pull something like that off alone, especially with his body failing as it was.

Sean took a breath. "Alright. It's time."

They moved silently and efficiently, everyone knowing exactly what they should be doing. In a few short minutes, two longboats were lowered into the dark water below and they were rowing towards the lights that marked the *Audacity*.

Sean glanced behind him at the varen ship and those who were staying behind. Seadar and Smythee, because they were too young and too old, and Sean had ordered them to stay. Farley, because he avoided conflict any time he could, and his arm was still healing. Ayana, because her leg was also still healing. Grace, because she refused to leave Ayana's side. And Kess, because he didn't have much experience fighting and they needed a medic to stay safe in case one was needed.

Sean then glanced at the second longboat quietly rowing behind the one in which he currently sat. Rooney, Aleksy, and to Sean's disappointment, Billy, occupied that one. Sean had tried to convince Billy to stay behind too, but Billy had none of that. The ship had been a home to him even before Sean was born, back when it belonged to Sean's father and Billy had been his navigator and first mate. Billy wasn't going to let the *Audacity* go without a fight.

Sitting across from Sean, rowing in silence and armed to the teeth, was Cam. Behind her, Ranit was twisted in his seat so he could watch them approach the *Audacity*. And somehow, Emery wound up in the seat beside Sean, sitting excruciatingly close. With every wave their little boat glided over, her shoulder bumped his, and Sean had to close his eyes against the onslaught of fire of both desire and pain that hit him every time. He could only thank the gods they weren't able to speak, lest they give themselves away to Ashborne's crew. And perhaps this was some sort of gift from the gods, one last moment of physical contact with her before they parted ways forever.

Ranit lowered his telescope, signaling the all clear. Too soon, their longboats were bobbing quietly alongside the *Audacity's* starboard side, near her stern. Sean reached out to steady the boat against the *Audacity,* so the waves didn't crash the two vessels together and give them away. Rooney did the same thing as the second longboat approached.

A little spark of hope flared in Sean's chest as he laid hands on his ship.

Maybe their plan would work.

Sean continued to hold the vessels steady as Emery, the best climber of them all, began to scale the *Audacity's* hull, reaching for a porthole first and then whatever handholds she could find next. For once, she wasn't barefoot. She wore a pair of leather boots to keep her feet warm. As she climbed, Sean fought the urge to yank her back down and insist someone else go up first. Better yet, insist that she take one of the boats and go back to the varen ship. But Sean knew that, apart from possibly alerting Ashborne's crew to their presence, his attempts would be futile. Emery had never wavered in her determination to help get the *Audacity* back.

As silent as a shadow, Emery reached the *Audacity's* railing and paused, peeking through the gaps to make sure the afterdeck was still empty. It must have been, because a moment later, she slipped over the railing and disappeared.

An agonizingly long minute ticked by as Sean, holding his breath, watched the spot where she'd disappeared, his ears straining for a sign of what was happening above deck. Just when he thought his nerves would snap, Emery's head poked over the railing, and she gave the signal. Sean released his breath as Emery lowered a few ropes, and Sean's crew began to climb up the *Audacity's* hull.

Once Ranit and Cam made the climb, Sean grabbed the rope and kicked the longboat away before hauling himself up. Usually, he'd be able to do the climb easily, but by the time he pulled himself over the railing, he was out of breath and dizzy, every muscle aching. He only hoped no fight broke out because he didn't think he'd be helpful.

"Captain," Rooney whispered. "Are you alright?"

"I'm fine." Sean pointed forward, signaling for him to keep moving.

Thankfully, no one else noticed. The others were all busy crouching in the shadows, weapons drawn, peering down at the deck below, where only a few men milled about. Sean silently drew his dart gun. The varen ship they'd stolen, of course, had plenty of those aboard for them to plunder.

But as Sean scanned the lower deck, counting only three men, each of them with his back turned, a new sense of foreboding prickled his spine. This was too easy. Nothing was ever this easy.

But his crew was already moving. On silent feet, they poured down the stairs onto the lower deck. With his heart in his throat, Sean followed. But he didn't even have to raise his weapon.

Cam took out the first man with a dart between his shoulder blades and a hand over his mouth to muffle his cry of surprise. Rooney paralyzed the second man in the same moment, and Aleksy, mere seconds later, shot a dart into the third man's neck, and palmed his mouth to keep him quiet until the curare took effect.

In just a manner of moments, the *Audacity* was theirs again. But Sean's unease did not waver.

Too easy.

A slow clap sounded, followed by the voice that haunted Sean's most recent nightmares. "How efficient."

Sean whirled to find Ashborne herself emerging from belowdecks, a smirk on her blood red painted lips. More of Ashborne's crew poured onto the deck after her—so many Sean knew it had to be almost all of them. They circled like sharks, swords and pistols drawn, forcing Sean and his crew to stand in a bunch together at the center of the ship.

A bang ripped through the night, causing Sean to startle nearly out of his aching skin. A burning light shot into the sky, arching over the water. Rooney had set off the flare to warn the others. Three men immediately pounced on Rooney, pinning him to the deck.

Sean fought his instincts to pull the men off his friend, knowing if a full fight started, they'd never win. They were too far outnumbered and not nearly as ruthless. He automatically placed himself between Ashborne and his crew, setting his expression to stone, so she didn't see the horror sluicing through his system, and the anger rushing at its heels.

Because how could he have not seen this obvious trap coming?

The *Audacity* had been the bait. The crew pretending to stand guard had been the decoy. The lights on the island were some sort of ruse. And he and his crew were the stupid prey that stepped willingly into the snare.

"I thank you for not making us wait long," Ashborne drawled. "You certainly made quick time."

"How did you know we were coming?" Sean asked, forcing his voice to remain steady. The last time she'd seen them, they were being captured by varens. How had she known they'd escaped?

"Did you forget I have a rather convenient tool at my disposal?" As she said it, an old man shuffled forward to stand next to her.

Sean's mouth went dry. The Wind Watcher.

Somehow, he *had* forgotten. Or at the very least, he hadn't considered that Ashborne would waste her time watching them. But he should have known. And now, his crew was going to pay for his mistake.

"While I admire your efficiency and determination, I obviously can't have such disrespect go unpunished." Ashborne raised a hand, and Sean braced himself for the fire.

But nothing happened.

"Sean!" Emery gasped and Sean spun towards her so fast, a wave of dizziness crashed over him. But at first glance, she seemed fine. She stood at the edge of their group, next to Ranit and Billy. Then he realized she was pointing out to sea.

The rest of his crew began murmuring with horror just as Sean realized what Emery was pointing at. It was difficult to see in the dark, but Ashborne's ship was moving. The *Crimson Vengeance* glided across the water like a silent specter, heading straight for the varen ship and the people they'd left behind.

Seadar, Farley, Smythee, Kess, Grace, Ayana.

The varen ship moved too, already fleeing at the sight of the flare as promised. But the *Crimson Vengeance* sailed faster, catching up at horrifying speed.

"Stop this!" Sean demanded, unable to tear his eyes off the two ships, unable to force his body to move.

But it wouldn't have mattered. Ashborne ignored him, and there was nothing they could do to stop it. Not when the deafening boom of cannon fire clapped like thunder. Not when the varen ship rocked violently with the shriek of cracking wood. Not when more cannons careened into her sails, effectively stalling their attempt at escape. Not when Ashborne's ship closed in, and the varen ship caught aflame, the orange-gold light of the fire so bright against the darkness, it seared Sean's eyes. Not when the loudest boom of all rattled the world, and the varen ship exploded.

Chapter Forty-Eight

A terrible stillness followed the explosion, the only movement the debris flying across the night sky like awful comets, the flames devouring what little was left of the ship.

Their friends, their family, had been on that ship.

And now they were...

Whatever restraint Sean's crew had earlier snapped. They lashed out in unison, united in their horror and grief and shock, taking out as many of Ashborne's crew as they could. But it seemed everything and everyone moved in the slow motion, the sounds all muted, as Sean watched the chaos unfold.

A few paces away, Emery screamed as she slammed her lim up into the jaw of the closest of Ashborne's crew, catching the man off guard and hurling him backwards. Another man tried to grab her, but she spun on one knee, dodging his hands and swinging her lim into the back of his head as hard as she could. He dropped like a stone.

Cam was a beast with her axes, screaming with rage for her lost brother as she took on three of Ashborne's crew at once. Rooney was still pinned to the deck but was struggling to rise as Aleksy slammed into one of the men holding him, gathering him into a chokehold and yanking him off her husband. Ranit and Billy fought back-to-back, blades flashing in the lantern light, slashing and slicing at anyone who came near.

Sean never raised his weapons. He was too stunned at first, but quickly realized he needed to stop this fight before they lost anyone else.

"STOP!" he tried to shout, but nobody could hear his ruined voice over the fray of the battle. He opened his mouth to try again when an all too familiar heat had him stumbling, sweat immediately breaking out across his forehead.

No, not again...

Fire flared in his veins, and it was worse than before, worse because his body was already so wrecked, so weak.

Screaming rose over the sound of battle, along with Ashborne's shout, "ENOUGH OR HE DIES!"

Sean realized belatedly that the screaming was coming from him, that he'd fallen to the deck, his back arching as fire raced through his veins. His world narrowed until all he knew was pain. There was only darkness and fire and nothing else.

Gradually, the pained waned. It didn't go away completely—there was too much damage inside him for that—but as he slowly came back to himself, he realized the remaining pain was the aftermath, and that Ashborne had stopped the torture.

Opening his eyes felt impossible, let alone moving any part of himself. If he'd been alone in a cell somewhere, he may not have bothered trying. He may have allowed himself to succumb to the darkness that had been waiting to claim him for weeks. But the knowledge that what was left of his crew still needed him, that Billy and Emery still needed him, bolstered the last of his strength.

He opened his eyes, finding he'd curled in on himself in the middle of the deck. His crew was now being held by Ashborne's crew, all of them having dropped their weapons and relenting their fights. Their expressions ranged from furious, to horrified, to grief-stricken.

For them, he rolled onto his hands and knees, ignoring the

way his entire body screamed in agony. For them, he rose to his feet.

He glared at Ashborne, even though his vision swam. "What do you want from us?"

"I want you to do my work for me," Ashborne said.

"What do you mean?"

"Well, judging by the last place this little treasure hunt led us, whatever is waiting for us on that island is going to be guarded by something dangerous. And I thought, why put myself or my crew in danger, when you were already on your way to do it for us?"

"Why on Roark's earth would we go to the island for you?"

At that moment, the hulking mass of Ashborne's ship glided up next to the *Audacity*. Ace—one of the men from the cemetery—shouted across the gap, his grin flashing in the lantern light. "There's no survivors, Captain."

The world tilted under Sean, as if he was falling with no end in sight. He wanted to scream. He wanted to cry. He wanted to break something. He wanted to break Ashborne. But he couldn't do any of those things.

"You'll volunteer because you've already lost a substantial chunk of your crew," Ashborne said, as if they were talking about a failed crop and not the family members she just murdered. "It would be a shame if you lost even more. In fact, let me give you further incentive."

Ashborne pulled a pistol from her belt, aimed at Rooney, and fired.

Screams erupted from Sean's crew, but Rooney merely grunted as the bullet struck him in the shoulder. He slumped forward in the arms of the two men holding him. Blood instantly flowed from the wound, staining his white tunic crimson.

"NO!" Aleksy cried, struggling against her own captors, kicking and flailing in her desperate attempts to get to her husband.

One of the men holding her struck her in the face. "Cut that out."

She kept fighting.

"Aleksy," Rooney's voice was calm, quiet, but it cut through everything, and everyone stilled. "I'm...alright."

"Indeed, he might be alright for now," Ashborne said mildly, holstering her pistol and smiling at Sean. "But he'll bleed out eventually. Here's the deal. If you can get to the coordinates and back before he bleeds out, I'll allow your blood healer to save him. If you take too long...well, I'm afraid he'll die too."

Chapter Forty-Nine

"You, you, and you. Join your captain in the long boat," Ashborne ordered, pointing at Emery, Cam, and Ranit with her pistol.

Feeling like she was watching from somewhere outside her body, Emery did what she was told, following the others into the longboat already prepared and waiting for them.

She wound up on a bench beside Cam, with Sean and Ranit on a bench behind them, and Ashborne's man, Ace, sitting at the bow. He sat back as if ready for a pleasure cruise, a pistol in one hand and a coin flitting across his knuckles in the other.

Ashborne tossed a bundle of weapons at Ace's feet and locked her stormy gaze on Sean. "These are so you don't die getting me my treasure. But if any of you try anything funny, like attempting to take those weapons and turning them on us, I will shoot more of your crew. And you're running out of people."

Sean said nothing, his face so awfully blank, Emery wasn't sure he'd even heard her.

Frankly, Emery was surprised Cam didn't immediately reach for a blade and stab Ace through the eye after watching her brother get blown up, but it seemed even she knew when to cede. Or maybe she was also in shock.

"Better get rowing," Ace drawled.

Emery and Cam each grabbed an oar and rowed across the dark water. Nobody else spoke.

Emery's entire body trembled, but she couldn't tell whether it was from rage, shock, or the cold. She'd never experienced cold before, not like this. Back home, the weather and temperature were regulated. It was never too hot, never too cold. But this island without a name was so far north, the air felt like frigid fingers against her cheeks. Every inhale seared her throat a little, and the wind currently attempting to yank her hair from its braid was as sharp as teeth. The extra layer of the cursed varen jacket she wore certainly helped, but not enough.

When they reached the rocky shore of the island, everyone silently climbed from the boat except Ace. He tossed the bundle of weapons onto the beach. "Best get going before your man bleeds to death," he advised. "I wager he doesn't have much time left."

Cam reached for the weapons first, rage morphing her expression, and Emery was certain her shock was over, and Ace was about to meet a bloody death. But then, with a shriek, Cam launched herself not at Ashborne's man, but at Emery.

Emery didn't have time to do anything before Cam caught her around the middle and they both hit the cold, rocky ground. Emery's breath exploded out of her, and her skull rang where it hit a stone.

"This is your fault!" Cam cried, punctuating her statement with a fist to Emery's face. "You caused all of this! You killed my brother!"

Pain lanced through Emery's cheek and the taste of copper flooded her mouth. She was so stunned, physically, mentally, and emotionally, she barely got her hands up in time to catch Cam's wrist before it came down again, this time with the dagger in hand.

The sharp point lowered closer and closer to Emery's eye. She pushed against Cam as hard as she could, but Cam was bigger and stronger, and had the advantage of being able to bear all her weight down on the weapon.

Plus, she had fury and grief lending her strength.

Just when Emery thought her arms were going to give in, the dagger disappeared, and Cam's weight lifted from her body as Sean and Ranit dragged her off.

Emery scrambled to her feet, blinking away the stars still exploding in her vision, and fell into a fighting stance. She instinctively reached for her lim, but Ashborne's men had taken it. She had no weapons at all.

"STOP, CAMULUS!" Sean commanded, struggling to keep hold of one of Cam's arms as he and Ranit wrestled to hold her back. "That's enough!"

"This is her fault!" Cam shouted. "She shouldn't get to live while...while..."

Her voice broke into a sob, and she slumped.

Sean and Ranit heaved her onto the ground and then both stepped in front of Emery, blocking her from Cam if she tried to start another fight. She stood up, wiping at her face with the back of her fist, but made no further move.

Ranit held up his hand in a placating gesture. "We're all hurting, Cam. But this will solve nothing."

"It would make me feel better to see her bleed," Cam snapped.

"Rooney is already bleeding," Ranit said. "Think of him."

"I *am* thinking about him!" Cam yelled. "I'm thinking about him and Farley and Seadar and Smythee and the *Audacity*. I'm thinking of all that's been lost because of her!" She pointed an accusing finger at Emery, and she may as well have thrown the dagger at Emery's heart. Then she pointed at Sean. "*You* were literally just tortured *again* because of her."

Emery felt as though she might shatter because it was all true.

"I'm sorry," she tried to say but it came out as a tiny whisper she didn't think anyone could hear.

"We don't have time for this, Cam," Sean said, his voice deadly calm.

"Tell me this isn't her fault!" Cam spat.

Sean said nothing and Emery was glad she couldn't see his face, glad she couldn't read his expression. He had to agree with Cam, had to hate her even more now. How couldn't he? After a beat, he said, "If you ever touch her in malice again, you will no longer be part of our crew."

Cam reeled back as if Sean had struck her. An awful silence swallowed the island as Ranit's gaze snapped to Sean. Cam just stood there, her throat bobbing, her eyes wide with shock and fury and hurt. "What crew? Half of us are gone. The other half may not see dawn. And we don't have a ship." She met Emery's gaze and Emery couldn't stop herself from flinching as Cam added, "Because of her."

With that, Cam spun on her heel and marched up the beach, stopping several paces away to cross her arms and await further instructions.

Sean and Ranit both turned to face Emery. But it was Ranit who stepped forward to examine Emery's face, and Ranit who asked, "Are you hurt?"

Emery shook her head, even though she felt a bruise forming on her cheekbone and tasted blood in her teeth. She deserved both.

Sean didn't approach, didn't say anything. When Emery built up enough courage to look him in the eye, he merely gazed back at her for a few strained moments. His face was pale but void of emotion, that mask of stone so secure, Emery had no idea what he was thinking. And yet, she knew him well enough to know he was likely drowning in emotions behind that mask after everything that just happened. Drowning, but not allowing himself to crack or gasp for air. He swallowed once, then bent to retrieve the supplies Cam had scattered, breaking their eye contact.

He dispersed the remaining weapons—a few knives, swords, and pistols—silently between the three of them. She noticed the way Sean's hand's shook, the way his breathing was slightly too fast. Was it from that night's events or something else?

Ranit must have noticed too. "Captain, are you alright?"

"I'm fine."

Emery gripped the long knife she was given, its pommel cold in her grasp. She twirled the knife a few times to get used to its foreign weight, before sliding it in her belt.

A map had also been included with the bundle of weapons and Sean unrolled it, his eyes scanning the landmarks, while Ranit held up one of the two lanterns they'd also been given.

"Emery, do you still have the compass I gave you?" Sean asked, and though he didn't look at her, that question was composed of the first words he'd said directly to her in weeks.

She tried to ignore the way her name on his lips flipped her heart, but also refused to say the truth out loud: *I never go anywhere without it.*

Silently, she dug the compass from her pocket and dropped it into his open hand, taking care not to let her fingers brush his.

She suddenly felt unanchored without the compass, and tried to ignore the way her chest ached when Sean went back to ignoring her.

Now was not the time to allow emotion in.

"Should we split up, Captain?" Ranit asked, eyeing Cam where she waited up the beach. "We could cover more ground that way."

'*And keep Cam away from Emery,*' he didn't add.

"It's too dangerous to split up in the cold and dark when we have so few supplies. Besides, thanks to Grace, we know exactly where to go. We stick together." When no one disputed him, Sean tucked the map and compass into his pocket, and pointed at a narrow path leading into a forest of scraggly pine trees. "We go east."

They hiked in silence, and Emery wondered if it was to conserve their energy, because everyone was still in shock from watching the ship explode, or if no one wanted to speak about any of it because it would all feel suddenly real, and panic would set in.

For Emery, it was all three.

She felt like she was in some sort of nightmare, watching herself from afar the entire time they hiked through the trees, searching for the cursed coordinates. They walked single file through the forest, since there wasn't really a proper path. The branches overhead blotted out any light the stars may have provided, and they only had the ever-shifting, orange lantern light to see by. The light and shadows flickered around them as they walked, making it impossible to know where to step. They tripped over hidden stones and roots poking out of the frozen dirt.

Cam and Ranit walked ahead, and Sean took up the rear. She was all too aware of him behind her, could hear his heavy breathing and the way he'd trip just like the others. But he seemed to trip more often, and sometimes, it took him a while to get back up. She tried to help him only once. He ignored her, using a tree to climb to his feet instead, and walked on as if she hadn't been there at all.

The terrain grew steeper, the pine trees bigger, and if it had been any other time, Emery might have felt more grounded at the familiarity of the landscape. It was wilder than home, but it still gave her an intense sense of nostalgia.

Eventually, the trees began to thin again, and a white crust of something smothered the rocks and moss. Emery bent to touch the crust and was surprised to find it freezing cold and wet. It felt solid too, but if she pressed hard enough, her finger went through it. "What is this?" she wondered out loud.

"Snow," Sean said.

Emery's head snapped up to look at him. He leaned against a tree, nearly panting. He watched her with an unreadable expression on his face that made her throat go dry. It was the longest he'd deigned to look in her direction in so long.

"Is there no snow in Orabel?" he asked.

He didn't sound angry. He didn't sound anything at all, and that was almost worse.

She'd seen snow in Orabel only once, when her grandmother had turned some water into great, big, fluffy snowflakes. They had been soft and beautiful, but this stuff below her feet was hard and unrecognizable.

Emery shook her head, and once again, was overcome by the compulsion to apologize. *I'm sorry I lied. I'm sorry I didn't tell you before. I'm sorry I got you tortured. I'm sorry you lost your ship. I'm sorry you lost your home. I'm sorry half your crew might be dead. I'm sorry, I'm sorry, I'm sorry.*

Her lists of regrets was endless.

The entire journey here, she'd oscillated between guilt, shame, rage, remorse, and acceptance. And she hadn't been able to do anything about any of it. She'd been so busy trying to keep the ship on course, so they could reach the *Audacity* as fast as possible, that she'd barely seen Sean at all. She knew he'd been avoiding her too, so she hadn't been able to apologize again. She hadn't been able to process the fact that she was angry that he thought so little of her after everything they'd gone through together. She hadn't been able to tell him she'd do anything to make things right—if it was even possible. She hadn't been able to tell him that she could not stand the thought that this was how things would end between them. Couldn't stand the thought that things would end at all. She hadn't been able to tell him that, if this really was what he wanted, she'd respect his decision. If he hated her so much now, she'd leave him alone and not bring him further pain. Even if it killed her.

Now, as their gazes held for longer than they had in weeks, her numbness was giving way to the same barrage of confusing emotions. She wanted to say everything she hadn't been able to say before. Instead, she asked, "Are you alright?"

Because not only was Sean panting, he also swayed on his feet, despite the fact that he was clearly holding on to the tree for support. Sweat shone on his forehead in the lantern light, despite the chill of the place.

"Maybe we should take a break?" Ranit suggested from behind Emery. He and Cam had stopped as well, and Ranit raised his lantern a little higher, so it illuminated more of Sean's face.

Sean immediately ducked his head and stepped forward, moving around the three of them to lead the way. "We don't have time for a break. Rooney doesn't have time."

So, they kept going. The ground grew steeper, and the snow got deeper, turning soft enough that they sank into it with every footstep. Emery was grateful she wasn't barefoot like usual, but even her boots didn't keep the cold from nipping her toes.

Sean led the way for a while, but slowly began to fall to the back again. No one said anything about it. Emery suspected they all knew he was trying to hide how much he was struggling and that he was failing at it. And they all knew saying anything would do no good. Emery wondered what, exactly, was wrong with him. Clearly, he wasn't alright. Did Ashborne's blood boiling leave him more injured than he let on? How unwell was he?

Eventually, they came to a stream where they could fill the one flask they'd been given and take turns gulping the icy water. Emery gasped as she took her first sip, the water so cold, it seemed to freeze all the way down her throat into her stomach.

Sean splashed the icy water on his face and the thought of doing such a thing made Emery flinch. But the cold didn't seem to be bothering Sean at all. In fact, his jacket was open, with only his tunic beneath, and sweat had clung to his forehead before the water washed it away.

Ranit crossed his arms, taking care not to skewer himself with his hook, and gave an exaggerated shiver. "I don't know how you do that, Captain. I'm frozen enough without the help of glacier water."

"This is nothing," Cam said, swiping the flask from Emery and taking a long swig. "We used to bathe in streams like this back home."

Emery couldn't stop herself from asking, "Where are you from?"

Cam just glared at her.

"Farther north, in Jokul," Ranit supplied for her. "Where it snows your height in a night, and you eat ice for breakfast."

Cam turned her glare on Ranit, tossed the flask to Sean, and stomped away in the direction they were heading.

"That certainly explains a lot about her personality," Emery mumbled, and immediately felt awful about it. Cam had just lost her brother, after all.

But to her surprise, a low chuckle sounded from behind her, where Sean was perched on a boulder. He covered it by drinking from the flask but she'd heard it. That one little sound sparked a flicker of hope in Emery's chest. Despite everything she'd done, and everything that was happening right now, maybe that laugh meant she had a minuscule chance of forgiveness.

Ranit laughed too. "It certainly does."

On they walked.

On and on and on.

Emery was simultaneously outraged that dawn hadn't arrived yet, so they could see better and possibly warm themselves, and relieved because if it was still night, then the evening was moving slower than it seemed, and Rooney hopefully still had time.

The terrain eventually grew so steep, they had to start climbing up boulders, sometimes slipping in the snow or sliding back down a few paces as loose stones fell away beneath their feet.

Finally, the ground levelled out into a sort of clearing atop a cliff, the grey stone mostly clear of snow due to the whipping wind having blown it away. A few pine trees and rocky bluffs dotted the area, but otherwise, there was nothing else to see.

Emery glanced at Sean as she bent double to take a few deep breathes. He was examining the map, holding it tightly as the wind tried to snatch it from his fingers, and then he checked the compass. A line formed between his brows as he slowly turned in place and scrutinized their surroundings.

"What is it, Captain?" Ranit asked, the hem of his coat flapping wildly in the wind.

"The coordinates should be here somewhere, but the compass isn't working. There's too much iron in the rocks, maybe." He glanced around again. "But we should be close, if we're not already here."

"It would help if we knew what we were looking for," Cam grumbled, glaring at Emery as if she was keeping such a thing secret.

Sean glanced one last time at the map and compass, and then stuffed them back in his pocket. "I suppose it might be time to split up and start searching. But we all stay on this bluff, and nobody goes far. If we can't find anything here, we'll move on somewhere else together."

After taking a moment to make a couple of makeshift torches so each of them had their own light source, their group of four scattered in different directions. Emery made her way to the trees, and held her torch high, searching for anything that might catch her eye. But all she could see was pine trees, rocks, snow, and ever-shifting shadows. All she could hear was the wind whistling through the branches. When she turned, the others were all out of sight. She could have been the only one on the island.

Emery sighed with frustration as she wandered, scanning the forest floor, the branches, the piles of snow that remained against tree trunks. She, too, wished they knew what they were looking for. The trees eventually spat her out at the edge of the cliff, where the wind howled even louder, and the night sky blanketed everything. She knew the ocean was out there somewhere, that the *Audacity* and a bleeding Rooney were out there somewhere, but the darkness hid it all.

She turned to head back into the trees and almost ran straight into Cam. Startled, she took an involuntary step backward, but her foot found nothing but air.

She fell.

Flailing, she managed to grab the edge of the cliff with both hands and scrambled to find a foothold. Her torch tumbled into the darkness below.

Clinging to the cliff, she stared up at Cam. The flickering light of Cam's torch cast her face in skittering shadows, causing her grin to look positively murderous.

"Oh dear," Cam said. "Quite a predicament you've found yourself in."

Chapter Fifty

Emery tried to haul herself back up the cliff, but every time she moved, more rock broke away, until all she could do was hold still and cling to the side of the cliff with her heart hammering in her chest.

Cam glared down at her, grinning, and making no move to help her.

And Emery knew Cam would sooner kick her off the cliff than pull her up.

The cold quickly sapped the feeling from her fingers, making it harder and harder to hold on. Taking a deep breath, she tried to steady her racing pulse, and mentally reached for the earth, urging it to stay together long enough for her to climb up. She reached for the closest tree too, commanding it to lean forward so she could grab hold of one of its branches. But neither earth nor tree seemed to be listening to her. She couldn't concentrate through the primal fear flooding her system.

"Teralyn's Teeth," she cursed. She'd spent her entire life standing at the edge of a cliff, staring at the horizon and imagining the outside world. Now, after surviving a storm, a sea monster and whole society that wanted her dead, she was going to die on another cliff. How stupid.

"It seems justice is about to be served," Cam mocked.

Emery did not want to beg, did not want to ask Cam for help at all. But she also desperately didn't want to die. "Cam, please..."

Cam crossed her arms and leaned against the closest tree. "Sean said I couldn't touch you. Now I don't need too. But at least I'll still have the pleasure of watching you die."

Anger flared inside Emery. "I saved your life! You owe me!"

"You killed my brother!" Cam cried, her calmness shattering in an instant. "You killed them all."

"I'm sorry," Emery said, and she meant it. Of course, she meant it. "I didn't want any of this to happen."

Her fingers were so numb now, she couldn't feel them at all.

"But it did," Cam said. "I knew from the moment Sean brought you on our ship that you were going to be his downfall. You wrapped him around your finger and there was nothing any of us could do."

"I didn't—"

"You did! And we'd only just gotten him back! We were so close to losing him and barely got him back, and then you showed up and I knew we were going to lose him again."

Emery's foothold crumbled and she scrambled to find another.

Cam either didn't notice or didn't care. She couldn't seem to stop talking now. "After Lily died, it was like he had died too. He was a specter of himself. For almost an entire year. He even tried —" She broke off and swallowed hard. "He was destroying himself. But then, slowly, he began to come back to us. Then you showed up and he actually smiled and laughed, and I knew we were all screwed because you basically brought him back and it would be so easy for you to take him away again. And that's exactly what you did."

Emery tried to process what Cam was saying, but her numb hands were slipping. "That's why you've always hated me?" she asked through gritted teeth. "You wanted to protect Sean?"

"Well, I did a piss poor job of that, didn't I? Because he's been destroyed. Again."

The ground beneath Emery fingers crumbled and her stomach disappeared as she fell. But then something grabbed her wrist, and yanked her up, practically flinging her up over the cliff, and onto the solid ground amongst the trees. She landed on her stomach, the air huffing from her lungs.

The cold of the ground immediately leeched into her body, and she tasted blood again.

But she was alive.

Emery quickly rolled onto her back. Cam stood over her, panting a little and glaring a lot. She wiped her hands on her pants, as if touching Emery had tainted her somehow.

Emery stared, unable to quite believe that Cam just saved her. "Thank you."

Cam spat on the ground, narrowly missing Emery's boot. "The only reason I didn't let you fall is because that stupid idiot is so in love with you and he doesn't deserve to lose anyone else."

With shaking knees, Emery picked herself off the ground, and mumbled, "He isn't, actually."

"Excuse me?" Cam said.

Emery squeezed her eyes shut. She wasn't even sure why she was saying this to Cam of all people, not when it hurt so much to force out. "He doesn't love me."

Cam scoffed. "I'm not blind. He loves you and you shattered his heart. You don't think I noticed the way he used to look at you, and now the way he suddenly *can't*? You broke his heart, just like I knew you would."

"He doesn't want me, Cam!" Emery shouted, her nerves snapping. "He told me he doesn't want me. He *hates* me."

Cam blinked, as if confused. "He told you that?"

"Yes." Emery blew out a breath, trying to bring her anger back down. "He can't forgive me for...any of it."

Cam's expression shifted into something else. Something like...alarm. "He *would* forgive you, though."

"What?"

She shook her head slowly. "Sean would never hate you for any of it. He's too... He's too good."

Emery crossed her arms. "Well, he does."

"No..." Cam's eyes flared wide. "He's protecting you."

Now Emery was confused. "Protecting me from what?"

Cam's face drained of colour, and then rage contorted her features. "That idiot!"

She took off through the trees, and Emery chased after her, tripping over rocks and roots as she followed. When they reached the clearing, Cam paused, scanning the area with wild eyes.

"Cam, what—"

"Shut up!"

Then they heard Ranit's voice, loud and...angry.

Cam rushed towards his voice and Emery followed at her heels.

"How could you not say anything!" Ranit's voice was closer, louder, angrier. "Why would you keep this a secret from us?"

Cam and Emery rounded a crop of rocks to find Ranit and Sean standing close. Ranit's face was a riot of emotion. Sean's remained stone.

Cam marched right up to Sean and shoved him square in the chest. Sean reeled backwards and fell hard to the ground.

"Cam, what the—" Emery cried, rushing forward to get to Sean. But to her surprise, Ranit caught her shoulder, holding her back.

"Wait," he said. His fingers shook where they gripped her shoulder.

"Get up!" Cam shouted at Sean.

Sean slowly sat up but didn't stand.

"Get up." Cam demanded again, her voice growing more frantic.

"Cam..." Sean's voice was quiet, too quiet, and his breathing too shallow.

"Get. Up." Cam's voice shook, and her eyes filled with tears.

Dread flooded Emery's veins as Cam's words back at the cliff and her actions now finally clicked together in her head. Cam hadn't shoved Sean out of anger. Well, not purely. It was a test.

Emery stepped forward. "You can't get up, can you?"

"I...can." Sean used a nearby boulder to pull himself to his feet, but he swayed dangerously, that sheen of sweat gleaming on his forehead again. He gritted his teeth as he said, "I'm...fine."

"That's enough, Sean," Ranit snapped. "Stop lying to them. Tell them what you just told me."

Sean swallowed once, twice. He wouldn't look at any of them. "Ranit, please..."

"Fine, I'll tell them!" Ranit insisted. Emery had never seen Ranit angry before. She'd begun to think maybe he never lost his temper. But he was furious now. "He's dying! He's been dying for weeks, since Ashborne tortured him, and he didn't bother to tell anybody. He's just letting himself die."

"I'm not letting myself die, Ranit," Sean said, his stony face finally cracking. "There's nothing that can be done."

"Bullshit," Ranit said. "You're doing what you always do. You're protecting everyone else at your own expense. And now we're going to lose you too."

Ranit turned and stomped off into the dark.

Cam marched up to Sean, so they were nearly nose to nose. "You're an idiot."

She shoved him again and turned to follow Ranit before Sean even hit the ground.

Emery was left standing there, staring at Sean as he slowly hauled himself into a sitting position. He rubbed his hands on his pants, his palms scratched and bleeding from catching himself on the rocky ground. He didn't bother standing again. Maybe he couldn't.

Because he was dying.

He was *dying*.

One of the lanterns had been left on the ground next to Sean, and the light played off the side of his face as he angled his head away, refusing to look at her. She stared at him while Cam and Ranit's words bounced around her head.

You're doing what you always do. You're protecting everyone else at your own expense.

He's protecting you.

A hurricane of horror and guilt and anger and hope churned inside her as the truth finally set in. She crouched in front of him but didn't touch him. He stared at the ground.

"Sean," she whispered, "is it true?"

She knew it was. Gods, she knew. Everything made sense now.

But she needed to hear him say it.

He was silent for so long, she thought he might refuse to answer. He shifted, placing a bloodied hand against the ground as if to prop himself up because even sitting was too difficult. Finally, he whispered too: "Yes."

The earth began to tremble, to shake.

Sean finally looked up, their confused gazes locking.

Something groaned and then cracked. And the ground beneath them split open, swallowing them both whole.

Chapter Fifty-One

Liam could taste the panic clogging the air of Orabel. It was sour, cloying enough to gag on. He'd thought when the time came to finally tell the truth, he would feel better. That it would all be better.

But it was so much worse now.

It had been about a week since the islanders burst into their leader's home, only to fine one dead from the Withering and the others simply gone, as if they'd vanished into the wind. Were the Arch-Elemists powerful enough to literally do that? No one quite knew. Liam remembered Emery's story about how their supposed Aunt Lilith had burst into flames before Emery's eyes only to vanish immediately after. Perhaps they'd done something like that. But most of the islanders figured they probably made themselves a ship and sailed off into the night.

In the end, it didn't matter *how* the Arch-Elemists left. It mattered *why*. But the islanders didn't have the answer to that question either. Did they fear facing the consequences of their lying and manipulation? Or did they fear staying in Orabel to wait for either the Withering or Tavor to destroy them?

Because Orabel *was* going to be destroyed. It was only a matter of what did it first.

Liam wondered if perhaps the Arch-Elemists had simply grown tired of leading and decided to save themselves, leaving their people to flounder.

And flounder they did. The first day without leaders was chaotic as the islanders argued amongst themselves over what to do. They'd never had to decide things on their own before. The Arch-Elemists had always done it for them, after seeking consult with the gods and the elements first.

Eventually, it was decided that they'd vote in four new Arch-Elemists to lead the islanders. The first to be voted in was Aran, as he was one of their top healers, had an efficiency with water, especially when it came to blood healing, and he had been openly against Tavor and his plans from the beginning. Second to be voted in was Liam's grandmother, due to her exceptional skills with wind and her overall high standing amongst the community. Third was a woman named Dhara who was greatly skilled with earth and was largely in control of the Gardens. Last was a man named Sulien, who had proficiency with fire.

Once the new Arch-Elemists had been established, the panic waned slightly. But that had been their smallest problem. Now, they still needed to figure out what to do about the Withering and about Tavor. The new Arch-Elemists had huddled away together in their tree, to attempt to communicate to the gods, to seek answers. That had been five days ago.

During this time, Liam had mostly hidden in his bedroom again. Now that the truth was out there, everyone wanted to bombard him with questions. Questions he either didn't want to or didn't know how to answer. And he didn't want to keep living it all over again. He was wrung out and exhausted. His job was done now, wasn't it? He just wanted to sleep and let someone else deal with everything.

But as Liam glanced out the window at a sky streaked with crimson and violet, he knew this one night he couldn't hide away. The new Arch-Elemists had come up with a plan, a solution to all their problems, and they were going to announce these plans in the clearing after sunset.

Liam knew he should be there to learn what his future held, but he had waited until the last minute, waited until most of the islanders would already be at the clearing and he could skulk along the shadows in the back, so no one would see him and be tempted to speak to him.

As he'd hoped, he saw no one as the glowing light of the fungi flanking the paths led him to the clearing. And as he hoped, it seemed everyone had arrived. His people sat in rows of wooden benches growing directly out of the grass. He had a strange sense of deja vu from the day when Tavor showed up on their shores and they had a meeting just like this one. Everything looked the same, until one looked closer. Tavor, of course, was not present this time. But many others were missing too. Like Emery and Ayana and Grace. Like the many islanders who had succumbed to the Withering. Like the Arch-Elemists, inexplicably gone.

Instead, the new leaders sat upon the chairs on the dais before the crowd. It was so strange seeing his own grandmother up there, garbed in a robe of woven leaves and a crown of twisted branches resting upon her dark braid. Liam couldn't decipher the expression on her face, but she seemed...displeased.

Liam remained standing in the shadows instead of finding himself a seat. He wanted to hear what the new Arch-Elemists had to say, and then flee back to his room.

"I knew you'd be hiding back here," a voice whispered in his ear.

Liam nearly jumped out of his skin.

Fia stood behind him, her eyes sparkling mischievously in the dying light.

Caelin was there too, arms crossed, his sword sheathed at his hip. "Good to see you're still alive," he murmured.

Guilt washed over Liam. He hadn't just been avoiding the others. He'd been avoiding his friends too. "I'm sorry. I was just—"

"I know," Caelin said. "Me too."

With that, he turned to watch the dais. Fia patted Liam on

the shoulder and turned to watch too. Liam let out a breath of relief, struck by how much he loved his friends, and then he, too, turned to learn of their fate.

The new Arch-Elemist Dhara was already talking. "We have spent the last five days and five nights communing with the gods and discussing amongst ourselves about what we should do about our two largest problems. The first being that the Withering has gotten stronger. It has now taken one of our most powerful and we now know no cure is likely coming."

"What about Emery?" someone asked from the crowd.

Liam's grandmother answered. "While my granddaughter is indeed searching for a cure, there are no guarantees she'll find one. And if she does, it could take years. We need a solution now."

"Our second issue," Dhara continued, "of course, is Tavor Thantos. There is a chance that he is dead, but there's also a greater chance that he is alive and still coming for us. He could very well be on his way right now, to destroy us and turn our home into a prison for elemists."

There was a horrible silence as the words fed the flames of fear amongst the islanders.

"We've come up with a simple solution that should solve at least one of our problems," Sulien said. "And that may give us insight into the other. We're leaving Orabel."

Silence swallowed the island as the world tilted beneath Liam's feet. Then voices shattered the silence, echoing Liam's shocked thoughts.

"But Orabel is our home!"

"We can't just leave! Where would we go?"

"How does leaving solve anything?"

Aran stood, raising his hands for silence, and eventually, the crowd quieted enough for him to say, "Yes, Orabel has been our home for one hundred and fifty years. It has been our safe haven. But it is not safe anymore. Outsiders know about us. They might be coming for us as we speak. Orabel only exists because we created it. So, we'll make a new island somewhere else, somewhere they'll never find us. We will let Orabel fall back into the depths from which we raised it, like it was never here."

Liam hadn't realized he was moving, hadn't realized he was shoving his way to the front of the crowd until he stood right before the dais. "We can't just leave! Emery, Ayana, and Grace are still out there! How will they find their way back to us?"

Aran and the two other Arch-Elemists exchanged uncomfortable glances, while his grandmother stared down at her tightly clasped hands, lips pursed.

"We have taken this into consideration," Aran said, "and we feel it might be safer if Emery can't find her way back."

Liam's jaw dropped open. "What?"

"While the fact that Emery is searching for a cure is admirable, she may never find one. In the meantime, who knows how many people she may divulge Orabel's secrets too."

"She would never—"

"You don't know that. It might not be on purpose. It might not be her fault. Either way, we now know what can happen if outsiders find us. We kept ourselves a secret for so long. To stay safe, we must do so again."

Liam opened and closed his mouth, too stunned for words.

Aran continued. "As for Ayana and Grace, they know the rules. It is forbidden to leave, but they did so anyway. They're no longer welcome back. And that's *if* they even made it anywhere. The Arch-Elemists may have stopped them. They may not be a factor at all."

Liam stared at Aran, and then shifted his stunned gaze to his grandmother. "Grandmother..."

She could barely look at him. "It has been decided."

Again, Liam lost his words. Behind him, the crowd was growing louder, rowdier. Someone shouted, "But how does leaving solve the Withering?"

"Leaving the island may not completely solve the Withering," Aran began. "But it can help us learn whether the disease is environmental or not. It's possible that there is something here that's killing us, and if we leave..."

Aran's explanation continued, but Liam lost track of it as he forced his way back through the crowd, back to the shadows. He couldn't catch his breath, couldn't steady his steps. When he finally broke free of the crowd, he slumped against a tree, sucking in breath after breath that never seemed to reach his lungs.

They were leaving. They were leaving the only home he had ever known, the only home his sisters had ever known. Emery and Ayana would never be able to make their way back to him. They could sail the Barren Sea forever, searching for an island that had been left behind to crumble into the sea.

If they were even still alive.

Fia and Caelin found him again. Fia's fingers brushed his back, causing him to shiver slightly.

"We can't leave," Liam said immediately. "I can't leave. I can't not be here if Emery, Ayana, and Grace come back. Even if the others go, I can't. Stay with me." The last part just slipped out.

Fia looked at him sadly. "I can't stay, Liam. My mother must go, and I need to take care of her. She'll die alone without me."

Liam's stomach hollowed out. If Fia left, and he stayed, would he be allowed to find them again? Would he ever see her again?

"I'm leaving too," Caelin said, his voice oddly calm.

"What?" Liam gasped. "What about Grace?"

"I'm not leaving with our people," Caelin said. "I'm not going to the new island. I'm going back out there to find our sisters. Our job was to warn Orabel, and we did that. Now it's time to leave again."

Liam stared at his best friend. "Did you forget how we almost died sailing back here? Or how big the world is? How will you find them?"

"I don't know. But I must try."

"But if you leave now, how will you find the new island?" Liam asked.

"I don't know that either. Maybe I won't."

Liam felt like his entire world was collapsing around him,

which it soon would, literally, once the islanders left. Everyone he loved was scattering in a hundred directions. He felt like he was being pulled in each one, like he was about to be ripped apart at any moment.

And he had absolutely no idea what to do.

Chapter Fifty-Two

Emery groaned as she rolled onto her back, the ground cold and hard beneath her body, her bones battered and bruised. Her brain too. It was working so slowly, too slowly, as she tried to piece together what just happened.

She'd been kneeling before Sean, reeling from his confession that he was...

Her mind couldn't even think the word.

But then the ground had split open, like a gaping mouth, and had swallowed them both. Had she done that by accident? She didn't think so, but she didn't have any other explanation.

She opened her eyes, her gaze immediately falling to the only source of light barely illuminating her surroundings. Sean's lantern, which must have fallen into the earth with them, was shattered across the stone ground. Only a puddle of oil was left burning, the only thing keeping her from being plunged into complete darkness. Because there was no hole in the earth above them now. Whatever hole they'd fallen through had sealed itself back shut, allowing nothing, not even light, to get through.

As Emery scanned the tiny cavern, she realized there was no debris littering the space either, no fallen rocks or layers of dust like there should have been if the ground had collapsed naturally.

There was nothing at all, except her and Sean.

Her breath hitched as she spotted him, lying on his back, unmoving in the shadows, almost out of reach of the tiny flame's light. She crawled to him, heart in her throat, ignoring the way her whole body felt like one giant bruise. He didn't stir as she approached and she couldn't tell if he was conscious or even breathing in the dark.

She hovered over him, scared to touch him, scared to move him in case she hurt him any more than he already was. "Sean?" When he didn't reply, she gently lifted his head, placed it on her lap. She barely grazed his cheek with her fingers, his skin so hot under her touch. "Sean?"

He winced, turned his face away from her touch. She withdrew her hand as his eyes fluttered open. He stared at her blearily, stared past her at the dark ceiling of rock above them. "Em?"

Relief flooded through her so strongly, she grew dizzy.

"Are you hurt?" she asked, resisting the urge to touch his cheek again.

He didn't answer right away, as if taking a moment to assess his body. "Honestly...it's hard to tell."

Because he was already hurt, already dying.

Emery closed her eyes at the sudden onslaught of emotions that hit her like a tidal wave. She wanted to cry, to scream, to hit him, to kiss him. She wanted to demand answers, wanted to continue to live in blissful ignorance. But all of it needed to wait.

"What happened?" Sean asked, his bleary gaze taking in the dark cavern. He didn't try to sit up, didn't even try to lift his head from her lap, and Emery knew that was not a good sign.

"I don't know. The ground collapsed and we fell. But it wasn't a cave in. And it wasn't me, I don't think. Was it you?"

Again, it took him a moment to reply, and Emery wondered if he was rallying energy just to be able to speak. "I don't think so."

"Maybe it has something to do with the treasure," Emery

said. "Maybe we're getting close, and we set off a defense mechanism of some kind, like those skeleton things at the cemetery."

"Cam?" Sean asked. "Ranit?"

"I don't think they fell."

She saw the relief wash over his features. And then panic. Finally, he tried to sit up. "We must get out of here. Rooney..." He rolled from Emery's lap onto his hands and knees, tried to stand but swayed and fell back to his hands and knees, his head hanging, hair falling over his face. He stayed like that, breathing hard.

"Sean?"

He shook his head, but otherwise didn't move.

"Are you trying not to pass out right now?" she asked.

He nodded once.

Gods. Holding her emotions at bay, she got to her feet. "Can I help you?"

"Alright."

The one word told Emery more than anything else. He didn't try to tell her he was fine like he normally would. He didn't try to hide how difficult simply standing had become for him. He knew he couldn't stand without her, and he admitted it, which meant things were dire indeed.

She took his elbow as gently as possible but didn't miss the way he sucked in a breath as if it hurt. She draped his arm over her shoulders and stumbled as Sean swayed again and she caught nearly his full weight. His breathing was shallow, fast, ragged in her ear.

Emery focused on the task at hand, scanning the cavern. They needed to get out of there. The walls were too far away from their meager light source, too shrouded in darkness for her to spot any openings. She looked at the flame, wishing it were bigger, brighter.

"Wait." She closed her eyes, concentrating on that tiny fire, sensing its fighting spirit, the way it was determined to keep burning until it couldn't possibly burn any longer. She allowed some of her emotions, a mixture of anger and hope, to feed the flame. The fire flared. Its light bathed every inch of their stone cage, except for a slice of shadow it couldn't quite reach, a gap in the stone that led into darkness and only the gods knew were else.

Forcing herself not to lose her concentration, Emery pointed at the gap. "There."

"I see it," Sean said, breathlessly. "We're going to...need light."

Emery wondered if she could manipulate the fire into moving through the tunnels, or to let her take a scoop and hold it. In the end, she knew she didn't have enough skill to do either of those things, that she'd likely burn one or both of them, or accidentally extinguish their only light source.

She ended up leaving Sean to lean against the wall, to set about making a torch. Again, the fact that he didn't even try to help terrified her to her core. And again, she forced herself to think only of the task at hand. She took out her knife and made to start cutting the hem of her jacket.

"Wait, use mine," Sean said. "You need yours."

"And you don't?"

He shook his head and Emery realized his jacket was still left open, and even the strings of his tunic beneath had been loosened, exposing some of his chest and the way it shone with sweat. Emery swallowed hard, realizing that whatever the blood boiling had done to him had left him perpetually overheated. She hated that she hadn't put that together until now.

She refused to look at his chest as she concentrated on slicing strips from the hem of his coat without slicing him too. He didn't bother taking the coat off. He trusted her enough not to cut him. Or maybe he didn't care about a cut at this point. She glanced up once, caught him watching her with a sad little smile.

"What?" she asked.

"Nothing."

She held his gaze. "I think the time for you to be hiding things from me is over."

He chewed his bottom lip before answering. "I was thinking about how I've imagined you ripping my clothes off me countless times, but I never imagined it would be like this."

Emery's whole body flushed, and she had to tear her gaze away again. She hacked through more fabric. But finally, she had to say it: "I thought you didn't want me."

Sean didn't reply, not until she looked up again. His expression was as serious as she'd ever seen it, his stare intense. "I lied."

She closed her eyes against his gaze and took a step back with her handful of rags. Not knowing what to possibly say to that, or how to even process it, she set to work making the torch. She didn't have a stick, so she tied the fabric to the sharp end of her knife, rubbed it against the ground where the oil from the broken lantern had splattered and then dipped the makeshift torch into the tiny flame. The fabric caught fire with a whoosh, and they had light. She only hoped it would last long enough.

She went back to Sean. He watched her with another intense expression, but this time, she didn't ask. She couldn't—not right now.

With Sean's arm once again draped across her shoulders, they made their way through the gap. It led to a tunnel just wide enough for them to shuffle through sideways. It seemed to go on forever, or maybe they were just moving painfully slow. Regardless, neither of them spoke, but Emery snuck glances at Sean's face. His eyes were squeezed closed, his breaths still shallow and fast. She wondered if he was fighting back pain or still fighting to remain conscious.

And then she remembered how he hated small spaces, realizing that he was likely doing both those things while trying not to panic.

"We're going to get out of here, alright?" Emery whispered. "Both of us. I'll make sure of it."

He nodded once.

Finally, the tunnel opened into another cavern, this one even smaller than the last. The walls were stone, but the ceiling looked to be made of ice.

"Thank the gods," Sean said in a rush.

"Rest while I look for another exit," Emery said.

Sean did not resist as she deposited him against a wall, and he slid down until he sat on the ground. Emery strode to the center of the cavern, held her torch higher. The cavern was strangely round, the walls as smooth as glass. Definitely not natural. Someone had made this place. Emery prayed to the gods that meant they were getting close to the treasure. That soon, they'd be able to find it and get back to Rooney before they lost him too...

Now that she wasn't moving, panic bubbled up inside her, the horror of everything threatening to erupt and drown her until she couldn't function anymore. She forced it all down. She'd feel it all later. If there was a later.

Her hands still trembled though, as she turned in a slow circle, causing the torchlight to dance across the smooth walls with jerky movements.

Sean swore softly, then pointed. "Up there."

And then she saw it. A hole in the wall about three times the height of herself. It was much too high to reach, even if she stood on Sean's shoulders. There was no way to climb up the smooth walls either. But it appeared to be the only way out.

Emery grew more certain they were nearing the treasure. This had to be some sort of puzzle or trick they had to solve to get to it.

No sooner had the thought crossed her mind when a grinding noise behind her made her jump. She whirled in time to watch the tunnel they had just come through seal itself shut, the rock melding together as if the tunnel had never been there at all.

Sean swore again.

And then she felt the soft grains of sand sprinkling down on her head. Shielding her eyes, she looked up. Sand trickled from several small holes near the ceiling, like tiny waterfalls of dirt raining down on them, slowly filling up the cavern.

"Oh no," Emery whispered. Dismay churned her stomach, because she knew if they didn't figure out how to escape this place, they were going to be buried alive.

Chapter Fifty-Three

"This must mean we're close to the treasure," Sean said, echoing Emery's previous thoughts. His voice was steady, but Emery heard the way he gritted his teeth, probably trying to keep his own panic at bay. Even though sand sprinkled down upon his head too, he didn't try to stand. Another bad sign.

"I suppose that is a bright side," she said, not sure who she was trying to convince. She stared at the smooth wall, contemplating whether either of them were skilled enough with earth manipulation to carve stairs or ladders into the stone, so they could climb up. Or even handholds. If they could just get up to that hole, they'd be fine.

Her torch sputtered, and then burned out, plunging them into a darkness so complete, Emery couldn't tell when her eyes were opened or closed. A gasp ripped out of her, and the panic she'd been holding back broke free.

The darkness transported her back to those dungeons, to that cell. She was trapped again. Trapped in the dark with no way out. Trapped, and unable to do anything but wait for someone to hurt or kill her.

Emery stumbled backwards and slammed her back against the wall before sliding down to the ground. She brought her knees to her chest, and threaded her fingers through her hair, squeezing her eyes shut, even though it made no difference. She couldn't catch her breath.

"Em?"

She didn't reply. She couldn't reply.

"Em, don't panic," Sean's voice was difficult to hear over the sound of the sand scattering across the ground around her and her own roaring heartbeat. "Dawn must be close and the ceiling above us is ice. That means when the sun comes up, light will filter through, and we'll be able to see again. Soon."

His words bounced off the cavern walls and Emery tried to grasp them, to cling to them like a life raft out at sea. Light would come soon. And Tavor was not here, was not coming for her. But what if the sand filled up the cavern before the light came? What if the time it took to wait for the light was time Rooney didn't have left?

Emery tugged on her hair, the pain reeling back some of her panic. But without the panic, everything else—the horror, the grief, the rage—welled up to replace it.

She needed to clear her mind so she could focus on getting them out of there. She needed to distract herself, to get rid of some of her emotions.

"How much time do you have?" she said into the darkness.

Sean misunderstood the question. "I think the sand will take an hour or two to fill the cavern—"

"No," she cut him off. "How much time do *you* have?"

He didn't respond.

"Tell me, Sean."

"You want to talk about this now?"

"I need to know. I need to talk about this, so I can concentrate when the time comes."

Sean sighed. "Aleksy gave me a few weeks...a few weeks ago."

Emery's heart sank. "And this is because Ashborne boiled your blood?"

He paused, the sand pouring into the cavern the only sound. "Aye."

"How... How many times did she do that to you?" She didn't want to know. But she had to know.

He didn't reply again.

"Sean, please tell me." She didn't mean for her voice to come out so quiet, so brittle. But it did.

Sean's voice was quiet too. "I lost count."

Emery squeezed her eyes shut again, trying to trap her tears inside. It didn't work. Sean was dying, and it was her fault. Rooney was dying, and it was her fault. Ayana, Grace, Farley, Seadar, Smythee...

"I'm sorry," she managed to choke. She shoved a fist into her mouth to keep from sobbing. Gods, she was falling apart now.

"I know," Sean said softly.

"Was there any truth to the things you said to me? Were you ever angry with me?"

She didn't understand how he couldn't be, how he couldn't possibly hate her.

Again, his voice was soft. "No."

This was worse. This was worse than if he did hate her. She wished he did. She wished he hated her and wasn't dying, and things were as she thought they'd been. Because this was so much worse.

Her rage flared. "Cam's right, you are an idiot!" she shouted into the darkness. "We could have helped you! I could have helped you! Instead, you said nothing and pushed me away? Why?"

She *knew* why, but again, she needed to hear him say it.

But he said nothing.

"You were trying to push me away so when...so I wouldn't hurt when you..." She couldn't say the word.

So he did. "When I die."

She flinched, angry tears welling again. "Well, guess what, Sean? You can be mad at me. You have every right to be. You can hate me. You can try to push me away, but I will *still* hurt. I will *not* be alright if you die. So, stop trying to protect everyone else for once and let us help you. Let us, at the very least, be there for you."

Sean was quiet for a long time. "It's not *if* I die. It's *when*."

Emery sniffed. "I refuse to believe that."

"Aleksy said the only way to save me is a blood transfusion and there are very few healers able to do that. The closest is a thousand leagues away."

"Aleksy isn't a god. She'd doesn't know everything. Maybe we can try something else."

"There isn't—"

"You don't know that!" Emery shouted, her voice too loud in the tiny cavern. "And I refuse to just let you die without even trying. When we get out of here, promise me you'll let us try to save you."

"Em—"

"Promise me!"

He hesitated once again. "Alright."

Emery lay her head on her knees, suddenly exhausted. The cold stone floor and wall were sapping away her body heat, and the cool sand was up to her ankles already. Now that she wasn't moving, the cold seeped into her bones. She shivered, her teeth chattering loud enough that Sean must have heard.

"Are you cold?" he asked.

"I'm fine."

"Come here," he said gently.

She thought about it, thought about crossing the cavern to sit next to him and share his heat. But she honestly thought being that close to him right now might shatter her composure even more. So, she stayed put.

Through the ever-sprinkling sand, she heard rustling, and then a groan. Sand shifted, and then warm fingers touched her ankle, moved up to her knee. Sean let out a quiet groan again as he pulled himself up against the wall next to her and sat down. Her heart tripped when she realized he'd *crawled* across the cavern to get to her because he couldn't stand on his own.

"Come here," he repeated, and she didn't resist as he pulled her onto his lap. He tucked her head under his chin and her cheek pressed into his chest. He wrapped his open jacket around her, his arms pulling her tight. The heat coming off his body was equal parts delicious and disturbing. She felt it against her cheek, but also through his tunic. He radiated heat like a fire.

She couldn't stop herself from snuggling closer to the warmth, even as her heart ached over what had been done to him, the damage that was slowly killing him and the knowledge that this could be the last time she felt his touch, because if the sand didn't suffocate them soon, then the damage to his body would take him anyway.

They sat in silence for a while, the sand sprinkling on their heads like heavy rain. Emery was acutely aware of every one of Sean's shallow breaths ruffling her hair, of the way his heart raced a little too fast against her ear, of the way he was holding her tighter than necessary, as if he feared he'd lose her in the darkness if he loosened his grip.

"Tell me about Orabel," he said.

The name of her home coming out of his mouth somehow sounded both foreign and familiar, wrong and very right.

"You're really not angry that I didn't tell you I'm from there?" Emery whispered, still not sure she believed it.

"No. Hurt, a little, to think that you didn't trust me enough to tell me."

Emery interjected quickly. "That's not why—"

"I know," Sean said. "Your sister explained that you couldn't tell because it's forbidden. I understand now."

Emery swallowed a lump in her throat, not sure what to say.

"Do you want to know what I really thought when I found out you were from Orabel?" Sean asked.

Honestly, she wasn't sure. "Alright."

"I thought it made sense."

"What did?"

"It made sense that the girl of my dreams was from the place of my dreams."

Emery sucked in a breath and didn't know whether she wanted to laugh or cry or swoon. "Sean..."

"I'm sorry. I know I shouldn't say things like that," he said.

"What—why?"

"Because I'm dying, Em." He said it desperately, as if he needed her to understand this simple thing. "And even if I wasn't, my life is a disaster. I'm a fugitive. I have *nothing*. I don't even have a home anymore. What can I possibly offer you but danger at every turn?"

This time she laughed. "You really are an idiot."

Sean was silent for a moment, obviously shocked. "Well, that was rude."

She sat up, and twisted so she was facing him, even though it was so dark she couldn't see his face. But she could feel his heat, his breath. She wanted to reach up and cup his cheek, but didn't want to hurt him, so she settled on gripping the collar of his tunic instead. "I meant what I said about wanting *you*, Sean. I don't need anything else. I don't want anything else. Plus, last time I checked, all of this danger we're in is because of *me*. And you want to talk about not having anything to offer? *I* have nothing. I don't even have my own clothes." She laughed again, feeling almost delirious to finally be saying these words. "Literally, all I have to offer is me and me alone."

There was another stunned silence, until Sean whispered, "You're all I want."

His fingers skimmed across her cheek, cupped her jaw, and pulled her closer. And even in the pitch black, he found her lips with his. He kissed her like he might never get to again, like she was his last gasp of oxygen before his head went under water. And she kissed him back just as desperately, because this could be her last chance to do so, still clutching at his collar to keep her hands from trailing down his chest and causing him pain.

He broke away first, unable to catch his breath. Emery placed a gentle hand on his cheek, and realized she could see him, just barely. Just the faint outline of his silhouette.

Gasping, she looked up. The ice above glowed with the faint, purplish light of dawn. It barely illuminated the cavern, but it was enough.

She kissed Sean one more time. "We'll finish this later," she promised.

She felt steadier, more determined. Ready. She'd get them out of there. They'd save Rooney and the others. They'd get the *Audacity* back. And then she'd save Sean. There was simply no alternative to any of these things.

Carefully, she rolled from Sean's lap and got to her feet, sand pouring off her as she moved. The sand was so soft, she sank into it. It reached her knees now, but since she'd been sitting on Sean's lap, and he'd, in turn, been sitting on some already fallen sand, she hadn't realized how deep it had gotten.

But she could see now. She could concentrate. She could get them out.

She slung Sean's arm over her shoulder once again and helped him to his feet. He couldn't suppress his groan and she couldn't imagine what kind of pain he was in, what kind of pain he'd been in for weeks, without letting anyone know.

Slowly, they made their way to the other side of the cavern, where the hole in the wall was, sinking into the sand with every step. At first, she'd hoped they could simply wait for the sand to fill up to the height of the hole and they could stand on it. But it was too soft.

Another grinding sound echoed throughout the cavern, and the rushing sound of falling sand grew louder as more of it poured from the ceiling. The cavern was filling up faster. Too fast. It already reached her thighs.

Sean swore softly under his breath, his hand squeezing hers. His whole body trembled, and she wondered if he was finally cold, if it was from too much exertion, or if it was his repressed panic finally showing itself. Possibly, it was all three.

"I won't let us die down here," she promised. "But I'm going to need your help."

Sean nodded.

"One of us needs to concentrate on keeping the sand directly below us hard enough to stand on," she said. "And the other needs to force the sand to build up underneath us, so it lifts us to that opening."

"I don't know if I can," Sean said, his voice trembling now too.

Emery swiveled so she faced him again. She wrapped an arm around his waist and placed a gentle hand against his cheek, forcing him to look down at her. She wasn't sure how much of her face he could actually see, since she could still mostly make out only his silhouette, but it would have to do. "You can do this. You must. Concentrate on me, and block everything else out but the sand below our feet."

Sean wrapped his own arms around her, pulling her tight and keeping his gaze directed at her. She couldn't see his eyes, but she sensed them on her like a physical touch. The sand beneath her feet grew harder and harder, until it felt more like stone.

"Good! Keep doing that."

Emery stared up at his silhouette, at the familiar shape of his jaw and his windswept hair outlined against the dawn. She shoved everything else aside but hope and determination, and mentally reached for the sand filling up the cavern, demanding every individual grain to do as she commanded. She willed the sand to move beneath them, to lift them.

And then they were rising, little by little, as Sean forced the sand directly under their feet to remain solid and Emery manipulated the rest of the sand to flow beneath that.

"It's working," Sean said in disbelief, his grip tightening on her as they rose ever so slowly.

Emery couldn't reply; she was too busy concentrating.

"We're almost there," Sean said.

When Emery finally opened her eyes, and twisted around enough to look, she found he was right. The hole was close, so close.

All they had to do was hold on a little longer.

As soon as it was within reach, they scrambled through the opening, both of their concentrations breaking. The sand collapsed a moment later. Emery felt a moment of relief—they'd made it! —before she realized the hole they'd crawled into was slick and steep, and there was nothing to hold onto. And it didn't lead up and out like they'd hoped. It led down.

She and Sean both screamed as they slid deeper and deeper into the earth.

Chapter Fifty-Four

Sean tried to grab for Emery as they slid deeper into the bowels of the earth, but he couldn't find any part of her in the darkness. The tunnel was smooth as ice and so steep there was no stopping their descent. All he could do was brace for impact whenever the tunnel ended.

It felt like eons before the tunnel finally spat him out. His momentum sent him rolling across another stone surface, until he slid to a halt on his back, the breath knocked out of him. Emery was flung from the tunnel a second later. She fetched up against him and for a moment, they both just laid there, staring at each other as their bodies got used to being still again.

"Are you alright?" she asked, her blue eyes an ocean of worry.

Sean blinked at the realization that he could actually see her eyes and glanced up. This newest cavern had another ceiling made mostly of ice, and pinkish gold light filtered through. Dawn had officially broken. His stomach dropped. What did that mean for Rooney?

"Sean?" Emery probed, her voice full of worry now too. "Are you alright?"

He looked back at her, belatedly realizing he hadn't answered her. Was she wondering if he was alright mentally, emotionally, or physically?

Because the answer to all three was: no.

He was wound so tight with panic—from the uncertainty of his crew's fate, from being trapped in such small spaces for so long, and from knowing his body would soon give up on him—he felt like he was about to implode.

His skin screamed from the abrasive texture of the sand that had nearly buried them alive. His bones bellowed in pain from his first fall into the earth and then the second slide deeper. His head hammered. His heart raced to keep his dying body alive. His lungs were losing their battle for oxygen with every breath.

He was certain if he closed his eyes now and allowed himself to drift off, he would never wake again. But he couldn't do that. *Wouldn't* do that. He refused to leave Emery alone down here. He refused to die until he knew his family was safe.

"I'm alright," he lied. "You?"

"I'm fine." She scanned his face, likely sensing his lies. But she didn't call him out this time. Maybe she needed the denial too.

She sat up, looked around, and her whole body tensed. She whispered, "Sean."

He sat up too fast, his alarm launching him upright before his body was ready. Dizziness crashed over him but he blinked it away so he could follow Emery's gaze. He sucked in a breath.

On the opposite end of the cavern, all on its own, sat a chest. "The treasure," he exhaled.

"It has to be," Emery said, but she didn't sound elated to see it.

He understood. Hope and weariness warred in his heart as he scrutinized the cavern. It was longer than the others, and appeared empty, save for them, the chest, and a pile of boulders and rubble strewn across the middle. "It's too easy," he said.

"I don't know about you," Emery managed to quip. "But that last part was not easy for me."

"What do you think will happen if we approach? More sand? The walls close in?" Sean asked.

"Well," she said, sighing, "there's only one way to find out."

She was right. They couldn't just sit there and contemplate forever, until Rooney bled out and Sean's body gave up and Emery was left alone to starve to death. Whatever awaited them, they had to keep moving forward. At least they could face it together.

"Can you stand?" Emery asked.

It was Sean's turn to sigh. He did not want to stand. "Aye."

Emery climbed to her feet, shaking sand from her hair and clothes. She gently took his arm, slung it around her shoulders, and heaved him to his feet.

Any other time, Sean would be embarrassed by his own feebleness. But his pride had long since been depleted and he was simply thankful that she was here with him, still inexplicably *wanting* to be with him after everything. He still couldn't quite wrap his head around the conversation they'd just had, couldn't let himself think about it too hard, because he knew any future they could have had together was lost because of Ashborne.

At least he could feel her warm presence by his side in these final moments, something he had craved and missed so much over the past few weeks. Now he wished he hadn't squandered that time by pushing her away.

Gods, he truly was an idiot.

He clenched his jaw against the pain that attacked his entire body inside and out as Emery helped him remain on his feet. His vision wavered, and he closed his eyes, willing himself to stay conscious, to stay with her.

He could not, would not, leave her alone.

They both gazed at the chest across the cavern, so far away, yet so close. What was in there that Ashborne wanted so badly?

Without another word, they slowly began making their way towards the chest, picking their way over the rocks littering the ground. They made it about halfway without anything happening. But then the noise began. A scraping, grinding noise that, at first, Sean couldn't place.

Then he realized the rocks were moving, rolling and sliding across the ground towards the pile of boulders just ahead of them. The stones molded together, forming a huge shape. The shape rose from the ground, standing on a pair of hind legs. Its front paws tore at the air with stone claws longer than Sean's dagger. It reared its huge head, baring stone teeth, sharp as steel, and roared.

"What is that?" Emery gasped.

"I think it's supposed to be a bear," Sean said, sighing.

The stone bear dropped onto his four paws, the impact shaking the earth, and began pacing back and forth, effectively blocking their path to the chest. But it didn't attack. Not yet.

"How are we supposed to get past that thing?" Emery asked. "We can't fight it. Our weapons are useless."

"Do you remember how, at the cemetery, the skeleton things chased us until you bled on the chest? How they just sort of disintegrated after that?" Sean asked.

"You think that will work again?" Emery asked slowly.

He shrugged and repressed a hiss of pain. "It's all I can think of."

"That still leaves the problem of us getting past it."

"Not us. Just you."

Emery's gaze snapped to him. "Don't even start—"

"Em, you must get to the chest. It's *your* blood that needs to touch it."

"We don't know only my blood works!"

Sean ignored her. "Besides, I can't walk on my own, let alone run. I'll distract it, while you find a way past it."

Emery's face paled. "Absolutely not. I'm not going to leave you here. We can think of another way."

"If you have another idea, by all means, suggest it."

Emery looked away, stared at the bear. "Damnit, no. I'm not doing this. Why are we always faced with this choice?"

She was panicking. Sean reached out, gently caught her chin, and turned her face towards him again. "You're not leaving me. I'll be right behind you. Just get to the chest."

"Sean, I can't—"

He leaned down and kissed her—hard—knowing that despite everything he was saying, it could be the last time he was able to. Then he shoved her away, firmly enough that she stumbled backwards and fell behind one of the remaining boulders.

Already sweating with exertion, Sean roared and charged at the bear. It roared back, the sound reverberating off the stone walls so loudly, he felt it in his bones. It charged for him too. It ran on three paws, raising the fourth in anticipation of swiping at Sean. But Sean knew one blow from that stone paw would likely be lethal. At the last second, he dove out of the way, flinging himself behind another boulder. The bear leapt after him, crashing into the boulder. Chunks of rock flew. Sean covered his head as debris rained down on him and took a quick moment to peek at the spot where he last saw Emery. She was gone, hopefully climbing her way towards the chest, unobstructed by stone monsters.

Sean clambered to his feet and ran back towards the side of the cavern where they'd entered, as far as he could get from the chest. The bear gave chase. Sean's entire body screamed in agony as he sprinted and scrambled over rocks, barely able to keep ahead of the beast. His vision darkened at the edges, his breaths searing his throat, his lungs.

He shoved the pain and the fear into the shadows of his mind and let pure adrenaline keep his body going. He concentrated everything he had left into the air around him. It was still and stagnant from being trapped underground for so long. But it was also willing, eager, and excited to finally move again, so it was surprisingly easy for Sean to muster up a twister to surround himself, one just big enough to swallow him in its center.

He tripped, fell hard to his knees, but the twister remained. And it was doing its job. He turned to see the bear hesitating on the other side, growling at the screaming wind as if confused. It pawed at the twister, then pulled its paw back when it was buffeted.

It wouldn't keep the bear away for long, but at least Sean was granted a brief respite to catch his breath. Only, he couldn't. He couldn't seem to get enough oxygen in his system, couldn't breathe fast enough or deep enough. He tried to stand, to get ready to run again, but he couldn't do that either. He could barely stay kneeling in the dirt. He was out of energy. A darkness tugged at him, pulling him towards the earth, insisting that if he only lay down, if he closed his eyes, everything would be better.

He didn't realize his body was slumping to the ground until the ground began to shake. He blinked, opening the eyes he didn't remember closing, and saw his twister had faded, and the shaking of the ground was from the bear charging right for him, mouth agape and teeth gleaming in the dawn light.

Unable to do anything else, he wondered if he'd be shredded by those teeth, or sliced with the claws, or crushed under the bear's feet. At least Emery could get the treasure and get back to his crew. She didn't need him anymore.

Sean stared the bear down and braced himself for impact as the beast closed the final distance.

The bear exploded into dust. Sean choked and coughed as the rocky powder that used to be the bear fell all around and on him. He tried to find the strength to lift his hand to wipe the dust from his face, but he couldn't do it. He barely had the strength to keep his eyes open, let alone feel relief that he wasn't dead.

Until Emery shrieked.

Chapter Fifty-Five

Emery had not meant to scream. It had slipped out.

She'd raced across the cavern as fast as she could, flinging herself up and over any boulder in her way, knowing if she arrived a second too late, it meant Sean's life. She hadn't allowed herself to look back, to worry about whether Sean could hold the bear off long enough in his sorry state. She'd ran and prayed that no other rock monsters reared up to block her path. Mercifully, none did.

She'd made it to the chest, sliced her palm with her knife and pressed the hand to the lid. She'd turned, keeping her hand on the chest, to watch as the twister Sean had made vanished, to see Sean slump to the ground, to witness the bear launch itself at him.

Something had clicked beneath her palm then, and the bear burst into a cloud of dust, the cloud so thick, she could no longer see Sean. She heard him cough though, which meant he was still alive. For now.

She had removed her hand from the chest, looked down at the now unlocked lid, flipped it open, and shrieked upon seeing the contents.

It was not a shriek of delight or fear or pain.

It was of outrage and disbelief.

Sitting in the chest was one single coin.

Nothing else.

It was hardly better than rocks.

Emery stared at it, momentarily frozen in shock, and then the rage ripped through her.

Everything they'd been through, everything and everyone they'd lost, had been for one single coin? She couldn't believe it and couldn't decide where to direct the fury that was building up inside her. At Ashborne for wanting this so badly, she tortured and murdered to get it? At her parents for pointing her in the direction of this stupid treasure hunt? At herself for so badly wanting to find out what became of her absent parents that she just had to follow this lead?

Her rage burst into dust much like the stone bear had done as she heard Sean's voice calling her name. She spun and saw him trying and failing to pick himself up off the ground. She snatched the stupid coin from the chest and raced back towards him, shouting, "I'm fine! I'm coming!"

He glanced up, saw both these things were true, and seemingly gave up, slumping back to the ground.

Oh no.

It took a few agonizingly long minutes for Emery to pick her way back across the rocks, her gaze never straying from Sean. He was covered head to foot in white dust, which made him look like a ghost of himself, something she didn't want to think about.

Finally, she dropped to her knees beside him, scanning him for new injuries. "Are you alright?"

He pried his eyes open with obvious effort and admitted. "I'm so...tired."

It was the first time Emery had ever heard him complain about...*anything*. Her skin grew cold with terror. She could not let his eyes close again, not down here in these caves.

She helped him sit up, a cloud of dust rising around them as he leaned against her.

"Why did you scream?" he asked, his voice alarmingly quiet, like he was fading away.

She held up the coin. "Because this was the only thing in the chest."

Sean blinked a few times, as if struggling to focus on the coin. He reached out and Emery dropped it into his open palm.

"It's not even gold," he said after a moment.

Indeed, the coin was a dull black, though Emery couldn't tell if that had been the original colour or if it was weathered. There were a few symbols around its edges and the figure of a woman in the center etched in gold, though.

Regardless, Emery couldn't tell whether he was angry or upset. Perhaps he was too far gone to feel anything at all.

He flipped the coin over, peered at the other side. "Perhaps it's something more priceless than gold? Or maybe it contains some sort of magic, like Grace said." His voice suddenly sounded ...stronger. "It doesn't matter. We must get this back to Ashborne immediately."

He tried to stand, and Emery leapt to her own feet, surprised by Sean's sudden new vigor. He still needed her help, still needed to wrap an arm over her shoulder to stay upright. But he was able to catch his breath.

When Emery's blood touched the chest, an opening had also appeared at the halfway point of the cavern. An exit, presumably, and they headed for it now.

The opening led to yet another tunnel, its icy roof allowing light to see by. Having no other options, they stepped into the tunnel and began walking. The going was slow, but no more obstacles appeared in their way until the tunnel split in two. They hesitated.

"Which way should we go?" Emery asked.

"Left," Sean said immediately, confidently.

Emery raised a brow at him. "How do you know?"

"I'm not sure," Sean admitted. "But I'm certain we need to go left."

With no reason not to, they followed the path on the left until they came across another split.

"Right this time," Sean said quickly. So, they went right.

They came across several more splits in the tunnels, and each time, Sean was immediately confident that he knew which way to go.

They didn't speak otherwise, both concentrating on putting one foot in front of the other, their heavy breathing echoing in the tunnels. Now that they'd found the treasure and didn't seem to be in any immediate danger, exhaustion weighed Emery down. After the rushed two weeks of getting here, the constant onslaught of adrenaline and emotion, the fact that neither of them had slept all night, and constantly having to bear a significant portion of Sean's weight for so long, Emery felt her body beginning to give out, to beg for rest.

She had no idea how Sean was still going.

But he was. He still moved forward, though slowly and with a lot of help from her, still giving directions as if he knew these tunnels by heart.

They had no way of knowing if his seemingly random guesses were correct until they rounded a curve in the tunnel and bright sunlight pierced their eyes. The tunnel sloped upwards, and the light filtered through another layer of ice and foliage.

Together, they kicked and bashed the ice until it shattered, and then shoved the foliage aside so they could finally, finally escape the earth. They crawled out onto a rocky beach and lay on their backs for a moment to catch their breaths, pine trees swaying in the breeze above them. The cold ocean lapped lazily at the shore, gulls cried in the distance, but otherwise, everything was quiet.

Sean pointed down the beach, to where the shore curved and hid whatever lay beyond from view. "That way."

They hauled themselves back to their feet and dragged themselves down the beach, the rocks crunching under their boots. The sun had fully risen now, casting everything in soft hews of pinks and golds. It could have been romantic, if it had been any other time, if Sean's heat at her side wasn't abnormally hot, if the way he leaned into her wasn't because, if he didn't, he'd collapse on the beach and possibly never get up again, if their destination wasn't their bleeding out—or possibly already dead—friend.

Sean gasped as they followed the curve of the beach and a boat wedged into the shore came into view, with three people standing around it: Cam, Ranit, and Ashborne's man, Ace.

Relief shot through Emery. At least those two were alright.

Cam spotted them first and ran the length of the beach to meet them, Ranit close on her heels.

"Thank the gods!" Cam cried as she skidded to a halt in front of Emery and Sean. "What happened? Where did you go? We looked everywhere!"

"Are you both alright?" Ranit asked. He immediately took Sean's other arm and Emery almost groaned with relief as some of the weight was lifted from her tired body.

"We're alright," Sean said. "You?"

"We're fine," Cam said. She pried Sean's other arm from Emery's shoulder so she could help Ranit keep their captain upright.

Emery didn't have it in her to protest. She trailed behind them as they made their way back to the boat, rolling her sore shoulders.

"We spent the rest of the night looking for you," Cam continued. "What happened?"

"It's a long story," Sean said. "Rooney?"

"We don't know," Ranit replied. "They wouldn't give us any updates. Did you find what was at the coordinates?"

Ranit glanced back at Emery, as if double checking he didn't somehow miss a giant chest of treasure in her arms. She winced. "Yes. We found it."

By that time, they'd reached the boat. Ace leapt from it with a little splash as they approached. "The treasure?" he asked, his coal-rimmed eyes roving over the four of them in search of it.

Sean removed his arm from around Cam's shoulders to dig in

his pocket. He held up the coin. Ranit and Cam stared at it, clearly as dumbfounded as Emery had been upon first seeing it.

But Ace did not look disappointed or even shocked. A gleam entered his dark eyes and he grinned. He took a single step forward, holding out his hand. "Give it to me."

Sean closed his fist over the coin. "No. I'll give it directly to Ashborne."

Ace glared but must have quickly realized they all had weapons now, and he was outnumbered. "Fine. In the boat."

The boat ride back to the *Audacity* was one of the longest of Emery's life. No one spoke, but Sean's hand found hers and she held on to him for what felt like dear life. The climb up the *Audacity's* hull somehow felt even longer. Sean only made it up with help from Ranit. And Emery climbed up after, terrified of what they were going to find on deck.

"Well, look at this! You made it back," Ashborne greeted them. "And with little time to spare."

Emery's eyes flew over the scene on the deck, which appeared similar to when they left, except Aleksy & Billy were now bound in rope and kneeling on the floor. Rooney, lay in a pool of his own blood, his skin stark white against the crimson puddle, his eyes closed.

Emery sucked in a horrified breath. They were too late. He was gone, he was—

Rooney's chest rose, fell, rose again in barely perceptible fractions and Emery's entire body numbed with relief.

"We did what you asked," Sean said, his voice hoarse from repressed emotion. "Let my medic tend to my man."

Ashborne gazed at Sean a moment, as if contemplating. "Oh, alright. I suppose he's waited long enough."

She snapped her fingers and one of her men cut Aleksy free. Aleksy flew to her husband, pressing her hands against the gunshot wound, murmuring words too soft for Emery to hear.

"There. I've granted some mercy. Now, where is my treasure?" Ashborne demanded.

Sean held up the coin, and just like Ace, Ashborne went

completely still, her eyes gleaming with want. She knew exactly what the coin was. "Give it to me."

"Release my crew first," Sean said.

"You really aren't in a position to negotiate, Denzel. In fact, I'm surprised you're even still standing."

Frankly, so was Emery.

"I'm not giving you this stupid coin until you release my crew and my ship," Sean spat, holding his ground.

"That stupid coin is probably the only reason you *are* still standing," Ashborne said, smirking. "You have no idea what you're holding, do you?"

Sean hesitated and glanced at the coin in his hand. "If you're not going to release my crew, and this coin is so special it's somehow keeping me alive, then why would I give it to you?"

"Because if you don't, I'll continue blowing holes in your crew. Your medic won't be able to stop them all from bleeding out." To emphasize her threat, Ashborne drew her pistol and aimed it at Billy.

Sean's face paled. Emery's breath stuck in her throat.

"I wouldn't do that if I were you," someone called out.

That voice.

Emery's heart leapt as she—and everyone else aboard the *Audacity*—whirled to face Ashborne's ship, which was still tied to the *Audacity*. There, standing at the railing, was Grace. And beside her, Ayana. All along the deck stood Seadar and Farley and Smythee and Kess, all of them armed, all of them very much alive.

Chapter Fifty-Six

Sean's knees nearly gave out with relief as he took in the scene before him. Grace, Ayana, Kess, Seadar, Farley, and Smythee all stood along the railing of the *Crimson Vengeance*, with Ashborne's crew bound and gagged at their feet.

They were...alive.

And somehow, they'd commandeered Ashborne's ship without her noticing. He could hardly believe it, and for a moment, he wondered if he was hallucinating again.

Ashborne stood very still, her pistol aimed at Billy as she scanned the scene aboard her ship. "What is this now?"

"If you start shooting more holes in our people," Ayana said, leaning on a crutch and aiming her own pistol at Torra's head, who knelt before her, as gagged and bound as the rest of Ashborne's crew. "We start shooting holes into yours."

Ashborne didn't lower her weapon. She released the safety instead and rested her finger on the trigger. "What makes you think I care about them? Shoot them. It doesn't matter to me. I'll be leaving here with two ships and that coin, and you won't be leaving here at all."

Sean's whole body stiffened, unsure if Ashborne was bluffing, his body automatically preparing to dive at Ashborne or in front of Billy or any number of stupid things.

Emery grabbed his arm, holding him in place. She whispered, "Trust Grace. She'll have back up plans."

Sure enough, Grace only shrugged. "I hoped you wouldn't respond that way, but I figured you would. So let me offer you something else: You let our people go and release the *Audacity*, and we won't burn this ship to ashes."

Smythee stepped up beside Grace, holding a lit torch. The flames travelled up his arm, down his body, until, like so many weeks ago now, he wore a suit of flames. Sean only hoped he stayed lucid long enough to remain helpful.

Ashborne's eyes narrowed, but she didn't lower her weapon. "You're playing a dangerous game, girl."

"Indeed," Ayana agreed. "Because this was your father's ship, was it not? It would be a shame to lose a family heirloom."

Ayana's words hit their mark. Ashborne's knuckles turned white as she gripped her pistol. "A ship is a ship. You burn that ship; I'll take this one."

"Yes, well, I guess the ship itself isn't that important to you. It's what's on the ship that you won't want burned." Grace bent to pick up something at her feet that had been hidden from view behind the guardrail. It looked like a leather-bound book, filled to bursting with loose pages stuffed into it.

Ashborne's face went white, and she gritted her teeth. She said nothing, possibly in fear of giving herself away, but her murderous expression did that anyway.

"This diary is important to you, is it not?" Grace asked, rifling through the book's contents carelessly. "It's priceless, irreplaceable. It sure would be a shame if something happened to it."

"If you touch even a single paper in that journal," Ashborne said. "I will boil the blood of every one of your people until their skin sloughs off and they're unrecognizable."

Sean flinched, and Ayana looked sick. Sean did not think she was bluffing. She would and could do such a thing.

"If you harm any of our people, I will light this whole book aflame," Grace countered, her expression betraying nothing.

Silence fell across both ships, both crews waiting to see what would happen next.

Ashborne did not lower the gun, but she did say, "I get the coin. You do not harm those documents. I'll allow your people to leave on your ship."

Relief once again flooded Sean's system until he heard Grace say, "No. Captain Denzel will be hanging on to that coin."

Frankly, Sean was tempted to toss the coin to Ashborne to get her to leave faster. But if it was truly the only thing keeping him alive...

Ashborne's face was turning red with rage. "If I don't get that coin now, I will hunt you down until I do. And I promise, I will not take it gently."

"So be it," Grace said. "Now leave our ship."

Another anxious silence stretched until Ashborne finally lowered her weapon. Sean let out a breath. Ashborne nodded once, and in unison her crew began climbing the ropes holding the ships together to get back to their own. Cam immediately lurched forward to cut Billy's bindings.

At the same time, Grace, Ayana, and the others lowered a plank and slowly made their way over to the *Audacity*. Grace still clutched the diary, and Ashborne glared at her the whole time, until she remained the only one of her crew left aboard the *Audacity*. Grace halted next to the railing and Ashborne approached her.

Grace calmly said, "You will take this, and you will leave our ship."

"I will kill you one day," Ashborne promised with a sadistic smile, reaching for the diary.

"See you then," Grace said, still so calm, holding up the book for Ashborne to take.

Ayana hobbled with her crutch to Grace's side. She snatched the diary before Ashborne could grab it and hurled it into the sea. For a slowed down moment, everybody on both ships watched the book drop until it splashed into the water and vanished beneath the grey surface.

Sean's entire body went cold. What had Ayana done?

"NO!" Ashborne shrieked. She grabbed Ayana by the arm and threw her to the deck. "You have no idea what's you've done!"

Ayana only grinned up at her with triumph. "I've killed you."

"Now I'll kill you!" Ashborne whipped out her pistol again and aimed it at Ayana's chest.

"NO!" Emery shrieked this time, letting go of Sean's arm to race across the deck.

Ashborne pulled the trigger, and once again, time slowed down. A bullet exploded from the chamber, heading straight for Ayana's heart. Emery ran but she wasn't fast enough.

Sean was.

His feet had moved before he'd made the decision and he used the very last of his energy to dive in front of Emery's sister, the bullet hitting him somewhere in the chest.

Time sped back up as chaos erupted. Screaming exploded from all directions. From Ashborne. From Grace. From the crew. From Emery. But not from Sean. Even if he wanted to scream, he had nothing left. Pain flared through his body as the bullet ripped through him, and he stumbled back, hitting the ground in front of Ayana just as Emery lunged for him, trying to catch him but missing.

All around him, people were moving in blurs, but he could only see Emery as she dropped next to him, the first to reach him. Hot blood poured from the wound, pooling around him, but the pain was already fading. Emery found the wound, which was just over his heart, and pressed both hands against it as if she had any hope of staunching the lifeblood that continued to flow between her fingers.

"Emery," he tried to say, but choked on blood.

He needed to tell her...to tell her...

"Aleksy!" Emery cried, but Aleksy was already there, hands

already stained with her husband's blood, hands that shoved Emery's out of the way so she could use her abilities to slow the flow of Sean's blood.

Most of the crew scurried around them, working to get the *Audacity* sailing away from Ashborne and the *Crimson Vengeance* as fast as possible.

Billy knelt on Sean's other side, taking one of Sean's hands in his. He couldn't feel it though. He couldn't feel anything anymore. Just a sort of weightlessness.

Billy sobbed, "My boy, my boy…"

"I'm sorry, Billy," Sean said weakly, blood trickling from the side of his mouth. He was so sorry. So sorry Billy and Luana were about to lose the last of their children, and it was, once again, his fault. But he couldn't regret saving Ayana. He never would.

Billy sobbed harder.

Grace paced back and forth behind Billy. "Don't let Sean let go of that coin! It's likely the only thing keeping him alive right now!"

Sean forgot he was still holding the coin. Somehow, it was still clutched in his fist. But keeping his fingers curled around the coin was getting more difficult by the second. Emery grabbed his hand, squeezed it so his fingers remained around the coin.

"Sean, you idiot!" she sobbed. "Why did you do that?"

"I couldn't let you…lose your sister," he said, every word a struggle, his breaths so ragged and shallow. His eyelids fluttered. They were so heavy, but he fought to keep them open a few moments longer. "Like I lost mine."

Indeed, Lily stood directly behind Emery, staring down at him with crossed arms. She had a sad little smile on her face, as if she approved of his last actions in life.

"I told you I would not be alright if you died!" Emery sobbed again, tears leaking down her cheeks. "You promised to let us try to save you!"

Darkness and weightlessness tugged at him with the promise

of a painless peace. But he resisted a little longer. He needed to tell her before he left...

"Em—" Sean tried to say.

But Emery couldn't seem to stop the panicked words from flowing. "You cannot die. Not now. Not like this."

Beside her, Aleksy was still attempting to stop the bleeding. Her eyes were squeezed shut and her face shone with the effort. She'd already spent so much energy on Rooney, on her efforts to get to Rooney before that. Maybe she didn't have enough left for this too.

It didn't matter. Even if she stopped the bleeding, his body was done.

More of the crew began gathering around as they finished their jobs. Cam, Seadar, Farley...Ranit was likely at the helm. Who knew where Smythee went. Farley had an arm around Seadar, tears streaking both of their cheeks. Cam mostly looked furious.

"I need you to live, Sean," Emery whispered, squeezing her eyes shut, presumably to try to stem her own flow of tears. "We all need you."

Sean let go of Billy's hand and, with extraordinary effort, reached to touch Emery's cheek one last time. Emery opened her eyes again and, despite the blood on his hand, she leaned into his palm.

"I wish I could have gone to Orabel with you," he said.

"Maybe we still can. Just stay!" she begged.

Behind Emery, Lily said, "It's time, brother. Come with me."

Sean coughed, the metallic taste of blood coating his mouth. His vision tunneled until all he could see was Emery's horrified face. His body was so numb he couldn't feel anything, not even her cheek beneath his fingers or the hole the bullet had ripped through his chest.

Another sob bubbled out of her. "Gods, why did you do this?"

Sean allowed his eyes to slip closed. He couldn't keep them

open and speak at the same time. But he had one last thing he needed to say before he left. "I am...so in love with you."

And he let go, allowing the bittersweet embrace of darkness to take him away.

Chapter Fifty-Seven

Liam stood on the shore of Orabel's bay, his bare feet in the soft white sand, his lim strapped to his back, the slight breeze tousling his dark curls. He'd stood in this spot a thousand times, when everything was always the same. But this day, everything was different.

The calm, turquoise water of the bay was usually empty, save for a few seabirds, jumping fish, and swimming islanders. But today, three enormous ships bobbed in the water, waiting to take Liam's people away from their home.

Using their elemental powers, it had taken less than a week to build the ships. If one saw them from afar, they looked like any other ships. But if one looked closely, they'd see the hulls were made of giant hollowed and smoothed redwood trees instead of individual planks. They'd see that the ropes were vines and the masts giant leaves.

Liam stood in the sand and watched as the people he'd known his entire life, his friends, his family, packed provisions and belongings onto the ships, preparing to abandon their home.

Not for the first time that week, rage seared Liam's veins. They weren't only abandoning their home. They were abandoning his sisters too. And though a few people had disputed this at first, in the end, they were outvoted, and no one wanted to be left behind. And that was that.

After the initial plan to leave had been brought forth, Liam had raced home to wait for his grandparents to return. He'd paced, and paced, and as soon as they stepped inside, he'd exploded. "How can you allow this, grandmother? We can't leave! What about Emery and Ayana? What about mother?"

He had not meant to let that part out. He'd long ago lost hope his mother and father would ever return home. But at least there had always been a minuscule chance that they could. But if they left and Orabel fell, there was truly no way for his parents to find them again.

Liam opened his mouth to yell some more, but the tears welling in his grandmother's eyes stopped him. She'd slumped in a chair, looking utterly deflated and defeated while his grandfather lit a fire in the hearth and began boiling water, presumably for tea.

"You must realize I know all this, Liam." His grandmother could be stern, but she rarely raised her voice. It was in danger of raising now. "Do you think I want my granddaughters ostracized? My daughter?" Her voice cracked. "I fought against this as much as I could have. But I was outvoted."

"But you said nothing when Aran was giving his speech," Liam said.

"Liam," his grandfather said placatingly, placing three steaming mugs on the table and sitting next to Grandmother. Liam could not sit. He kept pacing. "Your grandmother has been voted to lead our people. Do you know what a responsibility that is?"

"I fought behind closed doors," Grandmother continued, "but I couldn't say anything in front of everyone. We must show a united front right now or the panic and fear will only get worse."

"So that's it?" Liam asked. "We're going to just leave? Emery and Ayana can never come home?"

Grandmother took a deep breath and swiped at her eyes. "Not necessarily. I can watch Orabel for their return."

It had taken a moment for Liam to understand what she meant. *Watch through the wind.* Finally, Liam slumped into a chair himself, a little of his fury burning away. "But then what? We watch them wandering around a deserted island searching for us? Do we come back here and get them? Do we go against Aran?"

Grandmother let out a sigh. "I don't know, Liam. We'll have to solve that issue when we get there."

I don't know, Liam.

That seemed to be the only answer anyone had for him,

The next morning, Liam had gone looking for Caelin, ready to fight. He found him hacking away at his tree once again. And Liam did not waste time.

"How are you possibly supposed to find our sisters out there? Do you forget how massive the world is?"

Caelin continued to swing his sword at the tree. "I don't know. But I must look. And I can't go to the new island."

"Why not?"

Finally, Caelin turned to him. "I don't belong there, Liam. I didn't belong here. I never have. I've always been an outsider, the only Ungifted on the entire island. Do you know what that's like?"

He did not. But he'd known Caelin had struggled with this.

"I feel more out of place now than I ever did before. Out there, I wasn't an outsider. I was just normal. And maybe I can use that to my advantage. I might not be able to track down our sisters right away. But maybe I can look for a cure too. Or I can find another way to protect our people from Tavor."

Liam had felt the fight draining out of him despite his efforts to cling to it. Everything Caelin said...made sense. "How are you going to do those things alone?"

"I don't know, Liam. Honestly, I thought you'd be coming with me."

"You did?"

"Of course, I did. Before, this wouldn't have been a discussion. You would have made this plan yourself. But Fia's right. You haven't been the same since we've been home. And that's alright. It's alright to be scared. But you can't stay paralyzed forever. You must choose. Are you leaving with them? Are you leaving with me? Or are you going to stay on this crumbling island, waiting forever."

Liam had felt tears of frustration prickle his eyes. "I don't know."

He'd found Fia later, but by then, the fight had truly left him. And even if it hadn't, he knew he couldn't fight her anyway. She had to go with her sick mother. There was nothing to be done about that. And in a way, Liam was thankful for it. She'd be safe on their new island, where Tavor couldn't find her and where they might figure out a way to stop the Withering.

But if Liam chose not to go with his people, to leave with Caelin or to stay on Orabel, he might not be allowed to find the new island. He might never see her again. It had been so hard saying goodbye to her the first time. But back then, he'd been the chosen one. The gods themselves had chosen him to bring peace and to find a cure. And at the time, he had truly thought he could do it all. That he'd come back a hero. But now he was nothing and no one. And maybe, just maybe, it wasn't up to him to save his people anymore. Maybe he could go with them and stop worrying.

"What are you going to do?" Fia had asked.

"I don't know."

For the next several days, as he watched the ships be built and his people pack up their things, as he watched more of the island crumble into the sea, as he watched Caelin repair the boat they'd nearly died sailing back on, he'd repeated his own words: "I don't know."

Now he was out of time. His people were leaving that afternoon. Caelin was slipping away at the same time, the only ones aware of his plans his parents, Fia, and Liam.

And Liam had to make a choice. Stay and wait for his sisters, but possibly never see the rest of his friends and family again.

Join his friends and family on their new island, safe, but possibly never see Caelin or his siblings again. Leave with Caelin, journeying back to the dangers of the outside world to help his people, but possibly never see his friends or family again.

It was an impossible choice. No matter what he chose, he'd be scarifying things he couldn't bear to give up.

It was an impossible choice. But he made it. He knew what he needed to do. And he was going to do it.

Taking a deep breath, he tightened his hold on his shoulder pack, and headed down the beach.

Chapter Fifty-Eight

Emery had experienced death before. But not like this. People she knew had passed away at home, of course. Mostly people from the older generations. People she knew, though not well. She'd never been close to them.

But this, being so close to death now, watching someone you care about take their final breaths...it hurt more than she ever imagined. Her chest felt empty, save for the shredded pieces of her heart. Knowing she'd never see him smile again, never hear him speak in that accent of his—knowing it was all her fault...

They had at least gotten away from Ashborne and her crew, sailing blindly south for the past day, to get as far away from the *Crimson Vengeance* as possible. Grace, Ayana, and the others had destroyed the *Crimson Vengeance's* rudders before showing themselves to be alive, rendering Ashborne unable to follow, and granting the *Audacity* a huge head start.

But still, the mood aboard the *Audacity* matched how Emery felt on the inside: grim, with everyone drowning in their own grief and trying to deal with it in different ways. The crew took turns keeping the *Audacity* going and filtering in and out of Sean's cabin so they could say their goodbyes and offer any help they couldn't really give.

This was the first time in hours Emery had left Sean's side, her eyes swollen with tears, her chest empty, empty, empty. She'd gone below deck to fetch water, and now, stumbled across the main deck as she headed back towards the cabin with the heavy bucket, unable to avoid glancing at the two huge blood stains where both Sean and Rooney had lain dying.

She pushed through the cabin doors, trying not to gag on the coppery tang of blood and the sterile stink of alcohol. The room was crowded, but she headed straight for Aleksy. Aleksy perched on a stool, carefully running a wet cloth over Rooney's bare chest where he lay on a cot, cleaning the rest of the blood off him. She'd been doing it for the past hour, silently sobbing and refusing anyone's help as they came to say their goodbyes.

Emery quietly switched the bucket full of bloodied water with the fresh one she'd just fetched. It was the least she could do. She paused, gazed down at Rooney's still face. His already pale skin was so impossibly white now. Emery had always thought that a dead person would look like they were sleeping. But he didn't. He was too still, his skin and muscles too slack. Whatever had animated his body once was undeniably gone now.

Tears welled in her eyes, and she turned away. She didn't feel like she had the right to cry for Rooney, at least not in front of Aleksy. It was her fault he'd been shot. Her fault they'd been too slow to make it back in time to save him. He'd still been breathing when they'd gotten back with the coin. But he'd lost too much blood. By the time Aleksy was allowed to tend to him, it was too late. He had died quietly during the turmoil.

Still holding back her tears, Emery placed the soiled water bucket outside the cabin door and then reentered the room, this time heading for Sean's bed. Billy, Grace, and Kess stood and sat around him, softly discussing their next steps. No one had taken her stool in her absence, and she took her place next to his head. She ran her fingers though his golden hair to let him know she was back, and she wondered if he could feel it, if he was aware of anything. Could he hear them? Feel them?

Sean, at least, did look like he was sleeping. He still breathed, albeit shallowly. His skin still had a bit of colour, though not as much as it should. He looked like he was sleeping. But he wasn't.

Kess called it a coma, and he thought the bullet wound had been the final straw for Sean's body. Sean had lost a lot of blood, but Aleksy had arrived fast enough to stop him from losing too much. Kess had been able to get the bullet out, while confirming it hadn't hit anything vital. Sean had been lucky, but he also should have been awake by now. And he probably would have been had he not already been so close to death. Aleksy also confirmed that his blood was still riddled with infection, his organs failing from something called sepsis. In short, Sean was somehow still clinging to life, but the bullet wound had caused his body to shut down further to save his last precious dregs of energy.

Grace insisted the only thing truly keeping him from slipping away was the coin. "We cannot take it off his person."

And finally, she explained everything. How she realized Ashborne planned to ambush them and burn down the varen ship, so she'd ordered everyone to get the ship moving so it looked like they were still aboard and then to abandon it, taking the remaining longboats and rowing into the darkness undetected by Ashborne's crew. How they eventually infiltrated Ashborne's ship, climbing up the sides and slowly taking out each man until there was no one left standing. How Ayana knew they were still going to need some sort of leverage to get them out of this, so as they waited for Emery and the others to return, they snooped through Ashborne's cabin until they found the diary. Grace had skimmed the whole thing.

"I was right," Grace said. "Ashborne is cursed. And she's searching for the objects that will save her when Pyralis comes for her. It was all in the diary."

"The coin *is* magic?" Kess asked, looking skeptical.

"According to her diary, the coin grants the holder luck," Grace said, glancing down at where Sean's one hand lay open with the coin sitting on his palm. "I think luck is the only reason Sean is breathing right now."

"Luck?" Kess repeated, somehow looking even more skeptical. "All of this for a literal lucky coin? How...novel."

Emery was skeptical too, but she remembered how Sean had seemed reinvigorated after holding the coin for the first time, and how he'd known exactly how to get out of the tunnels with seemingly lucky guesses. How he'd taken a bullet for Ayana, and it had luckily just missed his heart.

"Luck is the only thing keeping him alive right now," Grace insisted. "But luck can run out. We need to get him to healers who can perform a blood transfusion immediately. It's the only way to save him."

They'd talked in circles about it. Not everyone was ready to believe a coin was keeping Sean alive, but none of them wanted to risk taking it away from him either. And all of them agreed that getting Sean to the closest medics was their most pressing matter.

"We can't go back to Audrye," Kess said.

"My old home and tribe are at least a month away," Aleksy spoke up from her position next to Rooney.

Grace looked at Emery. "I think we know where we have to go."

Emery nodded, knowing exactly what Grace meant. Emery had looked at the maps too, realizing which island was closest, had contemplated whether it was a good idea to go there or not. In the end, she didn't contemplate for long, because it didn't matter. If it was Sean's only chance to live, she'd take the risk and the consequences too. She would not let him die.

She ran her fingers through his hair again, wondered what he'd think if he knew that he'd finally be on his way to the place of his dreams.

"We have to go to Orabel," Emery said. "We have to go home."

AFTER THE PLAN had been set, which had taken a while because Emery and Grace had to confess to everyone that they were indeed from Orabel, and then had to answer a lot of questions about it, Grace had pulled Emery from the cabin, claiming she needed to speak with her and Ayana alone.

They found Ayana in the infirmary, where she was lying in a cot with her still broken leg propped up. She'd been in a lot of pain after the whole ordeal of escaping Ashborne's crew, commandeering the *Crimson Vengeance*, and then being shoved to the ground by Ashborne.

Ayana sat up a little straighter in the cot when they entered the room, looking hopefully at Emery.

But Emery couldn't meet her eyes. Not yet. She knew Ayana hadn't meant for Sean to get hurt. That she had not been the one to shoot him. But they'd been so close to escaping with no further harm to anyone. They'd been so close, and then she had to throw Ashborne's diary in the sea and cause one last altercation that had left Sean on the brink of death.

Now, Emery couldn't quite look at her without a spark of fury flaring in her chest.

Grace shut the infirmary door behind them and leaned against it. Without preamble, she said, "Ashborne's diary had a lot of...interesting information in it."

She almost looked...nervous.

"About magical objects and curses?' Emery asked. In truth, it was hard to care about any of that.

"Yes...and about your parents. I think."

Emery and Ayana stared at her. "What?" they said in unison.

"If I'm understanding correctly, you parents' disappearance had something to do with Ashborne's father. And Sean's parents were involved too."

Silence swallowed the cabin as Emery and Ayana gaped at Grace.

"What?" Emery asked again, her head spinning.

"Grace..." Ayana said, exasperated. "I don't think now is the time to get into all this."

Grace looked confused. "I thought you'd want to know all the information right away."

Before Emery or Ayana could answer, shouting and the sound of running feet exploded above decks, catching their attention.

Emery's first thought was that Sean had woken up, and she bolted for the door, sprinting for the stairs beyond.

But when she burst above deck, blinking in the dying light of day, it was to find most of the crew gathering starboard, staring at something on the crimson horizon.

A deep foreboding chilled Emery's bones and she didn't take a step further. She couldn't. Somehow, she knew what she was about to hear before she heard it.

"It's him!" Farley cried from the crow's nest. "It's Tavor!"

Don't Worry, Emery & The Crew Will Be Back!

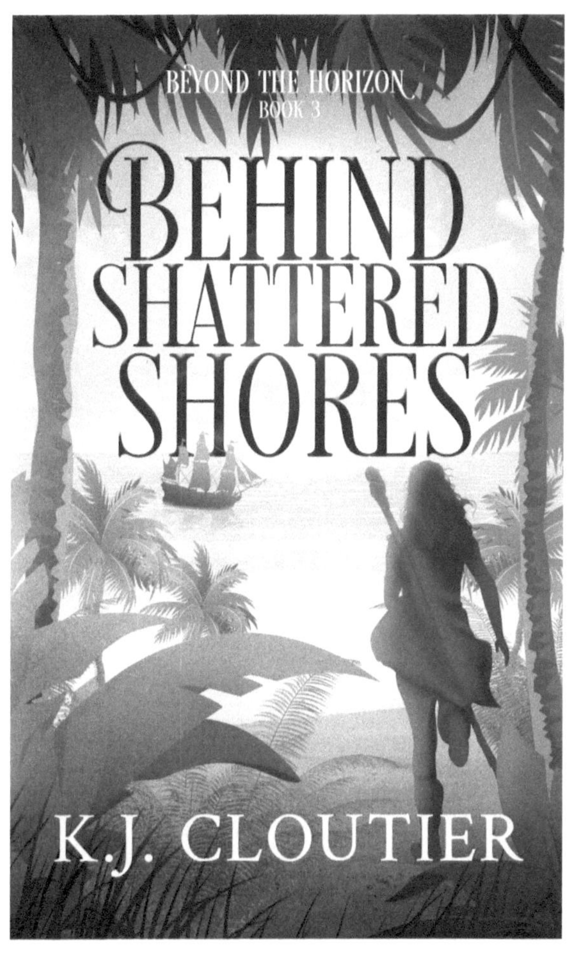

Out July 14th 2026!

Acknowledgments

When I began writing Beyond The Horizon, I was 14 and had absolutely no idea what I was doing. I certainly didn't understand anything about word count. Imagine my surprise, after writing ¾ of the story, when I found out it was WAY too long. I then split it in half and over the years, I went back and forth between the two books, rewriting both of them over and over. So, even though this is a sequel, it's technically taken me just as long to write is as it did the first book.

All of that to say, typing this up is tricky because my list of thank you's is almost identical to the one for the first book. But there are a few people who deserve to be thanked again, and a few new ones too add...

Thank you to my mom, who is still me biggest fan, and honestly, should become my agent with how many of my books she manages to peddle to everyone she knows, while also being the best grandmother to my boys and the best mother to me.

To my husband, who has always believed in my writing even before he ever read a word of it, and who was simultaneously terrified to read the first book because he worried he'd hate it. (He read it and loved it, eventually.)

To my oldest son, for reminding me to stay in the moment and to enjoy them while I can. Again, you did not make writing this book easy, and the entire first draft of the final version was written on my phone while I was nap trapped by you, but those are some of my favourite writing sessions.

To my youngest son, bless your little soul for being an amazing sleeper and allowing me to edit late into the night. And thank you for the cozy baby snuggles that remind me that nothing is as important as being present while you grow up.

To Loki, you're becoming a cantankerous old woman who doesn't listen to me at all anymore, but I'm glad you're still around and I hope you stay for a long time still. (But please stop barking at the neighbour's dog. You're driving me mad.)

To a certain manager at a certain indie bookstore in my hometown, thank you for supporting me in so many ways, including putting me front and centre on your website, placing my books on the shelf, and hosting me for all the signings.

To all the family and friends who supported me by reading Beyond The Horizon, or displaying it on your shelves without ever cracking the spine, or telling your own friends and family about it, or coming to visit me at my signings. It means so much to me that so many of you were excited to see my dreams come true.

To my cover designer, you absolutely nailed it once again! This cover turned out better then I imagined!

To my editor, for helping me polish the manuscript so it could shine as bright as possible.

To everyone who took the time to share about my books online, who took the time to rate and review, because those simple acts are so helpful to authors.

And finally, to you lovely readers! You took a chance on a little indie author and took time out of your life to read Beyond The Horizon. And if you're reading this, it means you came back to read Beneath Crimson Sails too, and I'm so grateful for you! I hope you return again.

Thank you.

About the Author

Legends say K.J. Cloutier was born with a pen in her hand. She wrote her first book at five years old. And now, as an adult, she still loves to write about fantastical worlds and torture her beloved characters (literally and figuratively.) When not writing, she's usually daydreaming about writing, while also cooking, travelling, and wandering near the woods or water. She's in real danger of one day being crushed under her forever growing collection of books. She lives with her husband, two sons, two dog and a bearded dragon in a tiny house by the lake in B.C., Canada.

For bookish updates:
https://www.kjcloutierauthor.com